RAVE REVIEWS FOR
PATRICIA J. MACDONALD
Best-selling author of *THE UNFORGIVEN*

"A terrific psychological thriller. Full of suspense and intensely readable."

—Mary Higgins Clark,
author of *A Cry in the Night*

"One of those rare books that, once started, you can't put down."

—John Saul,
author of *When the Wind Blows*

"Real and immediate . . . gruesomely effective . . . a scary, engrossing book. . . . MacDonald create[s] striking images that are far above the sort of stuff the genre usually produces . . . and use[s] familiar products to create moments of horror so real and immediate that they become almost hypnotic."

—Stephen King,
author of *Different Seasons*

"In the style of Mary Higgins Clark, the author weaves the plot adeptly . . . a quick read that holds your attention all the way through."

—New York *Daily News*

"A tight, well-crafted psychological thriller."

—*Book Week*

Also by Patricia J. MacDonald
THE UNFORGIVEN

STRANGER
IN THE HOUSE

Patricia J. MacDonald

A DELL BOOK

To the memory of my parents,
Olga and Donald MacDonald

Published by
Dell Publishing Co., Inc.
1 Dag Hammarskjold Plaza
New York, New York 10017

ISBN: 0-440-18455-X

Printed in the United States of America
First printing—July 1983

PROLOGUE

Propelled by a pudgy hand, the red sedan labored up the side of a pile of dirt and then zoomed down and tumbled into a trough on the other side.

"Mommy, look! The car crashed. It came over the hill, and it fell down."

Anna Lange halted the gentle rocking motion of the glider with her feet and smiled at her son. "You made it fall down, Paul."

The child beamed up at her, satisfied that she was paying attention. He wiped his dirty face with his equally dirty forearm and shook his head mischievously. "Unh-unh," he told her. "It just fell down."

Anna laughed in spite of herself at the picture he made, seated happily in the grass, his striped T-shirt and little blue shorts already smudged with dirt. Popeye winked and flexed a giant muscle from the crown of the sailor hat which her son was wearing. She had turned the brim down to protect Paul's face from the sun, so when he looked up at her, he had to bend his head back to get a clear view out from under it. Anna noticed that his socks had ridden down and were already disappearing into the backs of his miniature Keds.

Making a revving noise with his lips, Paul extricated the

auto from the ditch. "Have to hurry up and go to work now," he said. Waddling on bent legs, the child drove the car through the wooden gate of his play yard toward the sandbox, where a yellow steam shovel lay on its side. Paul abandoned the car outside the sandbox, clambered in, and plopped himself down beside the larger toy. He righted the steam shovel and carefully began to rotate the crank which lowered the scoop into the sand, all his attention now focused on his task.

Sunshine glinted off the stray amber locks which curled around Paul's hatbrim as he bent his head to his mission. Anna gazed fondly at her son and wondered briefly what new vehicles were in store for him on his fourth birthday next month. So far her parents in Michigan had provided their grandson with every simulated make and model that Detroit had to offer.

A breeze rippled through the sultry afternoon, and Anna lifted her face gratefully to greet it. She placed a protective hand on her slightly distended stomach. Summer was definitely the wrong time to be pregnant. She was three months along, and everything seemed to affect her more acutely. The heat seemed more oppressive, the humidity more stifling than it had been other summers. Excepting, of course, the summer Paul had been born. She shook her head at the memory. At least Tracy had had the good sense to be born in June. "Well, Roscoe," she said, patting her stomach, "looks as if you'll be ringing in the New Year." She and Thomas had dubbed the newest addition Roscoe about a week after she learned she was pregnant, just as they had referred to Paul as Mortimer and called Tracy Clem in the months before their respective births.

Paul, who had been mumbling and humming to himself as he dug, added one scoop too many to the mountain of sand, and the pile collapsed into the hole as if struck by an earthquake. The child let out a yelp of angry frustration.

"Shhhh, Paul." Anna reproved him. "Tracy's asleep." She cocked an ear toward the house, where the back door and windows were open. Her daughter had contracted a summer cold the day before and had spent a feverish night. The pediatrician assured Anna that it was nothing serious, but the child had been whiny and disconsolate all night long. Finally, in the morning, she had fallen asleep, after a series of witch hazel baths and a lot of soothing from Anna.

Paul looked up at his mother with wide, innocent brown eyes. "Can Tracy come out now?"

"Not today, honey. She doesn't feel good today. You play."

Paul resumed his digging, and Anna closed her eyes briefly. It had been a long night, trying to keep Tracy quiet so that Thomas could get some rest. He had a meeting with the chief financial officer of the company at nine o'clock, and she knew it was important for him to be alert. If Tracy's crying had bothered him, he did not mention it at breakfast. He had been his usual cheerful, preoccupied self. "It's amazing," she had told him once. "Sometimes I think you're at work before you even get out of bed."

Thomas had grimaced at her remark, but her smile reassured him. He worked harder than any man she knew, but it was all for her and the kids. Success was not so much a matter of pride to him as it was a means of providing for them, protecting them. It was virtually a passion with him, that need to take care of them. I'm a lucky woman, Anna thought.

She opened her eyes and looked out across the rolling, shady backyard, bounded by a woods which afforded them a sense of privacy and solitude. The only sound that broke the peaceful silence was the singing of birds and the occasional, almost inaudible whoosh of the cars which passed by on the leafy Millgate Parkway, a dignified, tree-shrouded old highway which cut through back Stanwich, adjacent to some of the loveliest and wealthiest homes in all of affluent Fairmont County.

It was Thomas's hard work which had landed them a home in this neighborhood. Theirs was far from the grandest house around. In fact, their lovely old home had once been the caretaker's house on an enormous estate. Their nearest neighbors, the Stewarts, lived in the manor house on the huge property, which had long ago been subdivided and sold separately. The Langes' home was small by comparison to the elegant Stewart mansion, but it was more than large enough for their young family and was magnificent in contrast with the other houses and little apartments they had lived in.

Anna smiled, thinking of the pride Thomas took in the home he had given her. She knew what it represented to him. His had been a chaotic childhood, with an absent father and an alcoholic mother who dragged him from boardinghouse to railroad flat and back. He had worked his way through college, where they met and married, and, after a lot of effort and long hours, had attained the position of assistant treasurer in the Phelps Corporation, which was based in New York. It was not long after his promotion was announced that Thomas had taken her to see the beautiful old Victorian house in the suburb of Stanwich.

"It's too much," she had protested. "How can we afford it?"

"We'll have to afford it," Tom had said, teasing her. "You have to have somewhere to spread all that junk of yours." She had laughed again at their old joke. It was true.

She had a collection of antique bottles, every dried flower he had ever given her, and she couldn't bear to throw away a magazine that had a sweater pattern or a recipe she might like to try. It had not taken long for them to fill up their new house. If Thomas worried about the cost, he never complained about it. But then, he was a master at keeping his worries to himself. After eight years of marriage she certainly knew that. Sometimes she worried that he would get an ulcer.

Tired of his job, Paul abandoned the sandbox and the play yard and went out exploring. She watched him as he tramped through the grass. He bent down to pick up a dandelion and blow on it.

Anna pushed herself out of the glider and walked toward her son. "Do you want a ride on the swing?" she asked him. Paul nodded eagerly and reached up to take the hand she extended to him. They walked along together toward the swing set at the back of the yard. When they were almost there, Paul disengaged his hand from hers and ran toward the swing, where he hoisted himself up on the seat and kicked his sneakered feet impatiently.

"Okay," said Anna. "Hold your horses."

Just as she approached the swing set, Paul squealed and slipped off the swing. He began to tear across the yard as fast as his pudgy legs would move, shrieking and laughing. "Look at the kitty," he cried. "Can we keep him?"

"That's all I need," said Anna, rolling her eyeballs skyward.

The fluffy black-and-white cat, which had appeared at the edge of the woods, stood frozen for a minute, whiskers on end, as the child barreled gleefully toward it, arms waving wildly. Then the cat turned and bolted into the safety of the trees. Paul started gamely after it, branches and leaves snapping against his short, bare legs.

"No, you don't, buster," said Anna, swooping down on her son and lifting him back into the civilized territory of the lawn.

Paul started to cry. "I want the kitty," he wailed.

"You're really getting heavy," Anna observed with a grunt. "I can't do this much longer. The kitty had to go home."

Paul continued to cry as Anna carried him back in the direction of the house. He stuck his thumb in his mouth and sucked noisily on it through his tears.

"What's this?" she chided him. "I thought you gave that up." He rubbed his eyes with small, dirty fists. Anna held him securely under his little rump.

As they approached the house, she heard the weak but unmistakable wailing of Tracy from inside. Anna placed Paul on the ground and offered him her hand. "Come on. We'll go and see how Tracy feels."

"No," Paul protested sullenly. "I don't wanna."

"Okay, then," she said, lifting him under the armpits and depositing him inside the large fenced play yard that Thomas had built. "You play quietly. I'm going to see how Tracy is. You be good." She wagged a finger at him and smiled as she lowered the latch on the gate. "You be a good boy, and I'll bring you a cookie when I come back."

Paul watched her forlornly, wiping his face again. Then he headed toward his sandbox. He threw one glance over his shoulder to the woods where the cat had disappeared. "Where's the kitty?"

"The kitty's gone, Paul. You play now."

Anna ran up the back steps and threw open the door to the house. "I'm coming, baby," she called as she dodged the

Wiffle ball and plastic bat in the foyer and mounted the stairs to her daughter's room.

Tracy was standing up in her crib, whimpering, when Anna entered the sunny pink and yellow bedroom. One look at her mother, though, and the child burst into wails of misery. Anna lifted the fretting child in her arms and began to murmur to her. The child's summer pajamas were damp with perspiration. "Oh, poor thing. It's too hot to be sick, isn't it? Poor Tracy." Anna put Tracy back in her bed, and Tracy immediately began to howl again. Anna spoke soothingly to her daughter as she rifled the brimming dresser drawer for a fresh pair of pajamas and then ducked into the bathroom and soaked a washcloth. Glancing at her watch, she realized that it was time for a few more baby aspirin.

After returning to Tracy's room, Anna removed the damp pajamas and sponged her feverish daughter gently with a soft cloth. She held out the new pajamas for Tracy's inspection. "It's Snoopy," she said, pointing out the pattern on the cotton fabric. "What's he doing?"

Tracy examined the pattern curiously as Anna put the pajamas on her. "Snoopy's sick," the child announced solemnly.

Anna pushed Tracy's soft hair off her warm forehead. "That's right. Just like my poor baby." Anna showed Tracy the two orange tablets in her hand.

"No," said the child, shaking her head.

"Better take them," said Anna, "so you and Snoopy can get all better."

The child reached for the proffered pills. She chewed the soft aspirin and took a gulp of water, her warm little hands helping her mother guide the plastic cup to her lips. "No more," she said abruptly, pushing the cup away. A stream of water dribbled down her chin.

"Okay," said Anna. "Hey, where's Fubby?" Anna hunted around under the crib for the stuffed rabbit which Tracy loved to chew on. She located the toy wedged between the leg of the crib and the wall and offered it to her whimpering child. Tracy clutched the rabbit and smiled wanly at her mother.

"You want a story?" Anna pointed to a stack of books piled on a table beside the rocker.

"No," Tracy said fretfully.

"How about a little song to sleep?" Anna asked her.

Tracy nodded. "The Winky song," she cried. She settled down in her crib, and Anna began to sing softly. The child's occasional hiccups of sobs died away with the verses of the song. By the time Winken, Blynken and Nod were out on the silver sea Tracy's eyelids were drooping. Anna gently patted the little form and tiptoed out of the room. Tracy sighed as she slept, her thumb planted in her mouth.

Anna headed down the stairs to return to Paul. Just as she was passing through the foyer, the phone on the hall table began to ring. She rushed to grab it and caught it on the second ring.

"Hello."

"Hello, Anna. It's Iris. Did I catch you on the run? You sound breathless."

"Hi, Iris. I was upstairs with Tracy. She's got a little cold, and I just got her off to sleep."

Anna's neighbor was immediately remorseful. "Oh, dear, I hope the phone didn't wake her up."

Anna listened up the stairs. "All's quiet," she assured her worried friend. "What's up?"

"Well, I've been meaning to call you about this. I have to go to a tea for the village green beautification committee, and I wondered if you wanted to go with me. Lorraine can watch the children. She can come over there if you don't want to wake Tracy."

Anna was bemused by the suggestion. Iris was a shy, ill-at-ease woman who trudged off reluctantly to countless social functions mostly, Anna suspected, at the behest of her status-conscious husband. Edward was a self-made millionaire with a passion for high society, while his wife, who came from a blue-blooded New England family, seemed more to dread than to enjoy the social set. She often invited Anna to the endless teas and charity functions, freely offering the services of her maid, Lorraine Jackson, to mind Anna's children. Occasionally, Anna took her up on the offer, for unlike Iris, she enjoyed the company of the other women at these events, and it was a nice change from being home. However, a sick child had a compelling hold on its mother, which, Anna thought, Iris probably did not understand, having no children of her own. Anna passed on the tea party without a second thought.

"Not today, Iris. I couldn't leave Tracy. Thanks all the same."

"Oh," said Iris, and Anna could hear her disappointment. "Well, maybe the next time."

Anna felt a little sorry for her friend, realizing how awkward she felt at these gatherings, casting about for something to say, especially without Anna to talk to. It seemed like a kind of sorry way to spend your life. If it weren't for Edward, she thought, Iris would probably be happiest at home, reading her books and dabbling with her watercolors. "I've got Paul outside," Anna said. "I'd better get back to him. Thanks for asking me, Iris."

The two women hung up, and Anna started toward the back of the house. On the way she remembered her promise of a cookie. Having detoured to the pantry, she rooted around until she located the butter cookies that Paul liked. Anna took two for him and then, after a moment's guilty debate, one for herself. It seemed, when she was pregnant, that she was always hungry. She returned to the back door, opened it, and stepped out onto the back porch.

"Paul," she called out, "I brought you a cookie." The child did not answer. She could not immediately see him in the play yard. He must be in the sandbox, she thought.

Frowning slightly, Anna descended the steps and hurried toward the play yard. "Paul," she called sharply. She rushed up to the fence and reached for the slats.

"Where are you?" she demanded. Gripping the top of the fence, Anna looked inside. She did not see her son.

Her throat constricted. Her gaze swept the play yard, searched the sandbox. The yellow steam shovel lay abandoned on its side. The red car leaned against the sandbox wall. The child was not there.

"Paul," Anna whispered through her tightened throat. Her frantic glance scanned the perimeter of the fence and then stopped short. She stared for a moment, disbelieving, at the gate, which stood ajar about two feet.

Anna held the fence for support, crushing the cookies between her hands and the slats. "Paul," she cried. "Paul."

At first she could not move. Her breath was short. Her limbs felt as if they had been set in cement. She looked out across the backyard, trying to breathe. Then her words came in a shrill rush. "Paul, do you hear me? Answer Mommy!"

The silent, empty yard shimmered in the heat of the July

afternoon. Dragonflies whirred across the sun-dappled lawn. Beyond the swing set and the garden shed at the back of their property, the woods rustled, dark and cool. There was no sign of the child. He was nowhere to be seen.

Letting go of the fence, Anna forced herself to walk. Like a stroke victim taking her first steps, she lurched away from the fence toward the back of the yard. Her eyes swiveled in every direction, starving for some brief glimpse of him. A swatch of his striped T-shirt, a splash of white from his sailor's hat, the glow of shell-pink skin through the trees. "Paul," she cried.

How could he get out? She stopped for a second and glanced back at the latch. One of the screws which held it to the fence was gone. It hung uselessly on the door. It mustn't have caught securely. I should have looked. Why didn't I pull on it to be sure? One tug was probably all it took, she thought.

Where was he? Immediately she remembered the cat. He had been fascinated by that kitty. He must have tried to follow it into the woods. He can't have gone far.

Running now, Anna plunged into the trees, crying out hoarsely for her child. She ran crazily in one direction, then another. A flash of waving brown-gold caught her eye. "Paul," she cried. A dried-out fern swam before her tear-filled eyes. She continued on, tripping through the mossy, leaf-strewn ground cover, her glance darting behind every tree. She could hear the sound of traffic beyond, on the highway, as she stumbled along. "Please, God," she whispered. "Please. Let him be all right. Paul, Paul, Mommy needs you." She could hear the choked bubbling of tears in her voice as she called out to him. The trees were silent in reply.

All at once she saw a sudden movement through the

trees. Heart leaping with hope, she whirled to face it. There, beside a tree, sat the fluffy black-and-white cat, staring edgily at her.

Anna's lips and chin began to tremble violently. She could feel the shaking spread down her arms to her hands, in her knees, all the way to her feet. She was bathed in sweat. She stared at the unblinking cat. Tears began to spill down her cheeks.

"Where is my baby? Paul!" she shrieked. Her anguished cry drowned out the intermittent drone from the highway, the rustle of the trees. It seemed to settle there on the dense, oppressive summer air.

"First thing in the morning," said Detective Mario "Buddy" Ferraro, neatly smoothing down his dark blue tie and buttoning his gray sports jacket over it. "We'll be here early, and we'll keep looking until we find your boy, Mr. Lange. I promise you. We'll do everything we can. Everything. But it's late now. We can't see anything, and these people need to get some sleep."

"I understand," Thomas said dully, staring out at the group of men and women who were milling about in his backyard, waving flashlights and talking quietly together. They were policemen, neighbors, people in town who had heard about it on the local radio station. There were even a bunch of teen-agers, members of the high school key club, who had volunteered to help in the search. Their numbers had swelled since three, when the search had started. Thomas gazed blankly at them, his face ashen above his white shirt. He was still wearing his suit, now rumpled and dirty from crawling in the woods and alongside the highway. His loosened tie hung like a slack noose around his neck.

"They need some rest, and so do you," advised the handsome olive-skinned detective earnestly, nervously adjusting the perfect knot in his tie. "Especially your wife. Did the doctor give her something to help her sleep?" he inquired.

"He was here a few hours ago," Thomas replied. "He gave her some pills to take. He would have given her a shot, but with the baby . . ." Thomas's voice trailed away.

"Try to get her to sleep," the detective urged. "We'll be back before she even wakes up. We'll find your boy, Mr. Lange. We will." The detective gripped the stricken father's shoulder for a brief second and then released it. "Let me say good night to your wife, tell her we're going now."

The detective nodded in the direction of the dining room. In a fog Thomas led the way.

Anna sat at the dining room table, her head resting on her arms in front of her. Iris Stewart sat beside her friend, her hands clenched together in her lap. Her plain, earnest face was distorted by a worried frown as she stared sadly at Anna. Her husband, Edward, dressed in a perfectly tailored pinstriped suit, hovered behind them, his shoulders stiffened into almost a military posture. There was a dazed expression in his pewter-gray eyes, and his sharp, sculpted, features seemed to be sagging. Both the Stewarts looked up anxiously as Thomas and Detective Ferraro entered the dining room. Anna kept her head lowered on her arms.

Thomas answered the question on Iris's face with a curt shake of his head. Iris blinked back tears and glanced up at her husband, who had averted his face and was staring down at the floor.

"Mrs. Lange," the detective said softly.

Slowly Anna raised her head. Her face was puffed up; her

eyes were red and swollen from crying. She flattened her trembling hands on the table and looked up at the detective.

Buddy Ferraro's stomach twisted at the sight of her face. "Mrs. Lange, I'm going to have to call off the search for tonight. Just for tonight. It's after two. We'll start again first thing in the morning."

"It's so late," she said. "We have to find him."

"We'll find him, Mrs. Lange. Tonight we need to get some rest."

Anna raised herself up shakily out of her seat. "I have to keep looking," she said. "You're giving up."

"Oh, no, Anna," Iris protested. "You mustn't think that." For a moment she herself looked like a lost child.

The detective cleared his throat. "We are not giving up," he said. "We are just going to take a break, and we'll be back at it as soon as there is light."

An expression of exquisite pain suffused the mother's face. The tears began to stream silently down her cheeks again.

"Try to get some sleep," said the detective helplessly. "I'll let myself out."

"You two should go, too," Tom said to his neighbors.

"Let me spend the night here on the couch," Iris implored him.

Edward cleared his throat impatiently. "Come along, Iris. We'll only be in the way here."

"It's okay," Thomas assured her. "You go on."

Iris hesitated and then clasped Anna's white hand in her own. "I'll be back first thing in the morning," she promised as Edward prodded her firmly toward the door.

"Thanks for everything," said Tom. Edward shook his hand with a quick, awkward jerk and then ushered Iris through the dining room doors.

The house was silent for a few moments. Anna moaned and hid her face in her hands. Then, without uncovering her face, she spoke softly. "I was gone for only a few minutes, Tom."

Thomas sat across the table from his wife, staring at the wall. "I know," he said in a choked voice. Then he looked over at her. "It's not your fault, darling. You can't blame yourself."

Anna did not reply. They sat in silence. After a few minutes he spoke again. "We'd better get to bed."

A feeble cry wafted down from upstairs. Anna started at the sound of the tiny wail. For a second she stiffened, and then she slumped over.

"Tracy's up," said Thomas. He watched his wife for a reaction, but she didn't move. "Do you want me to go?" he asked.

Anna avoided her husband's eyes. "If you don't mind," she said. "I want to clean up here." She waved a hand vaguely over the empty, stained coffee mugs that littered the table, left there by shifts of searchers.

"Don't bother with that, darling," Thomas said. "Come upstairs now."

"No, I want to." She got up from her chair and began to collect the cups and crumpled napkins with trembling hands.

Thomas opened his mouth to argue and then stopped. He lifted himself wearily from his seat and started to walk through the darkened living room toward the stairs and the sound of Tracy's complaints. Suddenly there was a crash.

"Ahhhh . . ." Anna cried out.

Thomas rushed back into the dining room. Anna was bent over double, clutching her stomach, pieces of broken china on the table and at her feet.

"Honey, what's the matter?" he cried, hurrying to support her in his arms. "What is it?"

What little color she had had was drained from her face. She breathed shallowly, holding herself around the middle.

"What is it?" he demanded. "Is it the baby? Should I call the doctor?"

Slowly Anna shook her head. She breathed more deeply. She began to straighten up. "It's better now. It's passing."

"Please come and lie down," he pleaded.

"I will. As soon as I'm finished here." Glancing briefly at her husband's troubled eyes, Anna turned away from him. Tracy wailed out, more insistently now.

"Anna?" he asked.

"I will," she said. She gestured at the mess around her. "I'll be right up."

Reluctantly Thomas released her and started again for the stairs. From the darkness of the living room he looked back at her fearfully as she sank onto one of the dining room chairs and stared beyond her own lonely reflection in the window into the yawning blackness of the yard.

"What a night." Buddy Ferraro sighed, opening the door to his car and sliding in.

"What time tomorrow?" asked a patrolman, leaning against the open door of the detective's car.

"Say seven," the detective suggested. "I'll probably be here six or six thirty."

"I don't guess half an hour's gonna make much difference to this kid," said the patrolman, shaking his head.

The detective glared at him. "It could make a lot of difference," he snapped.

"Hey, no offense," said the young man. "I feel the same way you do. I'll be here early."

Buddy gave his young colleague a conciliatory wave as he started his car. "I'll see ya in a few hours."

The young cop tapped on the detective's hood as the car rolled backward down the Langes' driveway.

Buddy Ferraro wondered if he would get any sleep at all that night. The sight of Anna Lange's face weighed down his heart. Her anguish had seeped into him, raging within him, giving the search an intensity that he had rarely felt in fourteen years on the force. To lose a child. It was a nightmare. The kid seemed to have just vanished in thin air. He thought of Sandy and of their own two boys, little Buddy and Mark. If anything ever happened to them . . .

He decided to take the Millgate Parkway home. It was faster than the back roads, even this late at night. He'd get off in two stops and nearly be at his door. He had called Sandy at around ten o'clock, ostensibly to tell her when he'd be home, but as the phone gave its third ring, he'd realized, by the tightening in his chest, that he just wanted to be sure they all were safe.

Following the signs for New York, Buddy crossed the overpass and drove down the curved entrance ramp to the full stop sign. He braked automatically and sat for a moment, lost in thought. They hadn't found a trace of the boy, nothing. There had to be something, some lead they had missed. If it was there to be found, they would find it. He was determined. He realized with a start that he was waiting for no reason. There was no other traffic on the parkway. He pressed his foot on the gas, and the car shot forward into the night.

Unnoticed by the grim-faced detective who sped off, not far from where he had stopped to yield, one small white sailor's hat was wedged out of sight in a drainage ditch beneath the lip of the road. The low-hanging boughs of a hearty evergreen helped to hide the little hat from view. There were dark patches of dirt on the crumpled brim. And something else as well. On the grimy crown, Popeye winked and held his spinach can aloft, while across his muscle, his face, and the balloon letters of his name, creases began to stiffen as the bloody fabric dried.

CHAPTER ONE

"You made that?" Anna exclaimed, running one hand over the shiny surface of the ceramic bowl which Iris held up for inspection.

Iris nodded shyly and carefully replaced the bowl on the tabletop between them.

"You're really getting good at this stuff," said Anna admiringly.

Iris beamed at the compliment and gazed down at the bowl's brightly glazed curves. "I was hoping you'd like it. You know how I value your opinion."

Anna smiled to herself. Ever since they met years ago, Iris had always treated her like the older sister she never had, even though the two women were about the same age. "It's beautiful," said Anna honestly. "I hope you'll make me something in your class one of these days."

Iris grinned with pleasure. "I will. I'm not good enough yet, though."

Anna took another sip of her iced tea. "How long have you been taking lessons now?"

Iris raised her eyes to the ceiling thoughtfully. "It'll be six months next week."

"And this is the teacher from the hospital?"

"Well, yes. But she has her own studio. She volunteers, teaching ceramics to the kids at the hospital. That's how I got interested originally in learning to do this."

"Well, I think you're really mastering it," said Anna. "I'm impressed."

"Thanks," said Iris. "I'm trying."

The two women were sitting at one end of the plant-filled conservatory of the Stewarts' opulent home. The sun streamed in on them, and a breeze from the open doors riffled the leaves of the plants.

"How do you like your tea?" Iris asked.

"It's great," said Anna. "Fresh mint. Is it from your garden?"

Iris nodded. "Henry brought it in this morning."

"I always mean to put some in my garden, and then I forget."

"I'll tell Henry to dig some up for you," Iris said eagerly.

"Would you? That would be great."

Iris and Anna relaxed in their chairs, enjoying the sun and the breeze. On the table between them the blue and ocher glazed bowl gleamed in the sun. Anna leaned over the glass table and picked up a pile of envelopes that were lying beside the bowl, addressed in Iris's careful hand. "What are you up to here?" Anna asked.

A pained look crossed Iris's face. "Oh, we're giving a party. For the Hospital Guild. It's going to be rather a large affair, to raise money for the new cardiac wing."

Anna nodded. "I read about it in the paper. I didn't know the party was going to be here."

"Well, Edward is the chairman of the fund-raising committee, you know."

Anna nodded, noting that Iris was clenching her hands

together in her lap. "You're good at organizing things," Anna reassured her. "It will be a great success."

Iris gave a small sigh. "I hope so," she said. "There's one for you in there." Iris pointed to the stack of envelopes.

Anna found the envelope addressed to the Langes and smiled. "Tracy, too?"

"Older children." Iris shrugged. "That was my idea. I thought they'd pep things up."

"Great," said Anna, feeling, as she often did, a twinge of pity for her childless friend. It was a subject they never discussed, but Anna sensed that Iris had wished for children, although she had trouble imagining Edward crooning over a cradle. "When's the party going to be?" Anna asked.

"A week from tomorrow. The thirtieth. I hope you're free. I'm a little late with the invitations."

"The thirtieth," said Anna softly, staring down into her glass of tea. "That's Paul's birthday." She looked up at Iris. "He'll be fifteen this year."

Iris's eyebrows rose slightly. For a moment she regarded her friend thoughtfully. "Is that so?" she murmured. Her blue eyes seemed to have darkened in her round face. "Well . . . that's good. Where's Tom today?"

"With Tracy. They're playing tennis. Is Edward home?"

"Oh, no. He had a business lunch today. He just bought another company. The Wilcox Company, I think it's called. They have something to do with helicopter parts."

"Will he be gone long?"

Iris shrugged. "You never can tell with Edward. I guess he'll be back in a few hours." Anna stirred the ice in her glass and looked up under her eyelashes at Iris. You would never know, to look at her, Anna thought, that her husband was a millionaire. Edward, whose company manufactured private aircraft, was always a model of correctness and elegance in his appearance, while Iris dressed in drab clothing and seemed to give only the minimum attention to her hair and makeup. Although Iris was the product of the finest finishing schools, she had none of the shiny, lustrous surface which that background produced in many women, while her husband was polished to the point of affectation.

Nonetheless, they seemed to get along together, and Anna had always ascribed it to opposites' attracting. She wondered now at the weariness in Iris's voice when she mentioned Edward. "Iris," she said tentatively, "is everything all right?"

Iris sat up even straighter in her chair. "Of course," she said, brightening. "Fine."

"Good," said Anna, relieved not to have opened a Pandora's box. "Well, I've got to be getting back." She placed her empty glass down on the end table and got up.

"Anna, I meant to ask you. How's Tracy's job at the vet's working out?"

Anna frowned, thinking of her daughter. "Oh, she loves being around the animals. She doesn't get paid for it, but she seems to enjoy it."

"There, you see! That's great," said Iris. "I had a feeling that all she needed was an interest. Didn't I tell you that?"

"It's helped," said Anna absently, although she felt a twinge of annoyance at Iris's simplistic solution to the problems she had with Tracy. Her shy, introverted daughter was turning into a moody, difficult teen-ager who seemed to resent her mother more each day. But Iris always acted as if a little change in the routine would solve everything. And perhaps in Iris's pampered, childless life, that was all the solution she needed, Anna thought ruefully.

"Why don't I ask Henry to get you those mint plants right

now?" Iris suggested, opening the glass door to hail the gardener in a straw hat, who was crouching in a flower bed beyond the pool. Anna realized that she had been unconsciously staring at him.

"No, no," she protested hurriedly. "Don't bother him."

"It's no bother," Iris insisted.

Anna shook her head but smiled at her friend's kindness. She felt guilty for her uncharitable thoughts about Iris, remembering how often she had taken comfort in Iris's confidence in Anna's ability to make things right. Often, when she had been down, it was a visit from Iris that had forced her up. She gave her friend a brief impulsive hug. "Not today," she said. "I'd better be getting along."

"If you have to," said Iris, fussing with the glass door, which was already halfway open. "Don't forget. Put that party on your calendar."

"I will," said Anna. She walked out the door and down the steps. Iris followed her and stood on the steps as Anna descended.

"Thanks for stopping by, Anna," Iris called after her. "I'll call you during the week."

"Say hello to Edward," Anna replied with a wave. She headed down the incline past the pool, greeting Henry, the gardener, as she went by. It was a long and meandering route through the Stewart estate that led Anna home, but it was a walk she always enjoyed. She followed the path through the gardens, skirted the frog pond, and wandered in the grape arbors until she came to the high hedges and the narrow stream which separated their properties.

Anna decided, before she went in the house, to get a few vegetables from her garden for dinner. She was proud of her garden this year. She had culled a few tips from Henry and had raised a bountiful crop of vegetables. Everything had grown vigorously, probably because much of the garden plot had lain fallow for so many years. She found that she had really enjoyed it this spring, digging in the dirt, encircled by seedlings.

Picking up her shears and a wicker basket from the garden shed, Anna strolled back to her vegetable patch and surveyed her crop. Lustrous, inky eggplants dropped low to the ground, almost hidden by the leaves. Tomatoes dangled invitingly from their stems, their pulpy ripeness in constant danger of plummeting to the ground and exploding. A host of beans were camouflaged by their vines. Being careful not to squash any of her carefully cultivated produce, Anna waded into the garden and crouched down. She began to pick off the vegetables, and they fell easily into her hands. She pulled out some weeds in a desultory fashion after filling her basket, but she realized that there was little left to be done to the garden now. The plants had borne their fruit. Now it was hers to enjoy. She had done her work diligently in May and June, and here was her reward. You could not, past a certain point, change the way things grew.

With a sigh Anna stood up and headed back toward the house. As she walked past the spot where the children's play yard had been, she stopped and sank down on the rusty glider, staring dully at the patch of lawn. It was green now and planted over with flowers. I'd better not mention Paul's birthday, she thought. Tom will only get upset.

She knew how much he didn't like to talk about it. But each year she felt compelled to bring it up, as if it were somehow vital that his parents speak his name aloud, acknowledge his birth. Every year Thomas would turn away from her with a grim look on his face. She didn't do it to pain him. It just seemed that it was important. Then, last year, when she mentioned it, he had suddenly gotten angry.

"Anna, I can't stand it when you say that."

"What? That it's his birthday?"

"Every year it's the same thing. 'Paul is eleven today. Paul is twelve today. It's Paul's thirteenth birthday.' Why do you always have to mention it?"

"Because it is his birthday," she insisted. "Because I want to remember it."

"It's like some grisly joke. Paul's birthday. As if he were still alive and about to walk in that door."

"But, Tom," she protested, "I do believe that he is alive. Don't you? I mean, we don't know any different. We need to have hope, darling."

But Thomas had turned away from her without another word, and the subject was closed between them once again, as it had been for most of the years since Paul was gone. She could not pinpoint the time when they had stopped any discussion of it. But the child's disappearance was like an amputation on the body of their marriage. Tom wanted to cover it, to hide it and pretend it hadn't happened. Or so it seemed to Anna, as she restlessly sought help, advice, some reassurance that she would one day reattach what seemed irretrievably lost. As if by agreement, they avoided talking about it. It was the best they could do.

Anna examined the ground from her seat on the glider, to see if any trace remained of the play fence, any faint outline of where it had been. The grass had grown over it. There was not a sign. It was as if it had never existed.

After getting up and clutching her basket of vegetables close to her chest, Anna walked up to the back porch and entered the cool, quiet house. She placed the basket on the butcher block beside the sink and turned on the tap, placing a copper colander into the clean porcelain basin. The only sound in the house was the rush of the running water.

Normally she liked nothing better than to be busy in her comfortable kitchen, but now a melancholy mood descended on her. She held her wrist under the water, like a mother testing a baby's formula, and gazed over the plants on her windowsill into the stillness of the sun-dappled backyard.

Suddenly she became aware of a sound like tapping. Turning off the water, she listened again. Someone was knocking at the front door. After wiping her hands off quickly on the soft terry towel next to the sink, she hurried through the house to the foyer and opened the door. At first she saw no one there. Stepping out onto the front porch, she observed the familiar back of a man descending the flagstone steps toward the driveway where his car was parked.

"Buddy," she called out, "come back. I'm here."

Detective Mario Ferraro started and then turned slowly around to face the woman standing in the doorway. He watched her face, smiling in welcome, for a moment without moving. Over the years he had come to know her well. Long after Paul's case had been officially abandoned, she continued to call him with questions about psychics, or other missing children, or any case that bore any similarity to her own. He had responded with what he hoped was patience and care to each of her desperate hopes, tracking down any fillip of a lead that came his way. "It's that poor woman again," a rookie named Parker told him, the last time she had called with news of a child who had turned up in Houston. That poor woman.

He knew that was how the others saw her, but secretly he admired her courage and her tenacity. After losing her son and then the baby, she had pulled herself together and committed herself to the search. Some people thought it was abnormal, but Buddy saw the logic in her efforts. But for the grace of God, he had reminded himself often, he would have had to make such a choice as hers. He had decided to help her. One night Thomas had taken him aside in the kitchen and apologized to him for Anna's relentless questions and leads. "There's no getting through to her," Thomas had said. In a way Thomas's reaction had bothered him more than Anna's. But he held his tongue. "I don't mind," he told Thomas. "I can imagine what she's going through."

"What's the matter with you?" Anna asked, squinting at him. "You look kind of sick."

Buddy Ferraro smiled with one corner of his mouth. "I'm glad you're here."

"I was out in the garden. I didn't hear your car come in. I hope you haven't been standing here for long."

The detective shook his head.

Buddy climbed the steps haltingly. When he reached the porch where Anna stood, he looked at her and frowned, pressing his lips together. Anna linked her arm through his and led him into the house. "My garden," she said, "is really terrific this year. I've got something for you to take to Sandra. Eggplants and tomatoes. You get that wife of yours to make you eggplant Parmesan. No excuses. I'll give you a big bagful to take home."

"Anna . . ." he began.

Arm in arm they had passed through the foyer and into the bright L-shaped living room, which was filled with flowers, baskets of magazines, and needlepoint pillows on the furniture. Anna released the detective's arm and gestured toward a chair next to the fireplace at the end of the room. "Please sit down," she insisted. "I haven't seen you in such a long time now. I'm glad you came by. I was just in

there starting to feel sorry for myself." She moved her
knitting bag off the chair matching his and sat down
opposite him.

Buddy perched on the edge of the seat and leaned
forward.

"Can I get you something to drink? Club soda or a
beer?"

The policeman shook his head. "It's good to see you," he
said quietly.

Anna smiled. "How are the boys?" she asked. "Mark
and little Buddy?"

"They're fine. Mark starts college next year. Sandy and I
are taking him up there for freshman orientation."

"Oh, Buddy!" Anna exclaimed, taken aback. "Already?
Is it possible?" Her eyes became distracted, and she bit her
lip. Then she shook her head. "That's wonderful. You and
Sandy must be so proud of him."

"We are," said the detective, folding his hands tightly
together. "Anna," he said firmly, "this isn't just a friendly
visit. I have some news for you."

Anna gasped as if he had slapped her. Over the years she
had been like a disappointed lover, waiting for a missive that
never came. In time she had grown to expect the postman,
not the letter. Now, suddenly, the detective was turning it all
around. She stared into the eyes of the policeman, trying to
read what the message might be.

"Is Thomas home?" he asked quietly. "I think he should
be here."

"He's not . . . he's out," she whispered, her eyes
riveted to the detective's face.

Buddy Ferraro frowned. "Maybe we should . . ."

"It's Paul," she said. She clasped her hands together and
pressed them to her lips. "Tell me," she whispered.

Buddy nodded and cleared his throat. "Anna," he said, "I don't know how to say this. It's going to be a shock."

Anna began to shake her head as she stared at him.

Buddy hesitated. "Paul's been found. He's alive."

Anna crushed her trembling fists to her mouth and squeezed her eyes shut for a moment. His words hung in the air before her, waiting for her to comprehend them. But a tingling fear suffused her, paralyzing her. She felt that if she tried to grasp what he said, take hold of it, it would somehow be snatched away from her. All hope, everything she had prayed for and clung to for all these years would vanish instantly and forever. "Don't lie to me, Buddy," she warned him in a shaking, nearly inaudible voice.

"I wouldn't, Anna. You know that. It's true. You can believe it. He's alive." Buddy was surprised by the tears which sprang to his eyes. He pressed his lips into a crooked smile.

Anna sat frozen in her chair for a moment. Then, slowly, as if in a trance, she slid from the seat to her knees on the floor, clutching her arms around her chest. Her head was bowed; her eyes were shut.

Buddy sprang forward from his seat, prepared to grab her, thinking at first that she had fainted. Then, understanding, he exhaled and sat back in his chair. Bowing his head, he crossed himself quickly. The room was silent.

When Anna raised her head, her face was like a flower opening, haltingly turning out fragile petals one by one.

Buddy offered her his hand. Anna reached for it and kneaded it between her icy fingers. "Tell me everything," she whispered in a choked voice. "Where is he? Is he all right? Is he safe?"

"He's fine," Buddy assured her.

For a few minutes the two people sat silently, hands

locked together. Buddy could feel the waves of shuddering going through her. Then he coughed and reached into his pocket . "Just let me do this," he mumbled, removing his handkerchief and handing it to her. "Here."

While Anna wiped her eyes, the detective began to explain. "It happened this morning. We got a call from the sheriff of Hawley, West Virginia. He had been contacted by a minister in town who had evidence that Paul has been living all these years in that town as the son of a couple named Albert and Dorothy Lee Rambo. It seems that the woman was dying of cancer, and last week she contacted this minister, one Reverend Orestes Foster, and gave him a letter. Told him to open it at the time of her death, which occurred day before yesterday. The letter amounted to a confession that she and her husband had abducted Paul and raised him as their own son, and it also revealed Paul's identity, which apparently they were aware of all along."

"You're sure it's Paul."

Buddy nodded. "It's your boy all right. She still had the little clothes he was wearing when they took him. Pictures of him. The works. Evidently the woman believed that this terminal illness was some kind of punishment for her crime. She wanted to set accounts straight, make sure the boy would be returned to you."

"What about her husband?"

Buddy grimaced. "Well, that's a problem. It seems that she told him what she planned to do because he cut out of there before she even died. Just left the kid and took off. He's been on the run ever since. The man is a little disturbed, I'm afraid. From what I understand, he's had a history of hospitalization for mental illness."

"Oh, God, no."

"As far as we can determine, he never hurt the . . .

Paul . . . in any way. He was just not quite right. The woman apparently was okay. She worked as a nurse and took care of them. Anyway, the police are looking for this guy, Rambo. And the FBI. They'll find him."

"Where is Paul now? Did you speak to him?"

"No, no, not yet. He's still being questioned by the Hawley police. They're trying to find out what they can. Getting the story in bits and pieces. You gotta remember, this has come as a real jolt to all of them. They've known these Rambos for some years. You should have heard this sheriff on the phone. I could barely understand him for his drawl." Buddy chuckled.

"But Paul is safe?" Anna persisted. "Is he okay?"

Buddy squeezed her hand. "They're taking good care of Paul. And he'll be home here with you before you know it."

Anna shook her head helplessly. "Why?" she whispered. "How did they take him? Why my son?"

"There's a lot we don't know yet. The boy was too young to remember it. But we're getting what information we can. All in good time, Anna," he said soothingly. "You'll know soon enough. At least he's alive. And we've found him."

"I have to see him."

"You will. Before you know it, you'll have your boy back."

Anna looked up at him with serious, tear-filled eyes. "I never gave up on him, Buddy. Sometimes I thought I was losing my mind over this. I always believed that he'd come home."

"You were right," the detective said.

Tears began to dribble down Anna's face again. For the first time in eleven years she pictured her son in her mind, and her heart did not twist in agony but was filled with joy.

What did he look like now? How would he be? Would he know her, and she him? Suddenly she looked up at the detective. "I have to tell Thomas. And Tracy. I have to find them."

"Do you know where they are?" Buddy asked.

"They're over at the tennis courts in the park. I have to tell them." Anna scrambled to her feet and looked around the room confusedly. "I need the keys. Where did I put the keys?" She wiped her tears away, but they continued to flow.

"Never mind," said Buddy, standing up. "I'll drive you over there. You're in no state to be driving."

"You don't have to do that, Buddy."

"I think I'd better. Your mind is not going to be on the road."

Anna raised her hands in a gesture of surrender. "You're right. Oh, let's go."

Anna and Buddy hardly spoke on the way to the park. Buddy devoted exaggerated attention to the rules of the road, as if he were drunk and had to negotiate with extra care. Anna sat straight up in the seat beside him, staring through the windshield, her thoughts ricocheting inside her head. She squeezed her hands together and continually squelched the urge to cry out, "Faster, faster."

The detective drove as fast as he safely could, sensing the urgency which emanated from his passenger's tense frame. He glanced over at her briefly and felt a wave of apprehension at the sight of her delicate profile. The suffering she had endured was visible in the lines on her face, especially in her forehead. Her soft brown hair was streaked with strands of gray. But her eyes were shining now, and her skin had a high color that had been missing for a long time. These years had taken a high toll on her and on that family, he thought. He offered a silent prayer that her ordeal would now be over. He wished he could dispel the uneasy feeling that had plagued him all day, whenever he thought of Paul's homecoming.

They passed through the stone columns which flanked the entrance to the park. Anna nervously directed him to the tennis courts, which were beyond the baseball diamond. As they pulled up to the courts, Anna could see through the climbing roses and the green chain links of the court walls the flash of Tracy's white shirt and her swift, coltish legs and the back of Thomas's compact, muscular figure in white across the net.

"Okay," she said aloud, as if preparing herself.

"Do you want me to wait?"

Anna stirred and faced him in a daze. Then she shook her head. "Tom will drive home. Buddy, I can never thank you enough." She leaned over and embraced him fervently for a second. Then she began to slide out of the car. As she put her hand on the door handle, she turned back to him, a worried frown on her face.

"What is it?" he asked.

"Buddy, I keep thinking about this man, this kidnapper . . ."

"Rambo?"

"Yes. You say there's something wrong with him mentally. We don't know what he might do. . . ."

Buddy dismissed her fears with a wave of his hand. "I have a feeling that Mr. Rambo is trying to get as far away from you and your son as he can. There's nothing to worry about, Anna. We'll bring Paul back to you safe and sound. Don't get yourself worked up over nothing. Go tell your family the good news. Go on."

Anna smiled and slammed the door behind her.

"Good luck," Buddy blurted out, not quite knowing why. He watched her as she hurried toward the court, bearing her precious piece of news. For a moment, incongruously, he thought of the eggplant and tomatoes she had promised him. Next time she would have them waiting for him. She wasn't one to forget. He tracked her graceful, straight-backed figure thoughtfully as she rushed toward her family. He had not told her all the Hawley sheriff had had to say about the severity of Albert Rambo's mental illness. Nor had he conveyed the sheriff's disturbing description of the sullen, uncooperative youth whose return Anna was anticipating with such joy. Why worry her? he thought. Things will all work out. But Buddy could not shake off the feeling of anxiety that had crept up on him again.

"Now you're in trouble," Tracy cried out as the racket connected with the ball at the sweet spot, with a hum and a thwack.

Crouched down and weaving, Thomas watched the ball and leapt for it. He slid into position and drew back his arm to swing, but his concentration was broken by the sight of Anna, who had thrown open the door to the court and was rushing toward him. He smiled and waved when he saw her, and then he frowned as he saw the expression on her face.

"Mo-ther!" Tracy cried in a voice shrill with exasperation. "Get off the court. You're not supposed to be here."

Anna did not even seem to hear her daughter. She ran up to Thomas and then stopped short, a foot shy of him. She clasped her hands together and stared into her husband's baffled face.

"Tom, I have to tell you something."

"What is it, darling?" he asked worriedly. "What's the matter?" He took a step toward her.

"It's Paul."

Thomas's mouth tightened, and his eyes narrowed with wariness. He raised his racket and held it across his chest. "We're right in the middle of a game, Anna," he said.

"What's going on?" Tracy screamed across the court. The players on the adjacent court looked over at them through the mesh wall and then back at one another before resuming their game.

"Tom, Buddy Ferraro was just here. At our house. Thomas, Paul's been found. He's been found alive. The woman who kidnapped him died and left a confession. Tom, he's alive. He's coming home. Paul's coming home." Anna's face crumpled, and she buried it in her hands.

Thomas stared at his wife in disbelief. He lowered his racket, and it dangled uselessly from his hand. "What?" he whispered.

Anna nodded. "It's true. I'm telling you it's true. Paul is coming back to us."

Thomas's heart swooped down and thudded inside his chest like a bucket let loose in a well. His eyes registered the azure sky, the green summer's day, and his wife's tearstained face and he knew that it was real. But it seemed to him that the pulsing of blood in his ears was muffling the words she was saying. They were words he had never expected to hear. When he tried to picture the boy, there was only a blank spot in his mind, only the black hole with which he had willfully replaced his son's image through the years.

Anna was gazing at him now, gripping his hands, which he had unconsciously freed by thrusting his racket under his upper arm. The warmth of her hands and the intensity in her eyes seemed to revive him. Feeling returned to him, in the form of an acute tenderness for her. She stood bravely before him, like a sapling that had withstood a pitiless gale.

He slipped his arms around her and drew her to his chest, his hands resting awkwardly on her back. "I knew it," she said, her cheek pressed to his sweaty tennis shirt. "I knew he was alive. I knew he would come back."

Thomas stroked her hair, staring out over her head. "Paul's alive," he murmured. "You always said that. I never thought . . . I can't believe it."

Anna pulled back and looked into her husband's eyes. The tears were starting again in her own. "Oh, darling," she whispered.

Thomas squeezed her arms, wishing he could find his tears, but he felt as if they were trapped in a knot in the pit of his stomach. "It's wonderful," he said. "God, it's unbelievable."

"Forget it," Tracy screamed from across the court. She threw down her racket, which clattered to the ground, and started to stalk off the court. "I don't know what's going on here, but you can find yourself somebody else to play with."

"No, Tracy," Anna cried, disengaging herself from Thomas's arms and hurrying toward her daughter. She grabbed hold of the top of the net and leaned over it. "Tracy, wait. We have to tell you something. Wait for me." Anna did not want to yell the news out in front of the other players. But Tracy reached defiantly for the door of the court and yanked it open.

"Tracy, listen to me, darling," Anna pleaded. "Your brother has been found. Paul. Paul is coming back."

Tracy turned around and faced her mother, who leaned toward her, clutching the top of the net between them.

Behind her mother her father stood, immobile, his arms hanging limply at his sides.

Slowly the blood drained away from Tracy's tanned and freckled face. She seemed rooted there, staring at them, her eyes wide and blank. The skin around her lips was a white ridge. For a moment her hand remained frozen to the door of the cage. Then her hand dropped, leaden, to her side. The chain link gate swung back and clanged shut behind her.

CHAPTER TWO

"All right, sleeping beauty, rise and shine."

Anna forced her eyes open like someone coming out of anesthesia and looked up groggily. Thomas was standing beside the bed in his bathrobe, holding a tray of food, decorated with one of the dahlias from her garden propped up in a juice glass.

She pulled the sheet up over her breasts and sat up with a sleepy smile. "Honey, what's this?"

Thomas looked down at the tray. "It's eggs, toast, coffee, and Bloody Marys!" Then he shot her a smile. "I forgot the milk. Here, hold this," he said, placing the tray on her knees atop the sheets. "I'll be right back."

"What time is it?" she called after his disappearing back.

"Almost eleven. I figured you needed the sleep."

Anna leaned back against the pillows and smiled at the tray on her lap. Then she gazed around the sunny bedroom. The wedding ring quilt was wadded up at the end of the bed, and their clothes were strewn on the bedpost and the floor, the telltale trail of lovers' impatience.

Yesterday, after they had gotten back from the tennis court, they had spent the balance of the day on the telephone and having visitors, talking to family, friends, and reporters. Thomas had gone out for Chinese food and brought it home about nine o'clock. Tracy had pleaded an upset stomach and closeted herself in her room for the rest of the night. At about midnight Thomas had unplugged the phone and hustled Anna up to the bedroom, where, with an urgency she had not seen from him in a while, he made love to her as if it were their last night together. At his moment of climax he had let out a cry so close to anguish that it startled her. She soothed him until he fell asleep, but she was awake most of the night, thinking about the miraculous news with a heart and mind so full that they would not admit sleep. It was nearly dawn when exhaustion finally claimed her.

The door to the bedroom opened again, and Thomas came in, carrying a small creamer of milk. He placed it on the tray and sat down carefully beside her on the bed. "Damn the crumbs, let's eat!"

Anna reached over and stroked the side of his face. "What a sweet thing to do," she said.

Thomas shrugged. "I thought we should celebrate. Besides, we hardly had a moment together yesterday. It was so crazy around here."

"Where's Trace?"

"She took off early on her bike. She left a note saying she was going to Mary Ellen's."

"I think she's upset by all of this," said Anna.

Thomas stirred the Bloody Mary with a celery stalk and handed it to his wife. Anna obediently took a sip. "It's a big change," said Tom. "It's a big change for all of us. But she'll be happy about it when she sees what a difference it's going to make in our lives."

Anna sighed and smiled at him. "I think so, too. Our son. Back home with us, and safe."

Thomas nodded and took a bite of the eggs. "We'll have a normal life again. Like other families."

Anna nodded, but she spoke a little defensively. "Well, we've had a pretty normal life, under the circumstances."

"I know," said Tom quickly. "I didn't mean that."

"It will just be that much better a life for having Paul back with us," she explained.

"I just meant," said Tom, "you know, that all that awful business will be over. You running off to every corner of the country every time we heard of a child somewhere. Those late nights on the phone and all that endless searching, contacting people. Nuts calling up every hour of the day or night with useless information. Reporters and police and psychics. If I never see another one of any of them, it will be too soon."

"They were all trying to help," Anna said.

"I'm sure they were, but they put you through a lot. You have to admit it. Now the boy will be back, and we can stop thinking about it. We can get back to living our lives the way we should." He reached over and squeezed her arms. "You don't know how I've missed it."

Anna looked at him seriously. "I missed it, too," she said. "But what other choice did we have?"

Thomas picked up a napkin and wiped his lips. "Right. Right," he said. "Now you eat those eggs," he ordered, "before they get cold, and then I think I might just crawl back under those sheets with you."

Anna laughed and picked up a forkful of eggs. "These look good," she said. "I may let you have this job since you do it so well."

"I'm talented," he said. "And modest."

"Has Buddy called yet?" she asked. "He was going to

arrange for us to talk to Paul today. I'm surprised we haven't heard from him."

Thomas poured some cream into his coffee. "I don't know if he tried," he said. "I've still got the phone unplugged."

"Tom," Anna protested, "Paul may be trying to reach us."

"I wanted you to sleep," he said ruefully. "You were so tired."

Anna put the tray to one side and leaned over to the phone on the bedside table. "Plug it in for me, will you, darling? I'm going to call Buddy right now."

"Why don't you eat first?"

"Just let me find out."

Thomas removed the tray from the bed with a soft sigh and placed it on the floor. Then he bent down beside the night table and plugged the phone into the jack.

Anna leaned over the edge of the bed and kissed him on the cheek. "Thanks." She picked up the receiver and started to dial.

Thomas sat on the rug, resting his head against the mattress. Anna finished dialing and placed one hand on his shoulder. He stared dully down at the tray beside him, where the eggs were hardening on the edge of the plate. He picked up a piece of toast and began to chew it slowly. The bread was getting cold now and tasted like greasy cardboard in his mouth.

The week of arrangements, red tape, and waiting seemed interminable to Anna, but finally they passed. Now, by the light of the early-morning sun through her kitchen window, Anna sat planning the homecoming dinner. The butcher-block surface of her table was littered with open cookbooks.

Glossy photographs on their pages pictured special dishes for every festive occasion, and Anna pored over them, seeking inspiration. She rubbed her eyes with the back of her hand and yawned. But it was a nervous gesture. She was not really tired.

She could feel her cotton shirt already beginning to stick to her back. The August day had started to heat up early. There was usually a breeze that ran through the house, keeping it comfortable, and there were only a few days a year that she even thought of air conditioning. She hoped to herself that this would not be one of them. She wanted everything to be perfect for this, his first day home. She wanted him to like it here.

Anna returned her attention to the cookbooks. He was not coming until dinnertime. It was bound to be cooler by then. She slowly turned the pages, studying the recipes, wondering which occasion most closely mirrored this unusual celebration. It was hard to know what to make, what he liked to eat. There was a recipe for lobster that looked good. Lobster was something special, and cool. But what if he had allergies to seafood? Lots of people did. She realized that she had no way of knowing about her son.

She rested her chin on her hand and looked out over the profusion of plants on the kitchen windowsill. Her mind drifted to its recurrent preoccupation of the last week. She wondered what he was like now, how he looked. During the last eleven years she had seen him everywhere. On every playground, swinging on the swings, at street corners as she whizzed by in her car, coming toward her down the corridors at Tracy's school. Her heart would leap to her throat as she spied him, sure it was Paul. His name would be on her lips when, as she looked harder, the vision of his face would dissolve, and she would see before her some strange child with honey-colored hair whom she did not recognize at all. She would turn away quickly, before the little one could see the horror and woe in her eyes.

But tonight she would open the door and he would be there. Tonight.

She shook herself out of her reverie and returned to the recipes. There was a lamb dish that looked appetizing to her. It was resting on a bed of yellow rice. The meat glistened, brown and juicy, on the page. Anna held the pages between two fingers. The thought of turning on the oven in this weather was unappealing. Through the open kitchen door she could see a haze of sultry air hovering over the yard. For no good reason she remembered the maggoty mutton stew which Lizzie Borden's mother was said to have served several hot days in succession to her restive daughter. Anna flipped the page over. It's too hot for lamb, she thought.

Tracy, wearing tennis whites and sneakers, entered the kitchen and slumped into a chair without a greeting. Anna pushed the cookbooks aside.

"Did you have a good sleep?" Anna asked.

"It's been so noisy around here it woke me up."

"Oh, I hope I didn't disturb you, darling. I got up early because I had so much to do," said Anna, ignoring Tracy's gloomy expression. "I dusted, waxed the furniture, and then I baked this." She got up, walked over to the counter, and lifted the lid on the cake dish. She held up the cake she had baked for her daughter's inspection. It read "Welcome home, Paul" in blue letters arching around the top half of the cake's chocolate icing. "I made chocolate. I figured all you kids like chocolate. Well, what do you think?"

Tracy stared at the blue writing and then looked up at her mother. "You made that?"

Anna nodded. "Does it look good?"

Tracy folded her arms across her chest and stared sullenly in front of her. "Yeah. Sure."

Anna returned the cake to the counter and replaced the lid after one last look. She wiped her hands on her apron and turned to Tracy. "What do you want for breakfast, sweetheart?"

"Nothing," said Tracy.

"Well, you should have something. You can't go out on an empty—"

"Juice."

"How about some cereal? I can get you some—"

"No!" Tracy shrieked. "I said juice."

Just then Thomas walked into the kitchen, still buttoning a cuff on his shirt. He stopped short and looked at his daughter.

"It's too hot to eat," Tracy insisted to him. Her tanned face was mottled, and her chin trembled.

"All right," said Anna.

"There's no need to scream," said Thomas.

"She tries to force me to eat when I'm not even hungry," Tracy muttered.

Anna placed a glass of juice in front of her daughter and turned to Thomas. "You had such a restless night," she said. "I hope I didn't wake you getting dressed this morning."

"I woke up for a minute. It was pitch-black out. What time was it anyway?" he asked.

"Oh, it must have been about four thirty, maybe quarter to five."

"Quarter to five," Tom repeated incredulously.

"I couldn't sleep," said Anna. "I was too excited."

Thomas put his arms around her and squeezed her, kissing her on the forehead.

"What do you want for breakfast?" Anna asked.

"I'm running late. I'll get something off the cart."

"Oh, Tom . . ."

"What's all this?" he asked, glancing at the pile of cookbooks.

"I'm looking for something to make tonight. I guess I should look through some of those magazines of mine, right?"

"I thought you were saving those for a special occasion," he said.

Anna smiled happily at the appropriateness of one of their standard jokes. "I'm so worked up I can't even think straight."

Tracy scraped back her chair and stood up. Anna tried to get her daughter's attention. "What do you think we should have, Tracy?"

"I'm leaving," Tracy announced.

"Playing tennis this morning?" Anna asked.

"Mmmm . . ." Tracy mumbled.

"Before you go, dear, I want you to get upstairs and take your stuff out of the guest . . . out of Paul's room so I can clean up there."

"I'll do it later," said Tracy. "Bye, Dad."

Thomas smiled at her. "Good luck," he said.

Anna picked the glass up from the table. "I want you to do it now. I need to get into that room."

Tracy stiffened in the doorway. "I have a game this morning."

"It won't take you long," Anna insisted. "You've known you had to do this all week."

"I told you I had a game this morning."

"And I told you," Anna reminded her sternly, "that I need that room emptied out so I can get it ready for Paul.

Now I mean it, Trace. Get up there right now. There are things more important than your game. Your brother is coming home tonight."

Tracy turned on her mother, her small jaw hardening stubbornly. Her hazel eyes were icy with rage. "I don't care," she said. "I'm leaving."

Anna was momentarily speechless, stung by the cold defiance in her daughter's eyes.

"Tracy," Thomas ordered, "do as you're told."

"Shit!" Tracy exclaimed, stamping out of the kitchen. "You both stink."

Anna shook her head and sat down. "God, she is really in a state about this thing. I don't understand it. Have you tried to talk to her? She just puts up a wall with me."

Thomas sighed, putting his newspaper in his briefcase. "No," he admitted. "I don't know what to say to her."

"Maybe she's jealous of all the attention to Paul. You know, she feels usurped," Anna speculated.

"Well, it does seem to be the only thing anyone has talked about all week," he said.

"I know," said Anna, "but that's only natural. I mean this has just happened. Naturally we're all excited about it."

"She might be feeling it's going to stay that way once he gets here," said Thomas.

Anna looked at her husband quizzically. "What do you mean?"

"I don't know," said Thomas, dismissing it. "Just talking through my hat. She's been a little hard to deal with for some time now."

"I think any parent would feel the way we do," said Anna.

Thomas looked at his watch. "She'll come around," he said. "Listen, Anna, we'd better run."

Anna nodded, even though she wished they could continue the conversation. She got up and found her car keys in the little teacup she kept beside the sink. Their second car was in the garage for repairs; that meant she had to drive him to the station.

Thomas shrugged into his jacket and picked up his briefcase. She glanced at him and saw that he was looking at her with a kind of accusation in his eyes. She raised her eyebrows in surprise.

"Your apron, Anna," he said.

Anna looked down at the apron stained with chocolate and blue icing. She untied it and hung it on a hook behind the door. "Okay," she said. "I just forgot."

Leafy limbs of ancient maples canopied the quiet back roads of Stanwich. Stately houses overlooked manicured lawns, separated by orchards and stone fences. Few cars passed to disturb the tranquillity of the morning.

Anna drove and Thomas rode in silence. He had his briefcase open on his lap and was leafing through the reports it contained. She watched the road unwind and the houses get closer together and smaller in size as they neared the center of town and the railroad station. She glanced at him out of the corner of her eye. He seemed to be absorbed in his papers.

"Tom . . ." she ventured.

"Yeah . . ."

"Are you looking forward to tonight?"

Thomas rested his hands in the open briefcase and nodded slowly. "Yes, of course I am."

"I still can't believe it. It's a miracle, really," she

continued cautiously. "Our son finally coming back to us. We'll all be together again, the way it used to be."

"I hope so," he said. "I really do."

"It's a wonderful thing. We're so lucky."

"Yes, we are," he said. He reached over and rubbed her thigh for a moment.

"I'm just afraid . . . I hope that Paul will be . . . all right."

Thomas removed his hand from her leg and looked at her warily. "Why shouldn't he?" he asked.

Anna twisted her lip and did not reply. She could sense him stiffening slightly, his eyes on her face.

"Ever since we heard about Paul, I've been thinking," she began. "Worrying actually."

"About what?"

Anna hesitated. "Well, I was thinking it might be a good idea if we had some protection . . . for him."

She kept her eyes on the road, but she could feel his eyes scrutinizing her.

"What for? I don't follow you."

"Well, I just can't help worrying about him."

"Paul?"

"That man." She shuddered.

There was a silence. "Rambo," Thomas said.

"He's running around loose somewhere. We know the man is mentally unbalanced. We have no idea what he is capable of. He might decide to come after Paul. He might have some crazy idea that Paul is really his and come looking for him or something."

"I don't think we should borrow trouble, Anna. We have no reason to think he'll do anything of the kind."

Anna turned and stared at him. "How can you be so sure of that? He took our son once, didn't he?"

"Watch the road, Anna," Thomas cried.

The car swerved slightly as Anna came around a curve and then evened out.

"Look," said Thomas, "the police have told you . . . even your friend Buddy told you . . . the man is probably going to run as far and as fast as he can. He has a kidnapping charge to face if the police get him. The last thing he's going to do is come around here. Even Rambo is not that crazy. I think you should just forget about him."

"I understand all that about the kidnapping charge. But I also think that we're not dealing with a rational, predictable person. I mean, was it rational for him to take our son? How can you predict what a person like that will do? We know that he had a history of mental illness—"

"All right," Thomas interrupted her, "but if he knew enough to run away when he found out that his wife was planning to spill the beans, I think we can be reasonably certain that he is not going to walk directly into the arms of the police."

Anna gripped the wheel tightly. "I don't know," she said. "Maybe you're right. But I have a bad feeling about it."

"For God's sake, Anna," Thomas said quietly as the railroad station came into view, "I thought now that you had the boy back, you would finally stop all this. I mean, do you get pleasure out of this constant worrying? Why can't you leave well enough alone?"

Anna pulled the car up beside the platform and shifted into neutral with the motor still running. "No, I do not enjoy the worrying, and you know it. But I won't just forget about this. Not after all we've been through. And your criticizing me about it doesn't help."

"All right, I'm sorry, I'm sorry," said Thomas. He opened the car door and got out. A rush of uniformly dressed, neatly barbered commuters passed on each side of the Volvo. Anna slid across the seat and looked up at him as he closed the car door. She opened her mouth to speak. Thomas glanced at his watch and then bent down beside the open window.

"Try to come home early," she said. "It's going to be a very happy night. You'll see."

"I know." Thomas gave her a strained smile and turned away from the window. Clenching his fingers around the briefcase handle, he started up the steps to the platform. Anna watched her husband disappear into the ranks of men in gray suits with attaché cases and newspapers under their arms who milled around restlessly on the platform, their eyes searching the tracks for the train to the city.

The mingled smells of toasting bread and greasy bacon and potatoes frying oozed through the grimy wall fan in back of the luncheonette and into the parking lot behind the little row of stores. The man who stood in the early-morning shadows behind the stores was tantalized by the smells. He plucked at the skin on his face with rapidly moving fingers, leaving red blotches across the surface of his pasty skin. Inside the diner, the waitresses and the short-order cook ribbed each other above the clatter of dishes. Although he heard their words, the man could not understand their joking. He never understood what was funny about the things people said to one another or why they laughed.

None of the other stores on the street was open yet, and the only car in the lot, besides his own blue Chevy, was an aquamarine Cadillac with gray velvet upholstery that came from DeRosa Motors, Kingsburgh, New York.

The man in the shadows remembered passing the Cadillac dealer on his way into Kingsburgh the night before. It was a couple of miles up the road from the cheap little motel court he had found, traveling slowly in the dark. This morning he had been up with the dawn, hunger summoning him, driving him out. He glanced around to see if anyone was watching him. The man wore a stiff gray hat, pulled low over his eyes, and dark sunglasses. A short-sleeved polyester sport shirt revealed wiry white arms covered with blondish hair. He knotted the probing, jabbing fingers into fists and thrust them deep into the pockets of his ill-fitting pants.

Another wave of heavy breakfast smells reached him, like a cat rubbing against his ankles. His stomach growled in instinctive response. He looked down the line of stores. There was a stationery store, a pharmacy, a bowling alley with a bar, and, two doors down from the luncheonette, a grocery store. Behind the grocery store sat a squat green metal garbage Dumpster—the reason he was here.

After detaching himself from the shadows, he moved deliberately across the backs of the stores to where the Dumpster stood. For two days he had had nothing to eat besides candy bars purchased in gas station machines. He had hardly any money and had been sleeping in his car in cul-de-sacs he found off the main highway. Finally he had had to stop. The voices had been so distracting him that he had almost driven into a divider on the highway. He decided to put up for a few nights in that dumpy motel, but if he did that, he didn't have enough money for food, too.

Grocery stores threw out food, though. There was bound to be something in the Dumpster. Looking all around him, he lifted the heavy metal lid and held it up with one hand. The smell of rotting and decaying food wafted up from inside, convincing him of his own cleverness. He stuck his head under the lid and looked inside. Loose garbage rested atop plastic trash bags in an unsightly array. Below a rumpled newspaper he saw an open egg box with three cracked eggs and two whole ones in it and, beside that, an open box of crackers with paper stuffed inside it. He reached in past a ripped and soggy milk container and fished for the egg box. He pulled out the newspaper first and threw it on the ground, As it fell, he saw the picture on the front page of his son, staring up at him.

Albert Rambo heaved a disgusted sigh and bent down to pick up the paper. Propping the Dumpster lid open against his shoulder, he read the latest news article about Paul Lange's happy reunion with his family which was about to take place. His lip curled as he scanned the story. On the inside page was a picture of the Langes' house, a monstrous palace to his eyes in the town of Stanwich, Connecticut.

A fit place for that scheming heathen to do the devil's own business, Rambo thought. Among the rich and godless up there in Connecticut. If the truth were known, he belonged in hell with the other devils, he thought. He did not know that he was muttering aloud. Rambo's stomach growled again, more insistently now. After all those years of giving up things for him, raising him as his own. He could still hear his wife's voice in his head. "The boy needs shoes. He needs a coat. Billy needs . . . Billy needs . . ."

Rambo gazed down at the house in the picture in the paper where the blaspheming little infidel, that acolyte to Beelzebub, would now be living.

Paul Lange. He snorted. Sounds like a young prince. Like a little boy-king. Dorothy Lee's voice faded away as other voices began to grip him like a siren song, whirling up through the hole in his stomach, haranguing him in insistent tones. The voices spoke of God's wrath against the wicked,

His desire that they should be plundered, trodden upon like the mire of the streets. Urging him, urging him, arming him with conviction.

A squeal near his elbow made Rambo jump and the voices disappear. A bloated rat scuttled down the wall of the Dumpster and into the garbage. Rambo's stomach squawked again, reminding him of his purpose at the Dumpster. He threw the newspaper back into the trash and shifted his shoulder out from under the lid and held it up with his hand. Then, with a furtive look around, he reached into the bin to pull up the crackers and the eggs.

Stanwich was only about thirty miles from there, he thought, as he sucked the cracked egg greedily from its shell. He knew the exact spot. Billy's new home. He remembered it well. Stuffing the cracker box under his arm, he crossed over to his car. He wanted to get out of the parking lot before anyone saw him and before the day's commerce began. He wanted to get back to his room before the voices came back, suggesting things to him, telling him what to do.

CHAPTER THREE

The gray towers of Manhattan were enveloped in a barley-colored haze of heat and soot. Thomas stared out his office window, dreading the prospect of going into the streets again. The air had been thick and nauseating at lunch, and the asphalt in the streets threatened to turn viscous from the heat. He knew what it would be like tonight, walking to Grand Central Station. Pedestrians, like human bumper cars, dodging and colliding with one another, knees slamming into swinging briefcases. Teen-agers on roller skates, wearing satin shorts and headsets, slicing through groups of startled walkers. Vendors, with carts of plastic boxes filled with dried fruits and nuts, blocking strategic intersections, forcing people to fan dangerously over the curbs.

Even from the twentieth floor, where he sat, Thomas could hear the whiny bray of the snarled traffic below on Madison Avenue. It was the start of the rush hour, which meant that buses and taxis and cars with Jersey plates were now securely lodged in the midst of cross streets, making it impossible for anyone to move in any direction.

With a sigh Thomas turned away from the window and looked again at the clock on his desk. His office, by contrast, was cool and air-conditioned, the temperate air shut in tight by large, clean, hermetically sealed windows. Even the decor was cool: beige carpet, beige walls, a muted blue print on the sofa and drapes. Some of his colleagues had tried to make their individual offices more homey by hanging favorite prints and bringing in plants. To Tom, that had always seemed a futile exercise. The coziness of home could not be duplicated with a few decorations. The only ornament which broke the sterility of the room was the framed picture of Anna and Tracy on his desk. The interior designer hired by the firm had mentioned to him that it was no longer fashionable to keep family pictures on one's desktop. Thomas had greeted this piece of information with stubborn disinterest. Glancing at the laughing faces of his wife and daughter in the photograph, he realized that he would now have to put a picture of Paul there, too. At that thought Thomas felt an unpleasant tightening in his stomach.

He picked up the report on his desk without enthusiasm. He knew that he really should finish it before he went home. It concerned the computer system that was being installed and how it could benefit his department. It was nearly five o'clock now. He counted the pages that he had left to read and calculated the time it would take him. Then he flipped the top page over and read the first paragraph.

There was a soft rap on his office door. He looked up, and his troubled expression dissolved into one of boyish pleasure at the sight of the smartly dressed young woman with wavy black hair who was leaning into his office.

"What did you think of my computer report?" she asked briskly.

Thomas indicated that the report was still in his hands.

"You're not finished with it yet?" she asked.

"I'm almost finished," Thomas said apologetically.

The young woman came into the room and eased herself onto the sofa across from Thomas's desk, then threw one arm across the back and crossed her trim, elegantly hosed legs. "So much for my brilliant analysis," she said, pouting.

"I think you're right about it," Thomas said earnestly. "I think we should have done it two years ago. You've done a very thorough job on this report, Gail."

"If you like, I'll give you a private summary over a martini," she said. "Save you all that boring reading," she said, running one hand lazily up and down her shin.

"Oh, I want to read it," he assured her.

"I'm only teasing you," she said.

"Oh," he said, embarrassed and flattered at once. He could feel her eyes on him, and his scalp prickled at the sensation. He tried not to look at her legs. "Were you teasing about the drink?" he asked.

Gail Kelleher laughed aloud at the ingenuous sound of the question. "Nope. That was a solid offer."

For a minute Thomas could envision himself sitting in a cool dark bar with her, talking and laughing, a piano playing languidly in the background. Even as he thought of it, he remembered what awaited him at home, and he shook his head. "That sounds nice," he said absently. "I wish I could." He frowned and looked down at the report on his desk.

Gail caught the wistful note in his voice. Like everyone else in the office, she knew about Paul's imminent homecoming, even though Thomas hadn't referred to it voluntarily. Although their relationship was still only light and flirtatious, she had tried to let him know that she would welcome his confiding in her. A couple of times he had. Twice, when Anna had gone off on one of her missions in search of the boy, they had shared a drink after work, and dawdling over a second Scotch and water, he had vented a little of his frustration at Anna's relentless pursuit of the missing child. As soon as Gail expressed any sympathy for his point of view, Thomas had immediately withdrawn. But Gail had spotted an opening there. This man, whom she had found terribly attractive from the first time she met him, was not entirely happy with his lot. And today she saw the same glum, distracted look on his face that she recognized from those nights when he had gone so far as to linger for a drink. She found his reaction to the boy's homecoming interesting.

"You seem a little . . . down," she observed. "Are you worried about tonight?"

"What?" Thomas asked. "Oh, worried, no. Not really. Well, it's been a long day. Everyone's been either congratulating me or tiptoeing around me."

"It's hard to know what to say."

"I guess so." He sighed.

She bit her lip. "I'm just concerned about you," she said.

"I'm okay," he insisted, swiveling his chair and looking out the window. "I feel great. Happy."

His voice fell, and he gazed blankly out the window. Gail reached up and toyed with one of her earrings. "I guess Anna must be in quite a state over all this," Gail ventured.

Thomas grimaced. "Well, it's been hectic, kind of. Anna—she's just . . . it's so important to her."

"I imagine she's been awfully busy trying to get things ready for Paul."

"Yes," said Tom. "She doesn't think of anything else."

"Well, I guess she's never been quite normal since that happened."

"Anna!" Tom exclaimed, looking at her incredulously. "She's normal. She's perfectly normal. She's just . . ."

"Obsessed," Gail offered.

Thomas seemed to balk at the word, and Gail could sense that she had gone a little too far. He began to retreat from the conversation. She moved quickly to smooth it over.

"It's a great strain on everyone, of course. You just have to give yourself a little time to adjust."

Thomas ran his hand over his eyes and then nodded. "I'm a little bit tired, I guess."

With slow and deliberate movements, Gail uncrossed her legs and rose out of the sofa. She walked over to where he was sitting and slid around behind his chair. "What you need," she said with mock sternness, "is a good relaxing massage." She placed her hands lightly on the back of his neck and then pressed down in a circular motion. She could feel his muscles tense up at her approach and then begin to relax at the pressure of her touch.

Thomas laughed nervously. "That feels good," he said, and then released a soft, involuntary groan.

Gail smiled to herself and kneaded his neck. "I took a course in massage one summer," she said.

"You must have gotten an A," he said. He wanted to speak in a carefree, flirtatious tone; but the pressure of Gail's hands on his back and neck seemed to be loosening something that was tight inside him, and he had to stifle a sob which rose unexpectedly to his throat. He closed his eyes in guilty enjoyment of the soothing manipulation, and as he did, he felt the sudden impulse to turn and embrace her, to bury his face in her stomach. His eyes shot open, and he pulled away.

"That helped a lot," he said as Gail released him. "Really." He made a point of looking at his watch. "God, I'd better run if I'm going to make the five forty." He looked down at his desk. "I guess I'll take this home with me."

Gail shook out her fingers and headed for the doorway of his office. "Well," she said casually, "if you should want to talk about it over the weekend, just give me a call. Or drop by. I'm in the book. I hope everything goes okay with Paul."

"Thanks," said Thomas. "It will."

Thomas watched her walk out of his office, admiring the sensual way she moved in her very correct business clothes. He realized that he did not feel his customary eagerness to get home. Instead, he wished he were going to a dark bar with her, and having a few drinks, and forgetting everything. Everything but the feeling of her fingers on the back of his neck. Thomas shivered at the thought. He wished he could feel happy or, at the least, hide the sense of apprehension with which he greeted this night. Perhaps he would not have to hide it, he reminded himself. Anna might be too preoccupied to notice. He opened his briefcase, put Gail's report inside, and snapped it shut. Then he pulled on his suit jacket, buttoning one button, and with a last look around his cool, orderly office, he started for the door, steeling himself for the chaos of the street.

Anna unwrapped the silver foil and cocked her head to one side with a crooked smile. Then, holding the bottle by the neck, she reached over and embraced her friend. "Champagne. Iris, that's so thoughtful."

Iris looked at the label uncertainly. "Edward selected the vintage. He says it should be an excellent bottle. Are you all set?"

Anna glanced around the unnaturally tidy kitchen. "I guess so. I think I've done everything twice."

Iris nodded approvingly. "It should be just wonderful."
The two women walked through the quiet house toward the
front door and stood out on the porch steps. "It's going to be
a lovely evening," Iris observed.

Anna nodded, scanning the sky for clouds.

"Don't worry, Anna."

"I'm getting nervous now," Anna admitted. "Maybe I
should go in and wash the floor again."

At that moment a black Cadillac appeared around the
corner, rolled down and pulled into the Langes' driveway.
The car's finish was lustrous, and above the grille, in place
of the characteristic Cadillac trademark, the hood ornament
was a gleaming golden eagle, its wings outstretched to full
span, its talons extended as if the bird were landing on its
prey. "Look who's here," said Iris. "They must have
caught the same train."

Thomas emerged from the passenger side of the Cadillac
and shut the door carefully. He came around the front of the
car as Edward turned off the engine and slid out from behind
the wheel. Both men were smiling, and that took Anna by
surprise. As a rule they were polite but not friendly. Thomas
found Edward to be too cold and demanding for his taste.
"He always looks at me as if I have tuna fish on my tie,"
Thomas would say to her, and she always laughed at his
impression of their neighbor, as with one eyebrow raised
and his nose slightly wrinkled, Tom would brush an
imaginary crumb off the front of her shirt with a curved
forefinger. Now, however, it made Anna feel good to see
them walking, shoulder to shoulder, up the lawn.

She raised the bottle which she was cradling in her arm.
"Look what Iris and Edward brought us," she called out to
Thomas.

Edward smoothed down the silken fabric of his suit jacket

and shook Tom's hand briefly. The two men approached their wives. "Thanks, Iris," Thomas said. "We appreciate the thought."

"Well," said Iris, awkwardly grasping his hand and squeezing it, "we are very happy for you, and we will be thinking of you all tonight."

"Indeed," Edward agreed stiffly. Anna looked fondly at them both, remembering that they had been present and ready to help on another night, the night that Paul had disappeared.

"Would you like to come in for a drink?" Anna asked.

Edward waved a perfectly manicured hand. "We have to be getting home. I have a lot to do tonight."

As Edward spoke, an aqua-colored van with a network logo printed on the side pulled up in front of the house.

"What's this now?" said Thomas as a man in a knitted sport shirt slid out of the front seat and they heard the door slam on the other side. A blond woman in a tailored suit and silk shirt came around the truck and skirted around the man in the sport shirt, who was opening the doors in the back. She hailed the Langes and started up the incline toward them, the heels of her shoes spiking down into the soft summer lawn.

Anna groaned softly, recognizing the reporter, Camille Mandeville, who had interviewed her several times in the years since Paul's disappearance. Anna hurried down the lawn to intercept her as another man emerged from the back of the truck and began to help the driver unload camera and sound equipment.

"Camille, you promised me," Anna said. "Not today. We want a private homecoming for our boy."

"Hello, Mrs. Lange," said the reporter, flashing her dazzling, practiced smile. She glanced down and made a face at the dirt still clinging to her lizardskin shoes. "Oh, we've been crazy all day. I was hoping to get here earlier."

"I made myself very clear," Anna went on. "Everyone else has been very cooperative."

"Calm down, calm down," Camille said soothingly. "We're not staying. We just want a spot for the ten o'clock report with you and your husband, about how excited you are and all that."

Thomas, Edward, and Iris had made their way down the lawn and were now surrounding Anna like reinforcements. "Are these relatives?" Camille asked pleasantly.

"These are our neighbors, Mr. and Mrs. Stewart," said Anna.

Camille gave Iris and Edward a brilliant, if distracted, smile as she shook their hands while sizing up the conditions for shooting on the lawn. "Pleasure to meet you. Hello, Mr. Lange."

"Camille, I don't know about this. We have so much on our minds right now," Anna protested.

Camille, who was signaling to her cameraman to join her on the lawn, turned to Anna and wagged a finger at her. "Mrs. Lange," she chided, "the people in this area have been very concerned about you and your family for a number of years now. Don't you think that you owe it to them to share your feelings with them on this occasion? I mean, a lot of people have hoped and prayed for this day, just as you have."

Anna sighed and nodded. "You're right," she said. People had been kind to them. Sometimes their curiosity had upset and infuriated her. But there were other times when their support was all she had to cling to. Letters from other mothers, strangers, urging her to have faith, trying to offer a clue. She glanced at Thomas, who was wearing an impatient expression. He met her eyes and shrugged his shoulders.

"All right," said Anna.

"Why don't you all gather around Mrs. Lange?" Camille suggested, directing them with her melon-painted fingernails. "This won't take long. Come on."

"I'm sorry about this," said Tom to his unprepared neighbors.

"That's right," said Camille. "Gather 'round her. It looks good. People will like this. Friends, sharing your joy and so on. Everybody look cheerful."

"Can you keep it short, Camille?" Anna pleaded. "Our friends here—"

"Don't worry, Anna." Iris reassured her. "I think it's kind of fun!"

Camille raised both arms to indicate that speed was no problem and then accepted a microphone from a cameraman who was moving in on them. "Now," she said, "I'm going to introduce you all. I may ask each of you a question. Mr. Stewart, I may ask you how long you've known the Langes, if you remember Paul, that kind of stuff, okay?"

Camille hesitated, peering at Edward, whose face was like a stiff mask, his gray eyes widened with alarm.

Poor Edward, Anna thought as she glanced over at him. Television really isn't his medium. A discreet portrait photograph in *The New York Times* business section, perhaps, but not the ten o'clock news, sandwiched in with murders, fires, and city hall politics.

Edward licked his lips and nodded at the reporter.

"Now," Camille went on, "more of the same for you, Mrs. Stewart. And then we'll ask Mr. and Mrs. Lange to comment on their feelings tonight. All right, are we ready?" She smiled expectantly at them.

Anna nodded and tried to concentrate on all those people who had sent their prayers to her over the years.

"Folks, there's nothing to be nervous about. Just smile," advised Camille. "Mr. Lange, why don't you put your arm around your wife?" She turned to face the cameraman, raising the microphone toward her chin.

"Once in a while a story has a happy ending," Camille began, "and here at the home of Mr. and Mrs. Thomas Lange one of those rare happy endings is about to come true."

As Anna listened to Camille's introduction, she felt Thomas's arm encircle her, his hand descend heavily on her shoulders.

Anna picked up one of the tasseled pillows from the corner of the sofa and squeezed it to her chest as she studied the arrangement of her living room. She crossed over, placed the pillow against the cushion of a wing chair, and stepped back to look at it. Then she picked it up again and circled around behind the matching chair across the room by the writing desk.

Thomas, dressed in a clean sport shirt, stood in the doorway and watched her. It was still very warm. He felt a trickle of perspiration run down his neck and under his collar. He walked over and sat down in one of the chairs, picking up a magazine from a rack beside his seat. He glanced up at Anna, who had removed the pillow again and replaced it in the center of the sofa. "Is that a new dress?" he asked.

Anna looked down at herself and then back at her husband. "Oh, darling, I got it the other day," she said. "I forgot to tell you." She picked the pillow up again and held it in front of her.

"It doesn't matter," said Thomas, opening the magazine. "It looks nice," he said. "Anna, what are you doing with that pillow?"

Anna sank down onto the edge of the sofa and placed the pillow beside her. She straightened the blooming begonia, the ashtray, and the silver cigarette box and coasters on the coffee table in front of her. "I was going to move it," she said.

"How long did Buddy say they'd be?"

Anna glanced at her watch. "He said he'd try to get him here by nine. Is the front light on?"

Thomas nodded and looked at his own watch. "Where's Tracy?"

Anna gestured toward the foyer. "She's still upstairs."

Thomas flipped a few pages of the magazine. Anna folded her hands in her lap and tried to focus her attention on him. "How was your day?" she asked.

Instantly he thought of Gail's hands massaging his neck. He kept his eyes on the page. "Fine," he said.

"You and Edward took the same train?" she said.

"Yeah," said Thomas, his eyes still lowered to the magazine page. "I ran into him at Grand Central."

"You two looked pretty chummy when you drove in."

"He was actually pleasant," Thomas said. "Wanted to know about Paul and all that."

"They're both very concerned about Paul."

"Yeah."

Thomas buried himself in the magazine again, while Anna searched for a topic that didn't involve their son. "How's that . . . um. . . computer business going that you mentioned?"

Thomas looked up at her warily. He had guilty thoughts

of Gail, but at the same time he was pleased by Anna's interest. "The system we're installing?"

"How long before you can start using it?"

"It won't be too long, I think."

"What remains to be done?" she asked, absently twisting her wedding ring on her finger.

"Well, I was just reading a report on it today. The hardware is already in, but it's a matter or reorganizing information and also retraining some of our staff.

"People in your department?"

Thomas rolled up the magazine into a tube and clasped his hands around it. "Well, I want the people in my department to have a working knowledge of how to obtain information from it, but the main effort is going to be concentrated—"

A rapid series of thuds issued from the hallway stairs, and then Tracy shuffled into the living room, still dressed in her grimy tennis whites. Anna's eyes shot to the slim, disheveled figure and widened in dismay.

"Tracy," she blurted out, "why haven't you changed?"

Tracy looked from her mother to her father, who had turned his head to the empty fireplace.

"What's wrong with this?"

"You look like a mess," said Anna.

Thomas got up from his chair and walked over to the bar cart. "I'm having a drink. Do you want one, Anna?"

Anna tore her eyes from Tracy and looked at Thomas. "There's ice in the bucket," she said, gesturing toward the ice bucket on the polished surface of the bar cart.

"I asked you," said Thomas sharply, "if you wanted one."

"Yes, please," said Anna, taken aback by his tone.

"Well, I'm getting something to eat," Tracy said,

flouncing past her father and heading through the dining room toward the kitchen.

"You won't want your dinner," Anna called after her daughter.

Thomas carried a glass over to Anna and thrust it toward her.

"We'll eat as soon as he gets here," Anna said.

Thomas crossed over to his chair with his own drink and began to drain it.

"I interrupted you before," said Anna. "I'm sorry. What were you saying?"

"I've forgotten," he said.

"I'm having steak," said Anna.

"Oh," said Thomas, watching the ice cubes clink as he swirled them in his glass.

"I hope it will be all right," she said.

"Oh, I'm sure he'll like it," said Thomas.

Suddenly Anna shot up from her seat. "Tom, do you hear?"

Thomas placed his glass deliberately on the coaster and stood up. "It sounds like a car in the driveway." He kept his voice steady.

"Tracy," Anna cried out.

A crash from the direction of the kitchen was her answer. Anna ran through the dining room and threw open the kitchen door. "What happened?" she demanded.

Tracy faced her defiantly. Anna looked from her daughter's face to the ragged hunk of chocolate cake, upended and stuck to the linoleum by its icing. The pieces of the cake plate were scattered about the floor. Another huge piece of cake tilted precariously on the edge of the sink. Icing streaked the front of the sink cabinets.

"I was moving the plate, and it fell when you screamed."

Anna clenched her fists. "Clean it up," she said. "This minute."

"I didn't do it on purpose," Tracy spit out.

Thomas appeared in the doorway. "The police car is in the driveway. Hurry up."

"She has to clean this mess up," Anna insisted, backing out the kitchen door.

"Later," said Thomas. "Get in here. Both of you."

Tracy passed by Thomas, wearing the suggestion of a smirk. Anna gazed, as if mesmerized, at the lump of chocolate on the floor. Then she got down on her knees and began mechanically to scoop up the cake with her hands.

"Anna," Thomas bent over and lifted her up gently by the elbow. "Leave it."

Slowly Anna rose to her feet and wiped her hands on the towel which he handed to her. She looked helplessly at her husband.

"We'll close the kitchen door," he told her. "It will be all right."

The doorbell rang through the house from the direction of the foyer. Thomas's and Anna's eyes met in a surge of apprehension.

"This is it, darling," he said softly. "Let's go."

Anna took his hand, and he led her out to the living room, where Tracy was sprawled on the sofa. Thomas reached for her hand, but she shook him off and jerked herself to her feet.

The doorbell rang again.

Anna approached the front door and then stood still, as if paralyzed by the sound.

Passing by her, Thomas strode to the front door and opened it. Holding her trembling hands clutched together, Anna walked up behind her husband's back and looked out.

The night was dark, but the coach lamp beside the door threw its light over the front steps and the figure standing there. Drawn by the brightness of the light, a battery of dun-colored moths swarmed to the screen door and flattened themselves against it, beating their dusty wings in agitation against the grid. Through the whirring, jumpy mosaic formed by the congestion of wings, Anna saw the pale, narrow face of a teen-aged boy. His brown hair was long and ragged, falling across his forehead like a dark scar. He wore faded jeans, black Converse sneakers, a T-shirt, and a worn and patched dungaree jacket. His deep-set amber eyes, ringed by grayish circles, looked warily from the couple in the doorway to the squadron of noctu.nal insects besieging the screen.

Thomas pushed the screen door out and motioned for the boy to hurry in. "Come in," he said.

Paul edged around the narrow opening and stepped into the foyer. On one shoulder he supported an old duffel bag. In his other hand he held a cardboard carrying case. For a moment they all stared at one another.

Then Anna took a step toward him and reached out her arms.

The boy lifted the cardboard traveling box and held it between them. A cat's meow emanated from inside the box. "I forgot to ask you on the phone," the boy said, "about my cat."

Tears filled Anna's eyes, blurring his face out of focus. She nodded, unable to speak.

"Welcome, Paul," said Thomas, stepping back to let the boy pass by him.

"It's Billy," said the boy.

For a minute Thomas stared at him, and then he felt a

chill as he noticed the name embroidered on the pocket of the boy's jacket.

"I'm really . . . I'm used to Billy," the boy said as he edged into the house, clutching his few belongings.

CHAPTER FOUR

Although the weather-faded wooden sign on the La-Z Pines Motel billboard promised air-conditioned rooms, the unit in Albert Rambo's window was nearly impotent, and the sheen of sweat on his skin from the outside did not dissolve inside the room.

Rambo sat on the edge of a straight-backed chair, his chafed elbows resting on his knees, as he smoked a cigarette. The stream of blue smoke undulated in the humid air, and the smell polluted the close room.

A combination of hunger and heat made him feel faint and slightly nauseated. Across the room, resting on the bedspread, was his treasure for the day. It was a red-and-white-striped box with a ripped cover that he had found in a garbage can outside Kentucky Fried Chicken. There was a leftover half-eaten breast and one little drumstick in the box. And he had managed to swipe a pack of cigarettes from the dashboard of an unlocked car in a parking lot. All in all, he had done pretty well.

The voices had almost ruined it, though. He had been working his way through the parking lot, keeping watch so no one would spot him and trying a door here and there, when the voices started speaking to him. Verses came to his lips, and he started saying a few things out loud. Then a lady pushing a baby stroller started giving him this funny look and said, "What's the matter with you? Get away from here." The voices had stopped then. They didn't always stop. But this time they stopped.

Rambo wiped the film off his face and heaved a sigh. The hair on his head was thinning, and his white scalp glowed in the gloomy room. The smell of the chicken in the little striped cardboard box made him feel faint again. He felt tired, too. Tired of running.

The thought of his predicament filled him again with a sickish feeling. He had always kind of stayed put after he married Dorothy Lee. When he was younger, he had bummed around, but then they had settled down and got that trailer. They had moved only once or twice after that: once when they got Billy and then again when they bought the trailer. And of course, there had been the times in the hospital. But he didn't like to count those. He had long since lost his taste for moving around. Besides, Dorothy Lee had liked to stay put and make a home for the boy.

Remembering his wife caused a brief rage to stir in him; it then subsided into the familiar dead despair. How could she do this to him? Tell the minister everything and leave him to the wolves. After all, he had done it for her in the first place. It was his biggest mistake. He'd known it almost from the start. After the day they got Billy, she cared more for that son of Satan than she ever had for him. That little bastard with his evil eye. She denied it, but Albert knew it. And this was the proof. His eyes narrowed bitterly as they took in the parameters of the shabby room.

Having dragged himself off the chair, he walked over to the old Magnavox TV set that was in the corner of the room. He did not want to think about it anymore. He wanted the noise of the television, and he wanted to eat his chicken and just sit. Tomorrow he would make a plan of what to do. He flicked on the set and walked back to the bed. There was some kind of movie droning to a conclusion. Turning his attention to the striped cardboard box, Rambo lifted the ripped paper lid as if it were a jewel case and stared hungrily at the meat inside. After untying his shoes, he shook them off beside the night table and sat cross-legged on the bedspread in his stockinged feet.

The ten o'clock news came on as Rambo lifted a drumstick to his salivating mouth. The announcer promised that a visit to the Lange home was coming up. Rambo thought of changing the channel and then decided to leave it. The story fascinated him almost as much as it infuriated him. He only hoped that they did not show his picture on the TV again tonight. He was fortunate that no one had ever cared much to take pictures of him. The ones they usually flashed were so grainy and distorted that you could hardly recognize him, his ever-present hat always throwing a shadow across his face. For a minute he wondered if he should get a different hat. Then he realized that he had no money to buy a new one. Maybe in the thrift shop. He might be able to pick one up for a quarter, although he hated the idea of wearing somebody else's dirty hat on his head.

The sweat began to stream off him again at the thought of the spot he was in. His stomach felt knotted, and he suddenly felt unable to eat. He sat immobile on the bed, the drumstick dangling from his fingers, lost in a miasma of fears. Two voices inside his head began to chant something unintelligible about death. Rambo strained to make it out. Then his stomach growled, drowning out words, reminding him of his hunger. He lifted the drumstick to his mouth and bit into it. The fat from the coating made his fingers slippery, and he could feel the slick grease spread out around his mouth toward his sunken cheeks. He took a few bites and then set the chicken back down in the box. It was too messy.

The reporter on the tube was talking about a happy ending at the Langes' house as Rambo got up and padded across the narrow room to the adjoining bathroom. Fuzz from the stained polyester shag carpet stuck to his damp socks. He threw on the overhead light in the bathroom, looking back at the TV set and the Langes' house, just visible behind the reporter. It looked like a mansion. Rambo thought of Billy, that evil little fiend, moving into all that luxury. A threadbare yellow fingertip towel hung neatly from the towel rack above the flesh-pink toilet seat. Rambo jerked it down and ran it under the faucet. Then he wrung it out with such force that his knuckles turned white. He ground the damp towel into his lips and the corners of his mouth and then wadded it up and brought it back into the room. He resumed his seat on the bed and dropped the towel down by the box of chicken. He picked up the drumstick with one bite missing and started to eat, his eyes returning to the TV set.

Suddenly the drumstick fell from his hand to his pants leg, forming an oleaginous spot there, as Rambo stared at the picture on the set. The bitter set of his mouth slackened, and his dull eyes flickered in amazement at what he saw.

Long after the report was over, Rambo still sat on the bed, his chicken forgotten, his eyes staring straight ahead, wide open in his stunned slack-jawed face. His mind raced furiously, though, trying to take it all in before the voices could confuse him, trying to figure out what it meant. He was suddenly aware, though he could scarcely believe it, that what he had just seen on the screen was his salvation.

* * *

With the side of his fork Paul pushed the mushrooms away from the steak on his plate and tried to scrape off the sauce. Anna sat across the table, her hands in her lap, and watched him. Paul looked up and caught Anna staring at him. He quickly looked down again, to avoid her eyes.

"Well, P—" said Thomas. "What's, uh, what's your favorite subject in school?"

Paul picked up his knife and began to saw away at the steak with some concentration. "I don't know . . ." he said. "I don't like school." He put a piece of meat into his mouth.

"You don't have to eat that," Anna said. "I can make you something else."

The boy studied the piece of meat on his fork and then put it into his mouth.

"Really," said Anna, getting up from her seat, "it's no trouble. I have things in the refrigerator. I'll make you a hot dog or something."

"No. I'll eat this."

"Well, I didn't know what you liked, and I have plenty of other—"

"No," Paul protested.

"Anna," said Thomas, "he doesn't want anything."

Slowly Anna resumed her seat. There was a silence around the table. "I didn't mean to interrupt your conversation," Anna said. "What were you saying about school?"

"Nothing."

Tracy pushed her plate away and rested her chin in her hands on the table, pushing her eyes up into a slant. "What did you use to do for fun?" she asked.

Paul shrugged and heaved a sigh.

"Don't you play any sports or anything?" Tracy persisted.

The boy glanced at her. "I like hunting," he said. "I used to go hunting a lot."

"That's not a sport," Tracy announced. "That's disgusting. Killing animals for fun."

"Tracy works at the animal shelter," Anna explained. "Animals are her favorite people."

"Don't make excuses for me, Mother," Tracy said in a shrill voice. "I think it's disgusting. And it is."

"I like animals, too," Paul said. "I have my cat."

"Yeah," said Tracy. "Well, how would you like it if someone went hunting for your cat?"

"That's enough, Tracy," said Thomas.

Paul blanched as Tracy leaned back in her chair, crossing her arms over her chest. Her eyes filled with angry tears, and two spots of color appeared in her cheeks. Anna reached a hand to her, but Tracy jerked away.

"Well," said Thomas, "I'll bet you're going to like school here. They've got all the latest equipment. Lots of activities . . ." As his words faded away, Thomas cringed at the sound of his own voice. You can't think of a thing to say to your own son, he thought.

Paul kept his eyes down and carved off another piece of meat.

Anna smiled brightly at him. "We're right near New York here," she said. "There are all kinds of museums and shows to see. We'll take a trip into the city soon, if you'd like that."

"I heard there's a lot of robberies and criminals there," said the boy.

"Well," said Anna, taken aback, "you have to be careful, of course."

"I'd like to go sometime," said Paul. "My mom always said she'd take me someday. . . ."

A silence fell over the table. Paul put the piece of meat in his mouth and started to chew it, swallowing hard.

"Can I be excused?" said Tracy, standing up.

"We're not finished yet," said Anna.

Tracy fell back into her chair.

"Let me get you something else to eat," said Anna. "Isn't there something you want?"

"Do you have any ketchup?"

Tracy stared at him, and Anna threw her a warning glance. "Of course," she said. "I'll get it for you."

Anna went into the kitchen and walked over to the refrigerator. She opened the door and reached in for a bottle of ketchup. Then she turned to the stove, put a kettle on, and quickly prepared the drip pot for coffee. From behind the door to the dining room she could hear an occasional muffled word. Mostly silence. The backyard was in total darkness now. Mercifully the worst of the heat had let up, and the night was merely warm. She gripped the edge of the sink for support as she stared over the flower pots on the sill out to where the play yard used to be.

As a toddler her son had always been on the chubby side, with folds in his glossy baby skin. He used to laugh at nothing at all. It had been the most amazing thing. He could make people who saw him laugh, just in delight at him. She looked over at the closed door of the dining room. This boy, her son, was thin. His wrists were bony and looked as if they could snap like a twig under strain. His hair was dark and limp. She had yet to see him smile.

From the box in the corner the cat meowed. The water boiled, and Anna poured coffee into the filter. She watched the water run through the grounds. She glanced at the ketchup bottle on the counter, knowing she should take it in, but still she stood there.

She realized now, with a sense of shock, that she had expected him to be the same. Gold in his curls and dimples of baby fat in his laughing cheeks. In these years of change she had lost the child. He was gone. She would never see her child again. She had lost her baby forever. Anna felt a sudden stabbing pain in her chest. Gone. Just as everyone had always said. Instead, this other boy, this stranger, sat at her table.

He is my son, she reminded herself. And he is here. It was all that mattered.

"My baby," she whispered. With a determined intake of breath Anna picked up the bottle of ketchup and pushed through the dining room door. The three of them sat at the table. Tracy leaned back in her chair with her eyes closed. Thomas was describing the town of Stanwich to the boy as if he were a member of the Chamber of Commerce. Paul kept his eyes on his plate, his face expressionless, as he cut another piece of meat.

"We have a couple of tennis courts, and there is a nice beach here in town. Plenty to do. There's no reason for a boy your age to be bored here."

Anna slipped into her seat and handed the bottle of ketchup to Paul. "Here's the ketchup."

"Thanks," Paul said, and doused his sirloin with the gloppy condiment.

"Tracy," said Anna, "don't sleep at the table."

"I'm tired. I need to go up and take a shower."

"We're almost finished. Then we can have some ice cream."

"I don't want any ice cream. It's so late already. Why can't I go?"

Anna looked to Thomas for a word, but he was staring down at the table in front of him. As her eyes swept past Paul, she noticed that he was holding his fork and knife rigidly upright in front of him, his eyes open wide. The veins on his neck were protruding, and he pitched forward in his chair.

"Paul," she said.

He made a gurgling noise in reply. Anna pushed her chair back and stood up. "Paul, what's the matter?"

They all swiveled their eyes to stare at him. As Anna watched him, his pale skin turned dead white, and then the area around his lips began to turn blue. His eyes were bulging, the whites visible all around the pupils. He made another low, gurgling sound.

"Is he having a fit?" Thomas asked.

Anna stared at Paul, unable to move, and suddenly she saw his hand dip slightly toward the meat on his plate. In an instant she grasped what was wrong. "He's choking," she said.

Thomas jumped up and began to thump the boy on his back. Paul was rigid now and not exhaling any breath.

"No," Anna cried, pushing Thomas aside. She pulled the boy off the chair and wrapped her arms around him from behind, just below his waist, jerking in sharply with her forearms as she bent him over.

"Breathe," she whispered, jerking again at his diaphragm. She could feel his heart hammering above her arms. He stared, unseeing, at the floor, his body stiff, except for his fingers, which were slowly tightening into claws.

Anna could feel sweat on her forehead, dripping into her eyes. She wrenched her arms in tight. Tracy whimpered in the dead silence.

"Please," Anna prayed, "breathe."

In the hushed room Anna could hear only the strangled whistle from the boy's throat. "Oh, please," she pleaded softly.

All at once he gagged. With a terrible retching sound he expelled a hunk of gray meat from his windpipe, and it shot out to the floor. Gulping for air, the boy began to cough and retch. His body fell limply in Anna's arms.

"Are you all right?" she cried.

Paul nodded, his eyes closed, the sweat popping out across his waxen face. Anna guided his slumping form to the chair. He breathed in great gasps as the color slowly returned to his skin.

"I'm okay," he whispered.

"God," Tracy breathed.

Anna buried her face in her hands for a moment as Thomas held the boy awkwardly by the shoulders. "Are you sure you're all right?" he asked. "Maybe we should call a doctor."

Paul shook his head weakly. "No, I'm okay." He drew himself up in the chair and sat with his shoulders hunched, his arms crossed tightly over his lap. The dark circles under his eyes seemed to have deepened in the last few moments.

Anna wanted to reach out and embrace him, but she knew that he would flinch at her touch. He sat as if he were trying to shield himself from their eyes. He would not look up to meet her eyes. "Thanks," he mumbled under his breath.

Anna nodded, unable to answer.

Thomas filled a glass from the water pitcher and handed it to Paul. "Here," he said, "have a sip."

Paul drank the water.

"Are you sure you don't want a doctor?" Anna asked him.

Paul shook his head. "No. I don't need anything. I just want to go lie down somewhere."

"Of course," said Anna. "Of course you do. I'll take you upstairs."

Tracy looked fearfully at the boy, as if he might suddenly collapse again.

Thomas stood up from the table. "Well," he said with false heartiness, "I guess I'll watch the news. Want to come, Trace?"

Tracy shrugged.

Anna turned to Paul. "You have your old room," she said. He looked at her blankly.

"It should be cool enough up there for you," said Thomas. "There's a fan in your window if it's not."

Anna reached out her hand and laid it on Paul's thin forearm. "You really scared me. I'm so glad you're all right."

"He looks fine now," said Thomas.

Paul looked from one to the other and then stood up. "Where's my cat?" he asked.

"In the kitchen," said Anna. "Why don't you put him out?"

Paul opened the kitchen door and searched for his cat under the cabinets. He scooped up the gray-and-black-striped animal and held it to his chest. The cat's legs flattened against his shoulder. The boy buried his face in the cat's fur. The creature appeared ready to leap from his arms, but it remained there, poised tensely in his grasp.

Tracy got up from the table and started through the living room. "I'm going upstairs," she said.

"Good night," said Thomas.

Anna tore her eyes away from Paul and looked at her

husband across the littered table. "Tom," she said, "that was awful. I was so frightened."

"You acted very quickly," he said, meeting her troubled gaze across the table. "You probably saved his life."

"He could have choked to death."

"I know," he said. "It was lucky." They fell silent, their fingers touching.

Anna bit her lip. "He's so thin, Tom."

Thomas turned and looked blankly into the kitchen through the open door at the boy. He began to run his fingers absently through his hair.

Paul placed the cat on the back step, and the animal stood uncertainly for a moment, scanning the darkness of the yard. Then it padded down the steps and out into the black yard without a backward glance.

Paul returned to the dining room. "Good night," said Tom.

"Come on," said Anna. "I'll take you up."

Paul picked up his duffel bag in the hall and followed her up the stairs to the room which she had readied for him. The garbled lyrics of a Billy Joel album emanated from behind the closed door of Tracy's room. When they reached the top of the stairs, Paul looked at Anna to direct him. She nodded toward a door down the hall, and Paul went over and pushed it open. He looked around and placed his bag on a chair beside the dresser. Anna felt for a moment as if she were showing a guest to a hotel room. There was no sign of recognition from him at all.

He turned and saw her watching him. "It's a big room," he said.

"The bathroom is at the end of the hall. Here're some towels." She patted a pile of terry cloth on the dresser. "Are you sure you feel all right?"

Paul stood by the head of the bed, his hands jammed into his pockets. "Yeah," he said. "Fine."

"Well," she said briskly, "I hope you sleep well." She stepped over to him and placed an arm around his shoulders. He drew away from her, and the kiss she had intended for his forehead skirted the top of his ear instead.

"Good night," she said, backing out of the room. He could hear the catch in her voice. He did not look at her.

For a few minutes after she had left the room, Paul did not move. He stood staring straight ahead of him. A silver cup was gleaming on the bureau in his line of sight. He walked over and picked it up to examine it. It was brightly polished, and on it was the name Paul, engraved in an elegant script.

He realized, with a queasy feeling, that the cup had been his. Someone had bought it for him, probably when he was born, years ago. When he had lived in this house. With these people. Paul looked around the strange room.

His mother had told him before she died that she had a terrible secret. So this was it.

Paul looked out into the darkness of the backyard, hoping for a glimpse of Sam, but the cat was invisible in the night.

He took another look at the cup. What was the use in fighting it? he thought. They were going to call him Paul if they felt like it. He threw the cup away from him, and it rolled across the floor and landed against the wall under a chair.

Slowly he untied his sneakers and shook them off. He pulled back the bedspread and crawled under it, fully clothed. He was still wearing the worn dungaree jacket which he had found in the woods two years before. Dorothy

Lee had washed it for him, and patched it in a few places, and sewn his name on it.

Despite the blankets, and the clothes he was wearing, and the heat of the night, Paul began to shiver. His teeth chattered, and he drew himself up, pressing his knees to his chest and wrapping his arms around him. No one had mentioned Dorothy Lee. Or his father. Not one word. Just as if everything were perfectly normal. Paul's lips drew back in a laugh. But his eyes were mirthless. He felt a pressure on his bladder, but he did not want to go out into the hallway. He didn't want to encounter any of them. His teeth were chattering more loudly now. He wondered if they could hear him.

Anna put the last dish in the dishwasher and wiped her hands. She turned the lock on the back door and then jiggled the doorknob to be sure it had caught. Then she padded through the quiet house and put the lock and chain on the front door. From the den she could hear the drone of the television late news. Anna looked around at the windows. She wished she could lock them, too. But it was too hot for that. They all would suffocate from the heat. It worried her, though, to think they were open. She looked up the stairs. It was dark and quiet. Maybe he's asleep, she thought.

For a moment Anna pictured him again at the table, his face ashen, the taut cords in his neck, his hands helplessly clutching the air. Her heart was squeezed by the remembered fear. Shaking her head, as if to dispel the image, she walked through the house and headed down to the cellar, where she locked the cellar door and windows from the inside. The light was on in the playroom adjoining the cellar, and she pushed the door open and went in. The room was still and empty. In one corner she spotted Thomas's golf clubs. She went over to the bag and, having disengaged one of the irons, pulled it out and turned it over in her hands. She just wasn't comfortable about the upstairs windows. At least she could lock the windows down here. No one would be down here. The heat wouldn't matter.

Anna leaned the golf club against the bag and made a circuit of the playroom, fastening the windows tightly shut. Then she returned to the golf club and picked it up again. The gleaming steel shaft and head of the club felt heavy in her hands. Anna hesitated, then gripped the club resolutely and started up the stairs.

As she turned on the landing, she saw a figure looming in the darkness above.

"Oh," she cried out.

"What are you doing?" Thomas asked.

"Locking up," she said, mounting the stairs to the top where he stood. He was holding the bottle of champagne from the Stewarts in his hands.

"I thought we might take this up to our room," said Tom. "Kind of toast the occasion. You about ready to go to bed?"

"In a minute."

Thomas noticed the golf club in her hand and frowned. "What's that?"

"It's one of your irons."

"I can see that. What are you doing with it?"

Anna edged past him and went through the hallway into the kitchen. Thomas followed behind her. "What are you planning to do with it?"

"I thought it would be a good idea to keep it up here," she said.

"What for?" he demanded.

"I don't know," she said evasively. "Just in case . . ."

"In case of what? Anna, give me that club. Let me take it back downstairs."

She drew the club back out of his reach. "No," she said. "We don't know what might . . . we might need it."

Thomas dropped his hand to his side. His jaw hardened. "Not this again."

"That man is out there somewhere, Thomas."

Thomas stared away from her, his eyes flinty. "I don't understand you, Anna. Don't you want to be happy? You won't leave well enough alone. You have your son back—"

"Our son," said Anna. Then she said quickly, "I'm sorry, darling."

Thomas glared at her and then turned his back. He looked down at the bottle in his hand. "I had thought you might want to have a drink with me, and talk over the day a little bit."

"I'll be along, Tom. Soon."

Thomas put the bottle of champagne down on the table and left the room. Anna waited until she could hear him climbing the stairs before she went into the living room. She pulled back the living room curtains and stared out at the street. The dim glow of one streetlight formed dark, shadowy patterns of leaves on the asphalt that shifted as the trees rustled. Anna turned off all the lights in the living room and sat down in the chair beside the window. She held the club in front of her across the arms of the chair, her hands gripped tightly around the cold metal shaft. The light of the moon threw a sheen on the blunt head of the club.

One blow from this would do it, she thought calmly. You have to be careful with children. You can't take anything for granted.

Anna looked up at the clock in the corner. She could barely discern that it was nearly twelve. I won't sit here long, she thought. Just for a while. She decided that by one o'clock she would go up and get into bed with Thomas. He would probably still be up reading. She could just slip the club under the dust ruffle on her side of the bed.

Soon. She would go up soon. Unless she heard something. If she heard something, she would sit here all night. If necessary. Anna glanced out into the foyer at the murky gloom of the staircase. She would do anything that was necessary. Anything at all. She ran her hand over the cold dense head of the club. She wondered if she could sink that deadly weight into the side of someone's skull.

Her eyes traveled around the room to the fireplace mantel, where a photograph of a pudgy boy with brown-gold curls laughed into the darkened room.

Anna gripped the club tighter. You could, she thought. If you have to, you will.

It was not until the cool gray light of dawn had banished the shadows that her wary eyes finally closed in sleep. Her head drooped to her shoulder, but she slept lightly, her fingers still curled around the shaft of the club.

CHAPTER FIVE

"Could you put out the cigarette, sir?"

Rambo looked up at the pig-tailed girl in greasy coveralls who was leaning into his car window.

"Sure, sure," he said, jamming the cigarette butt out in the ashtray.

"What'll it be?"

Rambo studied his narrow billfold and extracted a wrinkled five-dollar bill. "Five dollars' worth," he said.

The girl nodded and walked around to the back of the car. Rambo watched her in the side-view mirror, wondering why they let girls do jobs like this up North. It didn't make sense, what with good men out of work. He stuck his head out the window and called to her. "Pardon, ma'am. Do you have a phone?"

The girl pointed behind the station. Rambo adjusted his dark glasses, pulled down his hat, and got out of the car. Glancing around him in all directions, he walked self-consciously back to where the phone hung on the wall between the men's and ladies' room doors. He looked around; but it was early morning yet, and there was no one about. Reaching into his back pocket, he pulled out a slip of paper and deposited his money into the phone.

All night he had debated whether to call or not. He had waited for a word, a further sign, but none had come. He had read the Gideon Bible furiously, making notes in the margins and girding himself for his mission. At dawn he had decided to call. Now he dialed the number, which he had gotten from information, and put the phone to his ear. Before it could even ring, the door to the men's room opened, and a young man wearing blue jeans and a khaki shirt with the station's name embroidered in red on the pocket emerged and greeted him with a wave.

"Morning," said the young man.

Rambo quickly dropped the phone back into the cradle. His dime came clinking down into the change cup as Rambo returned the greeting with a scowl.

The young man walked off toward the pumps, and Rambo watched him go, waiting until he disappeared to pick up the phone again.

Once again he dialed the number, trying to go over in his mind what he was going to say. There were moons of perspiration forming under the arms of his shirt, and the fabric was sticking to his back. He had to speak just right, to make the heathen understand that there was payment due. That the wicked had been found out and had to be punished. It was the Lord's will.

He held the receiver to his ear and waited, his eyes darting around the service station plaza to be sure no one came near him. For a moment there was a clicking sound. Rambo took a deep breath. Then a busy signal squawked in his ear.

"Damnation," he said aloud, and slammed the phone back down on the hook.

The girl in the coveralls walked out in front of his car and signaled to him that his car was ready to go.

Rambo thrust his hands in his pockets, and his angry eyes bored into the phone. Then, suddenly, he realized what happened. It had been the sign, the one he had waited for. He was meant to go strike without warning. No time to lose.

With a sigh of relief Rambo retrieved his dime from the change cup and hurried back to his car.

It was a half hour's drive until he reached the Millgate Parkway, and Rambo kept his foot pressed lightly on the accelerator, his eyes shifting obsessively from the speedometer to the sides of the road the whole way. He was anxious to get there, but he did not want to attract the attention of any patrol cars which might be lying in wait.

The best thing about the Millgate Parkway, from his point of view, was that hardly anybody used it since the Connecticut Turnpike had been constructed. He entered the roadway with a sense of relief, even though the surface was gouged with potholes, which made it a risky ride, even for the sturdiest of automobiles. Rambo's blue Chevy, which had newspaper plugging the body rot underneath and four nearly bald tires, struck each shallow crater with a shimmy. On the seat beside him the Bible, which he borrowed from his motel room, bounced over and struck his thigh. Rambo gripped the wheel and watched the road, muttering verses under his breath as he drove.

Although he had been on the lookout for it, he still felt a small jolt when he saw the sign indicating the upcoming exit for Stanwich. Surveying the area, he slowed down as his car took the last miles.

It looked the same. More than ten years ago, and still, this anonymous exit was imprinted on his mind in precise detail. They had been coming the other way, of course, on that long-ago day, driving south after the funeral of one of Dorothy Lee's cousins up in New York State. That's what had made it all so simple. No one had ever questioned the story they made up that Paul was the child of the dead relative, left alone in the world. Rambo's eyes darted across the highway. That was the spot all right. They were just going to pull off the road so he could take a leak. That's when he had seen it. At first he had not understood what he saw. And then, before it was too late, he knew.

It was more than ten years ago since that day he had crouched there in the bushes, witness and then accomplice. And he had suffered since, although never more than now. But he had endured. And now he would have his revenge.

Rambo heard the voices like a knell in his ears. "Woe to those who turn aside the needy from justice and rob the poor of my people of their right."

The arrow for the Stanwich exit pointed right. His moment was at hand. Rambo turned the wheel and slowly exited onto the peaceful backcountry roads that cradled the homes of the privileged few.

"Buddy, I'm sorry to bother you. I know it's early. But I had to call you. I couldn't get any sleep last night, thinking about that man Rambo."

Paul stopped on the stairway. He could hear Anna's anxious voice on the phone, cutting through the silent house. He waited on the stairs, listening.

"I would feel so much better if Paul had some police protection. Just until that man is captured. Please don't tell me I'm being paranoid. I can't stand to hear it again."

Paul's lip curled as he thought of his father. He was probably off on some street corner somewhere, raving about the Lord. The thought of Rambo's wild eyes, his accusations, and his rambling discourses on the devil released a sluice of bile into Paul's stomach. The hunger which had awakened him subsided. He could hear Anna in the kitchen, still pleading with the policeman.

"Buddy, we don't know that he's not dangerous. Just because he never hurt the boy before doesn't mean that he won't try something. I don't feel that my son is safe while he is still on the loose."

Paul crept down the last few stairs and quietly opened the front door to the house. He stepped out onto the front porch and closed the door behind him. The dewy yard sparkled in the morning sun, and the quiet backcountry road looked like something off a calendar. Paul's stomach churned as he looked over the peaceful scene, and he was plagued by the sense that he didn't belong there.

"Sam," he called out softly, hoping for the familiar sight of his pet. There were birds chirping in the canopy of trees; that meant Sam was probably not in the immediate vicinity. Paul walked down the steps and circled the house, going out to the back.

"Sam," he cried.

He surveyed the rolling backyard, the glider, and the large vegetable garden which throve in the back. Out near where the woods started, was a small shed. He crossed the lawn to it and looked inside. Through the gloom he could make out a few rakes and some shovels. He closed the door and peered into the woods which spread out behind the lawn. Sunlight filtered down through the trees, and he could hear the distant hum of an occasional car passing on a highway which was not visible from the yard. He called out for Sam, but there was no movement in the trees.

After walking along the edge of the woods, he jumped across a small stream which meandered through the property on the other side. Beyond the stream was a long hedge of lilac bushes. Down at the end of it, and just beyond, he saw the top of a huge house, with a stucco surface and dark-framed windows, which had a series of gables and turrets like a castle roof. He stood still for a moment, struck by the fact that it was the biggest house he had ever seen. Then he crouched down and began to scout the length of the hedge, searching for movement in the bottom branches of the lilac bushes and making his way slowly down in the direction of the house.

As he approached the mansion, his eye was distracted from the search for his cat by a blaze of aquamarine beyond the hedge. He peered through the branches and saw a large rectangular swimming pool shimmering in the sun. A model sailboat with a gleaming wooden hull and white sails billowing floated across the tranquil turquoise surface. The pool was surrounded by a patio on which there was a collection of white wrought-iron furniture.

Crouched on one knee beside the pool was a well-groomed man dressed in expensive sports clothes. He was controlling the sailboat's progress with a pocket-sized device in his hand and watching the boat's graceful movements with obvious relish. He caused the boat to crisscross the aqua surface of the pool; its white sails full and elegant in the light breeze.

Beside him, at the pool's edge, stood an elderly man with silver hair and thick horn-rimmed glasses, looking uncomfortable in a conservative business suit, with a white shirt and a somber tie. The older man watched the man with the boat anxiously for a few minutes, and then he cleared his throat.

"I realize," he said, "that it may be inconvenient for you to see me like this, at home on a Saturday, but this matter seems to me to be of the utmost urgency."

"It's no problem at all," said the man with the boat,

although his rapt attention did not waver from the sailing craft.

The older man waited for the other man to get up and face him, but after a few moments it became clear that the man by the pool had no intention of doing so. Nervously adjusting his shirt cuffs, the old man began to speak to his host's back.

"Mr. Stewart, when I agreed to sell you the Wilcox Company, we made a verbal agreement that you would keep on the president and all our officers. Now yesterday afternoon they all received their notices and were informed that you are bringing in an entirely new staff. I can only assume that there has been a misunderstanding, some kind of mistake, and that's why I wanted to discuss it with you immediately."

"No, there's been no mistake," murmured the man by the pool. He directed the boat over to the edge, where he knelt and lovingly adjusted the rigging on the sails. Then he gently pushed the boat off again without looking up.

The elderly man's face reddened, and his voice began to shake slightly as he continued. "Mr. Stewart, the Wilcox Company is a family business. My father started it, as you know, and we have always treated our employees as family members. In turn, many of these people have devoted twenty years or more of their lives to our company. They think of it as their home. I explained all that to you before the sale. The only reason I sold the company at all was that my health does not permit me to continue running it. But you assured me that my people's positions would be safe."

Edward Stewart turned finally and looked up at the indignant older man. "Mr. Wilcox, your company is not an especially profitable one. I am in business to make money.

You and your officers have not done a very efficient job of making money. I intend to change that."

"But you gave me your word," the old man cried. "You promised me."

"Mr. Wilcox," said Edward Stewart patiently, "I thought it over, and I changed my mind. That is my prerogative. I am now the owner of the Wilcox Company."

The old man shook his head and clenched his hands into fists. "If I had known that was what you intended to do, I would never have sold the company to you. It is opposed to everything I have worked for and believed in. I took your word as a gentleman, and you lied to me."

Having risen to his feet, Edward Stewart walked around to the other side of the pool, his eyes, brimming with affection, glued to the sailboat. Under his command, the boat tacked back and forth across the gleaming surface of the water. After a moment Edward crouched down again beside the pool and shook his head in admiration. "Isn't she a beauty?" he said. "I believe this is one of the finest ships I've ever made."

Wilcox glared at the man by the pool, his eyes burning behind the thick lenses of his glasses. "I did not come here to admire your boats, sir. I demand that you answer me."

Edward tore his gaze from the model and looked up at him coolly. "Wilcox," he said, "these boats are my hobby. I relax by working on them and then watching them sail. They provide me with great satisfaction. I can think of few things more rewarding than seeing one of my ships on the water, responding to my every touch of a button."

The old man stiffened, as if he were considering a physical assault. Then his shoulders slumped, and he turned away from Edward's impassive gaze. He controlled the trembling of his muscles with an effort.

"You should take up a hobby," Edward advised him, smiling vaguely. "You'll have plenty of time now. No more business worries. I heartily recommend models."

"I will take you to court, sir," said Wilcox, focusing a piercing gaze on Edward's face.

Edward shrugged. "You'll find you have great difficulty making a case. A hobby, Mr. Wilcox. A hobby will calm you down."

The old man's eyes were full of fury, but his every muscle seemed to sag. He turned and stalked off through the patio doors and into the house.

"The maid will see you out," Edward called after him, but the old man had already disappeared.

Edward shook his head and then knelt down again beside the pool. He brought the boat about, and when it approached the edge, he lifted it out of the water and began to examine the hull.

Paul felt himself trembling all over, and he took a few deep breaths to calm himself. What's the big deal? he scolded himself. It's just some business thing. It doesn't mean anything to you. What are you getting all worked up for? But despite the lecture he was giving himself, Paul felt unaccountably distressed by the scene he had witnessed. The old man's helpless anger filled him with pity, and he felt a revulsion for the man with the boat for the way he had treated the old guy. It's none of your business, he told himself. But he knew for certain, after what he had seen, that he did not want to go up and ask the man if he had seen his cat. After a few minutes had passed and he felt steadier, Paul turned around and began to creep away. He had taken only a few steps when a gray-and-black-striped cat slipped under the bushes and into his path.

"Sam!" he exclaimed in spite of himself.

Edward Stewart's head jerked up, and the boat slipped from his hands, landing in the pool with a splash. "Who's there?" he demanded.

Sam darted off in the direction of the stream at the sound of Edward's voice. Paul hesitated, thinking of trying to run away, and then, lifting his hands in a gesture of surrender, stepped out of the bushes. "I'm sorry to bother you," he apologized. "I was just looking for my cat, and I saw him in those bushes."

The man blanched at the sight of the boy and stared at him without speaking. In his gray eyes Paul saw an anxiety which was close to fear, but then the man's left eyelid began to twitch, and the eyes grew colder.

"I was just coming along, looking for my cat," Paul repeated helplessly. "I'm sorry I disturbed you."

The man seemed to relax as Paul spoke, unclenching his fists and clearing his throat, although he still did not speak.

"I'm sorry . . ." said Paul.

"The next time you come over here, Paul," said Edward at last, "why don't you just announce yourself?"

For a second Paul was taken aback to hear the name. Then his face fell. "You know me," he said.

The man gave him a thin smile. "My wife and I have been neighbors of your family for some years." Edward looked at him closely. "Since you were a little boy, in fact. Perhaps you remember me."

Paul shifted his weight and looked at the ground. "Well, I was young then, when, you know, it happened. . . ."

"Yes," said Edward. "Of course."

The man began to stare at him again, and Paul had the uneasy feeling that the man was sizing him up, as if he were an escaped criminal. Paul cast about desperately for something to say. His eyes fell on the boat in the pool.

"Is that your boat?" he asked.

Edward removed a handkerchief from his pocket and blotted his forehead with it.

"Yes," said Edward distractedly. "I made that. I've made models of some of the world's great sailing vessels. I have a workroom in that windmill over there," he said, gesturing vaguely in the distance. The man looked at Paul as if demanding a reply.

"That's great," said Paul, nodding miserably.

The sound of a shrill, angry voice calling his name filled Paul with an unexpected relief. He and Edward both looked in the direction of the house and saw Tracy coming around the side toward the patio.

Tracy glared at her brother. "Mom's looking all over for you."

"I'm coming. I was just looking for my cat."

"I just passed him," she said.

"Hello, Tracy," said Edward.

"Hello, Mr. Stewart. You'd better get home." Without another word, she turned and headed back around the house.

Paul shrugged and started to back away. "Well, nice meeting you," he said.

"I'll see you later," said Edward.

Paul gave Edward a wan smile. "Okay." He backed off a few more steps and then turned and plunged through the lilac hedge, back the way he had come.

Edward watched him go, his cold gray eyes trained on the figure that flashed through the foliage. Behind him, the model boat bumped against the side of the pool and keeled over, the swamped hull of the ship beginning to sink below the surface. The gossamer sails were sodden flotsam on the water.

* * *

Tracy stomped up the porch steps past her mother, who stood clutching the railing and chewing on her lower lip.

"He was at the Stewarts'. He's coming," said Tracy as she slammed the screen door on her way into the house.

Anna closed her eyes briefly, and her tense frame relaxed. "Thanks, Trace," she said.

Thomas came through the porch door, dragging his bag of golf clubs. He set them against the railing and began to examine them without looking at Anna.

Anna watched him for a moment. "I replaced the iron," she said.

"So I see," said Tom coolly. "Did you find Paul?"

"He was next door. Tracy found him."

"Oh," said Tom. He unzipped the pocket on his golf bag, fished around inside it, and pulled out a couple of loose golf balls. "What was he doing over there?"

"I don't know," said Anna, leaning back against the railing and studying him. "When did Edward invite you to play golf?" she asked.

"Yesterday. On the way home from the station. I forgot to mention it to you."

"I'm surprised, aren't you?"

Thomas looked at her. "Why?"

"Well, you know him." Anna shrugged. "He's not exactly one of the boys."

Thomas smiled. "That's for sure. Although he's been very interested in Paul. He just wanted us to be his guests at the club. Maybe Iris put him up to it."

"Probably," Anna agreed, although she had trouble imagining Edward taking any of Iris's suggestions. "Well, it should be fun."

Thomas nodded. "I thought the boy might enjoy it."

Anna tried not to show how much his plans for Paul pleased her.

"I thought we might all go to the beach later."

Thomas counted the tees in his hand and then put them back into the golf bag. "We can go this afternoon," he said, "after we get back."

Anna walked over to him and slipped her arms around his waist. "I think it's great," she said. "You two will have a good time out there."

Tom sighed. "I hope so," he said.

"Honey," she said, "I'm sorry about last night. I meant to come up, but I guess I was so exhausted I fell asleep in the chair."

"It's all right," he said.

"Today is a fresh start," she said. She gave him a hug, and he returned it, holding on to her for a few moments after she had loosened her grip.

"Well," she said, "I'd better get inside and make breakfast, so you guys can get going."

She opened the door to the house and was about to go in when she saw Paul coming into the yard. She stopped and watched him as he walked slowly toward the house, murmuring to his pet.

Suddenly, as he reached the grassy spot where the play yard used to be, he stopped. Anna saw the expression on his face change from one of confusion to a grimace. All at once he dropped the cat, and it landed in a crouch on the ground beside him. Paul clapped his hand to his forehead and kneaded his eyebrow with one hand as the frown on his face tightened to a look of pain.

"Tom," Anna whispered, "there's something wrong with him." She let go of the porch door, and it shut with a bang. She hesitated for a moment and then rushed past her husband down the porch steps. She pressed her lips together for a moment, and then she called out to Paul.

"What is it? Are you all right?"

The cat looked up at her, but Paul did not meet her eyes. "Yeah," he said, lowering his hand and walking toward her, his eyes on the ground. He brushed past her and entered the house. She could see no trace of color in his complexion. She watched him go into the kitchen and greet Tracy, who was seated at the kitchen table. Tracy mumbled in reply.

Anna clenched her fists and looked back out to where the play yard had once been. The cat sniffed in the grass, carefully traversing the area. It picked its way across the unfamiliar territory, suspicious of every stone and weed.

CHAPTER SIX

Dry branches snapped sharply against his bare forearms and flying bugs hovered around Rambo's hatbrim as he worked his way through the dense growth of trees and bushes known to golfers as the rough.

It had not been difficult to find Hidden Woods Lane when he got off the parkway this morning. He had parked his car in a little dirt road which forked off it and waited. He had seen the boy and his father being picked up by the man in the Cadillac and had trailed them to this golf course. He had climbed over a fence to conceal himself in the trees and overgrown bushes along the fairway. He had already gone six holes through the thickets, following the progress of play. It had made him laugh to himself to see the way the boy lagged behind the two men, clearly disinterested in the game, sweating under the sun in that old jacket that he always wore. He could see that the Lange man was trying to be patient with the little heathen, but the boy didn't pay attention to the instructions, trudging along without a smile, his shoulders slumping. He wondered bitterly if the man was satisfied now to have the stubborn little monster back again. The voices began to speak to Rambo once more, railing at the child's ingratitude and at his return to the land of silver and gold, where evil was called good. His own lips moved to form the words he heard, and he tried to control the muttering which rose from his throat, threatening to expose his hiding place.

Thomas picked up a club and whacked his ball far into the distance toward the seventh green.

"Good shot," said Edward.

Thomas shaded his eyes with his hand and watched the ball drop. "Not bad," he admitted, "considering how out of practice I am."

Edward waved him off. "You might birdie this one."

Thomas turned and handed Paul a club which he had lifted from his bag. They had been trading off shots for the first six holes, Thomas instructing the boy on how to set up a shot and how to swing. Thomas had tried to ignore the boy's sullen expression and had complimented him frequently on his playing. "Probably want to use this club for this shot. We could be on the green with this one."

Paul stared at the iron for a minute and then held it away from him. "I'm getting pretty tired," he said. "Is it okay if I go back?"

Thomas replaced the club in his bag, carefully arranging the heads. "Sure. I guess so." He looked up at their host. "Can he wait at the clubhouse, Edward?"

Edward Stewart nodded. "Of course," he replied. "Can you find the way?"

"Yeah," said Paul.

"We're almost done," said Thomas. "We have only two more holes after this. Are you sure you don't want to hang in there?"

"No," said the boy.

"Okay, fine." Thomas watched Paul as he started slowly back toward the clubhouse.

Rambo thought that he didn't blame the kid. It seemed a dull game to him. He swatted a bug that was humming around his head and waited impatiently for Edward to shoot.

Edward addressed the ball in front of him, rocking a little on the sides of his feet, and then drew back his club. Rambo shifted lower to watch, and the bushes crackled. Edward swung a little wildly; the ball spun off in a curve down a hill and into a sand trap. Edward colored slightly and cleared his throat. "Did you hear those bushes rustling?" he asked. "Terribly distracting." He looked around at the bushes as if to excoriate them. Then he walked over to the crest of the hill and looked disapprovingly down at the ball, as if it were a badly behaved child. "I guess I'll have to chip it out," he said. "Go on up."

Thomas rolled his eyes behind his dark glasses and then looked up the fairway to where his ball was a tiny speck. "All right," he said. "I'll meet you up there."

Thomas began to stroll by himself up the fairway.

Seeing him pass by, Rambo tingled with anticipation. This was his chance. He licked his lips nervously and peered out between the leaves.

When Thomas was halfway up the fairway, Rambo edged his way over to the sand trap. Edward was treading gingerly into the middle of the sinking surface, his face screwed up into an expression of distaste at the grains of sand which were sliding into his shoes. Rambo parted the bushes and scurried to the lip of the trap. After looking in every direction, he cleared his throat.

"Mr. Stewart."

Edward stiffened and stuck his chin out, humiliated at being observed in this predicament. He looked around coldly, prepared to wither with his glance whoever was summoning him. He frowned at the unexpected sight of the pale, nervous man in front of him. The man wore a cheap sport shirt, a dark hat, and sunglasses. He might have been an aging caddie but for the shiny, plastic-looking black shoes on his feet. Edward relaxed at the sight of him. The man was clearly not someone of importance.

"Yes."

"You better come over here," said Rambo, his eyes darting around the sloping emerald hillocks of the course. "I want to talk to you."

Unaccustomed to being ordered about, Edward glared at the man and replied with an icy, imperious formality.

"If you have a message to deliver to me," he said, suspecting that the man had been sent from the clubhouse, "please do so immediately and then leave. You are interrupting my game."

Rambo stared at him, taken aback by Edward's response. He raised one finger and shook it at him. "The word of the Lord is my message," Rambo chanted at him. "The Lord's justice is my aim!"

Edward heaved his shoulders in a sigh and shook his head. The man in the sunglasses looked too old to be one of those Moon people. A Jehovah's Witness, perhaps, or some other sect. It infuriated Edward that people like this were allowed to roam around the golf course. With the prices that this club charged, it should at the least be able to guarantee privacy for the members. He made a mental vow to deliver a blistering complaint to the greenskeeper.

"If you know what's good for you, sir," said Edward, "you will go peddle your shibboleths elsewhere and get off this golf course this instant." He turned his back on Rambo and began carefully lining his club up with the half-buried golf ball.

"The Lord has spoke to me. The Lord has given me a sign, not once, but twice, that I must render His justice unto you."

"I'm warning you," said Edward in a menacing voice.

"Your evil, your wicked ways. Easier for a camel to go through the eye of a needle than for a rich man—"

"That's it," said Edward, jamming his club in the sand and turning around to shake a finger at Rambo. "I'm having you bodily thrown out of here."

Rambo took a step back. "I saw you," Rambo hissed at him. "That day on the highway. Eleven years ago. I know what you did."

Edward stopped short. His face turned ashen under the brim of his golf cap. His knuckles went white as he gripped the shaft of the club for support.

"I don't know what you're talking about," Edward whispered.

"To the boy, your friend's son," said Rambo, flinging his arm wildly back behind him, the direction in which Paul had gone. "I was there in the bushes. I saw it all."

Edward stared at the man, his body vibrating like a violin string. Suddenly he realized why the man looked vaguely familiar. Newspaper pictures of the wiry man, always wearing a hat. "Rambo," he breathed.

"That's right," cried Rambo triumphantly. "Albert Rambo. The voice of the Lord on this earth."

An incredible gnawing had started in Edward's stomach as he tried to absorb the shock of Rambo's words. It occurred to him, as his mind raced, that Rambo must be mad to have dared come here with Thomas and the boy so close by. He is mad, Edward thought.

But he knows.

Edward licked his lips several times and tried to think.

But his brain seemed to able to register nothing but flashing, glaring lights, offering only exposure, not refuge.

"What do you want?" he gasped, his eyes glued to Rambo's wild face.

"The Lord has a mission for me," Rambo cried. "I have work to do. I can complete His work with the help of your money. And you can be saved by giving it to me."

Blackmail, Edward thought. He wants money. Somehow that realization steadied him slightly. At first, with the shock, he had felt as if an avenging angel had swooped down on him, threatening to destroy all he had gained. The dread day which he had always secretly expected had now come to pass. The mention of money brought him around like a slap. He stared at the man in front of him, who clearly had no money. He spoke again in a flat voice. "What do you want?" he repeated more forcefully.

Rambo gazed down at the man in the sand trap. The question seemed to have jolted him from his ravings. "Money," he said. "Enough money to get away."

"And if I don't give it to you?" Edward asked in a cold voice.

"I'll tell the police what you did."

A shudder raced through Edward at the force of the man's threat. With a shaking hand he wiped his forehead under his cap. His stomach was churning, and hot flashes were passing through him; but even in his torment, his mind registered one important thought: If Rambo were to go to the police, they would arrest him immediately.

"Who else knows about this?" Edward asked.

"Don't worry about it. Nobody but me now. My wife knew. She was with me at the time. But she's gone now. And the boy knows, I guess you could say."

"You told him what happened?"

"Of course not," Rambo shouted. "But he was there, wasn't he? Maybe he remembers. I don't know. Otherwise, nobody."

"Why did you wait so long?" Edward whispered. "Why now?"

Rambo smiled slyly. "I didn't know it was you. Not until I saw you on the TV yesterday. Then I recognized you. And that fancy car of yours, with the eagle. Not a very good driver, are you?"

"The TV?" For a moment Edward was confused. Then he recalled the interview at the Langes', his Cadillac visible behind them in the driveway. He stifled a groan, remembering how he had been convinced to appear in the interview. Get hold of yourself, he thought. Use your head now. He gazed in silence at Rambo for a moment. The man's a lunatic, he thought. He has no proof that any of this ever happened. Edward could feel his heart thumping loudly, and there was a roaring in his head; but he spoke calmly.

"So," said Edward, picking up the golf ball and rolling it around in the palm of his hand, "if I don't pay you this . . . blackmail money, you will take your story to the police. Is that it?"

Rambo seemed drained but jumpy. "That's right."

"You," said Edward quietly, "who face a life sentence if you are caught will walk right into the nearest police station with this tale."

"Well," Rambo dissembled, "I might not tell them directly."

Edward stared at his tormentor, and for the first time he began to feel his power, his control, returning. Rambo was a shabby, pathetic little man. A weak, sniveling creature. He reminded himself that he was infinitely superior to this nobody who threatened him. "How are you going to tell them?" Edward inquired. "Are you going to send them a telegram? Maybe an anonymous tip?" He spit out froth on the *p*.

"I've got a way," Rambo insisted defiantly. He kneaded one bony hand with the other.

Edward trained his steely gaze on Rambo, who was shifting his weight nervously from foot to foot. He seemed disoriented and a little frightened, as if he were the one who had been cornered. Propelled to this confrontation by his information and his delusions, he had not bothered to reason out a plan. A cold satisfaction began to supplant Edward's fear as he watched the man fidget. He is a worm, he thought. You could crush him with the toe of your shoe. He felt his own trembling subside. "I don't think so," said Edward in a cold voice. "I don't think you do."

Rambo's face sagged as his voice rose. "Just give me the money," he cried, "or I'll show you." He fumbled in the pocket of his shirt and pulled out a cigarette and some matches. He thrust the cigarette in his mouth and lit it. He drew on the cigarette furiously, as if it were providing oxygen, rather than cutting it off.

"Let me tell you something, Mr. Rambo," said Edward in a cutting voice. "I belong to the finest social circles in this town. I have money and power, to be blunt. Who do you think would take your word over mine?"

A dose of spirit seemed to revive Rambo at Edward's words. "What will you do on the day of punishment?" he railed. "To whom will you flee for help, and where will you leave your wealth?"

Edward drew himself up and thundered over Rambo's chant, "You are a criminal on the run. A fugitive. A wanted man."

Rambo's shoulders slumped, as if his last outburst had exhausted him.

Edward felt the battle waning. "When you really think about it," said Edward slowly, "it's a preposterous idea."

Rambo stared helplessly at his intended quarry. "I need that money," he whined.

"I'm sure you do," Edward snarled. "But you won't get it from me. I'm not afraid of you. Now get out of here, before I call the police."

Rambo gaped at him for a moment as if trying to formulate a reply. "The day of punishment is at . . ." he mumbled.

"Now," Edward commanded.

Rambo began to back away. When he reached the bushes, he turned and bolted into the trees. Edward could hear him crashing through the rough, like a rabbit fleeing from a pack of hounds.

Although he watched Rambo go with cold eyes, Edward could feel his heart racing. He had taken care of him, and very efficiently, too. He had turned the situation around and gotten rid of him, he reminded himself. But he could not deny the feeling of shaky distress that made his stomach churn. Edward looked down at the golf ball in his hand. Drawing his arm back behind him, he threw the ball up and away, as far as he could toward the fairway. Then he scrambled out of the sand trap.

He saw Thomas standing up near the green, scanning the course. Plastering a smile on his face, Edward began to wave to Thomas, indicating that he was out of the trap and would be making his next shot. Thomas waved back in reply.

Edward walked over to his golf cart and selected a club from his bag. You took care of him, he tried to assure himself. You are safe. He won't come back.

As he was about to position himself over the ball for his next shot, he suddenly noticed a little square of white on the edge of the grass bordering the sand trap. He walked over to it, squatted down carefully, and picked it up. Then he examined it. The object he held in his hand was a matchbook with "La-Z Pines Motel, Kingsburgh, New York" printed on it in letters formed by miniature logs. "Gus deBlakey, Prop."

Edward licked his lips and then gazed into the bushes where Rambo had disappeared. He saw it all, Edward thought again with a shudder. He saw me. He knows what I did.

He stuffed the matchbook deliberately into his pocket. Then he returned to his ball and lined up his shot. Carefully he adjusted his weight and touched the ball with the head of the club, to be sure that the hit would be clean and direct. With every ounce of his concentration he drew back the club, and then he swung it down and struck the ball with all the power in his body. The sound of the ball connecting with the club produced a whack that reverberated through his frame. Before he could look up, the ball was gone from sight, sailing toward the green. Perfect, he thought. You never fail. You must never fail. His heart was still pounding as he started up the fairway.

"Do you like the beach, Paul?" Anna asked as Tracy and Paul got out of the car and Tracy started across the narrow road to the boardwalk which protected the dunes.

"I've never been," he replied, shouldering the aluminum-framed beach chair.

He looks like a waif, Anna thought. He was standing beside the car, wearing high sneakers without socks, a pair of cutoff khaki pants, and his dungaree jacket, despite the heat.

Anna lifted the plastic picnic basket out of the truck. "I'll bet you'll be coming to the beach a lot from now on. We'll get you a beach pass and a bathing suit. Right, Tom?"

Thomas shut the door on the driver's side and adjusted his sunglasses over his eyes. "What?"

Anna handed the picnic basket to Thomas as Paul followed Tracy across the road. "You're awfully quiet," she said.

"Just thinking," he said as they followed the path of the teen-agers.

"You didn't say much about your game this morning," she observed. "Did Paul enjoy it?"

Thomas peered at the boy, who was disappearing over the ramp down to the beach area. "I don't know. I guess he did."

As they came over the dunes, they could see the calm waters of Long Island Sound stretching out across the horizon. Anna walked up beside Paul.

"Well, what do you think?" she asked him.

The boy looked out over the pleasant summer landscape and nodded. "I like it," he said.

Anna felt a surge of happiness at his reaction. She turned to Thomas, who was setting up their chairs on the sand, to see if he had noticed, but Thomas did not look up.

"Well, spread your towel out," Anna instructed Paul matter-of-factly.

Tracy had found a group of friends who were oiled and giggling, sunning themselves at the foot of the lifeguard's chair. She avoided looking back at her family.

"You'd better put some lotion on," said Anna, eyeing Paul's pale skin as he removed his jacket.

"I'm going to look around," he said.

Anna could see from the corner of her eye that Tracy's

friends were whispering among themselves. One of them pointed to Paul's sneakers and snickered. This started the whole group of them laughing. Paul did not acknowledge them, but Anna was filled with the sick feeling that he knew what they were up to.

Anna watched her son as he gazed across the shoreline, planning his route. He made a funny face at a child in terry-cloth trunks who was shoveling sand not far from the foot of his towel. The child laughed delightedly and pointed his shovel at Paul. The young mother, who was keeping a close eye on her toddler, smiled at Paul and then glanced over at Anna as Paul passed by.

"Is that your son?" the woman asked Anna.

Anna watched the boy making his way down the beach toward the water. He carried his jacket over one arm, his skin a sickly white in contrast with the browned bodies on the blankets. She tore her eyes from Paul and smiled at the young mother. "Yes," she replied.

"Nice young man," said the woman.

"He's fifteen tomorrow," Anna said softly. "How old is your little fellow?"

The woman rolled her eyes and laughed. "Just two years, and he's into everything." As if to prove her point, the little boy waddled down and began to wrestle a pail away from a girl who was playing near a tide pool.

"Jeremy," the woman cried, and rushed over to separate them. "Give the little girl back her bucket," she said.

The child settled in a heap near his new friend, and the woman returned to her towel. Anna smiled at her.

"You're so lucky," the woman said. "You don't have to watch him anymore. I can't wait until Jeremy's old enough that I don't have to keep my eye on him every minute."

"They grow up so fast," said Anna, her eyes traveling

back to the water's edge, seeking Paul. For a moment she could not find him. Her heart began to race. She scanned the shoreline anxiously. Then she spotted him. He was wading near the edge of the water, looking out at the ocean. She sighed and turned toward Thomas, who was sitting in a low beach chair, looking through the newspaper.

Anna sank onto the blanket next to his chair. She patted her husband on the knee, and he lowered his paper.

"Do you want me to put some lotion on your back?" he asked.

Anna nodded and handed him the bottle. He squirted some lotion into his palm, and he began to massage it in a circular motion on her bare back.

"Oh, that feels good," said Anna, leaning her head back, although she kept her half-closed eyes on the shoreline, where Paul was standing ankle-deep in the sea. "I think I'll lie down here and read a few pages of my book."

"You look tired," said Tom. "Why don't you catch a nap for a few minutes?"

"I don't know," said Anna. "I want to keep an eye on him."

"What for?" Thomas cried, tossing the bottle of lotion down on the towel. "He's not a baby, Anna."

"I forgot to ask him if he could swim."

Thomas pursed his lips and stared at the boy wading in the shallow water. "It's not like he's going to be swept out to sea," he said.

Anna heard the edge in his voice and tried to appease him. "I do need to relax," she said. "You're right." She stretched out on the blanket and opened her book, but she looked up surreptitiously every few sentences.

The sun was hot and soothing on her body, and it began to have a soporific effect. After laying the open book on the blanket, she rested her chin on her hands and gazed out across the blazing sand. She had hardly slept all night, and weariness stole over her. The sounds of laughter and radios merged into a pleasant hum as her eyelids started to droop. She began to dream of a small boy in a pool of water and light.

Suddenly a horrible shrieking pierced her dream, frightening the dream child and then dissolving him, as Anna awakened with a jolt. The shrill squawking continued as she scrambled up from slumber, foggy and disoriented, searching for the source. The wail of a child filled her with dread. She looked around and saw a sea gull, perched on the edge of a wire mesh trash basket, a fragment of food in its beak.

"I'll get you another cookie." Jeremy's mother soothed him as the child decried the audacious bird's theft.

"Shoo," cried the mother, flapping her hands at the impassive bird, which eyeballed them from its perch.

With a sigh Anna sank down again to her towel. Then she remembered Paul. Immediately she turned over, and her eyes scanned the beach. For a moment she could not see him. Then she realized why.

Paul had not moved far from where he was before, but now a man wearing a loose-fitting shirt, dark glasses, and a wide-brimmed hat was standing directly behind him. Both Paul and the man in the hat had their backs to her. The man's hands were clamped on Paul's narrow shoulders.

"Tom!" Anna exclaimed. "Look."

"What?" Thomas asked, lowering a corner of his paper.

"That man," said Anna, rising to her feet, her heart beginning to hammer.

"Where are you going?" Thomas asked as Anna started to walk down the beach, her eyes fixed, trancelike on her son and the man behind him. As she got closer to them, she began to hurry, her pace beginning to keep time with her speeded-up pulse.

She approached the man and the boy and spoke in a voice so loud it made them both jump. "What are you doing?" she demanded.

Paul and the man in the hat turned around and stared at Anna. Paul lowered the binoculars which the man had offered to him and backed away from her. The man, who had been guiding the boy's sights, looked stunned.

"I was showing him . . ." the man said.

Anna tried to grab her boy's arm, but Paul squirmed away from her. The confusion in his eyes turned to anger.

"What's the matter?" the boy cried out. "He's letting me look."

Anna turned on the man, whose ruddy face sagged from the unexpected confrontation. "What do you want with my son?" she asked suspiciously.

"Nothing . . ." the man protested.

"He was showing me those fish," Paul screamed.

The people nearby on the beach were staring at them now. All activity around them seemed to have stopped, as the bathers watched the scene.

"I'll call a policeman," Anna threatened, trying to shepherd her son away.

"Leave me alone," Paul cried, pulling away from her. "Get away from me."

Anna's hands dropped, and she looked helplessly from the boy to the man.

The man in the hat drew himself up and took a deep breath. "Look," he said severely, "I didn't do anything wrong. I let your boy look through my binoculars. Now I think you owe me an apology. You're embarrassing me in front of all these people."

Anna felt herself shrink as her fright and anger oozed away. She passed her hand over her eyes. Her shoulders drooped. "I'm sorry," she whispered.

"I should call the police on you," said the man, more boldly now, slinging his binoculars back around his own neck.

"I'm sorry," Anna repeated. "I'm not myself. I was afraid . . ." Her hands hung limply at her sides. She stared down at an air hole in the sand where some clam was burrowing, wishing she herself could sink into the cool, dense muck.

"All right," said the man, pulling down the tails of his shirt. "You should be sorry."

Anna turned around, her eyes downcast, as Paul staggered up the beach, his pale cheeks flaming. Thomas stood in her path. He was watching her with grim, disbelieving eyes.

Anna shook her head, as if she could not begin to explain.

"Let's go," he said.

They walked in silence up the beach, past Tracy, who was hiding her face from the curious stares of her friends. "Do you want a ride home, Tracy?" Thomas asked.

Tracy kept her eyes averted. "No."

"Call me later, and I'll pick you up."

Anna walked up to their blanket. Paul had disappeared over the dunes. He was probably already in the car, hiding from the humiliation she had caused him. Her lips trembled as she bent over to pick up the picnic basket, still heavy with their uneaten lunch.

CHAPTER SEVEN

Gus deBlakey, the proprietor of the La-Z Pines Motel, was sweeping off the office front stoop as Albert Rambo pulled into the shady courtyard and headed back toward his secluded white cabin with the forest-green trim. Gus stopped his sweeping and leaned on his broom as Rambo passed by in his battered old blue Chevy. He wondered how long that guy was going to stay. But that was really all he wondered. He did not expend much of his limited imagination on the guests who passed through his motel. With his oldest daughter giving birth in a few days to his first grandchild, Gus had other things to think about.

But he did give a passing thought to the length of this particular visitor's stay. Lord knew, he needed all the business he could get. His wife had mentioned buying the baby one of those little warming dishes with different compartments for the different things to eat. Gus thought that sounded like a good idea. He didn't like to eat his food cold after all; no reason why his grandchild should. He straightened up and put his broom back to work.

Rambo slammed the door on his Chevy, unlocked the door to his cabin, and slammed that, too. He did not bother to turn on the light, although he did switch on the feeble air conditioner in the window. Then he flopped down on the sagging bed and sat there, staring at the drawn venetian blinds. He pulled out a cigarette from his pocket and stuffed it in his mouth. His matches were not in his pocket. He opened the drawer of the night table and picked up the matchbook which he had seen in there before. He lit his cigarette.

In his mind's eye he kept picturing Edward Stewart glaring at him. He shivered, remembering Edward's stony eyes. A gloomy sense of failure descended on him as he relived their conversation on the golf course. Rambo now realized that he had confronted Edward without much of a plan. After all, he didn't have any actual proof that the man had done anything. He had just been counting on his being so surprised and scared that he'd give in without a fuss. Besides, he'd had a sign that he should do it. He had been sent.

Rambo reached across the bed, picked up his Bible, and began to pore over the marked chapter in the dim light of the motel room. But his eyes refused to focus on the words. After a few moments he snapped the Bible shut and put it aside. Slowly he pulled out his wallet and opened it. He stared at its meager contents a good long time without moving. The room was silent. No divine voices spoke to him, suggesting what he might do next. He faced the bald fact that his money would be gone in a day or two.

He folded the wallet over, to insert it back into his pocket. A picture poked out from one of the loose flaps inside. He started to push it back in. Then, instead he drew it out and looked at it.

There was Dorothy Lee, wearing her nurse's uniform, smiling up at him. It was an old picture, from when she got her cap. She had been so proud of that.

He held the picture gently at its worn corner and thought about his wife. He had done it for her after all. Taken the boy. She wanted a baby so badly, and he couldn't give her one. The adoption people wouldn't even talk to them because of all the times he'd been in the hospital, locked up. So he had taken the kid. And look where it got me, he thought.

Dorothy Lee had always been after him to carry a picture of the boy, but he never wanted to. He wouldn't have a picture of that devil child anywhere on his person. It was bad enough when he'd had to look at his actual face. It set Rambo's teeth on edge just to think of the boy, who had ruined his life like this.

Once she had gotten that kid, it was almost as if she'd forgotten her husband, he thought. As if she hadn't cared for him anymore, just the kid. He could picture her, sitting there in the dark trailer on the daybed, watching TV, the kid cuddled up in her lap. She'd be crooning to him, and playing with his hair, and just ignoring her husband. Rambo looked down again at his wife's picture, half-tempted to tear it up. Then he slipped it back into his wallet and folded the wallet over.

You'll never know what it's like to be a mother, she used to say to him. Albert, a mother'll do anything for her child. Even when he reminded her that Billy wasn't really hers, Dorothy Lee had just ridden right over him. I am his mother, she would say, and it's up to me.

And then a voice spoke aloud in the room. Not the Lord's voice, but his own. "That's it," Rambo said. "The mother. She'll pay. The mother."

For a long time he sat still in silence, turning his idea over and over in his brain. Then he crossed one leg over the other and rested the open Bible on his bony knee. He mumbled

aloud as he flipped the pages furiously, seeking chapter and
verse to petition the Lord for aid in this, his last chance.

"Edward?" Iris asked timidly.

Edward closed the pages of the Princeton alumni magazine which he had been staring at and put it down beside his
dinner plate with a sigh. They were seated at the table in the
gloomy, cavernous dining room of their mansion.

"I'm sorry?" he said.

"I asked you how Paul enjoyed the golf game today."

"Well enough, I suppose."

Iris reached across the table to an untouched basket of
rolls and picked one up. She tore off a piece and held it in
her fingers. "What's he like?"

Edward peered disapprovingly at the roll in her hand and
then picked up his fork and held it poised over the seafood
salad in his plate. "I don't know," he said. "He seems like
an ordinary boy."

Iris slipped the piece of roll into her mouth and chewed it
with tiny bites. Then she leaned forward and looked
earnestly at her husband. "I'm so anxious to meet him.
Does he seem to be adjusting to the situation all right?"

Edward's eyes traveled from his wife's questioning face
down to her dress, where one of the seams revealed a small
gap just above her thickening midriff. Edward gripped the
fork he was holding by the tines and reached over toward
her.

Iris looked at him in confusion and then flinched as she
felt the cold end of the fork handle press into her skin
through the hole in her dress.

Edward's nose wrinkled in distaste as he poked at the spot
where the fork handle was pressed. "Iris, you are splitting
the seams of your clothing."

Iris drew back from the table, her face flushed, and folded her arms across her body in an effort to cover the gap in her dress. "I didn't notice it when I put it on."

"It would behoove you to be a little more observant when you dress," said Edward, resuming the correct hold on his fork.

"I know, I'm sorry," she muttered.

Edward finished off his seafood salad in silence as Iris picked at the food on her plate.

"Are the arrangements complete for the party?" Edward asked without looking up at her.

Iris bit her lip and nodded.

"Well?" Edward demanded, gazing at her impatiently.

"Yes!" Iris exclaimed.

Edward sighed. "You needn't shout, Iris."

"I . . . I talked to the florist and the caterer today, and everything is set."

"Oh, you may cross the Wilcoxes off your guest list," said Edward. "They won't be coming."

"That poor man seemed so upset when he left this morning. Is something wrong?" Iris asked.

"It is business, Iris," said Edward. "It does not concern you. Simply cross them off the list."

The maid came into the dining room to clear off the dinner plates. Iris lifted her plate and offered it up to her and then noticed Edward staring at the hole in her dress. She quickly lowered her arms to her sides.

Edward picked up his alumni magazine again and turned the pages. He found that he could not really concentrate on the articles, however, for his mind was distracted by the day's events. But it was easier to pretend to read than to look at his wife and the maddening hole in her dress. She had no shortage of clothes, although she had to squeeze herself into most of them these days. He wondered for a moment what she planned to wear to the party. He did not want her to shame him in front of the most important people in town.

"Iris," he said, "I hope you have a decent dress for the party."

"I do," she said.

The maid returned to the dining room and quietly put a bowl of ice cream down in front of each of them.

Iris smiled gratefully at the maid and picked up her spoon. "It's that blue dress," she said, "the one I wore to the ballet benefit. I received several compliments on it."

Edward watched with revulsion as she lifted a spoonful of ice cream to her open lips. He stood it as long as he could, then with a deft movement he rolled his magazine up into a tube and rose slightly from his chair. Thrusting his wrist forward, he plunged the tube of slick paper into Iris's bowl of ice cream. Iris let out a cry as the melting cream splattered up over the front of her dress, and magazine page corners curled into the dessert bowl.

She looked up incredulously at her husband, who kept the magazine planted in her plate.

"Iris," he said evenly, "why, when you are already bursting out of your clothes, are you eating a bowl of ice cream?"

Iris shook her head, and her lip trembled.

"You don't need that," Edward informed her. "It will only add to your weight problem."

Iris stared down at the bowl as Edward lifted the rolled-up magazine and placed it gingerly on the serving tray on the table.

"Now," he said, "why don't you go upstairs and change out of that dress?"

Wiping her lips and the front of her dress hastily with her napkin, Iris stood up shakily from the table. Edward picked up his spoon and began to eat his ice cream as she left the table. In the dining room door Iris stopped and studied her husband for a moment with a resentful gaze. Then she left the room.

Edward glanced over at the magazine with its one soggy end on the tray. He rang the bell impatiently for the maid to come and remove it. It was a shame, really, that he had had to sacrifice the magazine to teach Iris a lesson. He always derived such satisfaction from reading it, for each issue confirmed his suspicion that few of his classmates had done as well as he had, although most of them had started out with advantages which he hadn't enjoyed.

It had not been easy for him. While the other boys frittered away their time on football games and the camaraderie of their posh eating clubs, he had held a job in a local diner to supplement his scholarship and had been forced to live off campus in the home of an old woman who was bringing up her orphaned grandson and needed the money.

At least it had been quiet there, and he had been able to study. He had paid no attention to the woman or her grandson, until that one bad time. He had left his term paper on the kitchen table for a few minutes, and when he came back, the child had accidentally spilled a glass of chocolate milk on it. Edward had been forced to retype it and turn in the paper a day late.

He had taken care of the child for that, though. When the old woman and the boy were out shopping, he had gone into the garage and loosened the wheels on the boy's bike, so that the next time he went out for a ride, the wheels fell off, and the child hit the pavement on his head. Edward had watched from behind the curtain in his room as the child lay, still as death, the blood from his head running down his face and pooling on the sidewalk. The boy had a dozen stitches and a black eye as a result, and Edward felt satisfied. The old woman never accused him of anything, although she did ask him to leave the next day. It was an inconvenience, finding another room, but it had been worth it.

Edward shook his head and looked back at the magazine, which the maid was now lifting, tray and all, from the table. He had certainly come a long way since those days. He wanted to make a note to send the alumni magazine a notice of his purchase of the Wilcox Company.

He reached into his pocket for his leather note pad and pulled out, as well, the matchbook cover from the La-Z Pines Motel. Instantly his mind returned to his preoccupation of the whole day. At first he thought he had handled it so well, scaring Rambo off like that. Watching the would-be blackmailer shrink into a frightened, whining little worm had filled Edward with elation and a renewed confidence in his own power. But as the day wore on, he was not as sure of himself.

The man might be a lunatic; but he was on the loose, and he knew a terrible secret about Edward. Paying him the blackmail money was no solution because there was no guarantee that Rambo would keep silent if the police caught up with him. There was no way that Rambo could prove the story, of course. The police would have no case against him. But, Edward realized in mulling it over, there were other dangers besides the legal one. There was his position in society to think of. There was the possibility of scandal. More than a few people would gloat to see him disgraced. So many people were envious of him. He thought, for a second, of the alumni magazine, shuddering at the thought of an item in it about him, detailing the ugly accusations that could be made against him.

His concentration was so absolute that he did not hear Iris when she returned to the dining room. She inched into the room and stood behind her chair, wearing a different dress.

Edward gave her an annoyed glance.

"I was thinking," said Iris tentatively. "Perhaps I could go to a health spa for a few days next week. I've been thinking of doing it anyway, and I could trim down a little."

Edward picked up the coffee cup which the maid had brought in to him. "It's unfortunate that you didn't think of going before this party," he said.

Iris shrugged. "I think I'll go on Tuesday."

"Fine with me," said Edward, whose mind was on other things.

"Tuesday then," said Iris. She walked around behind him toward the door.

Edward opened his hand and looked down at the matchbook in his palm. There was only one way, he mused, that Rambo's story would never reach the wrong ears. He had no choice, really. As long as Rambo was alive, nothing was safe.

"You're sure you don't mind, Edward?" Iris asked from the doorway.

"Iris," said Edward, "I'm sure I don't care."

He knew what he had to do now, and he would do it, he thought. He had never been one to balk at doing what was necessary. Albert Rambo would regret the day he had ever tried to blackmail him. In fact, he would pay a dear price for his mistake.

Thomas wound his watch and placed it on the top of his bureau. Then he went to the bed, pulled back the sheet, and climbed in, picking up the book which was lying on the nightstand. He switched on the lamp beside him and opened the book.

Slowly Anna hung up her skirt and then removed the rest of her clothing. She lifted her summer nightgown off a hook in the closet and held it to her breast. She turned around and looked at her husband, but he did not glance up at her. He seemed to be concentrating on the book he was holding. She pulled the nightgown on overhead with a small sigh and walked over to her dresser to pick up her brush. The back and handle of the brush were sterling silver, with her initials engraved on it, a gift from Thomas on their first anniversary. The matching comb lay on the dresser beside it. Anna lifted the brush and began to draw it through her hair.

Thomas lowered his book and watched her as she pulled the brush back, her hair fanning out and then drifting softly to her shoulders. Then he shook his head and lifted the book again. "I assume you're sleeping up here tonight," he said in a gruff voice.

Anna pulled the bristles hard against her scalp. "I've locked up," she said. "I guess it will be all right."

Thomas stared over the top of his book at the foot of the bed. Then he looked back down blindly at the words on the page.

"I can't tell how he feels about being back . . . with us," said Anna. "I think he's a little confused by all this." She turned on the stool of her dressing table and looked at Thomas. "What do you think?"

"I don't know," said Thomas, staring at the print on the page.

Anna came over to the end of the bed and placed a hand on his leg, which was covered by the sheet. "Tom, I'm sorry about what happened at the beach today. I'm sorry I embarrassed you. And the kids."

Thomas kept his eyes on his book and spoke in a tight voice. "You didn't embarrass me," he said.

"I think I was just overtired." She climbed into the bed beside him and pulled up the sheets. "I'm hoping we can have a quiet, relaxing day tomorrow, although we've got that party tomorrow night."

"I need to go to the garage and pick up the car tomorrow," he said. "And I want to get some stuff for the lawn."

"Maybe when you get back, we can all do something together," Anna ventured.

"I told Tracy that she should take Paul to the animal shelter with her tomorrow afternoon."

"Oh, no, Tom. Why?"

"Why not? Those two need to get acquainted."

"But to go over there alone, just the two of them? Something could happen."

Thomas glared at her. "You let Tracy go over there alone all the time. You know it's perfectly safe around here."

"Well, yes, it's safe, but what about . . . you know . . . that man?" Anna shuddered at the thought of Rambo.

Thomas clenched his fists outside the bedcovers. "Anna, when are you going to let up? That's what it was at the beach today, wasn't it?"

Anna bit the inside of her mouth and did not reply.

"You're not doing the boy any favors with this," he said. "You know you can't watch over him every minute of every day. Why don't you let him go about his business? Let him be."

"I'm concerned for his safety," she said. "I should think you would be, too."

Thomas's jaw hardened. He turned out the light and slid down beneath the sheets with his back to Anna.

She put one hand over her eyes, then reached out and touched him on the shoulder. "I'm sorry," she said. "I didn't mean that."

Thomas stared into the darkness. "It doesn't matter."

"You're probably right," she said. "I can't seem to help myself. You were right about Tracy. You were always warning me, reminding me not to smother her because of what happened . . . to Paul. And you were right." She spoke softly to her husband's back, remembering their arguments over Tracy. How hard it had been for her to do what he said and let their daughter live normally. She caught her breath for a moment, remembering the constant fear. Reason had told her to listen to him, although everything inside had struggled against his advice. Once, when Tracy had gone on an overnight trip to Washington with her fourth-grade class, Anna had spent most of the night in the bathroom, throwing up from fear.

"I know you're right," she said, "but it's so hard for me. I can't just wipe it out, all the years of worrying and being scared."

"I know that," he said.

"It would help so much if I felt you understood. I need you now. I need to share this with you." She reached her arms around him tentatively and cupped his wrist, which was pulled tightly to his chest, in the palm of her hand. "We've always shared things before. If we could kind of . . . get together on this."

Thomas squeezed his eyes shut as she ran her fingers up his forearm. "I don't really know how, Anna. Maybe it's just that it's new. I have to get used to the idea of the boy's being back here and everything."

"It's not easy, darling," she crooned. "I know. But once they've caught up with Rambo, I promise you I won't be so anxious. I'm going to try not to worry. I only wish you seemed happier about all this. . . ."

He bridled reflexively at her suggestion. But at the same time he could feel her breasts pressing against his back, and that gentle pressure affected him like a clamp on his chest, squeezing out the air. The tumult of his feelings caused an ache in his throat. He wanted to roll over and press his stinging eyes to her soft breasts and clutch her to him with all the strength in his rigid arms.

Suddenly she loosened her hold on him and sat up in the bed. There was a cold spot on his back where her body had been. "Do you hear something?" she said.

Thomas rolled over and looked at her, sitting up in the bed, the moonlight outlining her body in her thin night-gown.

"What?" he said.

"Downstairs. I'm sure I hear something."

Thomas buried his face in the pillow.

"Don't you hear it?" she whispered. "There's someone moving around."

"I don't hear anything," he said, pulling the sheet up to his ears.

Getting out of bed, Anna pulled on her wrapper and tied it, straining to hear the faint sounds which came from the floor below. "It's probably one of the kids," she said uncertainly, but Thomas did not look up.

He lay, unmoving, shrouded in the bedclothes. "It's your imagination," he said dully.

Anna moved to the doorway and looked out into the hall. The doors to Paul's and Tracy's rooms were shut, and the house was completely dark. She could sense her husband's irritation, but she could not help herself.

"I'm going to have a look," she said.

Thomas did not reply. Anna slipped out into the hall and turned the light on over the staircase. She went down quietly, one hand pressing against the wall, as if to ground herself.

The downstairs was silent and dark. She stood at the foot of the staircase, thinking that Thomas was right. She had imagined it. She moved out into the dark living room, making her way by instinct toward a lamp. Suddenly she heard a soft thud from the direction of the kitchen. "Who's there?" she said, switching on the lamp. There was no answer. She looked around the room as if to reassure herself that she was alone, and then she peered into the dining room. The heavy brass candlesticks on the dining room table caught her eye.

Her heart thumped as she rushed to the table and grabbed a candlestick. It felt heavy and reassuring in her hand. "Who is it?" she said again. "Tracy?"

Gripping the candlestick in a sweaty hand, Anna pushed open the door between the dining room and the kitchen and threw on the kitchen light. The room was empty.

Anna looked around and then walked over to the back door and tested it. The door was securely locked. She turned back into the room and noticed the pantry door was slightly ajar. She walked over to it.

Drawing back the candlestick, as if to strike, she gave the door a kick, and it swung back. Anna looked in and let out a gasp. "Paul!" she cried, lowering her arm. "What are you doing?"

The kitchen light dimly illuminated the dark pantry. Halfway in, the boy crouched, looking up at her. The wide eyes of a cornered animal stared out from his pale, sickly face. His hands gripped the bottom shelf of the pantry, as if for support. He watched her warily, his eyes darting from her face to the candlestick in her hand.

"Why didn't you answer me?" Anna demanded, sharpness born of relief in her voice.

The boy shrugged, but his body was tense. Anna came toward him, worriedly examining his colorless face. She could see, as she approached him, that his body was trembling.

He scrambled to his feet before she reached him and sidled past her into the kitchen, keeping his back to the shelves.

Anna followed him and put the candlestick on the counter. She reached out a hand to him, but he pressed himself against the refrigerator. "I couldn't sleep," he said. "I was hungry."

"Paul, you don't need to hide from me," she said. "This is your home." The boy looked away from her. "Did you find something to eat?" she asked.

He nodded quickly.

She looked at him closely, not believing him, but decided not to press it. "What's wrong, Paul? Do you feel all right?"

He glanced at her and then took a deep breath. "I had a nightmare. It woke me up."

"Do you want to tell it?" she asked. "That helps sometimes."

The boy shook his head. "No. I'm going back up."

"Okay," she said.

"Night."

She waited until he had gone up the stairs, and then she turned off the lights and followed him. The thought of him, crouching there in the dark pantry, chilled her, and she tried to put it out of her mind. But she wondered what kind of dream it had been that had scared him so, made him cower from her like that.

Slowly she returned to her room. She opened the door. In the moonlight she could see Thomas's body, curled up with his back to her in the bed.

"It was Paul," she said. "He had a nightmare."

There was no answer from the bed. Thomas was making heavy, breathing sounds. She knew that he was only pretending to sleep. Anna took off her robe and got into bed beside him. In the silent dark house, his breathing was like the sound of trees, rustling in a graveyard. She sat with her back against the headboard, willing herself to be calm. After a while Thomas's rigid body relaxed, and she could see that he had actually fallen asleep.

CHAPTER EIGHT

The garage mechanic wiped his greasy hands on a ragged towel and rubbed his nose with his forearm. "Give me a few minutes, and then I'll add up the bill."

"No hurry," said Thomas, his hand resting on the hood of the car. "Was it bad?" he asked.

"Not too bad," said the mechanic. "About what I told you on the phone I expected."

Thomas shrugged. "I was surprised you were open on Sunday."

"Sunday, Monday, and always," said the man. "I'll be right back."

"Okay."

Thomas wandered away from the car and looked around the inside of the garage, which was filled with a dense, oily odor. On an aged bulletin board, there was a pinup calendar and scores of notes about cars in an illegible handwriting. Piles of tires were stacked across the shelves in the back, and there were huge black stains on the cement floor of the garage. A plastic pocket holding a few maps and some pens with the garage name printed on them lay on a counter.

It had a kind of appealing atmosphere to Thomas's mind. It was a place where a man could have a beer and tell a dirty joke over a hero sandwich. It was a place where a man could bring his son, lift a hood, and show him how an engine worked. If he had a son. He tried to imagine himself bringing Paul here, and then he shook his head.

He had slept fitfully all night and had hardly spoken to Anna when she dropped him off at the garage. It made him feel guilty when he thought of the look in her eyes as she left him. She was ready to apologize again for getting up in the night to check the house, but he had turned away from her before she could.

When he really thought about it, he admitted to himself that she shouldn't have to apologize for it. After all, Albert Rambo was still loose, and he was a criminal who had kidnapped their son. Maybe it was only natural that she was worried about it. Maybe what was unnatural was that he didn't care about Albert Rambo. But he didn't. Not about Rambo and not about the boy.

Thomas closed his eyes, sickened by his own thoughts. It was wrong. It was wrong to feel that way. It wasn't the boy's fault that he had been found. It wasn't the boy's fault that his own father could not feel anything for him besides a kind of churning resentment. Thomas drew his foot back and kicked the tire of his car as hard as he could.

"Tires are fine," said the mechanic, coming toward Thomas with the bill in his hand. "I checked 'em."

"Oh, good," Thomas said.

"Here's the damages."

Thomas looked the bill over and wrote a check on the hood of the car. "Thanks a lot," he said.

"No problem." The mechanic disappeared back into his office as Thomas got into the car.

He made a mental list of what he wanted to get in the

discount store. He needed some weed killer and some new hedge clippers.

He remembered, as he began to drive out of the garage, that there was a men's clothing store next door to the discount house. He decided to go in there if it was open and see if he could get something for Paul. He had to try. There was no excuse for not trying.

That was wrong, too, he thought. To give a gift out of guilt. To give your child a present because you could not give him your affection. He wished he could feel something, some kindness toward the boy. But he could not deny the fact that he felt cheated. At least before the boy had come back, he had a wife. Now it seemed he had lost her, too.

"Keep your hands off the animals," Tracy snapped. "You can look, but don't touch." She donned a dirty apron and disappeared into a small room attached to the kennels.

Paul watched her go and then wandered among the cages, talking to the dogs and cats. The smell was powerful, and they all howled as if in misery at being caged. Paul looked around to see if Tracy had returned and stuck his hand into the cage of a little terrier that was slumped against the wall of his cell. Paul patted the dog's wiry coat. The animal whimpered and seemed to wince under his touch. Running his hand up over the dog's muzzle, he felt the nose was warm. Paul frowned and touched it again. The animal just sank lower in his cage.

"This one here's sick," he called out.

Slinging a bag of dog food, Tracy appeared in the corridor between the cages. "What is it?"

"This one's nose is warm."

Tracy dumped the bag at her feet. "I said not to touch them."

Paul stared back at her coldly.

"Which one?" she asked.

Paul pointed to the terrier.

"Never mind him," Tracy said, but Paul noticed that she peered at the dog with concern. "Why don't you go outside? You'll just get in the way here."

Paul reached in and gave the terrier another pat. Then he left the kennel and emerged into the sunny yard behind it. A large, shady tree stood in one corner. Paul walked over and dropped beneath it. He was sweating in his dungaree jacket, but he didn't feel like taking it off. He sat under the tree, and a small breeze fanned him. After a while Tracy appeared in the back doorway and came over to where he sat.

Paul closed his eyes and pretended to be enjoying the breeze, so he would not have to look at her. He heard her plop down onto the lawn near him. He opened his eyes and saw her sitting cross-legged a few feet away. On the ground in front of her was a little plastic bag filled with what looked like dried herbs. Tracy folded a white cigarette paper in half and sprinkled a little of the marijuana into it. She began to roll it up between her fingers. Paul watched her from the corner of his eye.

Tracy held the joint up to him. "Do you smoke?" she asked.

"Sure," he lied.

Tracy rolled the joint on her tongue and bit off the end. Then she took a pack of matches from her nylon knapsack and lit it. Paul watched as she inhaled a large quantity of smoke and held it in. He had done some experiments with cigarettes and whiskey, but he had never tried grass before.

Tracy held out the joint to him, and he took it from her

fingers. He heard it was expensive, and he wondered how she could afford it.

"Do you get paid for this job?" he asked, gesturing toward the back of the kennel.

"What difference does it make," she said, bristling. "I like doing it."

"No difference." He took the joint between his teeth and inhaled, looking around first to make sure that there was no one in the vicinity. His cat, Sam, was sniffing around the kennels, but otherwise, there was nothing but the rustle of the trees. Paul handed the joint back to Tracy, and suddenly he began to cough.

Tracy eyed him disdainfully. "How do you like it?" she said.

Paul struggled to catch his breath. His eyes were watering. "Went down the wrong pipe," he explained.

"Take more," she said.

He recovered his wind and took another toke. He could feel a fuzziness in his feet and his calves and an unpleasant dryness in his mouth. The radiant blue of the sky suddenly caught his attention. For a moment he stared up, feeling enchanted by the fleeciness of the clouds as they slowly passed. Then he looked over at Tracy, who had flopped down on her back on the lawn. She was lying there with a perplexed look in her eyes, studying him. She quickly turned away. Paul sighed and hugged his knees. He passed her the joint, and she took it without a word.

"What's this party tonight?" he asked offhandedly.

Tracy expelled some smoke in a snort of disgust. "Some boring thing for charity, at the Stewarts'. Mr. Stewart is some big honcho in all the charities in town."

"He is?"

"Yeah."

Paul frowned and closed his eyes. He couldn't picture Mr. Stewart caring about good causes. He kept thinking about how mean he had been to that old man yesterday. It had been bothering him ever since it happened, and he felt he wanted to tell somebody. All the time they were at the golf course he kept looking at the guy, wondering if he was just pretending to be nice. He thought now of telling Tracy about what he'd seen. He figured he could tell it in a way that would make her laugh and then see what she'd say about it. But suddenly he realized that just to spite him, she probably wouldn't laugh. She was like a porcupine. He tried to pretend that she wasn't there. Sam, who had been exploring the yard, came over and climbed up into his lap. Paul began to stroke his fur, which was warm from the sun. The cat lay, heavy, in his lap, and started to purr.

"I think someone just drove in," said Tracy.

Reluctantly Paul opened his eyes.

"I heard a car," she said. "I better hide this and go see what they want."

"I didn't hear anything," said Paul. His limbs felt heavy, and even his eyelids drooped as he looked at her. "What time is it?" he asked.

"How should I know?" said Tracy, standing up and brushing herself off. She picked up her knapsack and stuffed the bag of marijuana in a side pocket. "I'll be back in a while," she said.

"Okay," said Paul. He watched her as she disappeared inside the kennels. The cat, roused by Tracy's sudden movements, got up and leaped off Paul's lap to follow her. Paul missed the warmth on his legs where the cat had been.

He closed his eyes again and started to drift. Prisms of light sparkled and dissolved in the backs of his eyelids. The breeze was just enough to make him comfortable. His body felt weightless and at peace. He tried not to think of anything, but only to enjoy the sensations. A peculiar feeling stole over him as he let his mind wander in a cross between memory and dreams. The feeling had come and gone fleetingly several times since his return to the Langes. It was not memory, he thought, because he had absolutely no recollection of any of it. Not the faces, not the houses or anything. But once in a while some elusive sense of familiarity would overtake him. Paul wondered if under the influence of the marijuana, he could force himself actually to remember. He pictured Tracy's face in his mind and tried to command his memory back, to picture her as a child.

He concentrated on her wary hazel eyes flecked with green and tried to picture them in a baby's face. In his mind's eye he roved over the house, trying to picture himself playing there with a baby sister. Suddenly the image of a wooden slatted gate burst in his mind like a flashbulb popping, leaving him with the uneasy certainty that he had remembered it, even though he had not seen such a thing at the house.

He tried to think about where he might have seen the gate, and as he focused on it, he was suddenly flooded by the memory of his nightmare from the night before.

Anxiety rolled over him in a wave as the nightmare replayed itself. He was lying on the ground, trying to move, but he couldn't. The ground was hard and cold beneath him. As he lay there, helpless, a huge black mass which he couldn't identify was moving toward him, as if to crush him. A large golden eagle appeared, flapping its wings and menacing him from where it hovered just above him. And then a man, familiar yet indistinct, was bending toward him, and he was awash in terror.

Paul's eyes shot open, and he scanned the silent yard

behind the kennel. He had almost forgotten where he was. He rubbed his hands together, as if the terrifying dream had turned them to ice. There was a nagging pain over Paul's left eye. He had no idea how long he had been sitting there. He frowned as he looked toward the kennel. It seemed that Tracy should have been back by now. Suddenly he was sure of that.

After staggering to his feet, Paul ran across the yard to the back door of the kennel. "Tracy?" he called out. Inside their cages the animals began to howl and yelp with renewed vigor. Paul walked quickly through the kennel and up the stairs to the waiting room and the vet's offices.

The examining rooms were still, the tables lying empty. All the glass medicine cabinets were closed and locked. At the receptionist's desk the appointment book was open to Monday. The waiting room was undisturbed. Tracy was nowhere to be seen.

For a moment he wondered if something had happened to her. What if the person in the car had come to rob the place? His throat tightened at the thought, that someone might have been surprised to find her there and abducted her. He ran to the front door and threw it open, his heart beating hard against his ribs.

There was no sign of a car in the driveway. Then he looked again. There was only one bicycle parked on the grassy side yard—his own. She had left him there.

Paul felt a surge of anger at her. He called out for Sam, but there was no sign of the cat either. She had just gone and left him. He realized just then that he did not know the way back. He had followed Tracy over, his eye trained on her red knapsack as she pedaled along.

He thought to call the house and then realized that he didn't know the number. He knew the street name—Hidden

Woods Lane. He could call information. But he did not want to admit that he was lost. His anger at Tracy filled him with resolve. She probably thought it was funny. He did not want to let her know that he was scared. He would find the way.

Paul ran down the front steps of the shelter and got on his bike. He remembered that they had come up on the sign at the end of the driveway from the left. He would take it from there.

He could feel the sweat rolling down his sides as he started down the driveway, but he already felt a sense of relief, too. He glanced back at the shelter, feeling as if by leaving it, he had left that terrible nightmare in the backyard, where he had recalled it. All that remained of it was a headache that wouldn't go away. Slowly he guided the bike down the long driveway and turned to the right.

The cardboard bin held a chin-high display of plastic packages of paper napkins. "Family size," read the poster written in Magic Marker. "Only 99¢. Stock up for picnics."

Anna drew her cart up beside the display next to the check-out counter and stared at the pile of napkins. As she gazed at the display of brightly colored napkins, she pictured families, like hers in Michigan when she was a girl. Gatherings on long holiday weekends, with pies and chicken barbecues. Everybody playing horseshoes and unwinding through the long, lazy summer days.

The first time she brought Tom to the annual July Fourth picnic he drank it in like a parched man at an oasis. "This is what I want for us," he told her then. "A family, like this."

Anna shivered in the nearly empty air-conditioned grocery store. Nobody shopped on Sundays, except for last-

minute items. But she figured she might as well. Tracy and
Paul had gone off together to the animal hospital, unhappily
yoked together by Thomas's command. Tom had informed
her that he had a lot to do when she left him at the garage.
Anna felt as if she just had to get out of the house and do
something useful.

"That's a pretty good price," advised the overweight
dark-haired woman in the uniform smock coat who was
standing behind the cash register. She had been watching
Anna staring at the napkin display and presumed that the
shopper could not make up her mind. Anna smiled blindly
at her and put a package of napkins in her cart, realizing, as
she did so, that she wanted the woman to think she had need
of them for a large gathering.

Anna wheeled the cart around and began to unload her
groceries so that the woman could check her out. One by
one the woman rang up the items and began packing them in
brown paper bags. Anna looked out the huge windows of
the grocery store between the backs of the sale posters into
the parking lot. Maybe, she thought, when she got back, the
children would be home. Or Tom would be back. Tonight
was the Stewarts' party. That will be fun, she told herself.
But even as she did so, she realized that she held out little
hope for it. With a sigh Anna lifted the paper bags into her
shopping cart and, after thanking the woman at the check-
out, headed through the electric eye doors and out of the
store.

"Buy a chance?" cried a voice to her left as Anna left the
store. She looked over and saw a man in a navy blue cap
and shirt seated at a card table, waving an arm at the end of
which was a hook, instead of a hand. Anna stared at the
curved steel claw, which the sun glinted off as the man

jabbed it at a pile of white tickets on the table. "VFW bazaar," he said. "You could win a station wagon."

The man beckoned to her with the gleaming hook, but Anna turned her head away. "No, thank you," she whispered, pushed her cart huriedly onto the hot asphalt, and headed toward her car, which was parked near the island in the middle of the half-empty lot.

She rested the cart against the rear bumper of the car and reached into her pocketbook for her keys. Her hands were trembling slightly, and she realized that she had been vaguely frightened by the man with the hook. She inserted the key in the lock for the trunk and turned it.

A few spaces down, a man in a blue car watched her movements. As she lifted the trunk hood, the man got out of his car and started toward her. He was wearing a gray hat and dark glasses, and he looked nervously around him in all directions.

Anna lifted the first paper bag out of the cart and placed it in the open trunk. The man walked right up to her and stopped.

"Mrs. Lange," he said.

Anna straightened up from inside the trunk and turned to face the wiry man standing beside her car. The instant she saw him, she knew who he was. Anna gasped and let go of the bag she was holding. Four oranges rolled out into the trunk, and a cereal box tipped over on top of them.

"Don't scream," he said

Anna stared at him. There he stood, the subject of all her worst imaginings: a thin, pale-skinned man with receding features, a dark-gray straw hat, and shiny shoes. She realized at once that she had no intention of screaming. It was as if she had always known that this meeting would come to be. Her eyes were locked on the face of the man who had stolen her son.

Rambo lit a cigarette and spit out some tobacco from the end. He began to speak in a rapid, nervous voice. "Now don't start hollering or anything," he said. "I don't want to hurt you. I ain't got a gun or nothing like that. I just want to talk to you."

"I knew you'd come back," said Anna. She did not recognize the sound of her own voice. It was even and absolutely cold. "You can't have him this time. I'll kill you first."

Rambo put up both hands and pressed them into the air. "I don't want him back. Naw, I don't want him. That's not what I'm here to say. No, sir, the Lord has given me a mission—"

Like someone released from a trance, Anna slammed down the door of the trunk and started back toward the store. "I'm getting the police," she said.

"Don't do that," Rambo cried, lunging toward her and grabbing her arm as she tried to pass him.

"Let go of my arm, you filthy . . . ugh." Anna struggled to get away from the man, spitting the words through gritted teeth as she landed a blow on his arm.

Rambo's eyes darted around the quiet parking lot. "No, listen to me. I got something to tell you about the boy." He held on to her with clawlike fingers. "People'll come running. Be still now."

A white-hot fury possessed her, and Anna turned and snarled at Rambo. For years he had been her absentee torturer. Now the fact that he seemed frail and ineffectual only angered her further. "You . . . you," she sputtered. "You won't get away this time."

With a swift motion she punched him in the sternum and

jerked her arm free of his loosened grasp. Staggering away from him, she looked frantically around the lot for a policeman or a squad car. The parking lot was nearly deserted of cars, and there was not a cruiser in sight.

"Help," she cried out. "Police."

Rambo caught up to her and grabbed her arm again. "Listen to me," cried Rambo. "Don't."

"Let go of me," Anna snarled. "Help." Her eyes swept the shopping center, searching for aid.

They were stumbling along together now, joined by Rambo's grip. "I'm telling you something," he hissed desperately. "That boy's life is in danger. Don't you want to know?"

Anna wheeled on him with vengeance in her eyes. "You'll never get near him. You'll be in jail." She jerked free of him again and bellowed for help.

"Not from me," Rambo screamed at her. "But you better listen. It's a matter of life or death." It was his last try. He knew in a second he would have to run, the way she was hollering.

As she was about to cry out again, the man's words registered in her mind. In spite of herself, the words arrested her. She hesitated, hating herself for stopping, and turned to him. "What do you mean?" she said. The question made her feel low and helpless.

"Listen here," he whispered urgently. "I'll tell you all you want to know. I have information about that boy that you better know. I swear to you. But I need some money. Five thousand dollars would do it. And then I'll tell you what you need to find out. After that I'll leave you alone. It's up to you."

Anna trembled and controlled the urge to spit at him, but

she could not take her eyes off him. "You are vicious," she said.

"I'm not lying to you, ma'am," said Rambo. "Life or death."

"What's going on here?" A voice floated toward them, and both Anna and Rambo turned to look as the veteran with the hook who was selling raffle tickets trundled toward them, his body puffed up with righteousness and military importance.

Rambo saw that it was too late to run, although the panic rising in him made him feel like wetting his pants. He glanced at Anna and saw the uncertainty on her face. The man was getting closer. Rambo clutched his car keys in his hand and hoped the old Chevy would turn over quickly if he had to bolt.

Anna watched the vet coming toward them, his face red and indignant, as if he were moving in slow motion. All she had to do was tell him and Rambo would be caught. Every reasonable sense told her to start screaming. But inside her, instinct warred with reason, telling her something alarming and awful. Rambo was not lying. He was telling her the truth. And he was the only one, the only person alive, who knew about Paul's lost years and could tell her.

Images of Paul filled her head: his pale complexion; the headaches that made him wince; the way he crouched in the pantry, trembling and disoriented, plagued by sleeplessness. He could be sick. He could be in danger. The last, lost eleven years could hold secrets she could never hope to learn any other way.

The vet was in front of her now, puffing and angry. "What's the matter, ma'am? Is this man hurting you?"

Anna stared at her would-be rescuer for a second. Then, with a sickening feeling in her stomach, she shook her head.

"It's nothing," she said. "Just an argument. I'm sorry I yelled out like that."

The vet glowered at Rambo, who was staring down at the asphalt, his hatbrim covering his face. "If she hollers again," he threatened, brandishing his hook, "I'll have the police here. I know just about every cop on the force. So mind your manners."

"Thank you," said Anna. "Thank you so much for coming over."

The vet grunted and gave a casual salute before he turned and started back toward his ticket table.

Anna watched him go and then turned to face Rambo. The bargain was made between them. Rambo was shaking.

"Tell me now," she said. "You have to tell me."

Rambo shook his head. "When I get the money." He handed her a slip of paper. "This is the address," he said. "Come tomorrow morning with the money. No police. No one but you. The door will be open. When I'm sure you're alone, I'll show up and tell you it all in exchange for the money."

"I can't," said Anna weakly, half to herself.

"Don't go fooling around," he said. "That boy's life might depend on it."

Anna searched the pale, shifty face of Albert Rambo. She reminded herself that this wreck of a man had brought up her son as his own. Paul had called him Father. Seizing on that, she appealed to him. "Look," she pleaded, "if Paul is suffering in some way, why won't you tell me, so I can help him?"

"I will," he said. "Just bring the money."

"You brought him up as your own son. Don't you care what happens to him?"

"Sure I do," said Rambo, backing away from her. He

glanced around and then looked back at her. "That's partly why I'm doing this."

But that, Anna realized with frightening conviction as he hurried toward his car, was a total lie.

CHAPTER NINE

Anna wiped her hands on a dish towel and glanced up at the clock. It was nearly five, and Thomas was still not home. In a way it made her angry, and in another way she was relieved. She wondered how she was going to conceal the turmoil she was feeling when he did come in. The less time they had before the Stewarts' party, the better.

Using the towel in her hand, Anna began to wipe the counter, which she had just finished cleaning. Usually she loved to be in her kitchen, which was her haven and the center of the house. But now, as she looked around the room, she felt a rising panic. Everything was neat and in its place, yet her life seemed to be in a state of chaos.

No feeling sorry for yourself, she scolded herself. You have to do it. What's the point of debating it with yourself a million times? Thomas had once railed at her that there was nothing she wouldn't do to get Paul back. Now she had him back, and she intended to protect him. I don't care what Thomas says when he finds out, she thought, although she was already apprehensive about his response. She could not tell him, though. She could not take the chance.

Anna heard the sound of the front door opening. She walked into the dining room and saw her husband coming in the front hallway. He was carrying a large white box under his arm.

"Sorry I'm late," he said sheepishly. "Where's Paul?"

"Upstairs in his room," she replied. Keep talking, she thought. "He's kind of upset. He thought his cat was with Tracy, but apparently she hadn't seen it. The cat still hasn't come back. You know, he seems so attached to that animal." Anna straightened out a pile of magazines as she spoke and then picked some dead leaves off a plant. "How's the car running?"

"Oh, fine," said Tom. "I did a lot of errands after I picked it up. I went shopping, too," he said. "I bought him a birthday present."

"You did? For Paul?"

"It is his birthday. After all . . ."

"Well . . ."

Thomas looked at her in surprise. "What do you mean, 'Well'?"

Anna spread her hands helplessly. "I wished him a happy birthday this morning, and he said his birthday was in October."

"What?"

Anna winced. "They made up a birthday for him."

Thomas's face puckered in disgust.

"It's not his fault."

"I know."

"What did you buy? Let me see." She came toward him.

He dismissed the package with a wave. "Oh, it's a jacket. I figured he needed something for the Stewarts' party tonight."

Anna smiled nervously at him. "Take it up to him. I'm sure he'll like it."

"I suppose," said Thomas. He peered at her for a moment. "Are you okay? I'm really sorry I took so long."

"Fine," she insisted. "I was afraid you'd forgotten the party."

"Do you want to see the jacket?"

"I'll see it on him," she said.

As Thomas started up the stairs, Anna turned away so that he wouldn't see the tears that rose to her eyes. He had remembered Paul's birthday and brought him a present. Maybe things would work out after all. He seemed less angry than he had been all weekend. Maybe once this whole thing was over . . .

Anna decided to make Thomas a drink, to welcome him home. She walked over to the bar and picked up a bottle of gin. Maybe she should tell him about Rambo, about what she planned to do. She filled a glass on the bar with ice. Just let him have the whole story. Thoughtfully she poured an ounce of gin into the glass, debating with herself. Then she shook her head. He would insist on the police. She couldn't take the chance. Once it was all over, she would tell him everything.

Anna was filling the glass with mixer when she heard the sound of raised voices over the wail and thud of rock 'n' roll from Tracy's speakers upstairs. Then a door slammed, and Thomas came pounding down the stairs. His face was dark and closed.

"He doesn't want it," said Thomas.

"Why not?"

"He wants to wear that filthy dungaree rag that he goes around in."

"Oh, Tom, I'm sorry."

"I told him he'll wear this jacket or he won't go. I'm not taking him anywhere looking like some bum."

"You didn't say that to him," she said.

Thomas glared at her. "Yes. That's exactly what I said. And I meant it."

"He's just so attached to that old jacket of his. Here, sit down and have a drink."

"I'm going to take a shower," he said.

"Don't you want this?"

"No," he said, and stalked off down the hall.

Anna replaced the glass on the bar. The ice was beginning to melt, making the drink watery. She wiped her hands on her skirt and then started toward the hallway, to go appeal to the strange boy upstairs.

The crescent moon hung like a sugar cookie in the violet sky, and garlands of pastel paper lanterns cordoned off a large area of lawn and patio behind the Stewart manor. A three-man combo in dinner jackets played mellifluous jazz on the patio near the French windows, although none of the guests were dancing. Clusters of sleekly dressed people talked and laughed in the falling evening light. A few teenagers, who had come with their parents, were huddled by the pool, the boys shoving one another into the girls, who shrieked as sodas splashed on summer cottons.

Anna fiddled with the bracelet on her arm and glanced at Paul, who stood stiff-shouldered in his new jacket in the doorway leading out to the patio. Tracy had already rushed past them, greeting the Stewarts on her way, and joined the tight little group by the pool. Thomas was shaking hands with Edward.

"Doesn't it look pretty?" Anna asked the boy.

Paul studied the glowing yard. "They must be loaded."

Anna nodded and then looked intently at him. "How do you feel?"

"Fine," he said shortly.

Anna watched his eyes shift nervously over the scene, the tables covered in white linen, waitresses hovering as the band played. She could tell that he wanted to back away quietly and just avoid it. Anna was all too aware of the knot in her stomach. She could not relax enough to make it easier for him. She watched him helplessly as he squared his thin shoulders and stuffed his hands in his pockets. She did not want to push him out into the throng. She just wanted to keep him there, standing still and safe on the edge of the party.

Anna looked away from the boy and saw Thomas watching them with indignant eyes.

"Shall we go say hello?" asked Anna.

Paul jumped and shrank back. At the same moment Iris spotted them. She was talking to a woman with strong features and short, wavy brown hair who was wearing an Indian caftan and long, dangling earrings. Iris motioned toward Anna, and the woman in the caftan accompanied Iris to where Anna and Paul were standing. Anna could see by Iris's high color and her nervous, fluttery gestures that she was in a state of total agitation about the party. She felt a sense of real empathy for her, but for once Anna felt as nervous as Iris herself.

"You must be Paul!" Iris exclaimed, extending a hand to the boy. "I'm so happy to have you here. I'm Mrs. Stewart."

"Thanks," said Paul.

"And I want you both to meet Angelica Harris. She's my ceramics teacher and one of the hospital's most prized volunteers."

Anna smiled at the woman and shared a firm handshake

with her. "You're quite a teacher. Iris has shown me some of the beautiful things she's made."

The ceramics teacher smiled broadly, revealing a gap between her front teeth. "Well, she's my most talented student."

Iris blushed and smiled. Just then Edward walked up and cleared his throat. He cast a critical glance over the ceramics teacher's flowing costume and then turned stiffly to his wife. "Iris," he said with a thin smile, "I hope you won't forget all our other guests."

Iris blanched and looked down at her clenched hands.

"If you'll excuse me," said Angelica, obviously aware of Edward's disapproval, "I'm going to mingle."

All but Edward smiled at her as she left. "Thank you for inviting us," said Anna to Edward, "and for taking Tom and Paul to play golf yesterday."

Edward nodded, although he wore a slightly pained expression. "My pleasure," he said. "Paul, why don't you go over there and join the other young people by that table? They seem to be enjoying themselves," Edward suggested, clasping his hands together behind his back.

"That's okay," Paul demurred, his eyes straying anxiously over the knot of laughing teen-agers by the pool. Anna placed a hand on his shoulder and then removed it instantly as he twitched his shoulder blade. She wanted to intercede for him, but she knew she couldn't say what she was thinking. I need to keep him here with me. I need to watch him every minute. He may be in danger. For the hundredth time that day she asked herself what Rambo had meant. Was the boy ill? She thought again of his headache the other day and his sleeplessness. She could just take him to the doctor and be done with it. But what if Rambo knew something specific about his condition? Or perhaps it was not illness at all. Perhaps it was a vendetta. Some enemy of Rambo's or his wife's. She felt as if she had thought of every possibility, but she would have to wait to know. Tomorrow. She looked at the back of Paul's head in front of her. She wanted to run a hand gently over his hair. She could not imagine anyone's wanting to hurt him. But surely nothing could happen to him here. She could feel Thomas's eyes on her as she struggled to hold her tongue.

Paul shoved his hands further into his pockets. There was panic in his eyes, which he strove to conceal.

"You know," said Iris, "I don't think Paul has seen the inside of our house yet. Would you like a little tour, Paul?"

Paul weighed this prospect against that of joining Tracy's friends and decided in favor of it. "I guess so," he said.

"Iris," said Edward, "you have scarcely exchanged a word with any of our guests. Don't you think it's about time you attended to that, rather than retreat back into the house?"

"Oh, well, I didn't think I'd be missed. I mean, I offered to show Paul . . ."

Edward studied the nervous boy with a critical gaze. "Go ahead," he insisted. "I will show Paul around the house."

Paul winced, realizing too late who his guide would be, but there was no way out of it. With a glance back at Anna, Paul followed Edward, who had started to march in the direction of the house.

A passing guest collared Iris, who turned and forced a smile. Thomas walked over to Anna, who was watching her son disappear into the house with Edward. He touched Anna on the arm, and she started.

"You're awfully jumpy tonight," he said.

"Oh, I'm just concerned about Paul. I think he feels a little out of place," Anna said hurriedly.

"I see Edward is giving him the grand tour. Rather an undignified chore for the lord of the manor, don't you think?"

"Maybe he likes the boy," Anna replied defensively. "He's just trying to be nice."

Thomas raised his hands. "Sorry I said anything."

Anna sighed. "You're right. I didn't mean to jump on you."

"Mmmmm . . ." said Tom.

"Do you think he minds?" Anna asked.

"What?"

"Edward. Taking Paul around."

Thomas shook his head. "I don't know. He probably loves it. A captive audience to show off all his possessions. It's just a shame that the kid won't realize how much everything costs. On second thought, Edward will probably tell him, in a subtle way, of course."

"Thomas Lange, that's unkind," Anna said with a smile.

"It's true, though."

Just then Iris returned to them, carrying a martini glass, which she handed to Anna. "I thought you might want this," she explained.

Anna thanked her for the drink.

"Anna," said Iris, "he's such a lovely boy."

"Tom brought him the jacket he's wearing," said Anna, glancing at her husband.

"He looks very handsome. I'll bet he was pleased."

"Mmmm . . ." said Anna.

"Will you excuse me?" said Tom abruptly. "I need another drink."

Iris frowned at her friend. "How are you doing? All this must be a strain. You seem a little edgy."

"I'm tired, that's all," said Anna quickly. "And you're right. It is a strain."

"Have you heard anything more about that man Rambo?"

Anna started, and the drink she was holding spilled over the rim of the glass. "No. No. Not yet."

"They will catch him, Anna," said Iris earnestly. "You should try not to worry."

"I know," said Anna, staring at the glass, which shook in her hand.

"Poor Paul," said Iris, glancing back at the house. "I hope he won't be too bored hearing all about the house."

"Edward's being very kind to him," said Anna automatically. She thought again of what she had to do the next day. The night ahead seemed interminably long.

"This is my room," said Edward, gesturing toward the closed door of the upstairs hallway. He opened the door, and Paul looked past him into the dark, heavily curtained bedroom with gleaming dark furniture and a leather chair in one corner.

Edward held on to the doorknob and closed the door again after Paul had glanced in. "And this is Mrs. Stewart's room," he said as they passed a room with eggshell-colored walls and rich floral chintz-covered furniture. The bed had a canopy over it.

Paul had never heard of married people having different rooms, but he decided that it must be something peculiar to the rich. "That bed's got a roof," he observed. "That's good for when it rains."

Edward stared at the boy, unsmiling, and Paul immediately regretted having made a joke. Music and laughter drifted up from the party through the open windows, and the strange party suddenly seemed infinitely preferable to this tour of the Stewarts' house. Edward, however, was oblivious to Paul's discomfort.

"Those are guest rooms and baths down the hall," said Edward. "Here, come in this room, and you can just see my pride and joy."

Paul obediently followed Edward into the bathroom and looked out the window. He looked toward where Edward was pointing, but he saw nothing but the darkness and the shapes of trees.

"My windmill," said Edward proudly. He noted the perplexed look on Paul's face. "I suppose you can't see it in the dark. You can scarcely see it in the daytime. It's quite a distance, and the trees cover it. Well, I'll take you out to it and show you."

Paul looked back up from the landing as they started down the stairs. "This is a really nice house," he said.

"Well, thank you, Paul," said Edward, descending the stairs behind him, twisting his wedding ring on his finger. "You used to come here as a small child. Do you remember that?"

Paul shook his head. "I don't ever remember being in a house as big as this. I don't remember anything from back then, really."

"Well," said Edward reassuringly, leading Paul through the winding hallways of the first floor, "it was a long time ago. Now," he said, "watch your step here. And follow me." The two stepped out into the night and skirted the edge of the party in the darkness.

Paul followed Edward up some terraced steps beside the house and up the graded lawn. He wished he had a flashlight to pick out the path, but Edward seemed to know the way and did not stumble or make any missteps as he negotiated the path. Paul dogged his footsteps as closely as possible, although once or twice he caught his foot under a flat stone and a low-lying tree branch smacked him across the neck. He glanced back at the island of sound and light in the dark where the party was rolling and hesitated.

Edward turned and looked back at him. "Come along," he said.

Paul continued up the path, watching his feet as best he could until Edward put up a hand to forestall him. "There," said Edward.

Through the trees Paul saw the stout, obelisk-shaped structure looming above him, the wide blades of the windmill outlined by the dim light of the crescent moon. The outer walls of the building were shingled in dark, rough slabs. The tiny windows were black holes gouged in its sides.

Edward walked over to the door and pushed it open, flipping on a switch inside. A weak yellow light warmed the doorway and lighted the panes of the windows. "Welcome to my workshop," said Edward, motioning for Paul to follow him in.

Paul slipped past Edward through the door. It was silent inside, and he blinked his eyes to adjust to the light. He rubbed his eyelids with his fingers and then looked around the six-sided room that formed the base of the windmill. It was colder inside the windmill than it had been outside. Edward stepped over to the workbench, which took up one of the six walls, and flipped on a light over the counter area. The workbench was a catacomb of drawers and compartments, each filled with a precise assortment of bolts, screws, and nails. The tiny floor space was immaculately clean, and a neat stack of plywood occupied one corner. Books, tools, sandpaper, and tiny boat parts were carefully organized into separate areas on the counter tops which lined the walls. A number of miniature boats, in various states of assemblage, were proudly displayed atop a shelf built into the sides of the windmill. Paul looked up and saw that the wooden floor of a loft formed a ceiling above them. A ladder going up to it rested against the side, surrounded at the top by sailing magazines and tin cans of paint. Edward gazed fondly at the orderly workroom. "This is where I am creating my fleet," he said.

Paul felt suddenly uneasy at the stillness in Edward's form, the faraway look in his eyes. He moved away from him toward the door. "Well, thanks for showing it to me," he said.

Edward looked at him strangely for a moment. Then he stepped into the center of the room. "Have a look around," he said. "Take your time."

After a moment's hesitation Paul began to pick his way through the assortment of ships. Edward stepped around him and closed the windmill door. He watched the boy as Paul stooped over to examine the boats.

"You sure have a lot of boats," Paul said.

"Sit down," said Edward, indicating a chair.

Paul sat down and glanced around the room. It looked too neat to work in, he thought, but he could see that Mr. Stewart really liked it that way. He shivered involuntarily.

"Are you cold?" Edward asked, leaning up against the workbench.

"It's kind of chilly in here," said Paul.

"Stone floors," said Edward. "I really should cover them."

Paul felt a little hemmed in, seated on the chair with Edward taking up most of the rest of the free space in the room. He wondered how Edward could stand to be so cramped up in the windmill.

Edward reached over the working surface of the tool bench and picked up a piece of bright, multicolored silk which was lying there in a heap. He unfurled it for Paul to examine.

"This," said Edward, "is a spinnaker for that sailboat over there." Edward indicated a large, delicate model with a deck of golden wood and a gleaming white hull. "I sewed the edges on that machine." Paul looked at the old Singer sewing machine which was nearly hidden in one corner.

"You can sew?" asked Paul, giggling nervously at the thought of Edward seated at the spindly machine.

"Indeed, I can," said Edward. "Here, take a look at this. Seven different colors in this one sail."

Paul reached for the sail in Edward's fingertips. The slippery material eluded him, and the sail floated from his fingertips to the floor. Edward started to bend over to retrieve it.

"I'll get it," Paul offered, sliding from the chair and crouching down to get the sail, which had fallen at Edward's feet. He put his hand on the sail, leaning over the toes of Edward's wing-tipped shoes. Edward stood over him, his tall frame blocking the light from the workbench and casting a shadow over Paul's huddled form.

Paul started to stand, but he felt a sudden dizziness come over him. He folded his body back into a crouch. There was a flash in his head and the fragment of an image on his eyelids. A golden eagle swooped toward him from a black cloud, talons extended, its eyes cold and enraged. Paul covered his right eye with a trembling hand. His complexion turned a chalky white.

Edward's cold eyes were riveted to the boy's bent head.

He injected a note of concern into his voice. "What's the matter? Are you ill?"

Paul shook his head. "I don't know."

Edward bent down toward him and reached out a hand to support him.

"No," Paul screamed, and scuttled away from him. In his haste he bumped into the table holding the white sailboat. The model teetered and then fell over. The delicate rigging crunched as the ship hit the stone floor.

Paul staggered to his feet, his breath coming in pants. He stared down at the model, but for a few seconds he did not seem to see it or to realize what he had done.

Edward froze where he stood, his left eyelid twitching as he fixed the boy with a gaze that dissected him. "That's too bad," he whispered after a moment.

Paul seemed to awaken at the words, and he looked, aghast, at the broken ship on the floor. "I'm sorry," he said. "I'm sorry."

Edward licked his lips and stared down at the broken vessel at his feet. "That model was the only one of its kind," he said in a low voice. "It was custom-made for me."

"I'm sorry," the boy cried, looking up at Edward with alarm in his eyes. "I don't know how it happened."

Edward's gray eyes were as blank as rivets in his head. "That was careless," he said, staring at the boy. "There's no excuse for carelessness."

"I know, I'm sorry," Paul repeated miserably. "Can I go now?"

Edward stepped over to the windmill door and held it open, looking out into the night.

"Maybe I could pay for it," the boy offered hopelessly.

Edward turned and watched him for a moment. Paul

began to feel again as if he couldn't breathe. Then Edward spoke. "You may consider it forgotten," he said, in a voice that did not sound forgiving.

"Thank you," the boy mumbled, and bolted out of the window and down the path in the direction of the glowing lights of the back of the patio.

"I'll be right along," said Edward. He watched the boy go, and then he looked back at the wreck of his ship on the floor. Carefully he crouched down and began collecting the broken pieces.

A dull throbbing in his head had replaced the feelings of panic and disorientation. Each time he put his foot down, Paul felt as if he were jarring the pain into a greater fierceness. His stomach had begun to churn in concert with the headache, and he kept on breathing deeply to hold the nausea down. Paul reached the periphery of the party and then hesitated, unwilling to enter the crowd of strangers. The light from the lanterns seemed to hurt his eyes.

From the edge of the patio Iris peered into the darkness and spotted the boy standing there. "Paul," she called out. "There you are." She came toward him, smiling. "Did Edward show you around?"

Paul nodded. His eyes searched for Anna in the group, wishing that he could see her and tell her he wanted to go home. He thought of asking Iris where she was, but he did not know how to refer to her. He could not bring himself to say "my mother."

Iris gestured toward the rest of the party. "Why don't you come along now and sit down with the young people and have something to eat?"

Reluctantly he let himself be led to a table occupied by teen-agers. Paul sniffed the aroma of marijuana as they approached the table, but Iris seemed oblivious to this. She indicated a chair, which Paul lowered himself into. "I'll send a waitress with some food," she said.

Paul smiled mechanically at Iris. Out of the corners of his eyes he could see Tracy watching him across the table.

"You have fun," Iris urged, patting his shoulder as she left. Paul nodded, but his head was throbbing with pain.

Tracy leaned across the table and looked at him with narrowed eyes. "Where were you?"

"Inside. With Mr. Stewart," Paul mumbled.

Tracy said something quietly to her friends, and their mocking laughter rang out. Paul tried to ignore them. A waitress walked over to the table and placed a plate of food down in front of Paul.

Paul looked down at the slab of pink fish on his plate. "What is this stuff?"

"Salmon," said Tracy. "Didn't you ever have it?"

Paul shook his head. "I'm not hungry." He tried not to look at the fish on the plate, but he imagined that the odor was overwhelming him, making him feel even queasier.

"Have some of this," said Tracy, producing a glowing joint from under the tabletop. "You'll be hungry."

A pretty brown-haired girl in a pink and white dress sitting next to Tracy burst out laughing at this and covered her mouth with her hands.

"I don't want any," Paul said, and pushed the plate of salmon aside, as if to remove it from sight.

"Mary Ellen wants to ask you something," said Tracy slyly.

Paul stiffened and quickly eyed the two girls. The girl in the pink stripes started to laugh, and Tracy punched her in the elbow. "Go ahead," Tracy ordered. "Ask him."

Waves of pain seemed to be surging through him now,

and he felt as if his eyes were aching from it. He could hardly focus on the girl's face.

"Did you ever . . ." Mary Ellen dissolved into laughter, and tears began to spurt from her eyes.

"Mary Ellen, you ass," said Tracy, elbowing her friend. Paul squirmed, but he tried to make his face impassive to whatever assault might come.

"Did you . . ." she cried, and collapsed into giggles again.

"Oh, shut up," said Tracy, "and let Paul eat his salmon in peace." She gave the plate a shove, and it bumped Paul in the arm. The slab of fish slid off the plate onto his jacket. The two girls started to laugh uncontrollably, although the sound of their laughter seemed far away because of the thudding pain in his head. Paul picked up the fish, and it felt cold and slippery in his hand. He thought he could smell the vilest odor off it. He tossed it away from him and stood up abruptly. All of a sudden he felt a lightness in his limbs, and black spots appeared before his eyes. He could see Tracy and her friend staring at him, but they seemed to be receding as the darkness descended in a cloud that came, then lifted, and then, in a rush, blacked out his sight altogether. He fell with a thud to the ground, pulling down a chair with him as he collapsed.

Tracy screamed, and there were gasps from the people all around him. The hum of conversation gave way to anxious murmurs as people began to crowd around the fallen boy. Paul came to in the midst of the worried crowd, his body feeling weak and drained. He tried to drag himself up on the edge of the chair seat without looking at the faces of any of the people surrounding him. He felt as if their warm bodies were imprisoning him, suffocating him. He was trapped there, still trying to remember what had happened to him.

Suddenly Anna was beside him, her hands firmly gripping his shoulders. "Paul," she said.

He looked up at her briefly. "I fainted," he said.

Galvanized by the helplessness in his eyes, Anna asked no further questions. "Okay now," she said in a firm voice to the people who surrounded him. "It's all right. We're going now." Resolutely she helped him to his feet. "Leave us alone." Paul stumbled to his feet beside her. Thomas took a step toward them and then stopped. Anna was miles away from him, completely in control.

"We're going," she said. Anna turned to Iris, who was shaking her head with concern. "I'm sorry. I'll call you, Iris."

She forced a path through the guests, and Paul followed her blindly, his young face haggard and deathly white.

CHAPTER TEN

Edward strode out across the sloping lawn of his estate. All the Japanese lanterns had been extinguished, and the extra people they had hired were cleaning up the remains of the party by the illumination of the terrace floodlights and the pool.

Edward spotted Iris just out of the floodlights' range. She was dressed in a flowered kimono and slippers, and she was eating a cream-filled pastry horn, which she had lifted from a tray that was still on one of the buffet tables.

She started as she saw Edward approaching her and quickly tried to put the pastry back down on the table. Edward glared at her and then turned on one of the women who were cleaning up at the other end of the table.

"Remove this food at once," he ordered. "Why is this cleanup taking so long?"

The woman looked up, surprised, and then quickly came over and collected the tray.

Edward turned back to Iris. "Well," he said, "I hope you're satisfied."

"With what?" Iris asked, baffled.

"The evening was a total disaster."

"Oh, I didn't think so, Edward. I thought everyone had a nice time."

"That child's display threw a pall over the entire party. As soon as that happened, everyone started to leave."

Iris shook her head. "The poor boy. I felt sorry for him. He was so embarrassed."

Edward snorted with disgust. "I was the one who was embarrassed. I was humiliated in front of my guests."

"I'm sure everyone understood," Iris suggested meekly.

"The question is, why did you invite those people in the first place?"

"What people?"

"The Langes, Iris. The Langes. They don't belong in our set. They are completely out of place here. And now they managed to ruin my party."

"Edward, that's not so. They're our friends."

Edward turned away from her in exasperation. Iris stood uncertainly, wadding up the belt of her kimono. "I guess I'll be going to bed," she said.

"And who," Edward demanded, wheeling around, "was that woman in that muumuu? Whatever was she doing here?"

Iris squirmed and looked down. "I invited some of the volunteers from the hospital. She's my ceramics teacher. She works at the hospital, helping the children."

"That outfit she had on was utterly disgraceful. She looked like something out of the circus."

Iris sighed involuntarily. "I'm awfully tired, Edward. I think I'll say good night."

"They won't be invited again," said Edward. "Any of them."

"Good night, Edward."

"I'm going to do some things in the windmill. I have to relax somehow," Edward announced.

"Oh," said Iris, surprised to be informed, "fine."

Edward watched her as she walked back toward the house, her dressing gown billowing out behind her like laundry hanging on a line. She was a graceless creature, he thought. She had always been that way, even when they first met.

He recalled that the first time he had ever seen her was at a party, much like this one tonight. The party had been given by a rich lawyer from one of New England's finest families to reward all the people who had worked on his victorious primary campaign for the Senate. Edward had joined the campaign in hopes of meeting some of the right people who could further his young career. The race had proved unsuccessful for him, however. He had done a thousand errands and ended up at the party without having gained any valuable contacts.

He was feeling irritable that evening and frustrated by the fact that just as they had at Princeton, these bluebloods closed their circle to him. The only reason he had noticed Iris at all was that she was behind the punch bowl, ladling punch in a drab dark outfit. He mistook her for a servant and was becoming increasingly angered, as he waited in the line, at the slow and awkward way that she was serving. When he reached the punch bowl, she offered him a glass which, unbeknownst to her, had a crack in it. Edward stared at the cracked cup, and the rage began to boil in him. He felt as if this low-class serving girl had somehow singled him out to receive the damaged glass. He drew the cup back and was about to toss the red punch at the front of her dress and slam the cup down on the table when one of the guests behind him asked her what she thought her father's chances for success in the actual Senate race would be. The chance remark saved him from an embarrassing faux pas and turned Iris from a frog into an heiress in his penetrating eyes.

All in all, marrying her had been a shrewd thing to do, he thought. It was true that she was an embarrassment to him, of sorts; but her family name still carried weight in society, and her father's money had helped him get started in his business. The rest he had done himself.

Now he had it all, all the things he had dreamed of and missed as a boy. He was important, rich, and powerful. And he had made it happen.

One of the cleaning women came by and gathered up the tablecloth off the buffet table. "It's about time," Edward muttered. "And take all that food out of this house." At least, he thought, there would be nothing left for Iris to gorge on before she went off to her spa.

Then he snorted in disgust. It was a waste of energy to think about Iris when he had much more important things on his mind. The night still held a difficult task for him, and he anticipated it with a twinge of anxiety, but mostly with excitement.

The cleaning people were beginning to leave the yard. It was almost time, he realized, to get over to the windmill and gather up the equipment that he needed for tonight.

He had spent the afternoon staking out the La-Z Pines motel and had been rewarded when Rambo drove in at four thirty in a disgusting old blue Chevrolet. He made note of the room number and then sneaked back to his car, which he had hidden up the road. Now he had to collect the things he needed, slip out, and make his way back to the motel. Tonight, he thought, he would put an end to the problem of Albert Rambo once and for all.

* * *

Thomas peered out the back window at the shape of the boy sitting on the glider, his shoulders hunched, in the darkness.

"He's still sitting out there."

Anna sighed and looked out the window again. "I don't know what to do."

"Maybe we should just let him be," said Thomas.

Tracy came into the kitchen and took a pear from the refrigerator. She rubbed it on her bathrobe and took a bite out of it.

Anna shook her head. "He's terribly upset. Maybe if we talk to him . . ."

"I think we should just let him alone. The air is good for him, and he might not feel like talking right now. He might want to be alone."

Anna seemed oblivious to his suggestion. She turned to Tracy, who was seated at the kitchen table, eating her pear and staring vacantly into the center of the room. "Tracy," she said, "what happened at the Stewarts'?"

"Nothing. Why? We were just fooling around, and then he just stood up and fainted."

"What do you mean, 'fooling around'?"

"Nothing," Tracy cried. "Just teasing."

Anna bit her lip. "Will you go out and talk to him?"

"Me? Why me?"

"Maybe it'll make him feel better."

Tracy shook her head. "I don't think so."

"Will you try? Please? For me?"

Tracy shrugged. "Okay, but I don't know . . ."

"Thank you, darling."

Tracy opened the back door and stepped out into the darkness. She waited for a few moments while her eyes got used to the dark. Then she walked over to where Paul was seated on the glider. She stood several yards away from him, waiting for Paul to acknowledge her. He did not look up.

She did not know how to get him to look at her. In movies people always coughed to get someone's attention. She decided to try it. She coughed. He continued to ignore her. She had no choice but to plunge ahead.

"Don't you think you better go in?" she asked in a soft voice. "It's pretty late."

"No," he said stonily, staring across the nocturnal landscape.

"Mom's worrying about you. Why don't you come in?"

Paul did not reply.

"Look, we were just kidding around over at the Stewarts'. I didn't know you were sick. You should have said something."

Tracy glanced back at the house. She could see Anna's silhouette in the kitchen window, watching them. Tracy sighed and tried again.

"I guess, you know, with your cat running away and everything, you probably feel bad. But why don't you come in now? If you want, I'll help you look for him tomorrow."

Slowly Paul stood up and turned to face Tracy. For a moment she felt relieved that she had accomplished her task. Then she saw the fury in his eyes.

"What did you do with him?" he said.

Tracy frowned and took a step away from him, drawing the tie on her bathrobe tight around her. "What?"

"What did you do with Sam? Where is he?"

Tracy shook her head.

"You did something to him. I know it."

"That's a shitty lie," she said through clenched teeth.

Paul took a menacing step toward her. "You and your friends probably had a good laugh about it."

Tracy stuck out her chin. "You asshole. I wouldn't laugh about that."

"I'm an asshole, right?" He turned his back on her, returning to the chair. "Get away from me. Leave me alone."

Tracy hesitated, stunned for a moment by his accusations. Then she approached the chair, fighting back the tears that were forcing their way out. "You're just acting like a baby. Blaming it on me. It's not my fault your cat ran away."

He kept his eyes averted from hers, staring coldly ahead of him. "Shut up," he said. "Just go away."

Tracy's face turned scarlet, and charging the glider where he was sitting, she landed a glancing whack with her fist on his shoulder that set the seat in motion. "It's not my fault," she cried.

Paul leaped from the swinging chair, grabbed her wrist, and whirled around to face her. "Don't touch me," he growled at her.

"It's not my fault," Tracy cried, her eyes widening as she flailed at him with her free hand. "Let me go."

Paul gave her a shake and then released her wrist. Suddenly he let out a groan. He gripped his head with his hands and slowly sank to his knees. Gasping for breath, Tracy watched in astonishment as he collapsed on the ground. The back door of the house slammed, and Anna sprinted across the yard.

"What's going on?" she cried out. "What are you two fighting about?"

Tracy looked up at her mother in bewilderment as Paul

rocked back and forth on the ground, holding his head. "I just slapped him. He was breaking my arm."

"Go in the house," Anna said grimly, bending down beside Paul.

"He said I laughed about his cat," cried Tracy, staring at the boy on the ground as he writhed.

"What is it?" Anna pleaded with her son. "Tell me what's wrong."

"My head," he groaned.

"I didn't even touch his head," Tracy insisted.

"Go inside, Tracy," Anna ordered. Tracy backed away from her mother and the boy on the ground, her eyes wide with fright.

"Let me help you," Anna pleaded with him. She put an arm under his and clambered to her feet, pulling Paul up beside her.

"Come on," she said, "we're going to the hospital."

"No," the boy cried. "No hospital." He tried to wriggle free of her.

"All right," she said soothingly, wondering what she could do for him. She held her cool hand to his forehead as he limped along beside her.

"I want to go to bed," he said.

"All right," she said. "All right. Come inside."

They approached the back of the house through the soft grass. The air was filled with the hum of crickets and other peaceful summer-night sounds. Anna could feel her son shivering in her arms. "I'll help you," she said.

"I feel better now," he said as they slowly climbed the steps to the house.

He was asleep as soon as he lowered his head to the pillow. She sat at one end of the bed and watched him fall away, his thin face white from the strain of the headache. His mouth fell open, as if he were gulping to breathe, and in the moonlight his face was all shadows and hollows. His hands fell open outside the sheet, weak and helpless. There was a sheen of perspiration on his forehead and upper lip.

He is sick, she thought. There is something terribly wrong with him. That's what Rambo meant. Try as she might, she could not stop thinking the worst. A brain tumor. Some kind of cancer. That had to be it.

She thought that maybe she should get up tomorrow and just take the boy directly to the doctor and never meet Rambo at all. It was utterly clear to her now that Rambo knew about this illness, and that was what he was going to tell her. A doctor would probably be able to diagnose it in no time. But the thought nagged at her that perhaps Rambo knew something about it that was vital. After all, the boy had grown up in his household. Perhaps he had sustained some injury, taken some kind of drugs, or something. She had to find out what Rambo knew. He might disappear, and she would never find out what he really meant. Anna felt her thoughts racing around her head like a dog chasing its tail. She did not want to waste precious time with Rambo if the boy was ill and needed to be hospitalized. But it was her only chance to find out. She tried to steady herself. Do as you planned, she told herself. Courage. Tomorrow you will know.

She wished for a minute that she could talk to Thomas. But she knew he would not let her go. She shook her head. She would do it alone. Anna stood up quietly from the end of Paul's bed. He was breathing normally at last. She opened the door and let herself out. She closed the door behind her and started down the hallway.

As she passed the door to Tracy's room, she noticed a

faint light emanating from the crack beneath the door. Still up, she thought. Then, from behind the door, she heard the sounds of gasping, as if someone were trying to catch her breath. For a moment Anna hesitated. Then she put her hand on the doorknob and slowly turned it. She pushed open the door to the room and peeked in.

A tiny reading lamp threw a pool of light on the floor of the darkened bedroom. Tracy sat at the edge of the circle of light. Her head was bowed, and in her arms she held a doll, dressed in white. Anna looked closely at the doll, and then her heart skipped as she realized that the doll was clothed in Paul's christening dress and hat, the little satin booties on its feet. Tracy's shoulders shook as she cradled the doll to her chest.

"Tracy," Anna whispered.

Tracy jumped and whirled around, hiding the doll behind her and staring defiantly at her mother. Anna could see that her daughter's eyes were pink, and there were tears still dribbling down the freckled face.

"Go away," Tracy cried.

Anna stepped into the room. "Tracy, what's the matter? Tell me what's wrong?"

"Just get out of here," the teen-ager wailed.

"Please, Trace," Anna pleaded, "talk to me."

"No," Tracy spit out.

Anna bit her lip and put a hand out to touch her daughter's flushed, contorted face. "I love you, Trace," she whispered.

Tracy jerked away from her touch and turned her back to her mother, hiding the doll in her folded arms. Anna sighed and put her hand on the doorknob.

A small resentful voice came from Tracy's huddled frame. "I'm just sick and tired of being blamed," she said.

Anna frowned and looked back at her daughter. "Blamed for what?" she asked softly.

"For what happened to him," Tracy muttered.

"Oh, Tracy, I don't blame you," Anna assured her, relieved to have an opening. "I'm sorry I yelled at you, darling. I was just worried about Paul. These headaches of his. I'm afraid it might be something serious—"

"Not only for that," Tracy interrupted her furiously. "For back then, when they took him."

"When they took him?" Anna looked at her daughter in confusion. "What—"

"You always blamed me," Tracy said accusingly. "You always thought it was my fault."

Anna's face slackened in amazement. Tracy was holding the doll tightly under one arm. Tears welled in her angry eyes, but she seemed oblivious to them.

"Of course, it wasn't your fault, Tracy. No one in the world ever thought it was your fault," Anna protested, wrenched by the sight of her daughter's misery.

"Yes, you did." Tracy corrected her bitterly.

Anna shook her head helplessly. "I never did."

"You always did," Tracy insisted.

"Tracy," Anna cried, "you were just a baby. It was something done by grown-ups. It had nothing to do with you." She reached out her hand to her daughter.

Tracy backed away from her, unconsciously guarding the doll.

"Why would you ever think that?" said Anna.

"You said so."

"I didn't."

"I was sick," Tracy cried.

Anna stared at her.

"I was sick."

Anna shook her head, uncomprehending.

"Every time you told it that's what you said. I was sick. And you came in the house to take care of me. And then he was gone. You said it every time. You had to come in because I was crying. Because I was sick . . ."

Tracy looked down at the doll under her arm as if she had just remembered it was there. "I was sick," she mumbled. "And so they came and took my brother."

Anna felt tears stinging her own eyes. "No, no," she whispered.

"I didn't want them to take him," Tracy said. "He was my brother."

Guilt sizzled through Anna as she stared at her daughter's unrelenting eyes. "I never thought . . ." she said.

"Leave me alone," said Tracy miserably.

For a moment Anna wanted to beg for forgiveness. But she was struck by the sense that she needed time first, to consider her crime, repeated time after time, for years, without thinking. She felt stunned by it, like someone who had learned that the cigarette she thought she had stubbed out had set a house on fire.

"I'm sorry," she whispered in a stricken voice.

"I'm going to bed," said Tracy.

Anna began to retreat from the room, then turned back to see her daughter climbing into bed; she tucked the doll in beside her on the pillow. "I'm sorry," Anna repeated. Tracy switched off the reading light beside the bed.

Anna stood there in the darkness, wondering how she could make it right. She gazed at her daughter's form, curled up and still in the bed. I'll make it up to you, she vowed silently. But she wondered, even as she promised, how she ever would.

*   *   *

Albert Rambo gave his head a shake over the empty basin, and a shower of coffee-tinted droplets hit and clung to the sides of the sink. Rambo stood up and smoothed his wet hair down on his head, speading the thin hair evenly over his white liver-spotted skull. Then he stepped back and examined himself in a three-quarter profile on each side of the bathroom mirror. His normally graying dirty blond hair was now a deep, robust auburn. It looked pretty good, he thought. He decided he would grow a mustache and dye that, too, the same shade. There was still plenty of dye left in the bottle. He hadn't liked the way the Lange woman recognized him so easily. Tomorrow, when he got the money, he would buy a new hat also, before he took off. Then he'd be all set.

After picking up a bathroom towel, he gingerly patted his balding head dry. He carefully combed the hairs into place and admired the result in the mirror. It had cost him his last few bucks for the hair coloring kit. But it was worth it. The fluorescent lights made his skin look grayish green, and the shadows under his eyes were gullies. But the hair looked good.

With the towel draped around his neck, Rambo screwed the cap on the glass bottle of dye and popped the plastic lid back on the squeeze bottle of stabilizer. He carefully washed out the brittle plastic tray they came in and put both bottles back in it. He wadded up the flimsy plastic gloves and put everything back in its box.

After looking in the mirror approvingly one last time, he shrugged on his shirt and buttoned it. Then he took the hair coloring kit with him from the bathroom to the bedroom and shoved it into a corner of his valise. He fingered his upper lip absently, wondering how long it would take him to raise a mustache. He had never been the hairiest guy. It might take a couple of weeks of looking untidy. By the time he grew it, he mused, he'd be far away from here.

If only he had some money, he thought, he'd go out to a bar and celebrate. But that was out of the question. Besides, the Bible lay open on the bed, and he got the uneasy feeling that he'd better get back to it before the voices came back to start hounding him. Obediently Rambo reached for the Good Book and settled himself in the stiff-backed chair by the bureau.

Just then there was a flurry of raps on the motel room door. Rambo froze, staring at the back of the door, his heart accelerating with fear. Police, he thought instantly. She had gone to the police.

But why would they knock? It must be a mistake. Maybe if he was quiet, whoever it was would realize that he was at the wrong door and go away. The onionskin pages of the Bible trembled between his fingers.

At the second set of knocks Rambo jumped from his chair and stood, feet apart, fists clenched, eyes riveted to the door. But then a low voice followed the knocking.

"Sorry to bother you. This is the manager, Mr. de-Blakey."

The manager. He exhaled with relief and then became immediately irritated. "What do you want?" Rambo barked.

"It's your car, sir. I'm afraid it's parked in front of the wrong cabin, and the other guest is making a fuss. I know it's late and all, but could you just move it over here in front of your place?"

Rambo shook his head in annoyance. "Okay, okay, I will," he answered in a gruff voice. He closed the Bible and put it back in the bureau drawer, and then he picked up his keys from the bureau top. I'd better do it now, he thought.

"Thanks a lot, Mr. Rambo."

"You're not welcome," Rambo muttered under his breath as he slipped on his shoes and unlocked the door.

Just as he was pulling the door open, he remembered. He had signed the register Smith. Mr. Willard Smith.

A force from outside shoved the door open, ramming him back into the room. For a second Rambo was paralyzed by the shock, his throat closing on him. He could not even cry out. The man in the doorway reached for him, and Rambo stared up into a pair of glittering gray eyes set in a chiseled, lifeless face. In that instant when he recognized Edward Stewart, his limbs came to life, and Rambo began to struggle, flailing the other man with ineffectual punches.

Edward seemed impervious to the blows which struck him. He grabbed Rambo's head and pushed his face into the rag he was holding in a gloved hand. Rambo gasped and tried to jerk his face away from the suffocating smell which filled his throat and nostrils. He staggered back, but Edward held on to him, crushing the cloth to his open mouth. In mute terror Rambo fixed on the eyes of his captor. They wore the same expression of pitiless determination that he had, seen in them once on a highway, years ago. Rambo began to hear the voices crying faintly in his ears, and then, as the eyes disappeared, there was silence.

CHAPTER ELEVEN

Anna watched the side of the road anxiously as she drove, looking for the sign for the La-Z Pines Motel. She was afraid to miss it and lose any more time. It was past noon already. She had gone to three different banks to get the money and had stopped twice in the town of Kingsburgh before she found someone who could direct her to the La-Z Pines.

The sign came up suddenly on her right, and Anna made a sharp turn into the driveway and slowly crossed the gravel courtyard. Driving at a crawl, she deciphered the cabin numbers, looking for Number 17. A tall gray-haired man in work clothes, carrying a pail and a mop, stopped and watched for a moment as she drove in. Then he turned and went down to the cabin at the front marked "Office."

Anna waited until he had disappeared inside the screen door, and then she pulled her car up and parked it. The motel courtyard was quiet and almost pleasant, shaded by dense pines. The walls of the little cabins were graying from their original white, but the trim on each window and doorway was freshly painted forest green to match the surrounding trees. Anna sat in her car, feeling the seat of her skirt and the back of her shirt sticking to the car seat. On the seat beside her, in a brown paper grocery bag, was the money. Five thousand dollars. It was ironic, she thought. There was a time when she would have welcomed a ransom note, some sign that the person who had stolen her son had done it for gain, that there was some possibility of an exchange.

Now here she was paying ransom for some piece of information—probably useless. She had already made up her mind. If it really were nothing, if he really had no information, she would not argue with him or try to hold on to the money. She would just hand it over to him, accepting the possibility that it might be gone forever. She would call the police when she got away from him and hope they could recover her money. If not, she would replace it somehow. Get a job. She could do that. It was a risk. He might have no information at all. But even as she reminded herself of this possibility, Anna felt the same certainty she had in the parking lot: that Rambo knew something important about the boy. And after Paul's attacks of the night before, she was more convinced than ever that she was doing the right thing in seeking out that information.

Anna glanced in her rearview mirror to see if she could spot Rambo skulking anywhere. He had said he would leave the door open and wait until she was inside. She saw nothing but a few scattered cars, closed blinds, and the unmoving foliage of the trees.

Okay, she thought. Here goes.

As she got out of the car, she pulled her skirt away from the seat and picked up the paper bag, which she put under her arm. Quietly shutting the car door, Anna looked all around and then hurriedly traversed the patchy grass to the doorway of Number 17. There was a single step outside the doorway. Anna mounted it and rapped twice on the door.

She glanced all around, but there was no sign of anyone watching her.

With one swift movement she reached down, turned the doorknob, and leaned forward to push the door open. It did not budge. The handle turned back and forth only a fraction of what it should. Anna stared at the doorknob and then rattled it as hard as she could. The door did not move.

Blood rushed to her face as she tried to force the locked door. Then she stopped and spun around, to search the surrounding cabins and trees with her eyes, in case he was watching her, enjoying her distress. Nothing stirred in the quiet courtyard. She put her face up to the door and softly called out his name. "Rambo. Rambo, open up." There was no answer from inside.

For a moment she stood staring into the courtyard, not knowing what to do. Over on her left she heard a door opening. She looked in the direction of the noise and saw a chubby man and a red-headed woman in bowling shirts emerge from a cabin two doors down and look her over. They got into a long Chrysler and started to back out. The woman arranged her hair in a visor mirror with the tail of a comb. The man ogled Anna as the car rolled slowly by.

Clutching the paper bag tightly, Anna retreated to her car. She slid into the front seat and slammed the door. Her eyes blistered the locked door of cabin 17 as she thought about Rambo, that weasel of a man, controlling her life once again.

For a moment she was tempted to treat it like a hoax and drive away. Just forget the whole thing. But even as she thought of it, she knew she could not let it rest like that. If she could only get into Rambo's room. Even if he had lost his nerve and was on the run, he might have left something behind, something for her to go on. She had to keep on trying.

Resolutely she got out of the car again. She hesitated about taking the bag of money with her. Then she decided that she'd better not leave it lying there. She walked down to the cabin marked "Office."

The La-Z Pines office consisted of two plastic-seated chairs, a high Formica-topped counter, and a wooden rack on the wall holding a few scattered brochures about the Kingsburgh area. The floor of the office was covered in a cracked brown and black linoleum. Behind the counter sat Gus deBlakey, absorbed in his favorite soap opera, *The Young and the Restless*. He'd been watching it on and off since it started a few years back. He felt a twinge of annoyance when he saw the woman with the Volvo coming into the office. He had a feeling that she had more than just a yes or no question on her mind. He had figured she was in the wrong place when he saw her come in. She didn't look much like one of his customers. Probably lost, he thought.

He tore his eyes away from the screen and looked up at her as she leaned over the counter. "Help you?" he asked, glancing back at the young man in a tuxedo who was making an impassioned declaration to a girl in a hospital bed.

"I'm looking for someone," said Anna. "A . . . friend of mine. He's in cabin seventeen."

Gus furrowed his brow and looked at her again. She didn't seem like the type to be friendly with the guy in 17. He was that sleazy guy who drove the blue Chevy.

"Didja knock?" he asked, his eyes drawn back to the small screen.

"There's no answer."

"Must be out. His car there?"

Anna hesitated. "Which car is he driving these days?" she asked.

"Blue Chevy," said Gus. "Look outside."

Anna stepped outside the office and looked down the row of cars. Parked not far from 17's door was a dirty blue car with a large dent in the front fender.

She called in to the man behind the counter. "Is that dirty blue car out there a Chevy?"

"What?" Gus called back, leaning forward as the couple embraced on the hospital bed.

Anna came in and approached the desk. "Could you turn that down for a minute? This is really important."

Gus glanced up at her troubled eyes and then, with a sigh, reached over and switched off the set. "Which one?" he asked, getting up.

He came around the counter and followed Anna to the door. She pointed at the battered fender just visible from where they stood.

"That's it," said Gus.

"But he doesn't answer the door," Anna protested.

Gus shrugged. "It's a free country. Maybe he changed his mind." Then, seeing the distress on Anna's face, he said more gently, "Maybe he went for a walk."

"He was expecting me," she said. "He's got to be there. His car is there."

"I don't know," said Gus.

"Please, sir, could you just open the door for me? I'm afraid he's ill or something. If he's not there, I'll just leave him a note with you."

Gus began to shake his head.

"Oh, please," Anna entreated. "If I could just look in."

Gus frowned. He knew better, but there was something about this woman that got to him. Whatever she wanted with this guy, it obviously meant a lot to her. And the guy really was paid up only until noon. And he was the proprietor after all.

"Okay," he said.

"Oh, thank you," said Anna. "Thank you so much."

She followed at a trot the man's long strides down the courtyard to cabin 17. He fiddled with the keys on the chain on his belt as he walked, finally locating the one he wanted.

"This is it," he said, stopping in front of cabin 17. He knocked on the door and called out, "Mr. Smith, you in there?" Then he turned to Anna. "I hope he isn't just passed out drunk or something. He's going to be hopping mad."

That's probably it, Anna thought. The explanation suddenly made perfect sense to her. And if she walked in with the manager, Rambo would never talk. She'd ruin everything. She watched the manager insert the key into the lock, wondering frantically if she should tell him to stop. "All right," said Gus. "I hope you two are real good friends."

He pushed the door open and walked into the gloomy room. Anna followed behind him, peering around his arm. All the blinds were drawn, and the lights were off in the room. The double bed was rumpled, but not unmade. Rambo's few belongings were heaped in an open valise lying on the floor beside the bureau. On top of the bureau were car keys and a tiny pile of change. Well, thought Anna, at least he didn't leave town.

"Where's the light?" she asked.

"There's a lamp beside the bed," said Gus, pointing to it.

Anna leaned over and turned it on. Its dim bulb illuminated only a small corner of the room.

"He probably went out for cigarettes," said Gus, pointing to the crushed packs and the pile of butts in the ashtray on the bedside table. "There's a little 7-Eleven store about half a mile down the road. He probably walked over there." Gus walked to the window and tried to raise it a crack. "Phew," he said. "It stinks in here."

Anna tried to take in as much of the room as possible, knowing that the manager would soon be insisting that they leave. She noticed that the bathroom door was ajar about six inches, but there was no light coming from the bathroom.

"Which direction down the road?" she asked. "I should think I would have passed him walking as I was coming in," she said, walking over to the bathroom door and pushing it open. She switched on the overhead light as she did so.

"We'd better clear out of here," said Gus impatiently. "You'll just have to come back and meet him another time. There must have been a mix-up." He waited, but there was no reply from the bathroom.

"Come on," he said, but there was still no answer.

Gus walked over to the door and stepped up behind Anna, who still stood in the doorway. "Holy Jesus," he cried.

A pair of shiny black shoes swayed only inches in front of Anna's face. The legs hung limp, pants stained wet in the crotch. The hands were open and stiff, the fingernails blue. A rope which hung from the light fixture cut deeply into the broken neck, and Rambo's tongue protruded, swollen and gray. His sightless eyes bulged from the bluish, mottled skin of his face. A few auburn-colored clumps of hair stood up messily from the white scalp.

Anna's face was as pale as tissue paper. Her eyes were blank and trained on the gruesome sight before her.

Gus pushed past her and nearly tripped over the straight-backed chair from the bedroom which was lying on its side.

"Christ Almighty," he breathed, standing the chair up with trembling hands.

"Oh, God," he heard the woman behind him whisper. "Oh, no."

"I am terribly sorry, Mr. Stewart," said the proprietor of the hobby shop. "I had no idea that anything was wrong with them."

Edward faced the balding, mustachioed salesman over the counter and shook the densely printed pages which he held in his hand at him. "I was halfway finished with framing the hull when I realized that the directions were incorrect. Fortunately I am skilled in this area, and I was able to discontinue what I was doing before the entire ship was ruined."

"I'm sure that was very frustrating for you, sir," mumbled the salesman, avoiding Edward's narrowed eyes.

"Do I have to remind you," Edward said, "that I am one of your most important customers? When I order a model from you, I expect it to be perfect in every detail. There is no room for error in precision work of this kind."

The salesman nodded. "I know, you're right."

"I am the manufacturer of jet planes, Mr. Martin. How would you like it if my company were to demonstrate this kind of carelessness on the products which we manufacture? How would you like to go off on your next little vacation with your wife to Miami or wherever in a plane put together with defective parts?"

"Not at all, sir," the salesman said. "You're right."

"That might be the last flight you ever took," Edward cried.

He looked up from the salesman's pale face to see a young man peering out at him with round eyes from the back of the store. The boy withdrew his head instantly when Edward spotted him.

The salesman fumbled with the glasses case that was hooked onto his shirt pocket and adjusted his glasses on his nose. "Do you mind if I just have a look at that?" he asked, reaching for the complex set of instructions which Edward held in his hand.

As the man's fingers reached the pages, Edward yanked them back and crushed the paper in his fist. He dropped the ball of crumpled instructions on the counter before the proprietor's startled eyes.

"Yes, I mind," said Edward. "You are wasting my time."

"Let me just go in the back and see if we've got another model for you with the correct instructions. I'll be right back."

Edward nodded curtly, and the man disappeared into his office. Other than this unpleasant problem, he thought, I am in a good frame of mind today. He felt a surge of pride, remembering how efficiently he had taken care of Albert Rambo. Now he was safe from the insinuations of that pathetic little madman. A smile began to play around his lips as he recalled the look in Rambo's eyes last night when he recognized him. It had been for only a moment, before Rambo had passed out from the fumes on the rag. He himself had been frightened, approaching Rambo's room, but now he felt an unexpected satisfaction.

"I'm sorry, sir," said the merchant, reappearing behind the counter, "but we don't have any of those models in stock. I'll have to give you credit toward your next purchase."

Edward turned a steely glance on the man. "Give me

cash," he said. "From now on I'll take my business elsewhere."

The salesman seemed to consider arguing; but then his shoulders drooped, and he silently opened the cash drawer and handed Edward his refund.

Edward jerked the money from the man's outstretched hand and left the store, slamming the door behind him. It was incompetence that infuriated him, he decided, the lack of attention to what was important. He would never enter the store again. He expected people to serve his needs properly when they were dealing with him. He was not someone to be trifled with. He thought again of Rambo at the golf course, demanding blackmail money. Well, he had certainly been punished for that indiscretion.

The blare of a taxi horn and the shouts of the driver shocked Edward, and he jumped back onto the curb, trembling, as the driver shook a fist and sputtered at him. Edward's heart pounded as he clutched his briefcase to his chest and stared at the driver, who scowled at him and then pulled away.

At least the man had been alert. For a moment Edward flashed again, as he had so many times over the years, on the accident which had started this whole thing. He had been coming off the highway, planning to stop home and change his clothes after a business meeting in New Haven. The deal he had made at the meeting had been a brilliant one, and his mind was preoccupied with reliving the strategy that had won the day. He did not notice, until it was too late, the child toddling onto the exit ramp. He had not recognized the child at that moment. All children looked alike to him anyway. But he could still remember the little sailor hat on the boy's head and the big, wondering eyes that met his through the windshield just before the car struck him and bounced the child off the grille and into the weeds beside the exit ramp. The thud of the impact reverberated through Edward's body, even today, when he thought of it.

Well, he couldn't have stopped himself in time even if he had seen him. The child should not have been there. His mother should have been watching him. It was as simple as that.

Edward looked both ways before stepping off the curb and into the street as he continued on his way back to the office. If only the boy had died that day, he thought. He would not have had to kill Rambo.

Well, it was done. There was no point in dwelling on it. It was done, and he was safe. Then another worry darkened his mind. He wondered, for a minute, if there was any chance of the boy's remembering what had happened. He had been only a toddler at the time, and he did not seem to have any recollection of it at all. Still, Edward wondered how anyone, even a child, could forget such an event. In a case like this, you had to be on your guard. Edward shook his head and drew in a deep breath. Needless worrying, he thought. Everything was all right now. He had taken care of it. His reputation was secure. It was a good feeling.

Buddy Ferraro looked from the piece of paper in his hands to Anna's tired face. "So that's all he said to you? That's everything?"

They were seated at Anna's kitchen table. A glass of iced tea, untouched, formed a wet ring by Buddy's elbow. Thomas stood with his back to the sink, his arms folded across his chest. The summer night had softly descended, and crickets hummed outside the screen door of the kitchen.

Anna nodded. She noticed as she looked at Buddy that the hair at his temples was turning gray. For a moment she wondered when that had happened. Buddy folded up the paper and put it in his jacket pocket.

"What do you think?" she asked.

"I think he was a desperate man," said Buddy.

"I don't understand why he killed himself before I even got there," she protested. "I was coming with the money."

Buddy gave her a baleful look. "I still can't believe you did that, Anna. You know better than that. How many cranks came to us over the years, offering information for money?"

"But this was Rambo. And he really did know something." Anna ran a hand over her eyes. "And now he's dead. There's so much he could have told us."

"Well, I grant you there are a lot of questions that I would have liked to ask Albert Rambo."

"Buddy, why would he do that? Say those things about Paul if they weren't true?"

"For the money," said Buddy firmly. "Anna, the man was up against the wall."

Anna nodded. "I know."

"Listen. Number one, the man was not right in the head. We know that. He was a kidnapper on the run. He was down, literally, to his last few cents. It all was closing in on him. And then you got there a little late. I guess he decided his scheme wasn't going to work. And he sure didn't have any other options."

"I understand about the suicide, I guess," said Anna. "But I'm convinced he really did have something to tell me. He wasn't lying to me. I'm sure of that. I'll tell you what I think," said Anna. "I think there's something physically wrong with Paul. And I think it had to do with that. I'm afraid he's ill."

Thomas quietly pushed himself away from the sink and

walked out of the room, without a word to either of them. Buddy watched him go. Then he turned back to Anna, who was frowning, deep in thought.

"Well," said Buddy, "I suggest that you get him to a doctor then. And while you're at it, you look like you could use some rest yourself."

"Oh, I'm taking him," she assured him. "First thing tomorrow."

Buddy stood up to go. "How's the kid handling all this?" he asked.

Anna sighed. "It's hard to say. I heard Tracy asking him about it, and he said he didn't feel anything about it. He's been up in his room for hours."

Buddy shook his head. "That kid has had it rough. Well, I'll be going. Got a busy day tomorrow. Sandy and I are driving Mark up to college."

"Tomorrow?" said Anna. "How great. How long a trip is it?"

"Coupla hours," he said. "We're going to go up and spend a few days there. They have a little inn. We have to go to all kinds of teas and cocktail parties and whatnot," he said casually.

"It sounds lovely." Anna beamed at him.

"It oughta be lovely, for what this year is going to cost me," Buddy observed, feigning exasperation.

Anna started to rise, but he gestured for her to stay in her seat. "I know my way out," he said.

Anna sighed. "I must say I'm glad this is all over. At least I can forget about Rambo lurking around every corner."

Buddy looked at her thoughtfully. "You take care of yourself while I'm gone."

"I will," she said, smiling at him.

Buddy frowned as he turned away from her. He had his doubts about this suicide, but he had decided not to burden her with them. He knew she would seize on them, and she did not need any more worries. He raised his hand in a relaxed salute as he left.

"Thanks," she called after him.

Anna could hear him going through the house and the sound of the front door closing behind him. She sat in her chair, her hands resting limply in her lap. She was afraid to close her eyes, even though she was exhausted. She was afraid to see it again in her mind's eye: Rambo, dangling there; the hideous color of death; the bulging tongue and eyes.

"Ugh . . ." She made a retching sound and forced herself to her feet. She did not want to sit alone there, thinking. She felt a sudden, urgent need to talk things over with Thomas. They had not really had a chance to talk yet. There had been the police, the reporters, the hospital, and Paul, all afternoon. Thomas had been quieter than usual, and it was hard to tell what he was thinking. As tired as she was, Anna felt that she had to explain it all to him now and make him understand.

Anna walked through the house to the staircase and trudged slowly up the steps. The door to their room was open, and the soft light of the bedside lamp spilled out into the hall. The house was quiet. Tracy had even kept her stereo off, stunned into silence by the strange events of the day. Anna walked quietly into their room.

Thomas stood by the bureau, his shoulders sunken, running his fingers over the back of the silver brush. The sight of him caused an aching in her throat, and Anna started toward him, ready to slip her arms around him from behind and rest her cheek on his broad back. But as she walked across the room, she saw the packed suitcase, standing at the foot of the bed. She stopped short. "Tom," she said.

He turned to face her, putting the brush down on the bureau top.

"What's this?" she asked incredulously.

Thomas did not reply, but his jaw tightened.

"Honey, what are you doing?"

He walked stiffly to the nightstand and picked up the book that was lying there. Then he unzipped the front pocket on his suitcase and shoved it in. "Packing," he said.

Anna sank down on the bed and sat on the edge, struck speechless for a moment. Then her words came in an urgent rush. "Tom, I don't blame you for being angry. But we have to talk. I probably should have told you what I was going to do. Believe me, I agonized over it. I wanted to tell you; but he threatened me and said I would never find out if I brought you, or the police, or anyone else into it, and I couldn't take the chance."

"I've heard the story," said Thomas in a dull voice. "All day."

"It's not a story, Tom. It's the truth," said Anna.

"Okay. It's the truth."

Anna leaned toward him. "But, darling, I'm still sorry for what happened. Can't you forgive me for not telling you?"

"You don't need to explain," said Thomas. "I understand why you did it."

Anna spread her hands. "Then what's this all about? Why are you packing?"

Thomas was silent for a few moments, and then he turned to face her, his eyes like ice-covered pools of pain. "Because it's endless, Anna. I can't take it."

"What's endless? What do you mean?"

"You. Your preoccupation with Paul. All those years he was gone, all the searching, and the phone calls, and the newspaper stories. All the times I felt you were only half with me, I didn't complain. But when I heard that the boy was coming back, I thought it might end. I thought you might finally let go of this . . . obsession. Only it's worse than ever."

Anna felt indignation flare at his accusation. "How can you say that? An obsession. I had to search for my son. I couldn't just say, 'He's gone,' and forget about him. I couldn't have lived with myself. Is that what you expected me to do?"

Thomas did not answer or meet her gaze.

"And when Rambo approached me and said he knew something of life-and-death importance about Paul, yes, I had to find out what it was."

"For Paul's sake," Thomas interjected in a flat voice.

"Yes," said Anna. "That's right. I had to try to protect him."

"And what about Tracy and me? What if something had happened to you?"

"Well, I intended to be careful. It seemed that there was never any real danger to me. All he said he wanted was the money."

"A criminal on the run. A lunatic . . ."

"Tom, I felt desperate. I had to know what it was that Rambo was hiding. He said our son was in danger, and I had to find out."

"Listen to yourself, Anna," he cried. "Don't you see? No sacrifice is ever too great for Paul. First it was the searching. Then it was Rambo. Now you've taken it into your head that the boy is sick, and it will be a round of doctors. And then what will it be after that? Where does it end, Anna?"

Anna stared at him for a moment, about to protest, and then she shook her head. "It doesn't end," she said quietly. "My concern for my own son—that will never end, any more than my concern for you and Tracy would end. . . ."

Thomas snorted. "Concern. Is that what you call it?" He stalked over to the closet, pulled open the door, and quickly inspected its contents.

Anna rose from the bed and shook her head in disbelief. "You know, have you ever stopped to think that maybe it's you who's being unreasonable? Ever since we heard that Paul was coming home, you've been withdrawn. You won't talk about it. You never once showed any real happiness about it. This should have been the best moment of our lives. Our own child coming back to us. Why don't I feel that from you?"

Thomas looked at her with tired, bleak eyes. "He's a stranger, Anna. He's someone we don't even know."

Anna stared at him. "How can you say that?" she whispered. "That boy is your son."

Thomas shook his head and slammed the closet door. "To me, he is a stranger. I can't pretend to love him. I don't feel anything for him."

Shocked by his words, Anna could not speak for a moment. Slowly she recovered her voice. "Then maybe you should go."

Thomas walked over to his suitcase and zipped up the front pocket. Then he picked up the handles. "I can't help it," he said. "That's the way I feel."

"Well, go then. Go," she said. She grabbed the bedroom door and pulled it open. "You don't belong here."

Thomas hesitated and then, carrying his suitcase, he

walked out. Anna heard his footfalls, descending the staircase.

"How could you?" she said softly as she stared at the empty doorway.

The sound of harsh voices filtered down the hallway through his bedroom door, but Paul could not hear what they were saying. He sat huddled up in the chair beside his bureau, his arms wrapped around his knees, which were pulled up to his thin chest. The only illumination in the room was the moonlight coming through the window, throwing the objects in the room into monstrous shadows.

Once, when he was younger, he and another boy had stumbled onto a body in the woods. The man was a hobo. They found him not far from the remains of a dead campfire. It was wintertime, and the hobo's rags had not been enough protection from the cold of the mountains. Paul had never been able to forget the sight of that stiff body, curling up into itself, the tattered clothes fluttering slightly over the man's blue limbs, the eyes and mouth open, and frozen into an expression of resigned terror. Every time he tried to imagine his father hanging in a motel room, he kept picturing that dead man in the woods. He could see his father's mouth open, like that, the stream of invective and religious ramblings silenced forever. Those agitated, angry eyes staring, fixed into eternity. Paul wondered uneasily if despite all his preaching, Albert Rambo would end up in heaven. If there was such a place, Paul suspected his father could get there only through the intervention of his mother.

But no, they both were kidnappers, doomed to be punished. And now they both were dead. He tried to decide if it was his fault that they were dead. The thought made him feel weak and woozy. They were gone, though. Both those people who had been his parents. And Sam was gone, too. Every trace of the life he had known seemed to have been swallowed up by the earth.

Although he felt that he should, he could not feel sad about the death of his father. Not the way he had felt when his mother died. But he did feel afraid. For as long as Albert Rambo had been alive, there had been someone who knew who he was. Now, with his father gone, he was truly alone. Alone with these people. The Langes. He was Paul. Their son. It was as if his life were a huge lie, and now he was forced, for the rest of his life, to live in that lie.

But even as he emitted a sob at that terrifying idea, he thought again about how Anna, the mother, had gone to meet Rambo with money, just to try to find out about him. It seemed like a kind of stupid thing to do, in a way. But Paul felt a tiny spot of warmth in the pit of his stomach when he thought of it. For a second the yawning loneliness lifted, and then it descended again.

CHAPTER TWELVE

Thomas drummed his fingertips on the surface of Gail Kelleher's cocktail table. "Thanks for inviting me over," he said. "I guess I needed to see a friendly face."

Gail tucked her legs under her and leaned back into the cushions of her plush sectional sofa. She took a sip of wine and gazed at him over the rim of her glass. "That's all right," she said. "I'm glad you called me."

"I wasn't sure you'd be home. I just took a chance. I figured a girl like you would be . . . I don't know . . . busy."

Gail smiled ruefully. "Out dancing till dawn and drinking champagne out of a slipper," she said.

Thomas shrugged. "Something like that," he said.

"Let's see," she said, throwing her head back as if she were reading something off the ceiling. "This past weekend I met a guy for a drink whom I knew from college. He had three stingers in a row and tried to maul me in the cab on the way home. I ended up in bed with a good mystery. One day I did my laundry and met my girl friend for a hamburger down the street. Yesterday I watched a hockey game on TV. Pretty glamorous, no?" She smiled at him, raising one eyebrow.

"I'm surprised," he said. "I pictured it differently. You're so attractive. And you're single."

"Oh, I meet a lot of men," she said. "Not many that I really like. They all seem to be preoccupied with their investments and their sound systems. It's rare to meet someone who is really warm. That you feel you can talk to . . ."

Thomas looked up at her and felt a tingling sensation at the intensity of her glance. He quickly looked away and gazed around the modern, elegantly appointed apartment. "I like your place," he said, although he felt a little out of his element in the sleek decor. He glanced again at Gail, who was barefoot and dressed in a V-neck summer dress that seemed to have only one button holding it closed at the waist.

"It's about time you got over here," she said lightly. "Want a glass of wine?"

"Yeah, okay," he said nervously.

He watched her as she walked over to the ice bucket on the bar, picked up a wineglass, and filled it. "You still haven't told me why you're here," she said. "You just said on the phone that you were spending the night in the city."

Gail walked back to the sofa and handed him the glass. Then she settled down beside him, somewhat closer than she had been before.

Thomas stared into the pale liquid in the glass. "I . . . I left home," he said, feeling, as he said it, like a small boy who had run away and was trying to appear to be brave.

"What happened?" she asked, watching him closely.

"Well, you probably heard about Anna's finding the kidnapper at the motel and all. . . ."

"It was on the news," said Gail.

Thomas sighed. "I don't know. I just couldn't take any more."

"Why did she do that?" Gail asked. "It was such a crazy thing to do."

Thomas felt himself shrink from the harshness of her judgment. He felt an instinctive urge to defend his wife. "She's been under a lot of pressure lately. She can't seem to stop thinking about the boy."

"It sounds kind of sick to me. I don't know how you've put up with it for as long as you have."

Thomas sighed and stared at his hands, which were clasped together. He did want to talk about it, and he knew that Gail was only trying to take his side in it; but he could not bring himself to say all the things that he felt about it. He felt guilty, talking about Anna that way. He felt only a kind of inchoate need for comfort. He had the urge to reach over and touch the skin on Gail's arms, which was smooth and gave off an exotic scent.

As if she had read his mind, Gail put a hand on his forearm, and Thomas gazed down at it. He started to speak several times and then stopped. "When Paul showed up on Friday . . ." he said. Then he shook his head and frowned. "He doesn't look anything like he used to." Thomas could feel a sob welling up inside him that he wanted to stifle at all cost. "I don't know what I was expecting. I feel so far away from him. . . ."

Gail tilted her head to one side. "It's been rough, hasn't it?"

Thomas was silent for a few minutes. Then he shook his head. "I'm terrible company tonight," he said. He finished his wine and put the glass down on the table. "I'd better be getting over to the hotel."

Gail put her glass down beside his and moved over to

him. As she came near him, he could see her bare breasts inside the plunging neckline of her dress.

"You don't have to stay at a hotel," she said.

Thomas looked up into her eyes, which were dark and deep and full of sympathy for him.

"I'm glad you came to me," she said softly.

Thomas closed his eyes and swallowed. Despite the air conditioning in the room, he was suffused with heat. He could feel her fingers burning into his arm. With a groan he reached out for her.

Sprawled on the bed in her rumpled clothes, Anna groped across the quilt for the familiar mound of Thomas's body and came awake, grasping a wad of the cotton mosaic in her fingers. Without lifting her head, Anna gazed at the undisturbed bedclothes beside her. The shafts of sunlight which fell on her made her wince, her eyes grainy from the angry tears of the night before. At least, she thought, the awful night was over.

Anna rolled over onto her back and stared up at the ceiling. The memory of Thomas's words, the vehemence with which he had disavowed their son still stung her. But with the morning and after a few hours of sleep, she felt more incredulity than anger.

She now admitted to herself that she had known for a long time that he had had no hope for Paul's return. Well, she thought, not to hope was one thing. But he seemed to be saying that he hadn't even wanted him back. Not at all. It made her feel that there was a whole side of him which she had never known about. She tried to think back, to the point where she had lost track of what he really felt.

In the year or so after Paul had been taken, and she had lost the baby, she would often come awake in the night, jerked from her fitful sleep by a sense of dread that was suffocating, that made the sweat stream from her body. Inevitably he would awaken moments later and turn to her, to encircle her tense, sleepless body in his arms, as if even in his sleep her needs were known to him. His embrace was meant to comfort her, but she could always sense that he was fearful of her dry-eyed grief, and his arms felt like a weight on her. One morning she complained of it to him. After that he still woke, but he would only take her hand, and gradually he learned not to touch her, but would lie there beside her, staring into the night, unable to help, unable to sleep. After a while he got a prescription and took sleeping pills. From then on she awoke alone. She was relieved, actually, to be alone with her thoughts, not to have to answer his unspoken anxieties about her. She would look at him dispassionately, lying there beside her, sleeping like an exhausted soldier, eyes encircled with shadows, mouth open. When had he stopped waiting for Paul? she wondered. Was it then, when he started to sleep?

For her part she had remained a sentry, without consolation, for a long time afterward. When she finally was able to sleep through the night, make love again, resume her life with him, they never mentioned those other times.

There were so many things that they had never talked about, subjects too tender to touch. Now she wondered if they ever would. She felt a stabbing pain in her throat, as if she were being strangled by the painful thought.

First things first, she reminded herself. She had to get ready and get Paul over to the doctor's office. She was convinced now of his illness, and as much as she feared the verdict, she could not bear to wait. In a sense she was grateful to have a mission of such urgency. It enabled her to get out of bed.

She dragged herself up and slowly shed the wrinkled clothes she was wearing. She grabbed a wrapper, went into the bathroom, and ran a hot shower. The water spilling over her felt good, and she marveled for a second at how such small pleasures were enough to keep a person going. She recalled those days after Paul had gone and she had lost the baby. She would focus on small, pleasurable sensations to lift herself up—the curve of a shell she found at the beach; the feeling of clean sheets on her legs; the blaze of an icicle struck by sun, hanging from the porch roof. These sensations would jolt her, sometimes forcing tears to her eyes, always reminding her that she was alive. The heartache had numbed her but not killed her. As she slowly dressed, she realized she thought that those days were over, that they had ended on the day she learned Paul was coming home. She shook her head, feeling pity for her own hopefulness.

Leaving her room, she noticed that the doors to Paul's and Tracy's rooms were still closed. She went quietly down the stairs, hoping not to disturb them yet. She had a feeling that Paul was dreading this doctor's appointment, although he had not actually said so. As for Tracy, Anna did not relish the prospect of telling her that Thomas had left. He had always been closer to Tracy than she had. She wished that they would sleep a little longer and give her some time to collect herself.

Anna went into the kitchen and put a few things for breakfast out on the kitchen table. She stopped short, thinking again of Thomas and wondering if he had eaten. He had never been able to take care of himself. He was probably having a doughnut at his desk and drinking black coffee till his hands shook. One thing was true of him: He had never taken for granted the way she took care of him, unlike most husbands she heard about. Anna sighed and poured some milk into a pitcher for the table.

"Mom?"

Anna turned around and saw Tracy, dressed in a Fleetwood Mac T-shirt and running shorts, standing in the doorway to the kitchen. They had not spoken to each other very much since Sunday night, when Anna had gone into her room, but Tracy's storm of accusations seemed to have eased her anger, as if an infection in her had burst and was draining away. Anna felt a sickening certainty that the news of Thomas's departure would create a whole new climate of resentment. She placed the pitcher of milk on the table and began to fuss with the gauge on the toaster.

"Hi, darling. When did you get up? I didn't hear you."

"Just now," said Tracy. "Where's Daddy?"

That was quick, Anna thought. She sighed a little. "He's not here."

Tracy picked up an orange from the basket on the table and started to peel it. "Did he go early?" she asked casually. She pulled out a section and slipped it into her mouth. She began to suck on it, her eyes warily trained on her mother's face.

Anna could sense the tension in Tracy's stance. For a second she realized that Tracy knew instinctively that something was wrong. She wondered how the child could be so perceptive, but at the same instant she understood, with a heavy heart, that Tracy had been bred on calamity. She must have a presentiment for it, based on experience. There was no point in trying to conceal the truth from her. Anna sat down carefully in one of the kitchen chairs and laid her hands, palms down, on the tabletop. She was not sure how to begin.

Tracy saved her the trouble. "What happened?" she

asked in a matter-of-fact tone, but Anna could hear a tremor in her voice.

"Tracy, your father and I had an argument last night, and he decided to go away for a little while."

"What do you mean?" Tracy asked incredulously. "You mean, he moved out?"

Anna was poised to deny it. Then her shoulders slumped, and she nodded. "For a little while." She mitigated the admission.

"What's a little while?" Tracy cried. "When's he coming home?"

Anna was silent for a moment. Then she replied, "I don't know."

Tracy spit an orange pit into her hand. "You mean, never," she said.

"I mean, I don't know."

"He just left, like that? He didn't even say good-bye to me."

"You were sleeping. He didn't want to wake you. You'll see him, Tracy. He loves you. It's not you he's mad at."

"What did you do?" Tracy asked accusingly. Then she blurted out, "I can't believe this." Tears spurted to her eyes, and she angrily wiped them away.

Anna stared sadly at her daughter, who was trying to be defiant about this, her latest loss. The scene in Tracy's room came back to her, as it had every day since. What have I done to you? she thought.

"Tracy, I'm sorry. I know you're going to feel as if I'm to blame, and I know how much you care for him; but I did what I had to do, and I'd do it again if I had the chance. I'm going to try to make your father see that, but if I can't . . . well, I don't know."

"Did what? What did you do to make him leave?"

Anna considered claiming that it was private. She felt too tired to face her daughter's reaction and the cementing of her conviction that her mother was to blame for all her misery. But perhaps there had already been too many things kept inside. Anna drew a deep breath.

"Your father was very angry at me for what I did yesterday."

"What do you mean? For finding that guy?"

"Not for finding him. For going to see him. I went to see him without telling Daddy what I was going to do. You heard the whole thing yesterday."

"Yeah, I heard it," she said. "He was going to tell you something about Paul."

"Yes," said Anna carefully. "He wanted money in exchange for the information, and I brought it to him. I did all this without telling your father."

"Is he mad about the money?"

"No, darling. He is mad because he thinks I acted recklessly. He feels that I didn't give any thought to his feelings, or to yours for that matter. That I just went ahead and did it without caring about the two of you. That's not true, but he didn't believe me."

Tracy inserted another orange section into her mouth and then sucked on it thoughtfully. "I don't get it," she said.

Anna looked up at her.

"Did he think we should have come with you? How could we do that?"

"No, he meant that if something had happened to me, I mean, if Rambo had been lying and done something to me . . . that I just took a dangerous chance . . . for Paul's sake."

Tracy nodded and picked another pit off her tongue. She deposited the pits in her hand into a ceramic ashtray on the table. Then she wiped her hand on her T-shirt. "Yeah, but you had to try to find out what he knew about Paul," she said simply.

Anna felt momentarily stunned by the unexpected endorsement. She looked up at her daughter with her mouth open. Then she bit her lip. "Yes," she said. "That's what I thought." She started to say more but stopped, afraid to break the fragile understanding with a load of explanations.

Tracy sank down into a chair beside her mother and rested her head in her hands. "Oh, this sucks," she groaned.

Gingerly Anna placed a hand on Tracy's back and rubbed it in a circular motion. Tracy let her do it.

"It'll be all right," Anna assured her softly. "We'll make him understand. Don't worry," she promised, gathering determination as she spoke. "You'll see."

Boarding the morning commuter train was like stepping through the open door of an inferno. Edward gasped and stepped back as the blast of heat hit him. Behind him, a pileup of briefcase-toting commuters began, and he could hear their murmured complaints. A trainman in a blue uniform came trudging up the center aisle of the car, bawling, "Step inside, plenty of seats, watch the closing doors."

Edward stood still, glaring at the conductor, as some of the other men slid by him, grumbling and flattening themselves against the seats. The conductor glanced at him and then shook his head, anticipating his complaint. "I know all about it," the conductor said in a bored voice. "Nothing I can do. The whole train's like this—a steam bath."

Edward bristled at the man's casual attitude about the

breakdown in the air conditioning, but it was clear that the conductor just didn't care.

Complaining under his breath, Edward marched down the aisle, settled himself in the window seat, and began removing his jacket. He cursed the chauffeur for being on vacation during this heat wave. From now on, he thought, I'm going to make a rule that none of the servants can take vacations in the summer.

Edward instinctively smoothed out the fabric of his suit to prevent it from being wrinkled by the man who sat down heavily in the seat next to him. He arranged his jacket carefully before glancing over at the man in the adjoining seat and stifled a groan when he recognized Harold Stern, a member of his country club in Stanwich. Harold had made his money in the department store business, and Edward did not consider him suitable for membership in his club. Edward looked quickly away and pretended not to see him.

"Hello, Edward," said Harold, disregarding the snub. "It's hot in here today, isn't it?"

Edward gave him a mirthless smile of assent, and the two sat in silence for a moment.

"Hey," Harold said as Edward began to open his copy of *The Wall Street Journal,* "this whole thing with Tom Lange's family is really incredible, isn't it. You're pretty friendly with them, aren't you?"

Edward gave Harold a rather patronizing nod. "We have been neighbors for some time, of course. The boy's coming home, you mean."

"Well, and then his wife's finding the kidnapper yesterday. They say he killed himself. My God."

"Anna found . . . that man?"

"My wife heard about it on the radio last night."

Sweat broke out at Edward's hairline and began to

bead on his face. "I don't understand. How could Anna. . . ?"

"I don't know the details. There might be something in this morning's paper, though. They love anything sensational, especially in the suburbs." Harold snapped open his briefcase and pulled out a copy of the *Daily News*. "My wife told me I'd better bring it home tonight so she can read about it. I just got it at the station."

Edward watched in horrified fascination as his seatmate pored through the scandal-ridden stories in the front of the paper.

"Here it is," Harold cried. "Page three."

"Let me see," said Edward urgently.

"Just a second," Harold said, frowning as he read.

"Let me see it," Edward demanded in a shrill voice. Harold looked up at him in surprise.

"They're friends. Neighbors. It upsets me terribly," Edward explained, tugging the paper from Harold's hands.

Harold released the tabloid, and Edward stared down at the account in the newspaper, the details just sketchy enough to leave his own fate hanging in the balance. Edward's face paled as he read, and the words seemed to throb in front of him. For an instant he imagined a phalanx of policemen waiting to meet him as he stepped off the train at Grand Central Station. His heart was pounding, and the gnawing in his stomach was almost audible.

Harold Stern watched Edward as he stared at the paper. "God," he said. "You look awful. Are you all right?"

Edward gripped the paper, the ink staining his dampened fingers black. "I'm all right. Shocking news," he mumbled.

"Well, it could be worse. At least nobody got hurt. Except that nut."

"It's this heat," said Edward, handing him back the paper and turning toward the window. How *could* Anna have found Rambo? She must have spoken to him at some point. And how much had Rambo told her? He had to get back to Connecticut and find out. He would not even leave Grand Central Station. He would just turn around and take the next train out. If the police were not already waiting for him, he reminded himself.

"Damned railroad," Harold agreed irritably. "They ought to pay us to ride on it."

"One can hardly breathe," said Edward, covering a clenched fist with his trembling hand.

CHAPTER THIRTEEN

A phone rang, and Anna looked up sharply as the nurse behind the desk answered it and spoke in a low tone. Anna's restless gaze strayed around the doctor's waiting room. Over in one corner a pair of neatly dressed girls with strawberry blond hair were squabbling desultorily over a jigsaw puzzle. In a chair beside them a man with red hair, dressed in khakis and a Lacoste shirt, alternated between glancing at the door and consulting his watch.

In a chair by the window a heavyset woman in a flowered dress was leafing through a *Ladies' Home Journal*, raising her eyes occasionally between pages.

Anna sighed and looked up at the clock. It had been nearly forty minutes since Paul went into the examining room of their family doctor. She wondered what Dr. Derwent could be doing with him all that time.

"Mrs. Lange," the nurse called out pleasantly as she returned the phone to the cradle, "Dr. Derwent would like to talk to you in his office." The nurse gestured toward the closed office door. Anna smiled wanly at her and got up from the sofa; her legs felt numb beneath her. One of the children by the jigsaw puzzle began to cry.

Anna passed through the office door and into the

diploma- and book-lined little room which the doctor used for conferences. She sat down nervously in a black leather chair beside the desk and waited. In a moment the door opened, and the plain, bespectacled face of the doctor appeared in the doorway. He gave Anna's shoulder a squeeze before he sat down in his chair. "Paul will be out in a few minutes, Anna," he said. "He's getting dressed."

Anna tried in vain to read the familiar but expressionless face. "How is he, Doctor?" she asked, steeling herself for any response.

Dr. Derwent leaned back in his chair. "Well, I did a number of tests on him today, and we won't have all the results of those tests for several days, of course."

Anna knotted her fingers together and stared at them. "I understand."

"But from what I have seen of him this morning, I would say that you have nothing to worry about, Anna."

Anna's head jerked up and her eyes widened in disbelief. "He's all right?" she whispered.

The doctor raised a cautionary hand. "I'm not a specialist in this area, as you know. But the presence of a tumor on the brain is something which can often be detected by an examination of the patient's eyes. Now I've done some blood work, taken X rays, and tested his reflexes. I'd still like to have some other tests done at the hospital, like a brain scan. But what I've seen so far looks quite normal. Now perhaps I shouldn't be telling you this without all the test results; but we've known each other for a long time, and I want to put your mind at rest about all this."

"But I don't understand," said Anna. "The headaches and fainting spells. The nausea . . ."

"Well, there are a lot of reasons for a person to have headaches which are not organic, Anna. The boy has been under a lot of stress. It's clear that he is exhausted. He needs to get some rest."

"He has nightmares," she said.

"I can give him something to help him sleep. And I do think you should bring him over to the hospital tomorrow afternoon to have these other tests done on him."

Anna gave him a puzzled look. "I just don't know what to think."

"Anna, you should feel free to take him to a specialist if that will make you feel any better. But I'm sure he'll put the boy through a lot, charge you a lot of money, and then tell you the same thing."

Anna shook her head and gave him a crooked smile. "I can't tell you how grateful I am, Doctor. This is wonderful news."

The doctor reached over and patted her hand. "Glad to be the bearer of good tidings."

Anna rose shakily from her chair. "I'll have those tests done on him tomorrow."

"Anna," said the doctor, getting up from behind his desk, "you might want to have the boy talk to a psychologist or a counselor or something. This whole thing may have an emotional origin. And I think the situation certainly calls for it."

"I suggested it to Tom before he even came home," she said. "He didn't really go for the idea. He thought we should just let things get back to normal without a lot of interference from outsiders."

"Suggest it to him again," the doctor advised. "Tell him I said so."

Anna nodded, not wanting to get into the fact that Tom had left home. She walked out of his conference room and back to the waiting room in a kind of daze.

All right. He's all right. Anna waited for the unexpected verdict to penetrate, but she felt numb all over. She had created a wall of readiness around her heart, so that she could tolerate whatever the doctor had to say without collapsing. She had endured for all these years, and she was not about to collapse now.

He is fine, she repeated to herself. No brain tumor. You were so well prepared for the worst that now you can't even grasp the good news. Anna looked up and saw that the others in the waiting room were eyeing her curiously.

She tried to force a smile, as if to let them know that she was happy with the news. I *am* happy, she reminded herself. He's all right. It's over. There's nothing more to fear. For a moment she wondered if everything Thomas accused her of was true. Maybe she needed the anxiety, just to survive. Maybe worrying was an end in itself, a way of life that she throve on. She should be hugging herself for joy. At that thought a tiny stab of happiness and relief suddenly pierced through her.

It's just a delayed reaction, she told herself. You'll feel it when you get home. I'll take him to a movie, she thought, or anything he wants.

But if the boy was not ill, she thought, why had Rambo said his life was in danger?

"Hi," said a quiet voice.

Anna started and looked into the drawn face of her son.

"Paul!" she exclaimed. "How do you feel?"

"All right," he said. "Can we go now?"

Thomas studied the array of muted silk ties which stood on the men's accessories counter. For a moment he held one between his thumb and forefinger and stared blankly at it. Then he let it drop and turned away from the display.

He stood in the aisle between the two glass counters like a stump in a rushing stream as women with their shopping bags brushed by him. His eyes traveled to the gilt clock above the elevators, and he tried to calculate how much of his lunch hour was left before he had to get back. But the numbers on the clock did not seem to make sense to him, and he felt as if he were in a stupor. A determined-looking young woman in an olive-green jump suit squeezed by him, muttering, "Excuse me," in an irritated tone. Her perfume remained in her wake, and Thomas recognized the scent with a start. It was the perfume he had chosen for Anna on their anniversary some years ago, and she had worn it ever since on special occasions. "Excuse me," Thomas murmured to the woman in drab, but she was already gone.

"I think this one will go," said Gail, coming around beside him and examining a silk tie with a maroon stripe in it. She looked up at Thomas's bewildered expression and smiled. "What's the matter? You look shell-shocked."

"It's so crowded."

"It's always like this at lunchtime," she said matter-of-factly.

"Let's get out of here," he said.

"What about the tie? You know you need something to go with that gray suit. You said so yourself. You haven't got anything."

Thomas shrugged. "I guess my mind was elsewhere when I was packing."

Gail felt a cold little knot form in her stomach at the faraway look in his eyes. She trained her eyes on the tie in her hand and spoke briskly. "Well, what about this one? This would go."

Thomas looked down at the tie in her hand without enthusiasm. "Yeah. That's fine. Let's buy it and get out of here," he said. He reached in his jacket for his wallet, but Gail brushed it off.

"I'll put it on my charge," she said brightly. "A present."

Thomas smiled briefly at her.

"You wait outside," she said, shooing him.

"Thanks," he said. "I'll be over at St. Pat's."

He watched her line up at the counter where a primly dressed saleslady with glasses on a chain around her neck was talking calmly into the store telephone. He threaded his way through the throngs of animated shoppers and pushed through the revolving door and out onto Fifth Avenue.

The crush on the sidewalk was nearly as bad as it had been in the store, but he heaved a sigh of relief to be outside. He inhaled the humid summer air, heavy with the smell of burned hot pretzels and automobile exhaust.

Thomas crossed the street over to St. Patrick's Cathedral and sat down on the steps outside, heedless of his well-pressed suit. On the opposite corner, a black man in a red knit cap was running a game of three-card monte for a crowd of gullible passersby. Behind him, a Puerto Rican family posed proudly at the portals of the great cathedral to have their pictures snapped. Thomas watched the father, who was wearing a sheer yellow sport shirt, a thin mustache, and black-rimmed glasses, ordering his children into the proper position for the snapshot. The mother draped her hands protectively over the shoulders of her little boys, while cradling her baby in the crook of her arm. The father motioned impatiently with his hands and then smiled broadly and nodded as he achieved the composition he wanted in the viewfinder. He pressed the button, and it clicked. The subjects of the photo relaxed, and they all laughed. Half a dozen pigeons rose into the air with a startled flapping of their wings.

Thomas turned away from the family and stared across the street at the occupied phone booth. They are probably back from the doctor's by now, he thought. All morning he had found himself wondering, with an intensity that surprised him, what might be discovered wrong with Paul. He did not like to think of Anna's dealing with bad news, if bad news it was, by herself. He realized, with a sickening sense of guilt that his leaving last night had probably robbed her of her sleep. She would be exhausted today. He could picture the weariness in her eyes. You wanted to punish her, he reminded himself. And it was true that last night he felt she deserved it. But with the morning had come the old impulse to hover near her.

The messenger boy in the phone booth across the street hung up the receiver and, transferring his envelopes to his other hand, headed toward the bus stop. Thomas stood up and gazed across the street at the phone. He rattled the change in his pocket absently. Then, from the corner of his eye, he saw Gail mounting the steps to where he stood, watching him. There was a flat package under her arm, and she was tearing a piece off a giant pretzel. She held out the pretzel to him, but Thomas shook his head.

"That saleswoman was infuriating," said Gail. "I thought she'd never get off the phone."

Thomas nodded. "Persistence won the day, I see." He glanced again at the phone booth.

Gail handed him the box, and he tapped it against his thigh.

"I guess we should be getting back," he said.

Gail nodded, and they started off together down the steps. He could sense that she was studying him, hoping that he had enjoyed their outing. He did not want to hurt her, but he could not seem to shake the melancholy mood which had descended on him. I'm hardly the picture, he thought, of a man on the town with his new mistress. He wondered if he was not so distracted whether he could concentrate on her.

"There's a nice little Mexican place in my neighborhood," said Gail brightly. "Does that sound like fun for dinner?"

"Sounds nice," he said with a forced enthusiasm.

Gail's high heels clacked on the stone as they descended the steps. As they got a little way down the sidewalk, she spotted a wire trash basket about five feet away from them. With a flick of her wrist she tossed the remains of her uneaten pretzel dead center into the trash.

Thomas squeezed her arm and smiled.

"College basketball," she admitted with a rueful smile.

Thomas shook his head. "You're a marvel," he said. "Is there anything you can't do?"

Gail did not answer but flashed a cheery, uncomplicated smile as she slipped her arm through his and held his forearm in a firm grip.

"Cutchee, cutchee, coo," crooned the proud grandfather, and his breath formed a cloud on the plate glass window in front of him. Gus deBlakey waved energetically and beamed at the newborn, swathed in a soft blanket, whom the nurse in a face mask held up for his inspection. The wails of the other babies were muffled by the window as they flailed their miniature red fists and feet drunkenly against the sides of their little beds. Gus's infant grandson blinked and yawned but did not cry as the nurse showed him off to his grandfather.

"What a good little fella. Yes, you are," Gus exulted, his

face distorted by a besotted grin, his eyes disappearing into crinkles. "You're a little angel, just a perfect little angel."

"Excuse me, Mr. deBlakey?"

Gus turned away reluctantly from the window and faced the handsome, neatly dressed man beside him. "That's me," he said. "Hey, does one of these belong to you?"

Buddy Ferraro shook his head, and Gus turned back for a last look as the nurse replaced the baby in the little bed. The child started to wail with his nursery mates as he was released onto the sheet.

"Have a stogie," said Gus, reaching into the pocket of his work shirt and fishing out a cigar. "His father's out on the road in his rig, so Grandpa gets to do the honors for him." He pressed the cigar on Buddy, who took it and slipped it into his jacket pocket.

"I'm sorry to bother you, Mr. deBlakey, but I need to talk to you."

Gus peered at Buddy with pursed lips. "Another cop," he said with resignation.

"I stopped by the motel awhile ago, and a chambermaid said I could find you here."

"Don't tell me," said Gus, biting off the tip of a cigar ferociously and spitting it into the palm of his hand. "That Rambo character again. What a mess this turned out to be."

"I'm afraid so," Buddy agreed.

Gus shot one longing look back at the babies, who twisted and burbled in their newborn slumbers. It took him a moment to locate his pride and joy. "Isn't he cute?" he asked.

"Fine boy," Buddy assented.

"All right," Gus muttered. "Come on outside. Can't smoke in here." Waving his cigar, Gus led the way out the hall and down the corridor to the waiting room. "I thought I told you guys everything there was to tell," Gus grumbled, but Buddy detected the familiar note of authority which being a witness to a crime often conferred.

"I'm not from Kingsburgh," Buddy explained. "I'm from Stanwich, where the Langes live."

"Oh," said Gus, shaking his head. "That was something. Well, what do you want to know?"

Now that Buddy had the man's attention, he was not precisely sure what he wanted from him. He could not fully accept the idea that Rambo's death was a suicide for two reasons. One was his gut reaction, which simply made him uneasy. The other, more specific reason was the observation by the medical examiner that Albert Rambo had dyed his hair on the day of his suicide. Despite all the other evidence of suicide, Buddy was plagued by that fact. He could not understand why any man, even a crazy man like Rambo, would dye his hair just before taking his own life. That fact and his gut feeling were making Buddy lose sleep. He was supposed to be on his way, right now, up to Mark's college, but he had kept his family waiting while he decided to make another stab at the motel owner's memory.

"I'm trying to find out if by chance, Rambo had any other visitors, if anything suspicious happened while he was staying at your place."

"Nope," said Gus. "The only one was the Lange woman. That I know of."

"Did you see any automobiles you didn't recognize in the area or anything like that?"

"Hey, mister," said Gus, "it's a motel. There's always cars there I don't know."

"What about when you went through the room?" Buddy persisted.

"Nothing," said Gus. "Anyhow, the police made a list of everything he left in that room. They kept all his stuff. They probably let you look at it."

"I've looked at it," said Buddy with a sigh.

"Well." Gus shrugged. "I wish I could help you."

"I know," said Buddy, "I know. Look, I've got to go away for a few days, take my son up to college, but I'll give you this card. It has my name and my number at the police station in Stanwich." Buddy had reached into his wallet and extracted a card, which Gus took and studied. Then Gus slipped it into his pocket.

"If you think of anything, even if it seems stupid or unimportant, would you just give me a call?"

"Sure, I'll call you," said Gus, "although I don't know why you'd care about this guy after what he done to that kid. I say good riddance."

Buddy grimaced. "I guess I've just been following him for so long I can't quite give up on it so easily."

"Okay," said Gus. He pulled his pocket watch out of his pants and consulted it. "It's almost time for them to bring the babies to their mothers," he said.

"I've got to be going anyway," said Buddy. "My wife and son are waiting for me."

Gus ground out his cigar carefully in the ashtray and put the unsmoked part back in his pocket. "I'll let you know if I think of anything."

"Thanks," said Buddy. He pressed the elevator button and watched as Gus passed through the swinging door into the maternity ward. A gaunt, unshaven young man in a rumpled sport coat burst out of the doors, passing Gus, sank into a chair in the lounge, and buried his face in his hands. Buddy trained his eyes on the floor indicator above the elevator door to avoid staring at the man huddled in the chair. As the soft bell rang, announcing the floor, Buddy heard behind him the chilling sound of the young man's muffled sobs.

CHAPTER FOURTEEN

A half-eaten tuna fish sandwich lay on the plate with a couple of potato chips beside it. Anna picked up the plate and put it on the counter beside the sink. At first, when they got home from the doctor's, Paul had said he wasn't hungry, but when she put the sandwich in front of him, he had managed to eat most of it. Then he had gone upstairs to rest.

I'm going to fatten you up, Anna thought. That's my next project now that I know you're all right. All right. She felt a thrill of happiness at the doctor's verdict, which had finally begun to register. He was going to be fine. Her strong, healthy son. And now that Rambo was dead, there was nothing more to fear from that quarter. For a moment Anna rested against the sink, counting her blessings. Her son was safe. She could stop worrying, despite what Thomas had said. Stop worrying and concentrate on putting her life back together.

A faint sound from the front of the house drew her attention. Tiptoeing through the dining and living room, she walked to the foot of the stairs and put her hand on the banister. She strained her ears to listen for him, but all was silent from the rooms above. He's all right, she repeated to herself. He's going to be fine. For a moment she wondered how Thomas would feel if he knew. She felt a sudden weakness, a need to share the news with him.

She stopped by the phone in the foyer, her hand hovering above the receiver. It would be a way to open up communication with him and to let him know that she still wanted to share her life with him. Then she remembered what he had said about Paul: that he was a stranger.

Shaking her head, Anna turned away from the phone and walked resolutely to the kitchen. She went over to the sink and with a fork began to scrape the sandwich and prod it through the garbage disposal, followed by the chips. She didn't really like using the garbage disposal. She hated the idea of those teeth inside her sink, so powerful that they could twist a piece of silverware like a coil of clay. But Tom had insisted on it when they had the kitchen redone a few years back, to make life easier for her. She sighed and shoved the last of the food through the rubber sleeve into the disposal. Then she turned on the water and flipped the switch.

The disposal went to work, its harsh din making Anna flinch, as it always did. She had seen forks tied into knots by that thing. She hated to think what it could do to human fingers. She noticed that a corner of bread was still in the sink. Gingerly she pushed it toward the opening of the disposal, ready to jerk her hand back as soon as it disappeared. Suddenly she felt a hand clap down on her shoulder, pushing her forward. She cried out and, bracing herself against the sink, jerked her head sharply around.

Edward Stewart drew back his hand apologetically and tried to shout her name above the racket. Regaining her balance, Anna leaned over and turned off the switch with a trembling hand.

"Edward!" Anna exclaimed, placing a hand on her chest as if to calm her heartbeat. "I didn't hear you come in."

"The front door was open."

"Oh," she said, exhaling a deep breath. "I was day-dreaming. Here, sit down, sit down." She cleared a pile of clean, folded dishtowels off one of her kitchen chairs. She glanced at her guest, who was wearing a business suit and tie. His complexion was pallid above his white collar. Seeing him sitting there in her kitchen unnerved her somewhat. It was the first time in their entire acquaintance that Edward had come calling on his own.

"Aren't you working today?" she asked.

"There was very little that needed my attention, so I came home."

Anna nodded, although she was surprised. She knew very well that Edward was a driven businessman, who spent as much time as possible at the office. She and Tom sometimes wondered when he and Iris ever saw each other.

"Anna," he said, "I came by to make sure that everything here was all right. I read the ghastly news in the paper this morning about what happened to you yesterday."

So that was it, Anna thought, both surprised and touched by his concern. Even the unflappable Edward had been shocked by this latest turn of events. Perhaps he was human after all. "It has been harrowing," she admitted. "It was so nice of you to come by."

"I . . . we had no idea you had been contacted by that monster," Edward said. "Whatever did he say to you?"

Anna rubbed her eyes with her hands. "Oh . . . this whole thing. He came up to me in the parking lot at the shopping center. Sunday, I guess it was."

"Sunday," Edward murmured, mentally calculating, "the day of our party."

"He said that he had something to tell me about Paul, that Paul was in some kind of danger. And he wanted money for the information."

"Good Lord," Edward said.

"I know," said Anna. "Are you sure I can't get you anything? A beer or a soda or something?"

"No, nothing," said Edward quickly. "Was that all he told you?"

"I begged him to tell me more, but he wouldn't."

Edward felt like laughing with relief, but he kept his expression grave. "But why did you go? Why didn't you just call the police?"

"Well, to be honest, I had had my own suspicions that there was something wrong."

Edward jerked forward in his chair. He began rapidly to massage the back of his left hand with his right. "I don't understand," he said.

"About Paul. He hasn't been . . . well, he's been ill, as you know. That incident at your house was not the only time. He's had these blinding headaches, nightmares. Ever since he got . . . home. I started to think . . . the worst. You can imagine. . . ."

"How terrible. But then the man was dead when you got there. He wasn't able to tell you any more."

"No," Anna admitted. "It was quite a shock. But I took Paul to the doctor this morning, and Dr. Derwent did a number of tests on him. He hasn't got all the results yet, but the doctor seemed to feel Paul is all right, that there is nothing serious to worry about."

"You must be relieved."

"I am," said Anna. "I am. It's a great relief."

"Well," said Edward, "it's probably best to just forget

about all this. Get life back to normal." He stood up from
his chair.

"You're right," she said.

"Please tell the boy that I stopped by to see about him."

"I will," Anna assured him. She found his interest in
Paul peculiar, but rather endearing, as if she were seeing a
side of him that she had never known existed. She had
always assumed that the Stewarts were childless by choice.
Edward's choice. Now, for a moment, she wondered about
it. Edward started walking through the house toward the
front door, and Anna followed him.

"And remember," he said, "if you ever need anything,
you can call on us. Iris and I are always—"

A wretched cry cut through their conversation. Anna
lunged for the staircase. "It's Paul," she cried.

"What's wrong?" Edward asked.

Anna was already taking the stairs two at a time. Edward
followed her up the steps, his breathing heavy.

Anna ran down the hall and threw open the door to her
son's room. Paul lay, fully clothed, on top of the bedspread,
whimpering and letting out intermittent moans. Anna sat
down on the bed beside him and took one of his clammy
hands in hers. With her free hand she pushed the damp hair
back off his forehead. The boy's eyes were open but glassy
and unseeing. Anna began to murmur to him.

Edward tiptoed up behind her. "Is he awake?" he asked
in a whisper.

Paul's whole head swiveled toward the sound of Edward's
voice as if he were blind.

"What was it?" Anna murmured. "Was it a dream?"

Paul's vacant eyes rested on Edward's face for a moment.
Then, all at once, he began to howl like an animal in a trap
and struggled to free himself from Anna's hands, crawling

away from her over the bed. "Help me," he cried. "Help." The word was barely recognizable, croaked out in a frantic voice.

"It's all right," Anna said soothingly. "It's all right."

The boy scrambled back and grabbed the bedpost, his dazed eyes locked to Edward's face as he cried out, "Help me, don't leave me."

"Paul," Anna cried, grabbing his wrists and shaking him, "wake up now. Stop it." Intent on her son, Anna did not notice her visitor standing frozen behind her, the sweat beaded on his ashen face, his eyes bulging. Like a man facing a rattler, Edward began to inch backward, his eyes trained on the dangerous beast in front of him.

"Please, Paul," Anna pleaded.

The boy's head rolled back, and he went limp in her grip. He seemed to awaken. He blinked at Anna and then relaxed against the headboard. "What's going on?" he said. She released her hold on his wrists.

"You had a dream . . . again."

"Oh," groaned Paul. He crawled slowly off the bed. "Oh. Oh, yeah," he said. "I remember."

"What do you dream of that scares you so?" Anna asked.

Paul walked over to the bureau and looked in the mirror. He began to flatten his unruly hair down with his hands, and then he pressed his palms to his forehead, his face screwed into a grimace. "It's always the same thing," he said.

"Can you remember it?"

"I remember a part of it. I know I'm lying on the ground. And there's this big black mass coming toward me, and there's a big golden bird flying over me, swooping down on me. It's got its claws out, you know. It's really scary."

"Is that it?" asked Anna.

"No. There's something else. A man coming toward me.

Leaning over me. Sometimes I think this really happened!"
he exclaimed, surprised at his own words.

"What's the man doing?"

"I don't know. But he's going to hurt me. I know that.
And I can almost see his face, but not quite."

Paul shivered and then shook his head. "Every time I get
to sleep . . ."

"It must be something troubling," Anna observed, "if it
keeps waking you up like that."

Paul shrugged.

"You really gave us a scare," said Anna.

The boy looked at her. "Who's us?"

"Mr. Stewart and I . . ." said Anna, turning around.
She stopped, seeing that Edward was no longer in the room.
"I guess he left. He probably saw how upset you were and
didn't want to intrude. He's very concerned about you,
Paul."

"Yeah." The boy nodded.

In the hallway Edward could hear their voices perfectly,
but he could not move. His arms felt stuck to his sides with
sweat, and his heart was hammering within his chest, so
hard that he was having trouble breathing. He felt the need
to urinate and a twisting in his stomach that made him feel
faint.

He wondered, as he listened to Anna soothe the boy, why
he had not realized it before. He had been so preoccupied
with Rambo that he had not really considered the boy. But
just because the child had not remembered him yet did not
mean that he never would. And if the memory surfaced and
he blurted it out . . . Edward felt a tightening in his chest
at the thought. Anna was a fanatic on the subject of that
child. Everyone in town knew it. If he were accused by that

urchin, she would never let it rest. She would pursue it to the bitter end and see him ruined before she was satisfied.

It was the kind of story that the newspapers would delight in. An important man like him, brought low by a child's accusation. There would be no end to it. All those who were jealous of him would laugh and gloat to see him cut down. It all was so clear now. Getting rid of Rambo was not protection enough.

Edward was almost swooning from the need to get some air, to sit down, to get out of there. He could not let anyone see him in this condition. Forcing one foot ahead of the other, he started quietly down the stairs. It was lucky, he thought, that he had been here and heard what he had. It had finally brought him to his senses, and none too soon.

As he descended the staircase with the lightest possible tread, he admitted that he had always known it, deep down inside. Ever since he had learned that the boy was coming back, he knew that he would have to silence him. At least that was now clear to him. He had no other choice.

A steady stream of people flowed by the glass doors of the phone booth in the skyscraper's lobby. Girls from the typing pool with magenta lips and high heels clacking laughed and chattered on their way to the subway. Sober, colorless men and a few women in business suits with briefcases, as well as the forest-green-liveried building staff, passed by without looking into the banks of darkened booths.

Thomas sat inside the middle booth, cushioned from the sound by the closed glass doors. It was close in the booth, and he knew he would have to make up his mind soon. Gail would come along soon, and once he was with her, he probably wouldn't call. By the time he got back to her apartment it would be too late.

He wished that he had not agreed to stay there again. It was obvious to him when he woke up that morning that his accepting her invitation implied something he didn't really feel. After tonight he was going to have to get a hotel room.

He didn't feel that Gail was trying to pressure him, one of her most appealing qualities to him. Still, he knew that she would not be pleased about his calling Anna.

He just wanted to talk to her. That was all. He wanted to find out how Paul had made out at the doctor's. And how Tracy was doing. He had left without even saying good-bye to her. Just those things, Thomas told himself, and I'll hang up. He lifted the receiver and rummaged in the briefcase on his knees for the credit card number.

Thomas dialed his home phone number and then waited for the operator to come on. Maybe Anna wouldn't even speak to him. It was possible. Thomas felt his stomach do a sickening flip-flop at the thought. He had never been able to stand it when Anna was angry at him. Part of the reason he had fallen in love with her was that she had such an even temper, and it was easy to make her laugh. On those rare occasions when she got angry, it turned him into a child again, helpless in the face of his mother's constant rages.

The operator interrupted his thoughts, scattering his demons. Thomas gave her the credit card number and waited for the phone to ring. You have a right to know about the children, he reminded himself. They're your children.

The phone rang a few times, and he felt a queer, sick feeling all through him. He was glad he was in a booth where he could sit because he didn't trust his legs to hold him up. He found himself half hoping that she wouldn't answer and then, as it rang again, panicked at the thought that he wouldn't be able to reach her.

"Hello."

Thomas started and thought of hanging up. He cleared his throat.

"Anna?"

"Oh," she said faintly. "Iii."

Her voice sounded guarded but not angry. Thomas took a deep breath and continued. "Am I taking you away from something?"

"Not really," she said. "I'm cleaning some vegetables."

He could imagine her there in the kitchen, looking over the windowsill into the backyard.

"What do you want?" she asked in a flat voice.

"Well, I . . . I've been wondering all day. Did you take Paul to the doctor's this morning?"

"Paul?" Thomas could hear the mistrust in her voice. "Yes, I took him."

"I was just curious. What did he say?"

"He said . . . I took him to Dr. Derwent, and he seemed to think that Paul is okay. He's going for some tests tomorrow, but he said there's not a tumor or anything."

"That was good news." He was surprised at the genuine relief he felt at her words.

Anna hesitated. "Yes, it is good news, but then this afternoon he had another bad dream. Woke up screaming and in a sweat. Well," she said coolly, "I'm sure that's not what you wanted to know."

He wanted to protest that he was interested, but the coldness in her voice daunted him. There was silence on the line for a few moments.

"How's Tracy?" he asked finally.

"She's all right. I explained to her that you and I had a disagreement, and she seemed to understand."

"Can I talk to her?"

"She's not here now. She went over to Mary Ellen's for dinner, and then she's going straight to the animal shelter."

"Oh, that's right," Thomas murmured. "She works tonight."

"How are you?" Anna asked after a pause.

"I'm all right."

"That's good," she said. He realized how unlike her it was not to question him further. He could feel, with a sense of panic, that the conversation was coming to an end.

"Anna," he blurted out, "I think we should talk."

She hesitated, and he winced at the silence. Then she answered carefully. "I think so, too."

Relief flooded him, and he felt like kissing the receiver. "Good," he said. "When?"

"I don't feel like discussing things on the phone," Anna said.

"No, not on the phone," he agreed hastily. "We should meet."

"All right," she said. He thought he heard relief in her voice also.

"How about tonight? Could you catch a train into the city? I'll make reservations at that Italian place we like on the West Side."

"Tonight?"

"Yeah. We can have dinner there and talk."

"I don't know about tonight," she said.

"Why not?" He withdrew, feeling wounded by her reluctance.

At her end Anna thought of Paul, who was listless after his day of tests and bad dreams. She did not like to leave him alone in the house. For a moment she was torn, but she realized that she could not use Paul as an excuse not to meet Tom. That would only drive them farther apart than ever. She had to make the effort.

"All right," she said. "I'll meet you at that place, Seventy-fourth Street, isn't it? I can be there by seven thirty."

"Good," he said. There was an awkward pause.

"Good-bye," she said.

"Bye." He hung up and sank back against the wall of the booth. His underarms were wet, and he felt weak, but the nauseated feeling had been replaced by one of anxious excitement. As he rested in the booth, he saw, through the glass doors, that Gail was leaning against the wall across the corridor, reading *The Wall Street Journal*. She looked up from the paper, and their eyes met. He tried to smile at her, but she gazed at him gravely for a moment. Her mouth was downturned, and there was an unfamiliar flush in her face. Then she lowered her eyes back to her paper.

Thomas could see her shoulders stiffen, as if she were readying herself for whatever he had to say. His relief at the phone conversation was tinged by guilt as he got up and opened the door to the phone booth. It was not going to be easy to tell her, he thought, that he was going to be meeting his wife for dinner, the night after their affair had begun.

CHAPTER FIFTEEN

"Please pack everything that's on this list," Iris asked the maid, handing her a cream-colored piece of notepaper. The maid looked at the list and nodded. "And then you can go," Iris continued. "We won't be needing you until I get back. Mr. Stewart plans to take his meals out and spend a few nights in the city."

Iris pulled her bathing cap over her hair, adjusted the top of her modest swimsuit, and dived into the pool. Edward, who was still dressed in his suit and tie, sat in a chair by the edge of the pool and watched her as she dutifully did her laps.

For once, he thought, her timing is perfect. I'll have the time and the opportunity to do something about the boy without her underfoot, volunteering their help to Anna in her time of need. By the time she gets back from the spa it will all be over. The realization relaxed him a little. He watched as Iris traversed the pool with even, determined strokes. She looked as stolid as a rowboat, thudding through the water.

At least she would not be questioning him about what he had done while she was gone, he thought. It was a well-established pattern with them that he told her virtually nothing of his activities, and she had always accepted that arrangement. It was the only thing that made living with her tolerable for him, he mused, eyeing her as one might eye an ill-favored animal that could perform one good trick. Iris pulled herself up, breathing heavily at his end of the pool, and began to peel off her bathing cap.

"If you kept your legs straight when you kicked," he observed, "you would not find it so difficult to swim such a short distance."

Iris sighed and stared out over the pool's surface.

Lorraine reappeared in the doorway, and Edward looked up at her. "Mrs. Lange's here," she said impassively.

Anna followed the maid out onto the terrace, and Edward started at the sight of her.

"Hello, you two," said Anna, walking over beside Edward's chair.

"Please sit down," he said, getting up.

"Hello, Anna," said Iris, her face lighting up at the unexpected sight of her friend.

"I can't stay," said Anna. "I've come to ask a favor."

"Of course," said Iris. "What is it?"

Edward urged the chair on her, and Anna sat down on the edge of the seat. "Tom called," she said, "and he wants me to meet him in the city for dinner."

"That sounds romantic," said Iris, picking up a towel from the edge of the pool and patting herself dry.

"Not really," said Anna with a grimace. "We had a pretty big fight last night."

"Did you make it up?" Iris asked.

Anna shifted in her chair. She was used to confiding in Iris, but she felt uncomfortable telling her marital problems in front of Edward, even though she assumed that Iris shared their confidences with her husband. "Well," she said, "he stayed in the city last night."

"Anna, no!" Iris exclaimed.

"So it's important," Anna went on hurriedly, "that I meet him. We have really got to work a few things out."

"Of course you do," Iris agreed. "How can I help, though?"

"It's Paul," said Anna. "I had him to the doctor today."

"Oh no," said Iris. "Is he all right?"

"He seems to be," said Anna. "Didn't Edward tell you?"

Iris looked surprised. "I didn't have a chance," Edward said hurriedly.

"Anyway," Anna continued, "he's tired tonight from all the tests, and I'm worried about leaving him alone there."

Iris bit her lip and grimaced. "I'm supposed to leave for my health spa tonight. I guess I could put it off until tomorrow."

"No, don't do that," said Anna. "I just wondered if Lorraine or anyone was going to be here; in case he needed anything, he could call."

"Well, Edward will be home, I think," Iris ventured, looking uncertainly at her husband.

Edward sat up very straight in his chair. "What about your daughter?" he asked.

"She's at the animal shelter until around ten," Anna explained.

"Well, I should be home," said Edward. "Tell him to call me if he needs anything."

"Thanks so much," said Anna. "I'd hate to have to tell Tom I couldn't come on account of Paul. That would not go over too well."

Iris's eyes were sad and worried. "Anna, I didn't know

there were problems between you two. I feel just awful about it."

Anna dismissed the subject with a shake of her head. "When will you be back from the spa?" Anna asked her friend.

"Sunday," said Iris, stretching out the bathing cap in her hand.

"Yogurt and massages, eh?" Anna said, teasing her.

Iris looked slightly pained. "It's not really like that."

"I'm only kidding you," Anna assured her. "I know they work you pretty hard at those places. I hope you'll enjoy it, though. Of course, we're all going to miss you," she said, turning to Edward for confirmation.

Edward gave her a tight smile of agreement.

"Well, I feel better," said Anna. "I'm going to go get ready." She bent over and gave Iris a pat on the shoulder. "Call me as soon as you get back," she said. She straightened up and smiled at Edward. "Thanks for everything. I'm sorry about this afternoon," she said. "Honestly, he's been so jumpy and upset. I didn't mean to abandon you like that."

Edward waved off her apology. "Think nothing of it," he said.

Anna smiled at both of them and then started off around the side of the house.

"Wait up," said Iris. "I'll walk around with you and go in through the solarium. I want to go take a shower."

Edward's eyes flickered as he watched the two women go off together around the side of the house. The boy would be alone in the house tonight. It was more than he had hoped for, and it had fallen right into his lap. He had to act quickly and without any hesitation. Edward's eyelid began to twitch, but he ignored it as he began to formulate a simple, brutal plan for the night ahead.

Points of light danced across the cut surface of the topaz earrings as Anna twisted her head from side to side, studying her reflection in the mirror. The earrings were her favorites—a gift from Thomas on their third anniversary. When she had protested his extravagance, he had laughed and told her between kisses not to get too attached to them, in case they had to hock them someday.

She had hesitated about wearing them tonight. In a way they seemed a poignant reminder of a happier time. But now that she had them on, they looked right. Be optimistic, she thought. Maybe there are better times ahead. She was about to turn away from the mirror when she remembered her perfume. He had chosen it for her. With all the deliberateness of a courtesan, she applied the scent to her pulse points. Then she straightened her dress and started toward the stairs.

She could hear the television in the den when she came down to the foyer. Following the sound, she went down the hall and into the den. Paul was curled up on the sofa, staring at the TV set, his head resting in his hand.

"I'm going to go now, Paul," she said. "Are you sure you'll be all right?"

The boy nodded, his eyes trained on the television.

"Tracy should be back around ten," said Anna. "If you need anything, Mr. Stewart will be home tonight. Just give him a call. His number is by the phone."

The boy continued to stare at the flickering images in front of him. "Okay," he said absently. Then he turned to look at her. "You look nice," he said.

Anna's anxious face broke into a beaming smile at the unexpected compliment. "Thanks," she said. "I tried."

"It was because of me, wasn't it?" the boy said.

"What?" Anna asked, surprised.

"He left."

"No," said Anna quickly. "It was something between us."

Paul looked back at the TV set. "He hates me," he said simply.

Anna felt shocked for a moment. Then she walked over to the control panel on the set and turned it off. The room was suddenly quiet. She stood in front of the set and faced the boy.

"That's not true," she said. "He doesn't hate you."

Paul shook his head. "He wishes I never came back," he said offhandedly. "That's why he left." He stuck out his chin at her, defying her to disagree with him.

Anna looked at him blankly for a moment, remembering Thomas's angry words about Paul and not wanting to reveal her thoughts by her expression.

The boy nodded, as if satisfied.

"Wait a minute, Paul," she said. "Your father . . . You don't know what it was like for him. For all of us. All those years of worrying and wondering . . . after you disappeared."

The boy's face was stony.

"It was terrible," she said. "Agony. We never knew from one day to the next."

"Maybe he started thinking he was rid of me," said Paul casually.

"Rid of you?" Anna flared. "How could you think that of your father?"

Paul did not look at her.

Anna shook her head. "I'm sorry. You don't really know him. He doesn't always say what he feels. But you . . . you meant the world to him. Why, when you were born . . . oh, he was in heaven," she said, seizing upon a memory that she was sure of. "You never saw anyone so happy."

"He's not happy now," said Paul. "I don't think he wanted me to come back."

"No," Anna protested, "I don't think he . . ." She stared unseeingly at the shelves of books above the sofa, trying to find the accurate description of her husband's feelings. The boy was silent, but there was a tension in his body as he waited for her to speak.

"You see, I always believed that you would come back to us. And he . . ." She groped for the right word. The fair word. "He couldn't."

Paul looked at her curiously.

"I remember," she said. "I don't recall when it was exactly. He began to think . . . he would say to me that I should try to prepare myself for the worst. But I always said that I thought you would come back. He couldn't understand how I was so sure of that." Anna shook her head, her eyes far away. "One day we argued about your room. He wanted me to clean out your room, and I wouldn't. He said it was unnatural to leave it the way it was and we could use the room." Anna bit the inside of her mouth and was silent, for a moment, her eyes darkening at the recollection.

"God, I was so furious at him. We hadn't really talked about you for a long time before that. But I guess I knew how he felt, although we never discussed it. Until this one day—it was just after one of your birthdays—and he started in on how we should clean up the room. I wouldn't have any part of it. I hated him for it. I remember that very well. He went upstairs, and I could hear him rummaging around, throwing things in boxes, and I just sat there in the living room, as if I were made out of stone. He began bringing boxes down to the basement, and I could hear him taking things out to the garbage cans in the garage. And I was just sitting there, watching all this and thinking that I would never forgive him for it." She gazed over at Paul, who was watching her intently.

"He was working, not saying anything, and then he came down the stairs, carrying a box under one arm, and under the other he was holding this elephant. It was a fuzzy blue elephant, stuffed, that he had bought for you when you were born. He brought it right to the hospital for you. He couldn't even wait until you got home. So he came downstairs, carrying this thing. And he was crying," she said quietly. "Tears were just streaming down his face." Anna's eyes filled suddenly at the memory. "He didn't say anything to me, and I was too angry to care. I remember thinking, Serves you right. You don't deserve to have your son back."

Paul studied her face as she remembered that moment. There was an expression in her eyes like that of someone trying to make out a sign from far away. She shook her head sadly.

"So why did he leave now?" the boy asked softly.

Anna squinted ahead of her. She hesitated for a minute. Then she said, "I think he's afraid."

"Of what?"

Anna looked quizzically at the boy. "I don't know," she said. "I don't think he ever expected things to turn out right."

Paul and Anna looked soberly at each other. Then Paul nodded.

"Well," she said, "I guess I'll go." She started to walk out, and then she turned back and flipped the TV back on.

"Good luck," said Paul.

Anna wanted to lean over and clasp the boy in her arms, but his wary glance forestalled her. She settled for kissing him lightly on the hair. Then, with a wave and a crooked smile, she headed for the door.

"It's getting dark earlier and earlier," Iris said wistfully as she gazed out the library windows. "I hate to see the summer end."

Edward looked at his watch. "Isn't it about time you were going?" He picked up a letter opener and began to tap it impatiently on the surface of his desk.

"As soon as Lorraine puts my bag in the car." Iris frowned and looked intently at her husband.

Edward squirmed a little under her gaze. "Is anything wrong?" he asked coolly.

"I just . . ." She faltered and then continued hastily. "I hope you'll be all right here while I'm gone."

Edward stifled the urge to laugh in her face. "I'll be fine," he said. "All you need to worry about is getting rid of some of that." He pointed the letter opener at Iris's stomach.

Iris sighed. "All right," she said. "What are you going to do tonight?"

"I'll probably work on my boats," he said offhandedly.

"All ready, ma'am," said Lorraine, coming into the library.

"Thank you, Lorraine." Iris turned to her husband. "Well, I guess I'll be going. I'll see you on Sunday."

Edward nodded and smiled at her.

"Don't forget about Paul," said Iris, turning back to him.

"What?" he said sharply.

"I told Anna he could call if he needed anything. Remember?"

"Oh, yes," he said. "I won't forget. Don't look so worried."

Iris hesitated as if she had more to say, but then she turned and left the library. Edward waited until he heard the slam of her car door and the sound of the car leaving the driveway. Then he looked out the library window toward the windmill. He could not see it from the house, but in his mind he visualized it. Tapping the letter opener on his palm, he went over all his tools in his mind, trying to decide which one to use. The idea was to use a tool that a burglar might have. He would break into the house, take care of the boy, and then mess the place up. Ransack it and take a few valuables, to make it look as if the boy had been killed in the course of a robbery. It was simple, and it made sense. These houses were isolated and clearly affluent. There was always the danger of burglary. A crowbar might be a good weapon, he thought, but it was large to carry. He didn't own a gun. He had thought of a chisel, but it did not seem part of a burglar's equipment. The best bet was probably a knife. In the windmill he had a set of large hunting knives he sometimes used. That would do, he decided. He could put it in a sheath under his jacket. It would be messy, but that was all right. He kept a change of clothes in the windmill anyway. He would just wait for a little while and then . . .

Lost in thought, he did not hear Lorraine enter the room and did not notice her until she appeared beside him like a dark ghost. He jumped a little as she said his name.

"What is it?" he asked.

"My brother is here to pick me up," the maid said apologetically.

"Fine," said Edward. "We'll see you next week then."

He walked with her to the door after she had picked up her suitcase in the foyer. He waited in the gloom until the taillights of Lorraine's brother's car had disappeared. Sweat gathered under his arms as he stood there in the silent house. He was keenly aware of each passing minute. His blood was singing in his ears, but the rest of the house was tomblike. Without bothering to turn on a light, he walked back through the house, headed out the patio doors and into the night.

CHAPTER SIXTEEN

Paul studied the *TV Guide* as the sounds of Anna's car faded away. He got up and stood in front of the control panel for a few minutes, staring at the images on the screen. Then he turned the set off. There was nothing on that he wanted to watch. He wandered through the house to the living room, where he sank into a chair and picked up a magazine from the brass rack beside it. He thumbed the pages restlessly and then dropped it back in the rack and got up again.

Anna had made him some dinner before she left, but he still felt hungry. He went into the kitchen and opened the refrigerator. Help yourself, she always told him. And there certainly was plenty to eat. His mother's refrigerator had never looked like that, except for the freezer, which had stacks of frozen dinners in trays in turquoise boxes with pictures of the food on the front. Dorothy Lee always worked the three to eleven shift at the hospital; he'd heat one up and eat it quick so he could be done before his father came around. Paul looked down at the shelf and saw a piece of cream pie left in a piepan. He could have eaten the whole thing standing there, but he felt uncomfortable about it. After getting out a knife and plate, he cut off about a third of the piece, only an inch across the back, and ate that. It was gone in an instant, and he thought about taking more; but he closed the door instead.

After taking his plate and utensils to the sink, he washed and dried them and put them back in their places. He surveyed the kitchen and then hung up the towel, satisfied that no one would be able to tell that he had taken anything.

The house seemed very still and strange to him, and for a moment he wished, more than anything, that he had someone to talk to. He thought of Sam and then tried to dismiss the thought of his lost pet from his mind.

He walked idly from room to room, looking at the furniture, the plants, and the pictures. It was like something from a magazine, he thought, or that you saw on TV. Probably if anyone from Hawley had seen him in this house, they would have thought he was the luckiest person on earth, living in a place like that.

Paul wandered to the living room window and pulled back the drapes. He looked out into the darkness. Every day he thought about running away. Every single day. He could just pack his few things in his bag and go. Maybe if he got away from here, the headaches would stop. And no one would miss him. Well, the mother maybe.

He sighed, realizing that he wouldn't know where to run. And he had no money, so he couldn't get far. There was probably money in this house, but he didn't want to steal from them. As much as he hated to admit it to himself, he was afraid to run. Yet he cringed at the thought of staying. I don't belong here, he thought.

With an impatient gesture he dropped the curtain and turned back into the room, to look for something to do.

Pressed against the window, the boy's pale face appeared to be melting against the pane. Edward's cold eyes focused

on the mournful visage as he crouched below the porch,
looking up at him. He had been making a circuit of the
house, scouting the best point of entry when he saw the
boy's face appear at the window. For a moment he thought
the boy had heard him in the yard, but as he watched, trying
to quiet his racing heartbeat, he could see that the boy was
not searching the yard but simply staring, his thoughts far
away.

Edward's knees ached as he crouched there, his pants
cutting into his legs. The indignity of the position made him
feel angry and impatient. He wished the kid would hurry up
and get away from the window. He did not feel like hiding
in the damp grass much longer. He wished to be done with it
and safely back in his studio.

The curtain dropped, and Edward breathed more freely as
he rose to his feet. He knew how he was going to get in. At
knee level there was a set of windows which opened into the
basement. He had seen them from the inside and knew that
they were latched with only a simple sliding fastener. It
would be easy enough to open one of them and slide himself
in. With the aid of his penlight he had seen a sturdy chair
below one of them. That was the window he would choose.
As he stole around the house to the window, he repeated his
plan to himself. The basement adjoined a playroom. He
would go through the door into the playroom and up the
stairs into the house. Edward reached the window that he
wanted and bent down beside it. He slipped his knife blade
through the side of the frame and began to worry it around
until he caught the hook. Carefully he jimmied it with the
knife point. After a moment the fastening began to move.

Paul passed by the door to the playroom stairs and
stopped, remembering that there was a stereo down there.

The silence of the empty house oppressed him, and he thought that perhaps some music would help. He opened the door and started down the stairs. An unfamiliar noise reached him, and he stopped on the steps, listening. It was quiet. Hearing things, he thought. Baby.

He wondered, as he shuffled down the stairs, how the big reunion was going. That story she had told about the father's carrying down the elephant had made him feel prickly at the back of his neck. He thought that the elephant seemed familiar. Maybe the father wasn't so bad. The mother was nice, and she liked him.

There was no telling why people liked each other. He had never been able to figure out his parents . . . the Rambos. His father had always been weird and crazy, although Dorothy Lee never said anything bad about him. Still, it had been so humiliating in school and all. Paul had actually been relieved to find out that Albert wasn't his real father. For a minute Paul felt a wave of pity, followed quickly by revulsion, at the thought of his father's hanging himself all alone in that hotel room. What a way to end up.

Paul cocked his head to one side and read the titles of the edges of the record covers. Most of the good records were Tracy's and they were up in her room. He didn't want to go up there. But there were a few good things in the playroom record pile. Paul picked out an old Beatles album and examined it. He didn't remember them; but he had heard of them, and he knew a lot of their songs. After putting the record on the turntable, he plugged in a set of earphones and separated them, planning to put them over his ears and lie back on the rug to listen. Just then he noticed, lying on the bookshelf above the record cabinet, a pair of fat brown leather books with photos sticking out under the covers. He reached up curiously and pulled the top one down, still holding the earphones in his hand as the lyrics of "Norwegian Wood" squawked from the headset. He opened the unwieldy book, and an envelope of snapshots fell out. The album was full of photographs neatly mounted and captioned. Crossing his legs Indian style, Paul opened the album on his knees and then settled the headset over his ears. Absorbed in the pictures, he did not see the door of the playroom across the room opening behind him a millimeter at a time.

The bright faces of the people in the pictures smiled, heedless of their images, which were fading with time. They were like people waving from the deck of a ship which was sinking noiselessly into the sea. Paul turned the pages carefully, tapping his foot and gazing at the photographs. There were pictures of Thomas and Anna toasting at their wedding and shy, smiling pictures of them, tanned shoulders touching, on a honeymoon in Florida. She was always smiling out at the camera, while Thomas kept his eyes on her face.

On the next page a baby appeared, and Paul realized, with a start, that it was himself. He traced the outline of the strange baby's head, which the infant struggled to lift from a blanket. There were pictures of him in every imaginable pose, one or the other of his parents holding him, in and around a house which was not this one. He laughed out loud at a picture captioned "Paul's 2nd birthday," in which he, a toddler now, was perched behind a lit cake, sporting, at an angle, a shiny, pointed foil hat. An older, dark-haired boy behind him was blowing a noisemaker right into his eager, squinting face. The music drummed in his ears as the Beatles sang about seeing a face they couldn't forget.

A shadow fell like a scythe's blow over the page, darkening the cheery faces in one swipe. Paul's head jerked up as he felt the presence behind him. He yanked off the earphones and twisted around to stare at the figure which loomed above him. For a moment he stared up, bewildered. Then he spoke.

"What are you doing here?" he said.

Tracy cocked her head and looked down at the book he was holding. "I brought you something," she said

Paul looked at her in confusion as she shrugged her backpack off her shoulders and carefully opened it. She reached in and pulled out the struggling, crying gray-and-black-striped cat.

"Sam!" Paul exclaimed. "Where'd you get him?" He lifted the animal from her grasp and crushed it to his chest. The cat protested angrily and leaped away from him.

"He turned up tonight at the animal shelter," Tracy announced with a satisfied smile. "The vet let me come home early, to bring him."

Paul's gaze lingered on the cat, which had dived under the sofa.

"Thanks," he said softly, not trusting his voice.

"That's okay." Tracy flopped down on the daybed. "You looking at those old pictures?"

Paul nodded.

Behind them the door to the playroom began to close, imperceptibly slowly.

"Would you like to walk a little?" asked Thomas, stuffing his wallet into his pocket as they left the restaurant.

"Yes, why don't we?" Anna agreed.

"I ate too much," said Tom. "The food there is always good."

Anna murmured agreement, although she had noticed

during dinner that he hardly made a dent in the meal on his plate.

They set off walking down Columbus Avenue, joining the meandering stream of pedestrians taking the night air on the West Side's most fashionable avenue. Although it was warm, it was not humid, and a few stars were visible above the city sky.

The dinner conversation had been halting but polite. Anna felt, as she faced him over the table, that she really understood the meaning of the word "estranged." Now, however, as they made their way side by side down the avenue, she felt more normal, their steps meshing neatly, turning automatically at the same corners, even though they had no stated destination. They both heeded the flashing "Don't walk" signs, while the New Yorkers around them spilled contemptuously into the intersections.

Anna stole a glance at her husband's profile as they waited on one corner. He had ordinary, rather blunt features except for his eyes, which were clear and expressive. The expression in them now was one of anxiety and a trace of sadness. She felt an impulse to slip her arm through his, but she restrained herself.

"Shall we go over to Lincoln Center?" he asked. "It's only a few blocks down."

Anna nodded. "I'd like to see the fountain."

They walked along in awkward silence, occasionally glancing at each other. "Is that a new tie?" Anna asked him.

Thomas reached up and fingered the knot at his throat. "Yes." He put a hand lightly on her elbow. "Light's changed," he said.

Anna noticed a slightly guilty expression on his face as propelled by the pressure of his hand, she crossed the street.

"I didn't pack too well," he said when they reached the

opposite curb. "I've got to go to Boston tomorrow on the ten o'clock shuttle, and I don't have the clothes I need for the trip."

"Are you going for long?" she asked coolly.

"Just overnight."

She stifled the impulse to say that he should have asked her to bring what he needed. He left you, she reminded herself. Walked out, remember. But she could not muster her anger against him. He seemed vulnerable to her. His hand burned on her arm.

"Where are you staying?" she asked.

"In Boston?"

"No, here."

Thomas squirmed visibly at the question. "On the East Side. Not far from work."

Anna nodded stiffly. They crossed the street and climbed the steps to the plaza in front of Lincoln Center. Anna caught her breath as she always did at the sight. The murals in the opera house were a giddy burst of color, the chandeliers sparkling through the huge panels of glass. In the center of the plaza ringed by theaters, a round fountain gave off sprays of water and light. Thomas and Anna walked slowly toward the gushing fountain.

A young couple sat on the wide granite lip of the fountain, embracing, while two short-haired, mustachioed men, one in stylish khaki, the other in black cotton, stared into the plumes of water as they talked, one pressing the other's arm discreetly as he made his point.

Thomas gave Anna a tight, pained smile and offered her a seat on the fountain's edge.

"Thanks," she said.

A silence fell between them, and Anna had the sense that their time was running out without their having made any progress. She cast about in her mind for some way of reaching him without starting a fight.

Suddenly Tom spoke. "I was really relieved to hear about Paul today," he said.

Anna looked at him in surprise. It was the first mention of the boy between them that evening. She thought of just agreeing with him but decided to plunge in instead. "We talked about you before I came down tonight."

"You and Paul?" he asked.

"Yes. He thinks you hate him."

Thomas closed his eyes, and Anna could see the pain in the grim lines around his mouth. He swallowed hard, as if trying to ingest some bitter tonic.

"I told him that wasn't true," she said.

Thomas looked at her in surprise. "You did?"

Anna nodded. "I was trying to explain to him. I was telling him about you. About when he was born and how you adored him. Things like that."

Thomas stared out across the empty plaza, his eyes pained and lonely. "I don't hate him," he said. "Poor kid." He was quiet for a long time. Anna watched him helplessly, wishing he would look at her. Finally he spoke. "I think I hate myself," he said.

"Tom," she protested, "don't say that."

He shook his head. "You don't know how I feel," he said. "It's different for you."

"What's different?" she said.

"Oh, you. You were always so sure he'd come back. Always believing he was still alive. Hopeful. Even the tiniest thing would make you hopeful." He turned and looked at her for the first time. "I never was hopeful, Anna. I never expected to see that boy again."

"But we had no way of knowing. Nobody did."

"I gave up on him, Anna. My own son." Thomas sighed and bent forward at the waist. He looked away from his wife and held himself around the middle, as if he were going to throw up. "When I see him, I feel so sick," he said. "I don't know. I feel so guilty—"

"Guilty! Tom!" Anna exclaimed. "You have no reason to feel guilty."

"I did love him," he said. "It's not as if I didn't."

"I know that," she said. "He knows it, too. I'm sure he does. Or he will. It will just take a little time."

"I could never stand the way you were always looking for some good sign, finding reasons to hold on to," he said.

"I know," she said. "I just had to."

"Sometimes," he said, "I wanted to scream at you because of it. But how could I? You were the noble one, the one who refused to give up."

"You never told me," she said. "We never talked about it."

"I know."

She groped for the words to try to explain it to him. "I didn't do it to be noble," she said. "I couldn't go on without hope."

Thomas reached over and put his hand on hers. They sat quietly at the fountain's edge. The meshing of their fingers was like a circuit completed. The consolation, the connection in their touch made Anna feel a sudden, fierce desire for him—her husband, her man. She closed her eyes and felt the heat throughout her body. She imagined turning to him, burying her face in the curve of his neck, feeling his hands on her again. She was trying to think of a way to say, "Come home." And then she realized that "Come home" was all she needed to say. She did not think she could speak aloud. She decided she could manage to say it in a whisper.

Suddenly Thomas released her hand. "That's not all I have to feel guilty about," he said quietly.

The portentous note in his voice was an icy bath over her. She sat up straight and stared at him. "What does that mean?"

The lovers who were sitting at the other side of the fountain got up and, arms around each other, began to stroll across the plaza. Thomas watched them walking away.

"Tom?"

"I don't know how to tell you this. But I feel I have to. I don't want this secret between us. I'd always be afraid you might accidentally find out." He licked his lips nervously. "I've been . . . There's been another woman," he said.

Anna rocked back on the granite ledge as if he had struck her a blow in the face. In all her concerns for him and for the children, the possibility that he had someone else had never even crossed her mind.

"I don't know why I did it," he was saying. "I was feeling lonely and angry at you. I couldn't talk to you. This sounds like a lot of excuses, I know."

"Who is it?" said Anna dully.

"It doesn't matter," said Thomas. "You don't know her."

"I see," said Anna. The young couple had traversed about half the plaza when suddenly the man stepped back and slid his arm around the girl's waist as he lifted her hand in the air. The girl looked momentarily startled, and then she laughed. The two began to waltz across the plaza, to music of their own devising.

"So that's why you left us?" said Anna, placing her pocketbook under her arm and sliding off the edge of the fountain to her feet.

Thomas, who had been rubbing his eyes with his hand,

looked at her in surprise. Anna was staring at him coldly, a pulse beating visibly in her neck. "No," he said.

"I can't believe this of you, Tom," she said. "But I'm not about to stand in your way. You can run off with your mistress for all I care."

"Wait a minute," Tom protested. "What are you doing?"

"I'm going home," she spit out at him. "To my children."

Tom stepped in front of her and blocked her way, trying to get into her line of sight. "Anna," he said, "you don't understand. It happened. Yes. But I don't intend to continue it. I felt I had to be honest with you. But I'm telling you it's over now, I want to come home, to you and the kids."

Anna brushed by him angrily. "I don't want to talk about it," she muttered. She dodged his open arms and started walking quickly across the plaza, passing the dancing lovers, who did not look at her. Anna descended the steps and held up her arm for a taxi. Through the blur of tears she saw the lighted sign of an empty cab getting closer to her.

Thomas approached her side. "Don't I get another chance?" he asked softly. "After all these years? I'm asking you to forgive me. Ah, I shouldn't have told you in the first place."

Anna glared at him but he stuck out his chin stubbornly. "I wanted to be honest with you," he said. "I thought you would be able to forgive me," he said.

Anna closed her eyes briefly, and then she looked at him. "I can't take any more right now," she said.

"We have to talk, Anna. I have to go to Boston tomorrow. I'm not going to be able to think straight for worrying about this."

"I can't help that," she said. "I have to do some thinking

myself." She got into the cab and slammed the door behind her. As the taxi pulled away from the curb, he reached out forlornly, as if to hold on to it, and then he disappeared from sight in the tangle of traffic and people.

CHAPTER SEVENTEEN

With anxious, stealthy movements Edward pulled the cellar window closed and crept across the lawn toward his own property, silently cursing the starlight. The sudden blaring of the stereo from inside the house startled him. He stopped for a moment, perspiring profusely, and waited. Then he continued on, his hand wound around the handle of the knife under his shirt.

It had crossed his mind, as he hid behind the doorway, prepared to strike, that he could try to kill them both. He considered it and then decided against it. It was too messy, too dangerous. Still, the rage he had felt when he saw the girl come in with the cat had almost been enough to propel him through the door and into a frenzied attack on the two of them. Everything had been perfectly calculated, and then the stupid girl had ruined it.

Despite his show of restraint, Edward still felt the anger churning inside him at the way his plans had been thwarted. He had been ready. Ready to finish this business. Now he was left with his anger, his frustration. Edward made a wide circle around the back of his house as he headed for the windmill. He could see the blades jutting up black against the night sky, beckoning him. There was still time. He would find a way to do it tomorrow. He tried to keep his mind on that as he skulked along, his jaw and his fists clenched.

Edward reached the door of the windmill and pulled it open. He had imagined himself all day, coming back here, hiding his weapon and changing his clothes, his business done. If only, he thought, it had been done. If only he had gotten it over with.

Stepping into the cool confines of the windmill, Edward pulled the knife from under his shirt and threw it onto a workbench, where it landed with a clatter. Then he turned back to close the door behind him.

"Edward."

Edward whirled around, slamming the windmill door shut, his face drained of color. Standing in the shadows beneath the loft, kneading her hands together and smiling tremulously at him, was Iris.

"Iris, what are you doing here?" he demanded in a shout. His whole body was shaking, his eyes bulging at the sight of her.

"I'm . . . I'm sorry," said Iris, recoiling at his outburst. "I didn't mean to startle you."

Edward stared at her, his mind racing. The thought that he might have walked into the windmill covered with blood and been surprised by her filled him with a terror that left him speechless. It didn't happen, he reminded himself. She didn't see anything. He tried to calm his pounding heart with that thought, but he was still unable to speak, his eyes glued to her puzzled face.

"I'm sorry," she repeated. "I thought you'd be here when I got back. Then, when you weren't, I just waited."

Edward shook his head as if he didn't understand, not trusting his voice.

"Where were you?" she asked. "Why did you have that knife?"

His natural impulse was to scream at her, to drive her from the windmill with a shaking fist. But he knew instinctively that she would only wonder more about what he had been doing. He needed to be calm, to invent an excuse. He needed time to think. He kept picturing the Langes' house, the boy in the playroom, and how close he had come to his aim.

"Whatever were you doing out there with a knife?" Iris asked. "Did you hear something outside?"

Edward looked at her with a sudden sense of relief. That was it. She had provided his excuse. "Yes," he said. "I thought I did. I thought I heard a prowler. So I picked up this knife and went out to look. That's . . . that's why it startled me so to find you here. For a second I thought that whoever it was had sneaked in here." Sweat was pouring from his forehead now, but he knew that he was safe. She was looking at him with anxious, sympathetic eyes.

"Did you see anyone out there?" Iris asked.

"No, no," said Edward finally, collapsing against the counter. "Nothing. It must just have been the wind. Or my imagination."

"I don't know, Edward. Maybe we should call the police."

"That's hardly necessary," he said. "I'm sure it was nothing."

Iris had another thought. "Paul!" she exclaimed. "He's all alone over there."

"I told you. There was no one outside."

"Perhaps we should call and check."

"Iris," Edward demanded, "what are you doing here? I thought you had gone to the spa."

It was Iris's turn to look first surprised and then uneasy. "Well, I was on my way," she said. "And then I came back. I'd been wanting to talk to you, and I thought I'd come back."

"Why didn't you just phone me?" he asked, as if it were the obvious solution that only the simpleminded would overlook. He was regaining his composure quickly now. It slipped only when he saw the mental image of himself bloodied from the kill and surprised by Iris. But he forced the thought down. You're safe, he reminded himself.

Iris bit her lip nervously. "I thought we should talk in person. Edward, I've been thinking a lot lately about us . . . about our marriage."

Edward tried to stifle the disgust which rose in him at her words. She wants to talk about our marriage now. It was almost laughable. He knew right away what had caused this crisis. Anna was having problems with her marriage, so naturally Iris had to jump on the bandwagon. Monkey see, monkey do. Sometimes, he thought, she is really a stupid woman. He assumed a long-suffering expression and stared at her. "Iris, what are you talking about?"

"This is so hard to say," Iris continued, looking pained and almost fearful as she spoke. "I don't think I am really making you happy anymore. If I ever did. I feel this very strongly lately. You deserve a wife who can be the way you want her to be."

Edward could scarcely believe his ears. The incongruity of her earnest confession made him feel almost amused, but he kept his expression grave. The trembling in his body had subsided by now, and he could barely concentrate on her words for the relief he felt for his narrow escape. All he wanted to do was to get rid of her, propel her back onto the road toward her spa, and sit down to plan his next move.

"Iris," he said, "is this really the time and the place to discuss this? Can't it wait until you get back?"

"I suppose it could," said Iris miserably. "I'm just—"

"I'm tired," said Edward. "I was looking forward to a peaceful evening, working in the windmill."

"But I feel sometimes that you would be better off without me," Iris blurted out.

Edward looked at her with an expression of amazement, as one would at a display of exceptionally bad manners. "I haven't complained about our marriage," he said coolly. "Why must you bring this up now? Must I spend my life reassuring you that your position as my wife is secure? I think that shows a rather pitiable lack of self-confidence, Iris. I am satisfied with our marriage. I see no reason for you to doubt that."

Iris sighed, and her shoulders slumped. "I suppose you're right," she said.

"Why don't you get on the road now, so that you can arrive at the spa before it is too late? It's not a good idea to be driving late at night. Go ahead now, and don't worry anymore about this. As far as I am concerned, everything between us is as it always has been."

Iris sighed again, and nodded, and walked toward the door of the windmill.

"Shall I accompany you to your car?" he asked.

"That's not necessary," said Iris.

"I think I had better," said Edward smoothly. "I'm still a little apprehensive, even though the noises turned out to be nothing."

"All right," said Iris.

Edward took a look behind him before he closed the door on the windmill. The hunting knife lay on the counter where he had dropped it. Tonight, once he was sure she was gone, he would sit down and make another plan to get rid of the boy. He could not stand any more delays. He had to do it right away, before Iris decided that she had had enough of her spa and wanted to come home for a second honeymoon. He shuddered at the thought, remembering the tedium of their first honeymoon. Putting her off would be no problem, he reminded himself. Meanwhile, he had more important things on his mind.

"Watch your step in the dark," he called out to her as he shut the windmill door behind her.

The plaintive harmonies of the Bee Gees greeted Anna as she opened the door to the house and walked in. She saw Tracy's jacket draped on one of the dining room chairs. Home early, Anna thought. She had not seen any lights on upstairs as she came up to the house. She walked over to the door beyond the kitchen which led down to the playroom.

"I'm home," she called out.

"Hi . . ." The voices of both children floated back up the stairs. Anna raised her eyebrows in surprise and then smiled. She walked over to the refrigerator and opened the door. There was an open bottle of club soda on the shelf. She pulled out the bottle and poured herself a glass of soda.

As she sipped it, she thought about their conversation. All the way home on the train she had gone over it again and again. He had slept with another woman. She wondered if there were signs she might have noticed, if she hadn't been so preoccupied with Paul. If she had been paying attention to him.

The worst part was the thought of him in bed, in someone else's arms. Probably someone who had no lines around her eyes or gray hairs. Someone whose body was trim and taut and very willing. It made Anna feel nauseated to think of it, and vaguely ashamed.

A warm swish, like a feather duster across her calves, made Anna jump and let out a little shriek. She looked down and saw Paul's cat, rubbing against her legs. Anna quickly bent over and picked him up.

"Sam!" she exclaimed. "Where'd you come from?" Anna went to the top of the stairs and thought of calling down. But the volume of the music discouraged her. She started down the stairs, carefully cradling the cat in her arms.

At the foot of the stairs she stopped, surprised by what she saw. Tracy and Paul were sprawled on the round braided rug, each studying a hand of cards.

"Ten," said the boy, laying down a jack.

"Twenty, for two," Tracy announced, savoring the move as she matched his jack with her own.

"Hey," said Anna, "look who I found." She held up the cat for their inspection.

Paul looked up and smiled with such unexpected sweetness that Anna drew in her breath. It was as if, for a moment, she had glimpsed her lost toddler again.

"Tracy brought him," said Paul. "He came back to the animal shelter."

Anna smiled into the cat's furry coat. "Welcome home, Sam."

"What did Daddy say?" Tracy asked diffidently.

"Well." Anna hesitated. "He sends his love. To both of you," she added pointedly.

Paul lifted his arms for the cat, and Anna placed the animal into them. The boy began to stroke the fur.

"Come on," said Tracy. "Play."

Still holding the cat under his arm, Paul reached into his hand and put down another card. "Twenty-six," he said.

Tracy glanced from the card to her hand, her fingers hovering above the fan of cards.

Anna wrapped her arms around herself and watched their game. She wished that Thomas could see them at this moment. She dropped down on the daybed, to be closer to them. "All quiet around here?" she asked.

"Yeah," said Paul.

"So, what else did Daddy say?" Tracy asked, playing another card and murmuring the point score. "Is he coming home?"

"I don't know," said Anna. She laid her head back against the sofa and gazed out across the room. I wish I could say yes, she thought. "I hope so," she added, surprised to realize that it was true. She turned her head from side to side, trying to release the tension that had built up in the back of her neck. As she rolled her head around, she noticed that the door to the basement was not completely shut. With a sigh she got up and went over to close it.

"Who left this open?" she asked.

"I don't know," said Tracy. "That's six," she corrected Paul, pointing to his cards.

"Did you, Paul?"

The boy looked up. "Not me."

For a moment she hesitated, and then she pushed the door open farther and walked slowly into the dark cellar. Skirting the boxes and old pieces of furniture, she walked over and pulled the light chain in the center of the space. Despite the bulb's illumination, the corners remained gloomy, while the rest of the basement's contents was revealed in all its dishevelment. Maybe I didn't shut that door tightly, Anna thought. She glanced around at the piles of neglected and forgotten objects which were stored in the damp cellar. I've got to clean this out one day, she thought wearily. She reached up to pull the light bulb chain again, and as she did so, her eyes fell on the window.

One of the short café-length curtains which she had made to cover the low windows was caught, partially trapped between the closed window and the frame. The twisted material ballooned out awkwardly. Anna walked over and touched the curtain. Then her fingers traveled to the latch, which was unfastened.

Anna felt her heart begin to race as she stared from the open latch to the snagged curtain. In a sharp voice she called out, "Who opened this basement window?"

"Can't hear you," Tracy called back over the sound of the music on the stereo.

Anna backed away from the window, her eyes focused on the captive curtain. Halfway across the basement she turned and hurried toward the light of the playroom.

Paul looked up, holding a card poised to drop between his fingers. "What's the matter?" he asked. Tracy, who was hunched over one bent, upright knee, turned and looked at her mother.

Anna stood stiffly in the doorway, staring at her children. "Did either of you open the cellar window?"

The two shook their heads no in unison. "Why?" Tracy asked.

"Somebody did," said Anna grimly.

Tracy and Paul looked at her blankly.

"Did you hear anyone outside there?" she asked. "Either of you?"

"No," said Tracy impatiently.

Paul frowned for a moment and then shrugged his shoulders.

"Paul?" Anna asked.

"No."

Anna stared at him, trying to remember when she had last checked that window, knowing that she had locked it when Paul came home and not opened it since.

"Maybe Daddy opened it," Tracy offered.

Anna looked at her daughter and considered the suggestion. "Maybe," she said.

"That's probably what happened."

"Probably." Anna nodded, wanting to reassure them, to convince them they were safe and had nothing to fear. As she watched them resume their card game, she knew that they really weren't fearful. They didn't think in terms of what could happen.

She shivered, worrying over the open window. It was probably Tom. It probably was. But she felt vulnerable all the same. You could not be too careful. Not where your children were concerned. That is one thing, she thought, I know for sure.

Iris tapped tentatively on the door with the "Closed" sign visible behind the panes. In a few minutes she heard movement behind the door, and then it was thrown open by a woman with short brown hair, wearing blue jeans covered with gray dust and a sweat shirt with the sleeves cut off near the shoulder. Long silver earrings with turquoise stones dangled below her cap of curly hair. The determined look in the woman's dark eyes softened when she saw Iris, and she smiled to reveal a gap between her front teeth.

"Are you working?" Iris asked timidly.

"Just firing a few pots. Come in." The woman stepped back, and Iris entered the studio. Coils of clay and chalky-looking pots occupied the counter tops. A potter's wheel sat in the center of the room, while two black kilns took up most of the back wall. The room seemed to have been dusted with a soft gray powder.

"Where are your suitcases?" the woman asked.

"I put them in the bedroom in the house," said Iris, turning to face her. "I'm sorry I'm late, Angelica."

The woman put her strong, clay-caked hands on Iris's shoulders. "I wasn't worried about you. Yet." She drew Iris close to her, and the two women kissed each other gently on the mouth. Iris sighed and pulled herself away from the lingering embrace.

Angelica released her and walked over to a little stove and sink on the side of the studio. She poured a cupful of boiling water into a ceramic mug and handed the mug to Iris, who sat down on a stool and rested the mug on the counter.

"Herb tea," said Angelica. "Looks as if you need it."

Iris sighed again, and Angelica cocked her head to one side and smiled at her. "What's the matter?"

Iris shrugged her shoulders like a dejected child.

"You didn't tell him, did you?" said Angelica.

Iris looked at the other woman beseechingly. "I tried to tell him. All day I wanted to tell him. But I couldn't find an opportunity. And then tonight I went back, after I had started out for here, and I told myself that that was it. That I was entitled to my happiness and that it was time to speak up and tell him. And I started to . . . but then I couldn't."

Angelica lit a cigarette and held it between her teeth as she shook the match out. Then she took a drag and removed it and had herself a sip of tea. "Maybe you don't want to tell him," she said. "Maybe you don't really want out of the marriage."

Iris looked up at the other woman with woeful eyes and

shook her head slowly. "Oh, no," she said. "I am going to get out of it. I promise you that."

"Don't promise me," said Angelica archly. "I mean, don't do it for my sake. If you can't take the pressure and the scandal, well, I understand. I'll be your back street girl."

Iris reached out and put a hand on Angelica's forearm, pulling it to her and then squeezing the dusty hand between her own. "No," she said. "I don't want it to be like that. This is the first time in my whole life that I have ever really been happy. I feel as if I were asleep before I met you. Now I know what I was missing in life, and I want to live with you. I don't care what people say."

The other woman squinted at her and took another drag on her cigarette. "It's not going to be pleasant. He will make it miserable for you."

"He's going to be so upset when he finds out," said Iris. "He told me tonight he was satisfied with our marriage."

"Satisfied." Angelica snorted. "Honestly, Iris, I don't know how you have put up with that man as long as you have. He's a hell of a snob, and the way he treats you is inexcusable. I don't see why you should care how he feels about it."

"I can't help it," said Iris apologetically. "I feel guilty. I'm afraid I never really cared for him. I haven't been much of a wife to him, you know. I know he has a bad temperament, but he's as demanding of himself as he is of anyone else. And the scandal of this is going to be awfully hard on him."

"You don't have to make a public declaration and do time in the stocks, you know," Angelica said. "Lots of people get divorced these days. The whole world doesn't have to know why."

Iris looked up at her friend with shining eyes. "I want the whole world to know," she said. "For the first time in my life I'm in love, and I feel like shouting it."

"You're so sweet, Iris," said Angelica kindly. "You're a little bit naïve, but that's something I love about you."

Iris blushed, and tears sprang to her eyes. She wiped them away quickly. "I will tell him," she said. "In a couple of days. Maybe I'll just call him and tell him I'm not coming home when Sunday comes around. I just don't want to spoil these next few days we have together," she said earnestly.

"All right," said Angelica. "Whatever you think will be easiest on you." She put out her cigarette and smiled. "I'd better check the kilns. Don't go away."

Iris shook her head and followed her raptly with her eyes.

The phone rang as Gus deBlakey was eating the last of his sweet and sour pork from a waxed paper carton with a plastic fork.

"La-Z Pines," he said, tucking the lid of the carton neatly together.

He was both relieved and apprehensive to hear his wife on the other end. He inquired immediately after the baby and learned to his relief that the infant and mother were fine. His wife was calling only to find out when he would be home because she worried that he was exhausted from all the excitement lately, between the coming of the baby and the suicide of the guest at the motel. She reminded him, although she knew he hated to hear it, that he was not as young as he once had been.

Gus held the phone to his ear and squinted out the office window through the letters of his modest neon sign. The parking lot was quiet, but he was still expecting a little more business for the night.

"That Methodist convention is in town," he explained to his wife. "I got a bunch of them rolling in here tonight. Spillovers from the Holiday Inn. I was over there tonight, by the way. I stopped on my way from the hospital and picked up some sweet and sour pork from that Chinese restaurant they've got there in the hotel. Pretty good stuff."

Gus's wife reminded him that sweet and sour pork gave him gas, but Gus was unruffled. "Never felt better," he assured her. "Hey, Millie, you know what? Saturday night's the last night of the convention. Ends after church on Sunday, and you know who they're going to have on Saturday night over at the Havana Room? The Champagne Lady from Lawrence Welk. I was thinking we should go. You love her."

Millie agreed that she did love the Champagne Lady and that she would consider the proposition. With a last warning to her husband to drive carefully, she hung up.

Gus got up from his chair and looked out into the parking lot again. Those Methodists tended to go to bed early. Probably wouldn't be too much more action tonight. And he hated to admit it, but he was tired. With a sigh of both weariness and contentment Gus began to roll down the blinds on the office window. He thought he might request "Danny Boy" if the Champagne Lady was taking requests. He loved that song, "Danny Boy."

As he was rolling down the front blind, he saw a sight that made him grimace. A pair of the Methodists, husband and wife, were striding up toward the office with that look on their faces that said, "The toilet's stopped up, and we're paying good money for this room." Gus looked at them reflectively. He recognized them all right. They were in cabin 17. Well, it surely was the cleanest one in the place. It had been scrubbed down pretty well after that guy was found swinging in there.

Gus had an inkling now of what the problem was. Someone probably had told them about the guy's hanging himself in their cabin, and now they didn't want to stay there. He hoped, briefly, that the word didn't get around on cabin 17, or he'd be stuck with one useless piece of real estate.

The door to the office opened with a jingle, and the middle-aged husband and wife stepped in.

"Evening, folks," said Gus, pasting on a smile. "What can I do you for?"

The husband, who had steel-rimmed glasses and hair the same color, cleared his throat. The wife just stood next to him, looking indignant. Gus could see that was going to be the way it was.

"Well, sir," said the husband, "my wife and I are staying down there in one of your cabins."

"Seventeen," said the wife.

"That's right," said the husband. "We're members of the Methodist Church. Here for a convention." The man held up the Gideon Bible as if by way of explanation.

"It's a pleasure to have you folks," said Gus. "How do you like your room?"

"The room's just fine," said the man, "but we aren't too happy about this." The man wrapped both hands around the Bible and gave it a little shake.

Gus looked at it with a frown, wondering if the Methodists used another version of the Good Book in their religion. He didn't know too much about their activities other than that they were going to be entertained by the Champagne Lady.

"Disgraceful," the woman stated, sniffing at the Bible.

"We put those in all the rooms," Gus started to explain. "It's an old custom. For the weary traveler."

"I know that, sir, and a fine custom it is. But this Bible in our room has been defaced."

"Defaced?" said Gus.

"My wife wanted to read a few passages this evening, and when she opened it up, this is what she found." The man opened the book and held it up for Gus to see. Gus swiveled around to have a look. The margins of the page he indicated were covered with scrawled handwriting lapping over onto the text. Gus could see at a glance that some of the words were of the obscene variety. He quickly lifted the Bible from the man's hands and put it behind the counter.

"I am so sorry about that, sir," he said, going into a drawer and bringing out another copy, which he offered the offended conventioneer. "You do get the occasional guest who has no respect for the Lord's Word. I'm terribly sorry."

The woman opened the new Bible and looked through it. "That's better," she announced.

"Will that be all?" Gus asked, worried that there might be more.

"That's fine," said the man, putting his hand on his wife's elbow. He turned to Gus as he reached the door. "I wouldn't keep that lying around here, you know. Some child could get his hands on it and have a terrible shock."

"I'll take care of it," Gus assured him.

After the couple had gone, Gus took the Bible out from under the counter and began to examine it curiously. He leafed through the pages until he found the offending section and turned the book upside down and sideways to read what was written there.

It was that nut, he thought, deciphering the passages in

Jeremiah which had been amended by Rambo's jerky handwriting. The writing did not make much sense; that figured, to Gus's way of thinking, and he soon gave up trying to figure out the gist of it. The only thing he noticed was that in one corner of the page was written, quite clearly, the name Edward Stewart and, beneath it, a phone number. Gus pondered it for a while, wondering if that name, or any of this crazy business, would be of any use to that nice detective who had come over to the hospital. He thought for a moment that it wasn't a good idea to get involved, but he didn't see himself as one of those kind of people you heard about in New York who never bothered to call the police, even when they heard their neighbors screaming bloody murder. Gus fished in the pocket of his shirt and pulled out the card with the detective's name and number on it. It wouldn't hurt to give him a call, he thought.

Picking up the phone, he dialed the number of the Stanwich police station and waited. He looked up at the clock while it rang. A gruff male voice answered, identifying himself as Sergeant McDonough and announcing the Stanwich police station. Gus squinted down at the card in his hand and asked to speak to Detective Mario Ferraro.

"He's not here now," said the cop at the other end. "Can I help you?"

"Off duty?" Gus asked knowledgeably. "When do you expect him?"

"Well, sort of," said the policeman. "He went away for a couple of days. Who's calling, please?"

Then Gus remembered. The detective had said something about taking his son off to college. "When'll he be back then?" said Gus, unwilling to go into a whole long explanation with somebody else.

"A couple of days. He's due back in on Friday."

"I see," said Gus, looking down at the writing in the Bible. He would be curious to see what the detective would make of it.

"Can anyone else help you?"

Gus shook his head. "No, I don't think so. I'll give him a call when he gets back. Friday, you say?"

"Want to leave a message?"

Gus hesitated. "No," he said at last. "It'll keep. I'll call when he gets back." He hung up the phone and put the Bible back under the counter. Then he picked up all his keys and switched off the light in the office, leaving the emergency number facing out on the door. He decided not to tell Millie about it. She'd tell him he should have minded his own business. But as he locked the door and went out toward his car, Gus felt a lot better for having done his duty as a citizen.

CHAPTER EIGHTEEN

The morning sun fell across Anna's shoulders as she crouched down in front of the clothes dryer, pulling out the warm laundry and folding it cursorily into a plastic basket. She heard Tracy's sneakered steps in the kitchen and called out to let her know where she was. Tracy appeared in the doorway and then came over to where Anna was working. She bent down and kissed her mother briefly on the cheek.

Anna felt a flutter of surprise and pleasure at the kiss, the first sign of affection from her daughter in what seemed weeks. She tied two socks together and affected a jaunty tone. "You're up early."

"Mary Ellen invited me to go sailing on their boat with her older brother and his girl friend."

"That sounds like fun."

"Are you wearing perfume?" Tracy asked.

Anna stood up and put the laundry basket on top of the machine.

"Lipstick and everything," Tracy said. "Where are you going?"

Anna took a deep breath. "To the airport," she said.

"The airport?" Tracy cried.

"Your father is going to Boston on the shuttle this morning. I've decided to see his plane off."

"Oh," said Tracy, trying to appear as if she understood.

"We have some things to talk about," said Anna. "Will you take these up to your room, darling?"

Tracy accepted the pile of folded clothes from her mother.

"I was thinking of asking Paul to go sailing with us," the girl announced offhandedly.

"That was a nice thought," Anna said seriously.

Tracy shrugged her shoulders.

"But I've got to take him to the hospital this afternoon. For some tests. We should be back from the airport before noon."

"Is he going to see Daddy off, too?" the girl asked, a note of petulance in her voice.

"I'm not leaving him alone in this house," said Anna. "He'll have to come with me." Mother and daughter were silent for a moment.

"Well," said the girl, "I'm going up and getting ready. Can you drop me at Mary Ellen's?"

"Sure," said Anna. "Wake him up for me, will you? We're going to have to leave before long."

"Okay," said Tracy. She glanced at the little stack of sweat socks and dungaree shorts on the washer. "Is that his? I'll take it up."

Anna rubbed her daughter's back between her shoulder blades for a moment. Tracy pretended not to notice. Clutching the two piles of laundry, she headed off through the house.

Anna walked into the kitchen and sat down at the table by the phone. She had been up most of the night, but she did not feel tired. On the contrary, her entire system seemed to be racing, and she was anxious to get going.

After her discovery of the opened window she had carefully checked the house and then called the police. The officer she spoke to could barely conceal his impatience. He explained to her that they did not generally come out to investigate windows that had been opened. He advised her not to worry, and said that they would send someone only if she insisted. Anna had debated it and then decided to insist. An officer had dutifully arrived, checked the house in a perfunctory manner, and assured her she had nothing to be concerned about. Anna had ignored the officer's indulgent manner and, after he had left, tried to put the open window out of her mind and concentrate on her other problem.

The long night, alone in her bed, had given her plenty of time to think about what Thomas had said. He had been to bed with another woman, and now he wanted to be forgiven and to make it up with her. All night she had wrestled with her feelings, unable to decide what to do. She had fallen asleep at around 4:30 A.M., and when she awoke, she knew.

Now that her mind was made up, she could hardly wait to get going. She closed her eyes and imagined his face when he saw her at the departure gate. She felt a warm wave of anticipation, thinking of him. It was the right decision. You didn't let a life with someone go for a mistake. She had made her share as well. She thought, guiltily, of Tracy, suffering all those years from her own telling and retelling of a tale. Yet Tracy seemed to have forgiven her. Now it was Anna's turn to forgive.

She opened her eyes and looked up at the kitchen clock. She had one phone call to make now, before they left. It was still early. In all likelihood Edward had not yet left for work. Anna dialed the Stewarts' number and waited for several rings.

* * *

The glass doors of the apartment house lobby were opened by a small-boned, balding man in aquamarine livery. "Good morning, sir," said the doorman politely. "Lovely day, isn't it?"

"Yes, isn't it?" Thomas mumbled, slipping into the elegant, chandeliered lobby trying not to catch his briefcase or his suitcase in the door on his way in.

"Whom did you wish to see, sir?" the doorman asked.

Thomas recognized the doorman as the same one who had been on duty when he had left with Gail the previous morning. He wondered if the man remembered him and was just being discreet. He felt as if the gold of his wedding band were blazing in the electric candlelight. "Miss Kelleher, please. On the twentieth floor."

"Who's calling, please?"

"Mr. Lange."

The doorman nodded and walked over to the house phone on the desk in the lobby. Thomas sat down in one of the velvet love seats and placed his bags on the floor. He had to be at the airport in an hour and a half, but he felt that he couldn't leave without talking to Gail, as much as he dreaded it. After having left Anna the night before, he had gone to a hotel, where he had been up most of the night with his thoughts and a bottle of bourbon. This morning he was weary, and his head ached; but at least he did not feel as guilty as he had the morning before.

"You can go up, sir," said the doorman.

"Thank you," said Thomas. He stood up, picked up his bags, and started for the elevator. It opened after a moment's wait, and he got in and pushed the button for the twentieth floor.

He figured that Gail would not be too surprised by what he had to say. They had hardly spoken after he told her he was meeting Anna for dinner. He had collected his bag from her apartment, telling her that he was going to a hotel because he needed to be alone that night to sort things out, and although she had tried not to let her feelings show, she had answered him in monosyllables.

He had considered not telling her anything at all. He knew he could just avoid her at work, and she would get the message in no time because she was a sensitive woman and she had her pride. He suspected that she would not press the issue. She would let him get away without an explanation. And the last thing he felt like this morning was having an ugly scene with her.

But it was too cowardly a way out. He didn't want to continue the affair, knowing that his heart wanted to go home, but at least he owed her an apology. No matter what her hopes for their affair might have been, she had been good to him when he needed someone, and now the guilt and reluctance that he felt as the elevator rose and opened at her floor were telling him that he would have to pay for accepting her offer.

He walked slowly down the carpeted hallway to her door and rang the bell. After a few moments the door opened, and she was standing before him in a suit, all dressed and made up for work. He met her eyes briefly and then looked down.

Gail looked him over quickly and gave a slight laugh. "Moving in?" she asked.

Thomas did not smile. "I'm going to Boston today," he said.

"I know," she said, stepping aside to let him in.

He did not look at her as he passed into the sunken living room. He could feel her eyes on him, appraising him, anticipating what he was about to say.

"I'm sorry about last night," he said. "I should have called you when I got back to the hotel, but I just couldn't think straight."

"I didn't really expect to hear from you," she said. She walked over to where he stood gazing out her windows at the morning, smog-covered skyline. He glanced over at her and saw in the harsh daylight that there were dark circles under her eyes which she had mostly concealed with makeup.

"How was your meeting with Anna?" she asked.

He thought about trying to explain it to her, but he did not know where to begin. How, he wondered, do you explain something, when you don't even understand it yourself? He turned to face her. "I've made a mess of things, Gail. I just didn't use my head. Now I'm afraid I'm going to hurt you, and I never intended to."

Gail nodded, but there was a remote look in her eyes, as if she were answering him from miles away. Thomas thought in that moment that she had prepared herself for this through a long night.

"No," she said softly. "I don't imagine you did."

Edward hung up the phone and returned to his chair in the dining room. What a piece of luck, he thought. What an incredible piece of luck.

Anna had called to ask him if he had seen or heard any sign of a prowler the night before. At first he had felt panicky, hearing her describe the open window, but he was able to assure her, as the police had, that there was absolutely nothing to worry about, that all had been quiet.

And then she had told him about the airport. She was taking the boy with her to the airport. What better place to abduct the boy than the sprawling, anonymous airport? He could easily think of some story to lure the boy off without being seen by either of his parents. Once he had the kid in his possession, it was just a matter of hiding the boy in the house and waiting until darkness fell to get rid of the body. It was so simple. So simple. He only wished he had known about this last night, so that he could have gotten some sleep. Edward brushed the crumbs from his croissant off his fingers onto his plate. He would have to get someone to come in tomorrow and clean up. He could not stand the sight of the dishes collecting in the kitchen.

Now, however, it was time to move. He checked his watch. They would be leaving soon. He decided to get ready quickly because he wanted to leave right behind them, keeping his distance, of course. Tonight, he thought, this all will be over. He felt a huge sense of relief at the thought. He would have dinner at the club in peace, knowing that his potential accuser was safely dead and buried, somewhere far enough away, and all his worries buried with him.

CHAPTER NINETEEN

Anna pulled the car up into the line of cars beside the traffic island outside the Eastern terminal. She glanced over at Paul, who seemed mesmerized by the rush of airport activity.

"It's a good thing you were with me," she said. "I don't know how a person is supposed to drive and read all those signs at the same time. I could have ended up on the runway, for heaven's sake."

Paul shrugged. He had sulked on the way down at her insistence that he accompany her and not stay in the house alone. "You could have found it," he said.

"Well, maybe so. But it helps to have a copilot." She didn't want him to feel smothered and overprotected. But the thought of that open window in the basement plagued her. She kept thinking of Rambo's threatening predictions, although she would not have admitted it to anyone. He's safe, she thought, chiding herself. He's perfectly safe. But the sight of that window last night had reminded her that you could never be sure.

Anna realized guiltily that Thomas would never approve of this precaution. But today she needed the assurance of the boy beside her. Once Thomas was home again . . .

292

She reached into her purse and extracted a tube of lipstick. She carefully applied it, checking it in the rearview mirror. Then she snapped the tube shut and turned to her son. "Will you come in with me?" she asked.

The boy shook his head.

Anna looked over at the busy entrance to the terminal. There were police directing traffic and uniformed airline employees streaming in and out of the sliding electric eye doors. "I guess you'll be all right here," she said. "Just keep the doors locked."

"What for?" he asked.

"This is New York, darling. There is a lot of crime around here. You have to be careful around here. You sure you don't want to get out and have a look in the terminal? It might be boring sitting in here."

"No," said the boy dispiritedly.

Anna frowned at him. "Do you feel all right?"

"Yes," he said, his voice rising in annoyance.

"All right," she said briskly. "I'll be back shortly." She slid out her side and locked the car door behind her. Then, giving him a wave, she looked both ways and hurried across the road to the doors of the terminal.

Paul leaned over and turned on the car radio. The announcer was talking loudly about back-to-school specials, and Paul's spirits sank as he listened. He was not looking forward to starting school. He had a feeling that everyone would be staring at him. He had no friends here, and while that wasn't so bad in classes, it was going to be creepy during lunch and free periods and stuff like that. He had a sneaking, newfound hope that Tracy might take him around a little. She had wanted him to go sailing with her today after all. It wasn't the best to be led around by your little sister, but it would be better than nothing.

A sudden rap on the window made him start, and he looked up, expecting at once to see Anna or some sinister-looking character with a gun trained on him. "New York," she had said. "Crime." Paul jerked his head around and saw the worried face of Edward Stewart peering in the window.

Paul gave him a bewildered look as Edward motioned for him to lower the window. Paul turned off the radio and slid over to roll the window down.

"Paul," Edward began abruptly, "where's your mother?"

Paul nodded toward the airline terminal. "She went in," he said, "to see my father's plane off. What are you doing here?"

"Oh, no," Edward groaned, straightening up and grimacing at the terminal.

"What's the matter?" asked the boy.

"Oh, dear," said Edward.

"Why?"

Edward leaned over again. "Paul, your father's not in there. There was . . . Well, he had an accident this morning in New York. He got stabbed by a mugger. He's in the hospital."

"Uh oh," the boy breathed.

"When they couldn't reach anyone at your house, they called ours. Oh, she's going to be frantic, looking all over for him."

"I can probably find her," Paul offered.

Edward seemed to consider the idea and then brushed it away. "Never mind. I'll find her. I've come to take you both to the hospital. To see him. My car is in that parking garage way over there." He indicated a building quite a distance down the road across from the main terminal. "It's in space H-thirteen. Can you find that?"

"Sure," said Paul.

"You go wait for me there. I'll find your mother inside."

"What about our car?" Paul asked, getting out of the Volvo and shutting the door.

"Leave it," Edward said. "I'll explain it to the policeman."

"Okay," said the boy.

"Get in my car and wait," said Edward. "The door's open."

"H-thirteen?"

"That's right."

Paul loped across the street and walked along the road until he finally reached the parking garage. It was dark inside, despite the brightness of the day, and very quiet. A couple of people were exiting as he came in, but mostly it was empty and looked like a graveyard for automobiles.

He noted that the letters marking the lot were low on the first floor, meaning he had go up. He climbed the ramp into the second crowded level, but the letters only went up to F. With a sigh he walked up to the third level, where the cars had thinned out and it was as silent as a tomb. He thought about Thomas as he walked, bleeding on some sidewalk while a guy ran off with his wallet. The thought made him feel nauseated and a little apprehensive. The gloom of the garage suddenly felt very unfriendly, and he hurried to find the car and get into it. He would lock the door and just wait for Mr. Stewart. He began to scan the letters and numbers, making his way down the row of cars. He passed the parking lot elevator. The light above it indicated that the elevator was on its way up.

The space next to the elevator was H-7. Almost there. He

counted the spaces as he walked and noted that he was coming up to a black car. As he approached it, he saw that it was a Cadillac, long and gleaming. He walked up to it and put his hand on the door handle. Then he stopped short and stared. The long hood of the car sloped down like a shining black mirror to the grillwork on the end. Perched on top of the grille was a hood ornament the likes of which he had never seen before. It was golden and in the shape of an eagle, its wings expanded, talons extended, its golden beak open, its eyes narrowed into angry slits.

Paul felt a pain shoot through his head, and he started to wince. His hand rested on the door handle; but all the muscles in his body felt limp, and nausea began to overwhelm him. His eyes riveted to the eagle, he began to back away from the car.

Suddenly he felt a thud on his back, and an arm reached around him and jerked the car door open. Paul toppled forward, through the open door, and fell into the front seat, his chin smacking hard against the steering wheel. He was momentarily stunned, and then he scrambled backward with a cry as he turned to face his assailant.

Edward Stewart's cold eyes floated above him in the gloom of the black car in the empty lot. Paul raised a fist, but Edward grabbed it and pushed it down, pinning him with his weight under one bent knee. Paul had started to cry out when a damp rag descended on his face and a sickening smell assaulted him.

In the few seconds before he passed out, he was a child again, lying limp on a grassy edge of the exit ramp, unable to move, as those cold eyes inspected him. He was pleading for help, but as those huge hands reached for him, he knew now, as he had known then, that they would only carry him deeper into danger.

* * *

Anna scanned the line of passengers waiting to have their bags examined to board the plane. Her eye was caught by the dejected slope of his shoulders—a posture, she realized, that she recognized from Paul, who had stood just that way in the kitchen door this morning. In that simple stance she felt that she recognized another signet, shared by father and son, which proved their bond beyond a doubt. Thomas shuffled forward in the line, unconscious of her scrutiny.

For a moment she wondered if she had the courage to proceed with her plan. The resolve which had propelled her from home to the airport now wavered as she looked at him moving toward the guards and the conveyor belt. Maybe she had misunderstood his intentions. Perhaps he intended to stay with the other woman after all. He was getting closer to where he had to leave his bag. In a few moments he would pass through the doorway frame and be headed for the plane. Anna felt her voice sticking in her throat.

It's Thomas, she reminded herself. Not some stranger. Even though she did not understand what he had done, she did know him. She could not be that wrong about his feelings. You're afraid, she told herself. That's all. Fight for him. You have to.

Forcing herself to move forward, Anna called out his name. Thomas turned and looked around with a puzzled glance. Then he saw her, and his troubled face was transformed by a smile. "Anna!" he exclaimed.

He broke from the line and rushed toward her. It's going to be all right, she thought.

"What are you doing here?"

Suddenly she felt shy under the warmth of his smile, unsure of what to say. "I . . . I wanted to see you off," she said.

He gazed at her, his tired eyes cautious but hopeful. He set his bags down on the ground and then rubbed his hands aimlessly on his trouser legs.

Anna realized that he did not know what to reply. She had always smoothed the way for him. He needed her to do it now.

"I hardly slept at all last night," she said. "I was thinking about what you said. It hit me pretty hard at first."

"I know," he said quickly.

"But I didn't want you to go off today with this misunderstanding between us."

Thomas nodded miserably.

"I know we can't talk about this whole thing now," she said. "But the more I thought about it, the more I realized that there was blame on both sides. I was so busy thinking about Paul that I guess I didn't give much thought to what you were going through. Anyway, you asked me to forgive you, and I want you to know that I do. That's the least I can do."

They stood awkwardly, facing each other. Anna's hands hung at her side. Thomas reached down and picked up her right hand. He placed it between his own hands, his eyes filling up as he stroked it and then, hesitantly, squeezed it in his palm. She watched his face as he clutched her hand, the determined set of his mouth an indication that he was forcing back some insistent tears.

Anna felt herself swallowing her own. She was suffused by the peaceful sense that she had done the right thing by coming. Whatever needed to be unraveled could be done in time. They were joined again, she thought, looking down at their intertwined hands.

An amplified voice cut through the corridor. "All

passengers for the ten A.M. shuttle flight to Boston must have their baggage checked and be ready for boarding."

Thomas sighed. "That's me," he said.

"You'd better go." She smiled.

"I'll call you tonight," he said, but it was a question.

Anna nodded. "Where are you staying?"

"The Copley Plaza."

"Yes. Do call. I want to talk to you."

He picked up his suitcase and his briefcase. "How is everything at home?" he asked. "All right?"

Anna hesitated, thinking of the opened window in the basement. But he was poised to go, looking for reassurance. Besides, it would be all right soon, when he came home for good. She smiled at him. "Fine," she said.

"Where are the kids?"

"Tracy went sailing with Mary Ellen. Paul's out in the car."

Anna could see a shadow pass over his face and knew that he felt hurt that the boy had not come in to see him. "He wanted to come in," she said, "but I asked him to watch the car for me. I'm parked right across from the terminal.

Thomas glanced over at the dwindling line of check-in passengers. In the waiting area he could see that people were standing, preparing to board the plane.

"Don't be late," said Anna.

"Give them my love, will you?"

Anna nodded and smiled.

Impulsively he dropped his bags on the ground again and leaned toward her. She met his embrace, and they held each other tightly, his face buried in her hair. She could feel him shaking. Her own knees felt weak.

"You feel so good," he said softly.

She smiled and gave him a pat on the rear end. "You'd better get going."

He kissed her hard on the mouth and reluctantly released her. Then he was gone, sprinting toward the conveyor belt, where he deposited his bags, and turning to wave at her as he passed through the electric eye doorframe.

Anna waved back vigorously, forlorn and happy at once. He would be gone only overnight, she reminded herself. Tomorrow he would be back. Back in their home, to start over again. She waited until he had disappeared into the passenger lounge, and then she turned and started back.

Men in suits streamed by, heading for the shuttles. At the ticket counters, people in a variety of costumes waited and looked around. One young man wore dark glasses and running shoes and looked glamorous and insouciant. A woman in a neat, tailored summer suit rummaged in her purse, while a couple in leisure suits examined their tickets and tugged on the wheeled harnesses around their large suitcases.

People traveling, she thought. Going on vacations and trips and important business junkets. But she didn't envy them their travel plans. She was delighted to be going home, getting her house ready for her husband's return, and looking out for the children. She thought of the house on Hidden Brook Lane with a longing she could not muster for any strange city. Tomorrow they all would be home together, safe under that familiar roof. Again her thoughts flashed to the open window in the cellar, but she pushed them away. Thomas would be there, to make sure everything was all right.

Anna crossed through the modern vault of a lobby, past hustling employees dressed in blue and hurrying passengers. She opened the sliding doors with her step and left the air-conditioned hum of the terminal for the warm, racket-filled roads out in front. The car was parked beside the island where she left it, and she was relieved that there was no sign of any policemen around it, issuing traffic violations for her questionable parking job.

Dodging the porters and the taxis that hovered in front of the terminal, Anna hurried across the street, craning her neck to see the top of Paul's head, which was not visible inside the car.

He's probably taking a nap, she thought. Teen-agers. They eat and sleep with such a vengeance. She approached the door of the car, ready to tease him about his ability as a sentry, but she realized, when she arrived at the vehicle, that her son was no longer inside.

For a moment she stood on the curb, staring into the car. Then she pulled the door open and got into the front seat.

There was no sign of him. She looked up through the windshield, half expecting him to come walking into her line of sight, but he was not there. He must have gone looking for me, she thought. Or gone inside to get some candy or something. After locking the car doors, Anna hurried back across the street into the terminal. Coming through the doors, she looked in every direction, searching for the blue dungaree jacket and the black sneakers, but she didn't see him. The same people were in the terminal, but the sight of them no longer intrigued her, like guests at an overlong party after the novelty has worn off. She rushed over to the candy counter and was finally able to get the attention of the proprietor, who was busily collecting fees for paperbacks and newspapers.

"Excuse me," she interrupted him.

The man looked owlishly at her through thick glasses.

"Did you see a teen-aged boy here, buying candy or anything? A kid in a dungaree jacket, brown hair."

"Nope," said the man, and turned to another customer.

"He's kind of a thin kid, about this tall."

"No, lady," said the man, and turned his back on her.

Anna whirled around and studied the terminal. Maybe he had gone to see the plane off after all. She checked on the information board to remind herself of the gate and then began to walk swiftly down the carpeted corridors toward the waiting area. I'll probably meet him coming back, she thought.

The shuttle area was empty as she rushed up to it, except for a few employees who were joking and enjoying the letup between crowds. The woman who had checked Thomas's bags gave her a suspicious look. Anna repeated her question about Paul, but the woman, after consulting her disinterested colleagues, assured Anna that they hadn't seen him, or if they had, they didn't remember.

Damn kid, Anna thought as she walked away from the gate. Why did he have to wander off like that? I told him to watch the car. She tried to ignore the other feeling that was rising in her, like a long-dormant specter. She returned to the waiting room and looked around. The men's room was next to the phone booths on the far wall. She rushed over to the phone booths but could see at a glance that he wasn't there. Just then a man in a gray suit emerged from the men's lavatory.

Anna hesitated and then accosted him, trying to appear perfectly natural and matter-of-fact. "Excuse me," she said, "but I'm looking for my son. We have a plane to catch. I wondered if he might be in there." She indicated the men's room door with a wave of her hand. "He's a teen-ager, about this height. He's wearing a dungaree jacket."

Anna could see the man's face going through stages of surprise and an embarrassed uneasiness. He shook his head quickly in answer to her question. "I didn't see him," he said gruffly, and edged away from her.

Anna turned away from the man and walked slowly back across the terminal. She could feel herself starting to shake, even though she reminded herself that it was ridiculous. He's probably back in the car by now. He'd better be. Wait until I get hold of him.

She kept looking through the terminal as she walked, her eyes like two divining rods, trying to cover every inch of the place. She moved slowly, out the sliding doors, giving him time to return to the car. As she walked, she twisted the car keys in her hand.

The street was jammed with cars, and she picked her way through them, trying not to look at her own car as she crossed the road again. When at last she reached the door, she already knew what she would see. There was no sign of him anywhere. She stared down at the empty seat. Slowly she unlocked the door on the driver's side and got into the seat. I'll just sit here and wait for him, she thought. He ought to be back in a minute.

She sat for a few minutes in the silent car, staring through the windshield, her mind as numb and blank as if it had been covered by a snowdrift.

A sharp rap on the window startled her, and she looked up to see a female security guard holding a pad and pencil and peering in at her.

"You're going to have to move this car, lady. This is a fifteen-minute only parking area. Just move it out of here."

Anna looked up at the officer and opened her mouth.

The other woman's face softened and then wrinkled up in concern. "What's the matter?" asked the airport meter maid, suddenly abandoning her official stance at the sight of the face, white as death, which stared up at her. "Are you all right?"

"Help me," Anna whispered. "My son. He's gone. It's happened again. He's gone."

CHAPTER TWENTY

Edward crawled on all fours across the surface of the loft, pushing piles of newspapers and half-empty brown cardboard cartons out of his way as he went. It was a small loft, but sturdily built. He had meant to house some of his finished work up there, but all that had ended up in the loft were broken pieces of ships and an assortment of garbage. Edward observed the post in the corner to which one side of the loft was anchored. That would suit his purposes. He sat back on his heels and folded his arms, lowering his head to avoid an overhead beam. There was no ceiling above him, for the windmill continued up with its narrowing sides. There was nothing to climb toward, just the dark, window-less tower above him. It looked satisfactory to him. He shifted awkwardly around to reach the ladder, and one of the cardboard boxes sailed off the edge of the loft and landed with a thud on the stone floor below.

Edward peered over the edge of the loft to the floor, where the box lay on its side, empty tubes of paint, brushes, and a coffee can of turpentine spilling from its open flaps onto the floor. The turpentine began to trail across the floor until it was stopped, and then absorbed, by the worn denim fabric of the jacket worn by the boy sprawled on the stones.

Paul's inert body did not react to this disturbance. He lay with his mouth open, his eyelids only half-closed, the whites giving off a sickly gleam in the gloom of the stuffy windmill.

Edward sighed as he gazed down at the frail body. He did not relish the thought of carrying the boy up the ladder to the loft. Not at all. But the body would be safer there in case anyone should stumble in here by accident before the night fell. It was unlikely but not impossible. He thought again, his eyes narrowing at the memory, of Iris's surprise of the night before. He continued to shove boxes aside, making a place for the boy among the trash. After it got dark, he could move the body to somewhere far from the house. A dump or possibly the landfill in Kingsburgh. It could be months before anyone found him.

A weak groan came from the figure lying on the windmill floor. Edward looked over the edge and saw the boy's eyelids flicker and his arm move slightly. Grabbing a few rags and a length of rope, Edward hurried down the ladder to the loft and approached the prone form.

"Help me," said the boy.

Edward reached down and stuffed a rag in the boy's mouth as a reply. Paul's eyes opened wider in that expression of recognition and fear which Edward had seen in those eyes before. Edward lashed the boy's hands and feet together and rolled him over onto his back. The boy jerked his head from side to side, his eyes sick with fear.

Edward did not look at Paul. He staggered to his feet and picked his way through his equipment until he reached the odd-shaped windows which were cut into each of the six walls of the windmill. It was a hazy, uncomfortable afternoon now, and the Stewart estate was in perfect stillness, no sight of anyone to disturb the peace. Satisfied,

Edward squeezed past his sewing machine and back to the body which was slumped on the floor. He looked up again at the loft. There was nothing to do but to take the boy up.

He took a deep breath and tried to ready himself for the unaccustomed exertion. It would all be over tonight, he reminded himself as he squatted down and reached under the sharp shoulder blades and the bent, lashed knees.

Edward lifted the boy and staggered to his feet. It took him a moment to regain his balance, and then he started toward the ladder, straining under the boy's weight.

As he did so, he was struck by the memory of the last time he had carried the boy. Paul had been much lighter then. Just a toddler. He had been lying in the grass by the edge of the exit road, just after the car had struck him. Edward paused at the foot of the ladder, remembering the frightened, pleading expression in the child's eyes as he bent over and recognized the injured, bleeding little form of his neighbor's son. He had been lighter. Yes. And that was good, for Edward had had to move quickly. It had taken only a moment to make his decision. And then he had acted on it.

Edward sighed. It had been such a bold action, and it would have worked, too, if Rambo had not seen it all and saved the child. Still, he reminded himself, for a long while he had been safe. Given the same choice, he would still have done the same thing.

Edward looked up the ladder and hoisted the boy up in his clumsy grip. Slowly he began to climb, resting with each step. The boy was stiff, but he did not struggle. His head lolled back, his mouth stuffed with the rag. Edward counted the stairs and made his ascent.

Anna closed her eyes and rested the base of her head against the back of the wooden chair. The area around her eyes stung, and she raised the heels of her hands to rub it, as if she could rub the pain away, but the piercing sensation lingered.

She blinked and looked around the Stanwich police station. There was a low level of activity which provided a constant hum, the blue-uniformed officers coming and going with papers in their hands, their holstered guns looking incongruous against their hips inside the station house.

Anna turned to the woman in the blue shirt and long black tie who was sitting at the desk beside her. She wore a name tag which read "M. Hammerfelt."

"May I use your phone?" she asked.

The woman smiled sympathetically at her. "Of course you can."

"It's long distance," Anna explained. "I'll charge it to my home phone."

"Dial nine first," the policewoman instructed her.

Anna placed the call to Boston as she looked around the station house for the young officer who was supposed to be helping her. She had already spent an hour with Airport Security at LaGuardia, and then they had kindly driven her car back to Stanwich for her, advising her to take a nap and not to worry. At her insistence they had taken her to the Stanwich police station, where she had now been for half an hour.

"Copley Plaza."

The operator's voice interrupted Anna's thoughts. She asked for Thomas but was not able to get an answer from his room.

"Do you wish to leave a message?" asked the operator, who had explained, unnecessarily, that there was no answer in Thomas's room.

"Yes," said Anna softly. She thought for a minute how to put it. "Please tell him that his wife called. Tell him, 'Please come home right away. Paul is missing.'"

The operator read back the message and promised to deliver it. Then Anna hung up. The policewoman at the desk beside her pretended not to have overheard the conversation. Anna sat back and closed her eyes again.

She had debated whether or not to call him. Their reconciliation was so fragile. It had not even really begun. She was loath to put on it the strain of yet another crisis over Paul. But she needed him now. She could not go through this without him. Something terrible had happened to Paul. She knew it in every fiber of her being, no matter what the police thought.

"Mrs. Lange?"

Anna opened her eyes and then rose to meet the young patrolman who had emerged from an office obscured by a clouded glass door. "Yes," she said anxiously.

"I think we have all the information we need now."

"What are you going to do?" she asked.

The young officer assumed a patient smile and put his notebook in his back pocket. "Well, there's not much we can do right now. We're just going to have to wait a few days and hope he turns up."

Anna stared at him incredulously. "What do you mean? Aren't you going to start looking for him?"

The young man shrugged apologetically. "We don't even know if he ran away or not. There was no sight of a note or anything. But that doesn't mean he didn't take off on a little jaunt. Kids do it all the time."

Anna could feel her anger rising, and she knew that her face was reddening; but she tried to control her voice. "This is not a case of a runaway, Officer Parker. I'm telling you that something happened to my boy. We can't just wait and see."

The young policeman folded his arms over his chest and distributed his weight, with a slight swaying motion, evenly over his feet. "Mrs. Lange, technically I shouldn't have even made out the report. The boy is not officially missing yet. And we have no evidence of any kind that anything happened to him."

"But he was right there in the car, and when I came back . . ." Anna heard her voice start to rise, and she made an effort to lower it.

"I know what happened," the officer said, more kindly now. "But there's nothing we can do at this point."

Anna gazed at the young man as if in a trance. Finally she spoke. "Officer," she said, "I imagine you must know about some of the troubles I've had with regard to my son."

"Yes, ma'am, I do know," said the young cop respectfully.

"It's my belief," said Anna carefully, "that my boy's life may be in danger. It is just possible," she said, shivering involuntarily at her own words, "that someone has kidnapped him again."

The cop smiled at her sympathetically. "It's only natural that you would think that, ma'am. But my advice to you is to go home and get some rest. This kind of thing happens frequently. I'm sure the boy will show up. He's probably back home already. Really."

Anna stared at the man's impenetrable smile for a few moments. Then she glanced over at the policewoman, who had ceased her paper work for a moment and was studying them. The policewoman quickly looked down at her desk.

Anna shook her head in disbelief, but there was no corresponding sign of understanding from the officer. "All right," she said. "I'll hire someone to find him if you won't help me."

The young officer drew himself up, a little stung by her remark. But then he renewed his smile. "Try not to worry, Mrs. Lange. If he doesn't turn up in forty-eight hours, we will begin looking for him. I promise you."

Without another look at him, Anna picked up her pocketbook and trudged toward the door of the station. Her face was tired and haggard, and her eyes were far away; but there was a flicker of determination in them that did not escape Officer Parker's notice.

He watched her go with almost a sense of awe. For years she had been something of a legend around the station, with her dogged pursuit of the kidnapped boy. Every cop on the force had known of her obsession, although he had personally never come into contact with her before. Well, she had turned out to be right about the boy. He had to hand her that, but now it seemed the whole thing was too much for her.

Officer Parker had been taking some psychology courses at NYU at night, and he had his own theory about her. He'd heard that she'd called the station the night before about an open window in her house, and now this. It confirmed what he had been thinking: She was so obsessed with the boy's disappearance that she couldn't accept it when she got the boy back. She had to keep the ball rolling somehow. It was a sad case, really.

He couldn't help feeling lucky, however, that he had been the one on duty when she came in today. It would make a pretty interesting story to tell his sister and his parents. They always got a kick out of the strange things he encountered. Even in a town as nice and quiet as this one, there was always some weird thing to report.

"I feel sorry for her," said the policewoman at the desk, interrupting his thoughts.

"Yeah, me, too," he said. "Well, I've got work to do." He started back toward his office, already composing in his mind the tale he would tell of his meeting with the notorious Mrs. Lange.

Marian Hammerfelt leaned back in her chair and tapped her pencil on her desk, thinking over the conversation between the distraught woman and Parker. The young officer had scarcely been able to conceal the fact that he thought Mrs. Lange wasn't operating with a full deck. But Marian wasn't quite convinced. She had often talked with Buddy Ferraro about the Lange case over morning coffee. He had once told her that he had a lot of respect for a mother's instinct, and Marian had to admit she agreed with that point of view.

Sliding her chair back, she opened her desk drawer and took out the folder with all the information about the on-and off-duty officers. The inn where Buddy was staying at his son's campus was listed there, along with a number where he could be reached in an emergency. She debated for a few minutes, and then she picked up the phone. It was his case, she thought. It always had been. And he'd want to know.

This is just the way it used to be, Anna thought as she sat limply in the wing chair, gazing around the living room. Everywhere she looked there were chores she could do. The plants needed watering, there was dusting to be done, and the refrigerator held nothing for dinner. But she could not move from the chair.

It had been that way for months after Paul had been taken and she had lost the baby. The house had been a prison to her; her household tasks, no matter how simple, had seemed more than she could do. It had taken every ounce of strength she had just to wait. Wait for the phone to ring, and when it did not, wait for the day to end. Wait in that numbed state of relentless dread that made inertia into a way of life. It was just as it had been then, but this time she doubted if she had the will to withstand it.

"The Lord doesn't give you more burdens than you can bear," her mother used to tell her. Anna turned her head and looked up at Paul's baby picture on the mantelpiece. She could not call her parents in Michigan and tell them this. Not yet. They were all excited, busily planning their visit to their long-lost grandson. They were old now. This news could precipitate another stroke in her father. You were wrong, Mother, she thought. It *is* more than I can bear.

But even as she sank deeper into her exhaustion, there was a sliver of will inside, nagging her to get up, to do something, anything, to try to recover her son.

There was that sheriff in West Virginia. She could call him up and try to find out if he knew anything. Or tell him to keep an eye out for the boy. If Paul *had* run away, he might be likely to go to a place he was familiar with, although even as she told herself that, she knew, with utter conviction, that the boy had not left of his own choice.

She recalled a psychic, a nice woman who was a New Jersey housewife, who had told her, some years back, that she saw Paul alive and in a warmer climate. She was right about that, Anna thought, remembering the prediction. Maybe she will know something.

The realization gave her the needed energy to get up from the chair. I have her number in the folders, Anna thought. She had kept voluminous folders in the years while Paul was gone, holding every scrap of information that had ever seemed useful. I'll dig them out and find the number.

The idea of going back to the folders overwhelmed her with a sense of despair that almost sent her back to the chair, but she marshaled her strength and headed toward the den, where she kept all her papers in a desk drawer.

The sudden ringing of the phone sent a shock through her that made her jump. She raced to the telephone and grabbed it before the second ring. "Yes. Hello," she cried into the receiver.

There was a second's pause before Iris's anxious voice reached her ear. "Anna, it's me, Iris."

Anna closed her eyes and fell against the wall. "Oh, Iris. Hi."

Iris hesitated a little before she spoke again. "Am I interrupting you? Can you talk?"

Anna felt tears that she had held back all day rushing to her eyes at the sound of the familiar voice. "Oh, Iris. I'm sorry. I'm in kind of a bad way."

"What is it?" Iris asked, submerging her own concerns in her eagerness to be of help. "What's the matter? Is it Tom?"

"No, it's not that," said Anna, unable to keep the tears out of her voice. "It's Paul. He's disappeared."

"Disappeared? What do you mean?"

"Oh, God, it's such a nightmare. I took him with me to the airport this morning to see Tom off on his trip to Boston, and when I came back to the car, he was gone. Gone. Just like that."

"Did you call the police?" Iris asked.

"Yes. I was there already. They weren't much help, I'm afraid. I thought this might be them now, on the phone with some news."

"I'm sorry," said Iris, feeling guilty for calling. "I won't keep you. I know how worried you must be."

"That's all right," said Anna wearily. "It's good to hear your voice. They probably won't call me anyway. They think I'm just an alarmist. I had them here last night because I thought someone broke into the house. And then today this. I just don't think it's a coincidence."

"Someone broke in?" Iris exclaimed.

"I'm not sure. I thought so."

"How about that?" Iris said, half to herself. "Edward was right."

"Right about what?" Anna asked half-heartedly.

"About last night," Iris said. "He thought he heard a prowler; but he went out to check, and there was nobody there."

"What?" Anna asked, gripping the phone tightly.

"He told me he heard someone outside, but then he decided it was nothing."

"But I called him this morning and asked him that very thing, and he said he didn't know anything about it."

Iris's voice took on a doubtful tone. "He must not have understood you, Anna."

Anna's heart began to thud in her chest, and she raised her voice. "I asked him specifically about it. He couldn't have misunderstood."

"I'm sorry, Anna," Iris said in a small voice. "I can't think what else could have happened."

"No, you're right. It's not your fault. I . . . I'll just have to call him again, that's all."

"Do you want me to come over and stay with you?" Iris asked.

"No, that's all right. I'll be all right." Her mind was already racing, trying to absorb this news about the prowler. Why had he denied it? He *had* denied it.

"Maybe he just didn't want to upset you," Iris suggested.

Anna seized on the explanation gratefully. "Of course. That was probably it." But she felt goose bumps rising on her flesh at the certainty she now felt. Someone had broken in. And Edward could confirm her story to the police.

"Are you sure you don't want me to come over?" Iris asked.

"No," said Anna. Then another thought intruded. "Where are you, Iris? I thought you were at the health spa."

Iris's courage failed her. This was no time to get into her own situation. "I am," she said. "I just felt like talking to you."

"Oh." Anna was lost in thought again. The fact was, she realized with a flash of anger, that if someone had been lurking outside the house, it might have had something to do with Paul's disappearance. How dare Edward keep that information from her, even if he meant well?

"Well," said Iris, "I won't tie up your phone. I'll call again tomorrow to see if there's any news."

"Thanks for calling, Iris," said Anna dully.

"Don't worry, Anna. He'll be all right. You'll see."

"Okay. Good-bye."

"Good-bye."

Before she had even hung up the receiver, she knew what she would do. She would go over to the Stewarts' and see if Edward was there. If he was, she intended to confront him with what Iris had said. If he would be willing to tell the police about the prowler, it might convince them to start their investigation right away. It could give them something to go on, more substantial, she thought, than a psychic's prediction. At least it was something she could do. It was better than just sitting here, waiting and wondering if she would ever see her son again.

* * *

Iris hung up the office phone and opened the door to the studio. Angelica sat beside the potter's wheel, a cigarette dangling from her lips, patiently helping a student reshape the pot he was working on. Iris sighed and looked back at the phone.

She had hoped she might be able to talk to Anna, to explain things to her, and maybe even ask for some advice on how to break it to Edward. Of course, Anna couldn't think about all that now, with Paul in some kind of trouble again.

Iris fiddled absently with her wedding band, which was caked with clay. She remembered how she had always watched in fascination as Anna did things around the house, happy to be taking care of her family. This is how it feels, Iris thought, like an explorer discovering at last the river's source, to want to take care of someone.

She had thought, when she picked up the phone, that she might be able to make Anna understand about her and Angelica. She had hoped she could explain it in a way that Anna would not be repulsed or think she was sick or something. But when it came right down to it, she hadn't been able to say it.

It couldn't be helped, she reminded herself. Paul's disappearing is much more important. But she knew, secretly, that she was relieved, that she still couldn't come up with the words to explain it.

Angelica looked up from the potter's wheel and removed her cigarette, giving Iris a smile as she did so. The smile made Iris feel stronger. Angelica was right. It was going to be a mess. But it would be worth it. It already was.

CHAPTER TWENTY-ONE

At the end of the driveway, which was almost as long as a private road, the Stewart mansion loomed dark against the afternoon sky. Anna walked slowly up the drive toward it, staring at the house. She had always felt that she could never enjoy living in a house like that, no matter how magnificent it might be. She often wondered if Iris, with her simple humdrum ways, felt out of place in that palatial house. It always struck her that the house must have been Edward's choice.

The thought of Edward made her feel angry once again. For a moment she stood there, gazing up at the house. The windows throughout the mansion were dark, and the house was quiet. She wondered if she would find him home. She knew that he only rarely spent a working day out of the city. Still, he had come home early the day before. Perhaps he had done the same today. She almost wished that Iris were here, to run interference for her. Anna never felt at ease with Edward and his stiff ways. She knew that he was only a few years older than she, but something about him made her feel many years his junior.

She decided to walk up and have a look in the garage windows to see if his car was there. The gravel crunched under her feet as she picked her way up to the expansive doors of the garage, which was in the same style as the house. Anna pressed her face to the windows and looked in. It took her eyes a few moments to adjust to the darkness. She knew that Edward's car was black, so she was unlikely to see it until her eyes were accustomed to the dark interior. In a few seconds she was able to make out the long lines of the black Cadillac. He always drove the same kind of car, year after year, although he often traded it for new models.

As she recognized the car, she also picked out the golden eagle which he affected as a hood ornament and which was always transferred from car to car. Privately she and Thomas had sometimes chuckled at this conceit since Edward's pompous nature bore so little resemblance to the majestic bird's. As she looked at it now, though, something about the bird bothered her. She stared at it through the window for a few moments, puzzled by her own feelings, and then turned away. It was a problem for another day, she decided. He was home. That was what counted.

Anna marched resolutely up the walk to the front door and rang the bell. She could hear the chimes echo through the halls of the house, but no one came in answer to her summons. For a few minutes she stood there impatiently, tapping her foot and trying to peer through the lead pane windows which surrounded the door. But the heavy silk-lined drapes were almost shut, and she would have had to pick her way through the rhododendron bushes to get a look inside. He might be taking a nap, she thought. She stepped down off the step and started back toward the driveway. Then she had another thought. He might be in the windmill. According to Iris, that was where he spent most of his free time. Anna glanced up at the huge Tudor structure. Maybe he didn't like the house either, Anna thought. You never know.

She walked over to the stone path which circled the Stewart mansion and walked around to the back of the house. She came upon the terrace, the white wrought-iron furniture facing the empty aqua pool. The top of the windmill was barely visible in the distance. He was probably out there. Skirting the assembled furniture, Anna started to cross the terrace. For a moment she hesitated, thinking that Edward might resent the intrusion. Then she continued on. She had something important on her mind, and she didn't think she would be too shaken by Edward's annoyance. Not if he might know something that could find Paul.

Behind her, the glass doors slid back on their track. Anna heard the sound and jumped, bumping her shin on the table legs as she whirled around.

Edward Stewart pushed back the doors until they stopped with a snap, and he came toward her across the patio, his eyes cold and fixed on her startled face. "Where are you going?" he said.

"Edward," said Anna, "I didn't think you were in the house. I rang and rang."

"There are no servants here," he said, as if that explained why the door had gone unanswered. Anna let the explanation go. Maybe he just hadn't felt like company.

"I hope I didn't wake you or take you away from something."

"No," he said. "Do come in." He indicated the glass doors, and Anna passed by them and then waited for him while he closed them tight and led the way into the library.

"I was just about to look for you in the windmill."

She noticed that his shoulders stiffened at the mention of his work room. He certainly is possessive of that space, she thought.

"Come in," he said. He gestured toward a brown leather chair in the library.

Anna sat down on the edge of it, and Edward seated himself across from her.

"I can't stay. I know you're probably working," said Anna. "I only came over to ask you something."

"Oh? What's that?"

Anna took a deep breath. "Iris called me just a little while ago."

Edward sat up. "Iris?"

"Yes."

"Whatever for? I was under the impression that they didn't have telephones at the spa she's staying at."

"I don't know about that," said Anna, realizing as she said it that she didn't really know why Iris had called. She had been so involved in her own concerns that she hadn't bothered to ask. For a moment it troubled her, but then she dismissed it. She couldn't worry about that now. She'd find out sooner or later. She looked back at Edward, interpreting the indignant expression on his face to mean that he was affronted that Iris had gone out of her way to call Anna, not him.

"What did Iris want?" he asked, his eyes narrowed slightly.

"I'm afraid I didn't give her a chance to say," Anna said apologetically.

Edward thought he knew. It was the same thing as last night, this kick she was on about not making him happy. Naturally she would pour out her heart to Anna. They could compare notes about their marital problems. It almost made him laugh to think about it, except that Anna's presence was making him extremely uneasy.

"I told her about Paul. Well, I guess you don't know what happened."

Edward shook his head and assumed an innocent, wondering look.

"I took him to the airport this morning, as I told you on the phone. I went to see Tom off, and when I got back to the car, Paul was gone. I haven't seen or heard from him since."

"Vanished?" Edward said. "It's unbelievable."

"He didn't vanish." Anna corrected him sharply. "Something has happened to him."

Edward was silent for a moment. Then he cleared his throat. "Well," he said, "how can I help?"

"That's why I'm here," said Anna. "Remember this morning on the phone I told you about someone trying to break into my house last night?"

Edward looked at her blankly. Then he pretended to remember. "Oh, yes. The window. In the basement, wasn't it?" Immediately he knew what Iris had told her that had sent her running over here. He kept his expression puzzled as he searched his mind for a lie.

"Yes," said Anna. "Edward, why didn't you tell me you heard a prowler last night?"

"What?" he asked in apparent confusion, stalling for time.

"Today, when I mentioned to you about calling the police and the open window, you never said boo about it. But Iris told me that you thought you heard a prowler last night."

Edward rubbed his hands together and looked at her apologetically. "I didn't think it was important. I mean, I didn't want you to be needlessly alarmed. After all, I didn't see anyone.''

The anger which Anna had been controlling blazed forth for an instant. "For heaven's sake, Edward, I'm not a child that needs to be protected. Why didn't you just tell me when I asked? It would have been a big help to me in dealing with the police to have known what really happened.''

"There's no reason to shout,'' Edward said, and Anna was brought up short by the chill in his voice. "I did what I thought best.''

Anna took a deep breath and nodded. "I know. I'm sorry. That's just what Iris said.''

"What?'' Edward asked suspiciously.

"That you probably kept it to yourself so I wouldn't worry.''

Edward tried to stifle a smile. Iris. Was it any wonder that his life with her had been so simple? She had never been able to keep up with him. He always had his own way.

"I need to know,'' said Anna. "What did you see or hear last night?''

Edward picked up the Dunhill lighter which rested in one of Iris's little clay ashtrays and fiddled with it. "I was in my workroom, and I thought I heard something outside. So I went out to look. But there was no one there. Everything was perfectly quiet.''

"Would you tell the police what happened?'' Anna asked him evenly.

"What for?'' Edward exclaimed, dropping the lighter back into the ashtray. "I don't see what possible difference it could make.''

"I think it could make a crucial difference,'' Anna insisted. "Right now the police aren't taking me seriously. They are treating me as if I'm half-insane with these complaints. If they were to hear it from you, they might start doing something to help."

Edward gave Anna a tight, chilly smile as he rapidly reviewed the options in his mind. If he refused her request, she might become suspicious of him, and he did not want to appear uncooperative. He loathed the idea of becoming involved with the police in any way on the subject of the boy; but if he didn't volunteer the information, Anna would simply take it to them herself, and he would be forced to answer their questions anyway. Reluctantly, with a churning feeling in his stomach, he realized that he had to do it.

"I'd be happy to call them," he said smoothly, "if you think it would help."

"Oh, Edward, thank you," said Anna, exhaling and falling back into the leather seat.

"I'll call them right now," he said. He got up slowly from his chair, trying not to reveal the agitation he was feeling and headed for the phone. As he picked up the receiver and dialed, he mentally rehearsed the offhanded way in which he would present the information. As he listened to the phone ringing, it occurred to him that this call might ultimately work in his favor. A little neighborly concern, prompted by the mother's distress, was appropriate in this case. And Anna would be pleased with him for trying to help.

Anna closed her eyes briefly and then listened with one ear as Edward called the station. His manner of reporting the incident was infinitely casual and in no way reflected the kind of urgency she felt. Ah, but that was Edward, she reminded herself. At least he was calling. She gazed around the library as she waited, thinking what a handsome, if somewhat forbidding, room it was. The leather furniture was all in perfect condition, as if no one had ever sat in it.

The antique wood furniture glowed from being polished and untouched. Several of the models which Edward had built adorned various tables and the bookcases. She had to admit to herself that he had a gift for it. They were elegant vessels, perfect in their details. Across from her, hanging on the paneled wall, was a series of engraved etchings of various birds of prey. There were owls, eagles, hawks, falcons, and others she could not identify. It struck Anna that it was an odd choice for decoration. Most people of the Stewarts' ilk had pictures of mallard ducks on ponds or sleek Thoroughbreds. She could not help noticing that the eyes on some of the birds reminded her a little of Edward's. Perhaps, she thought, that's why he likes them.

Then, as a strange sensation flooded through her in a warm rush, her eyes focused again on the center etching in the group. It was a golden eagle, much like the one which adorned Edward's car, and Anna suddenly remembered where she had recently heard of a golden eagle.

"There," said Edward, coming back around in front of her. "I've alerted the police."

"Thank you," Anna mumbled, tearing her eyes from the picture to look at him.

"Now," he said, "why don't you go on home and try not to worry? The boy will probably turn up before you know it. This is all probably some youthful prank."

Anna got up carefully from her chair, avoiding his eyes. "I hope you're right," she said. "I know that's what the police think."

"Well," said Edward, "we have to trust our men in blue."

"Yes," she said, and then she forced herself to laugh, although it sounded hollow. "I just can't help worrying."

"I'm sure they would, too, if they were you," Edward

said, thinking, with a great sense of relief, that the policeman he spoke to had not offered to come out and look around again.

Anna drew in a breath and started toward the door. She turned to her neighbor with a warm smile. "I really appreciate your calling them," she said. "I'm sorry if I disturbed you."

"No trouble," he said expansively, relaxing at the sight of her leaving the house. "I was happy to do it. I only hope you'll find the boy."

He accompanied her to the door and watched as she started to walk toward the driveway. Before she disappeared from sight, she waved to him. He smiled, and waved back, and then closed the door to the house.

As she walked down the path to the driveway, she relived her revelation in the library. The eagle coming toward him on a black mass was the image Paul remembered from his dream. The connection had stunned her for a moment when she made it. There were other eagles in the world, of course. It didn't have to have anything to do with the one on Edward's car.

She reached the driveway and stopped short. She knew she should start walking home, but she felt as if she were frozen where she was, her eyes fixed on the garage. She was staring so hard that she felt as if she could see through the doors to the car inside. She had the reckless, unreasonable sensation that if she could stand in front of that eagle and put her hand on it, she might almost be able to reach Paul, to remember something vital that could help her search. She felt suddenly compelled to get closer to that eagle, to stare at it and try to think. As if in a trance, she walked to the garage door, opened it, and slipped inside.

She knew that she should probably have asked Edward if

she could look at the car and explained about the dream. But as soon as she had made the connection in the library, she knew instantly that she would not mention it to him. It was an instinct, almost animal in nature, and she trusted it. For a moment she berated herself for it, but then she reminded herself that she had been right before. She was Paul's mother, and there were things she felt she knew. If that was madness, so be it.

The interior of the garage was dark and empty, except for the Cadillac. It was a beautiful car, in perfect condition. Anna placed a hand on its cold, shiny side, as if to steady herself, and walked around to the front of the car. The eagle was poised in flight, wings outstretched, its angry eyes focused on the pavement below, just as the boy had described it in his dream.

Maybe he had seen the car, and the hood ornament had made an impression on him, she reasoned. But that would not explain why it frightened him so or why the dream recurred. She felt her breath growing short as she stared at the bird. She wanted to get out of the garage before Edward realized she was there. She was loath to deal with him again. She needed to get home and think about the impressions which seemed to be colliding in her mind.

She started back around the car, admiring, in spite of herself, its glossy finish. Just as she passed the windshield, she noticed a piece of paper stuck under one windshield wiper. The letters *LaG* jumped off the paper in the gloom and caught her eye. Carefully she reached over the hood and extracted the slip from under the wiper.

The paper in her fingers was a receipt for parking, with the number of a space on it, for a parking garage at LaGuardia Airport. It was timed and dated that morning.

Anna felt her knees start to buckle as she stared at it. She willed herself to stand up, to recover from the fainting feeling that came over her as she crushed the paper in her hand.

In a few moments she thought she could walk. She stuffed the ticket into her pocket and hurried toward the side door of the garage, which she had pulled shut behind her as she came in. There was light coming through the window-panes on the door, and she kept her eyes on the light as she stumbled across the garage.

Reaching the door, she turned the knob and pushed it open. A force from the other side jerked the door back, and Anna fell forward. She looked up into the unblinking eyes of Edward Stewart.

For a moment she stared at the white, fine-boned face which was contorted with anger. Then she began to stammer. "I was just looking for something . . ."

He reached out a hand and grabbed her by the jaw. She felt her teeth crack together, and there was a clicking sound as if the bone were separating from her skull. The force of his grip lifted her off the cement floor, and then he tossed her inside the garage. She landed on her hands and knees, skidded across the concrete, and cracked into the side of the Cadillac. She felt the skin tear from her palms and her kneecaps. A foot came down on her back from behind. Anna lifted her head and cried out.

She heard Edward growl like an animal above her; then something sharp and hard caught her in the temple, and she passed out.

CHAPTER TWENTY-TWO

Buddy Ferraro took a sip from his plastic glass filled with pink punch topped by a disintegrating grapefruit section and gently nudged his wife with his elbow. "Look at Mr. Popularity," he said, nodding toward his son, who was huddled with a group of boys across the reception room crowded with freshman and their parents in the student union.

Sandy gazed wistfully at her eldest son and sighed. "He seems to like it here," she said.

"He'd better like it here if he knows what's good for him," Buddy said gruffly. "At these prices."

Sandy smiled and slipped her arm through her husband's. "I'm going to miss having him around the house."

"Yeah, me, too," said Buddy. "I'll miss him swiping my razor, and leaving his dirty socks all over the bathroom floor, and his girl friends calling and waking me up at midnight."

Sandy pressed her lips together in a shaky smile. "Seems like a long time until Thanksgiving," she said.

Buddy quickly looked in all directions and gave her a peck on the forehead. She squeezed her husband's hand.

"Come on," he said. "Let's go back to the hotel and take a nap before this dinner tonight. He doesn't need us."

Sandy raised an eyebrow at him, but she did not resist as her husband edged her toward the cluster of students where their son was standing.

"Hey, son," said Buddy. "your mother and I are going to take off for a while."

Mark tore his eyes away from a pretty blond girl who had joined the group and was tossing her hair. "Oh, okay, Dad."

"We'll meet you at the dorm tonight at six thirty for the dinner."

"Okay," said Mark. "See you then." He and his new schoolmates returned to their conversation as Buddy steered Sandy toward the door, smiling at the various relaxed-looking faculty members and the pairs of nervous, correctly dressed parents.

"That kid can't wait to get rid of us," said Buddy, as they left the student union and began to stroll across the campus toward the hotel on the other side of the street.

"I know," said Sandy sadly. Then, after a pause, she smiled. "I guess that's good, huh?"

Buddy nodded. They walked in silence toward the cobbled walkway to the hotel lobby.

"Mr. Ferraro," the desk clerk called out as they passed through the lobby.

Buddy looked over at him in surprise. The clerk held up a slip of paper. "There's a message here for you."

Buddy excused himself from his wife and walked over to the desk. Sandy thumbed through a blue folder which she found on one of the tables in the lobby. On the cover of the folder was a picture of the campus in fall, with students scuffling through the leaves and laughing as they passed a handsome old classroom building.

She looked up to see Buddy standing by the desk with a

grim look on his face. "What's the matter?" she asked, walking over to him.

Buddy shook his head. "That was from Marian at the station. She called to tell me that Paul Lange has been reported missing. She figured I would want to know."

"Oh, no," Sandy said. "How is that possible?"

"Listen, honey," he said, "we're going to have to go back right away. I'm sorry."

"But what happened?" she said.

"I don't know," said Buddy. "But I knew something wasn't right." He crushed the message slip in his hands. "I'm afraid for that boy, Sandy." He touched his wife's arm. "Come on, let's go."

Anna came to in the darkness, her head throbbing, her limbs stiff and painful. She tried to move her arms to rub her eyes and realized, through a groggy haze, that her hands were tied behind her and her feet were bound at the ankles. Her aching head rested on a cold stone floor. Her tongue felt like a lead weight in her mouth as she tried to maneuver it over her dry lips. For a moment she was tempted to slip back into the relative painlessness of an unconscious state. Scattered thoughts flickered and disappeared in her mind, and she was aware only of the pain and a desire to sleep.

Forcing herself to keep her eyes open, she gazed dully around her prison. The cold floor and the darkness led her to think she was still in the garage, and she was further disoriented when she saw that she was not. The piles of wood and pieces of boats confused her at first. It required all her concentration to tally her surroundings and finally understand that she must be in the windmill.

The recognition of Edward's workroom brought back, with full force, her confrontation with him in the garage.

Panic gripped her by the throat as she remembered. She gritted her teeth and waited for it to pass. Edward had done this to her. Everything familiar had suddenly been turned upside down. For one second she wondered if this was some kind of misguided practical joke. Then she remembered the parking ticket on his windshield and knew for a certainty that it was not.

A low moan from the loft above her startled her clouded senses into total alertness. In an instant she remembered why she was here.

"Paul," she cried. Her voice came out in a whispered croak. She did not dare yell, even if she could, for fear that their captor might be just outside. "Paul, is that you?"

"I'm up here," he said in a weak voice. She heard him make a thrashing motion, and a cardboard box and two pieces of plywood sailed off the edge of the loft and crashed to the floor.

Ann grimaced at the crash. "Don't, don't," she called out. "Stay quiet. Don't get near the edge of that thing. You'll fall over."

The thrashing sounds subsided, and then Anna heard a groan that caused her more pain than all her bonds. "Are you all right?" she cried. "Did he hurt you?"

He groaned again, and his voice was weak but steady. "I guess I'm all right," he said.

"Thank God," she said.

"He put a gag in my mouth, but I worked it off against my shoulder." She could hear that he was proud of his effort.

"Good. Good."

"He tied me up. I can't move too well."

"I know."

"Let's start screaming," he said. "Maybe someone will come."

"I'm afraid the only one who'll come is . . . is him. There's no one else around. Paul," she said, "how did he get you here?"

"He followed us to the airport," said the boy. "He tricked me into getting into his car. He told me . . he said my . . . father was in the hospital. Then he brought me here."

A sickening thought made Anna tremble. "He didn't do anything . . . you know . . . molest you . . ." she whispered.

"No, not that," said the boy emphatically.

Anna felt an unreasonable relief at this denial. The only possible explanation surfaced to her lips. "He's gone mad," she said.

"No," said the boy calmly. "He was afraid I'd remember him. And finally I did." He tried to laugh, but a sob caught him short. "A little late, I guess."

Anna shifted her aching body and stared at the floorboards of the loft above her. "Remember him?" She felt the confusion overtaking her again, like spots before her eyes.

"Yeah, from that day. Back then."

"What, darling? I don't know what you mean."

"I finally remembered today, when I saw the car, just before he knocked me out. I've been dreaming of it ever since I came back here. But today it came back to me."

"What did?"

"I got hit by a car. I must have been playing by the road. And I got hit by his car, a black car with an eagle on it."

"The eagle," she said, knowing now that she had been right about it.

"And then he was there, bending over me."

"Edward?" said Anna.

"Yeah. I was only little. I guess it hurt. I don't remember. I guess it did. I was lying in the grass by the road, and I couldn't move. And he was there. I was scared. That I do know. And I was reaching up to him. I knew him, and I thought he came to help me. I reached up, and I think I was crying. And then he picked me up, and he started to carry me."

"Paul, did this really happen? You were never hit by a car. Never. I would have known. Did he bring you home? Are you saying that Edward hit you in his car? It's impossible."

"Yes. He hit me, and then he got out and picked me up."

"But I would have known that. If you had been injured, I would have known. And you never played near the road. You were only a small child."

"He picked me up, and he carried me a little ways, and then he put me down again." Paul's voice was dull and matter-of-fact. "In the highway. He put me down in the highway. And then he left me there. I remembered it today."

Anna lay rigid on the floor, visualizing the scene her son had described. For a moment she could not speak. Then her voice came out in a whisper. "He left you . . . in the highway."

"Someone came and picked me up. Someone I didn't know. I think it was my . . . you know . . . him . . . Rambo. My father. Only he was a stranger then. He picked me up and carried me off the highway."

For a few moments the windmill was silent, save for the sounds of their breathing. The boy was quiet, relieved of his story.

It took Anna a few minutes to absorb what she had heard

and to understand its truth. Suddenly her body began to shake with a violence so fierce it seemed that the ground must be trembling beneath her.

"He did that to you," she said. It made sense to her now. This man, her neighbor, had hit her son by accident and then left the child in the road to die. Moved him, so that his death would not be left to chance. For a few intense moments Anna knew what it was to want to kill. With electrifying clarity she realized that she could plunge a knife into Edward Stewart's heart without remorse. Or cudgel him to death without pity. She closed her eyes as the murderous rage engulfed her helpless body, and then she began to breathe again as slowly it subsided. When the anger passed over her, like the angel of death, she was left with only an intense pity that brought tears to her eyes as she pictured her poor child, helpless in that open roadway. For a moment she blessed Albert Rambo with her entire being for saving her son from a certain death.

Anna began to inhale deeply, trying to will herself to be calm. She had to think of a way out of here. She had to survive this torture and rescue her son. That was what was important now. She did not have energy to spare on hatred. She needed her wits to get them free. And then, then she would see Edward Stewart punished for what he had done.

She counted backward to herself, slowly, trying to focus on something other than the vision of her child in the road, left to die by a "friend." Her mind refused to release the image. Then she heard Paul moan again from the loft above. She reminded herself of how scared he must be. Finally she found her voice. "Don't worry, darling. We'll get out of this. I won't ever let him hurt you again."

Paul was quiet for a moment. "Okay," he said. "What'll we do?"

In his voice was the innocent trust of a child turning to his mother for the answer. And although she did not know the answer, his trust made her feel strong, made her sure that she could find it. "We'll get out of here," she said.

But as her defiant promise hung in the air, the door to the windmill opened, and Edward Stewart appeared in the doorway. He was carrying a large suitcase. Anna lifted her eyes and stared at him, her loathing for him oozing from her body like sweat. Edward did not speak but turned on one small wall lamp and set down his valise. He began to search through the built-in cabinets. On one of the shelves he located an electric hot plate with one burner. He removed it and closed the cabinet door, then placed the hot plate on the workbench.

The sight of Edward's face made Anna's stomach churn with revulsion, but she understood the helplessness of her position. She kept her voice calm and steady as she spoke.

"Edward, untie these bonds and let us out of here. This has gone on long enough."

"Please don't speak to me, Anna."

"Be reasonable," she said coldly, "and stop this before it goes any further. Before you know it, people are going to be looking for us. This house is the first place they'll look."

Without answering her, Edward began pulling out drawers and emptying them on the floor, scattering papers and parts of boats around the room. Then he collected a bunch of rags that were in a bag on a workbench. They were stiff and stained with varnishes and turpentine. He examined them for a moment and then put them together in a pile. "By the time they find you," he said, "it won't matter."

"As soon as Thomas or Tracy gets home, they're going to come right over here and look for us. What are you planning to do? Take us away somewhere?"

"No," he said, "you're not going anywhere." He opened the suitcase he had been carrying and laid it on the trash-covered floor. He began to select the models which were finished, or partially finished, and load them into the valise. He was only able to fit about three boats into the bag. With a sigh he snapped it shut.

Anna watched him in fascination as he tested the weight of the suitcase. She thought she understood and felt a momentary relief. He only wanted a head start on getting away. She could not resist tormenting him. "What's the point of running?" she said. "You'll get caught in the end."

For the first time Edward looked at her incredulously. Then he started to laugh. It was a hollow laugh, over as soon as it began. "Oh, heavens," he said, "I'm not going anywhere. I'm just going to the club for dinner. No, no. I simply wanted to rescue some of these from the fire."

Anna's and Edward's eyes locked for a moment. At first she could not comprehend what he was saying. And then she recognized, in his steely gaze, the calm determination of one who had made an irrevocable decision. "The fire," Anna repeated.

Edward nodded and began to pile together some papers that crinkled. "I had planned to dispose of the boy somewhere else. But then you got involved, and it all became too complicated. So I thought it over and decided that the best solution was for a tragic accident to occur right here, while I was away from the house, of course."

"You wouldn't," Anna said.

"There's no one in the vicinity to alert the fire department. At least not before it's too late. I suspect you're right, that your husband or your daughter will eventually come looking for you and will find . . . what's left of you. Forgive me, that was crude."

Edward stepped over to the workbench and lifted the hot plate. He turned and looked at her, holding the hot plate awkwardly under one arm. "You shouldn't have interfered with my plan, Anna." He placed the hot plate on a low bench and plugged it into a socket on the wall. Then he picked up the pile of rags which he had collected. He carefully distributed them and the newspapers around the hot plate, with one corner of a rag overlapping the ring of the burner. "There," he said. "That will heat up and start to catch."

Anna's heart was hammering from fear, but suddenly the rage which she had held in check, hoping to reason with him, surged up from inside her, displacing every other feeling. "You loathsome, vile excuse for a man," she said through clenched teeth. "You disgusting pig . . ."

"Don't talk to me like that, Anna," he said tonelessly.

"Wasn't it enough that you left my son in the road to die?" she cried. "You weak coward. You scum . . ."

Edward wheeled around, his eyes blazing wildly. He took a step toward her and kicked her hard in the side. Anna gasped and cried out.

"Yell all you want," he said. "No one will hear you."

Edward turned around and picked up the valise. Then he looked up into the loft at the boy imprisoned there. "Goodbye," he said evenly. Paul spit at him, and the spittle landed on Edward's sleeve. He wiped his sleeve off gingerly with a paper towel and tossed the roll down next to the hot plate. Without another word he left the windmill and closed the door behind him.

Anna lay on her side, staring across the floor at the hot plate. The burner was starting to glow now. The edge of the rag rested on the brightening burner. Anna saw a faint brown border begin to appear on the dirty cloth.

Paul's small voice drifted down from above. "Did he hurt you?" he asked softly.

Gathering her breath to reply caused a sharp pain in her chest. But her voice was steady when she spoke. "I'm all right," she said.

Slowly, painfully, she began to inch her way across the floor toward the menacing burner. The edge of the rag was black now, and a tiny lick of flame began to flicker across at its rim.

"Don't be afraid," she called out to him. "Don't be afraid."

CHAPTER TWENTY-THREE

Thomas pulled his suitcase and his briefcase from the back seat of the cab and leaned over to pay the taxi driver his fare.

"Thanks, Mac," said the driver. "Have a good night."

Thomas nodded and watched as the driver backed slowly down the Langes' driveway. He turned and looked up at the house. He had somehow expected that Anna would rush out to the porch to meet him; but all the lights in the house were dark, and there was no sign of her, except for her Volvo parked in the driveway. He checked the garage window and saw his car parked inside. He walked slowly up the walk to the house and let himself into the front.

He stood for a moment in the silent foyer and looked around. It was not the homecoming he had anticipated, but, he reflected, it was probably the one he deserved. "Anna," he called out, but his voice was not answered by the empty rooms.

He went into the living room and turned on a light. It was getting late in the day, that hour which is neither dark nor light. He set his bags down on a chair and walked through the house.

It was just lucky that he had decided to go back to his

hotel room after lunch to pick up some papers. That was when he had gotten the message from Anna about Paul. His first thought upon reading it was one of dread. He had had a moment where he felt too disheartened to face it. But she needed him, and she was calling him home. It had not taken long to decide what to do. With a few phone calls he had canceled all his meetings and prepared for the trip back.

Now he walked into the kitchen and went straight to the counter where she always left her notes for him. There was nothing, no indication of where she had gone.

Thomas sighed and punched a fist lightly into the counter top. "Tracy," he called out, but he knew there would be no answer. For a moment he felt as if he were in every child's nightmare, when you come home from school and find that your family has moved. He shook the feeling off. He remembered that Tracy had gone sailing with Mary Ellen. Walking over to the phone, he dialed Mary Ellen's house and waited. The girl's mother answered and told him that the boat was still out. He told her to have Tracy call the moment she got in and he would come to pick her up. Mary Ellen's mother agreed, and Thomas hung up.

He loosened his tie and went to the refrigerator to get a beer. Anna was probably with the police, he decided. If Paul was missing, she would go straight to Buddy for help. She and Buddy must be out looking for him. Thomas took a swig of beer and swilled it around in his mouth. He could not help wondering, as he had on the shuttle back to New York, if the boy had decided to run away. And with that speculation came the guilty feeling that his own selfish behavior might be the cause. He gave a quick and silent prayer that his wife and son would walk in the door before he had finished his beer, but even as he prayed, he was dialing the phone number of the Stanwich police station.

The phone rang five times before anybody answered; it seemed to Thomas an unconscionably long time. When the receptionist finally answered, Thomas barked out his request to speak to Buddy Ferraro.

The woman on the other end explained that Buddy was not there.

"Well, this is Thomas Lange," he said. "My son is missing, and I was wondering if my wife might be out looking for him with Detective Ferraro. I just got in from Boston."

The woman at the other end was silent for a moment. "Oh, hello, Mr. Lange," she said finally. "I'm sorry about your son."

"Can you possibly tell me what is going on?" he said.

"Well, this is Marian Hammerfelt. I was here when your wife came in this morning. Your boy disappeared at the airport this morning."

"What's being done about it? Does Buddy Ferraro know about this?"

"Detective Ferraro was out of town when it happened. He just came back himself on account of it. He called me from home a few minutes ago, and he's on his way to the station right now. But your wife is not with him. We haven't seen her since this morning."

Thomas stared at the phone as if the instrument were deliberately confounding him.

"Detective Ferraro ought to be here in about twenty minutes," said the woman. "You want me to have him call you when he gets in? Or shall I tell him just to go on up to your house?"

Thomas sighed and thought for a moment, trying to decide what to do. "No," he said. "I may have to go pick up my daughter, and it's a long drive up here. I don't want him to get here if I'm not home. Just have him call me. That'll be fine."

Thomas hung up the phone and threw his empty beer bottle into the garbage can. His clothes felt wrinkled and uncomfortable. He decided to go upstairs and change them while he waited. Going back through the living room, he picked up his bags and climbed the stairs. He pushed the door open to his and Anna's room and looked inside. The room was orderly and welcoming as always, the wedding ring quilt spread neatly across the bed, a bedside vase filled with flowers. He walked over to the dresser and picked up the silver-backed brush, running his fingers over its smooth surface. Then he set it down and started to change.

It was unlike Anna not to leave him a message. Perhaps she thought that he wouldn't come home, wouldn't answer her call for help. It occurred to him again that he had done a lot of damage to their marriage, and along with the guilt he felt a powerful urge to make it up to her. He wanted to start right away, and the emptiness of the house filled him with a sense of impotence and frustration.

As he was tying on his sneakers, he suddenly realized where she must be. She would not bother to leave a note if she were only going over to see Iris. It might mean that she would be back at any time. That was it. A feeling of relief flooded him. She had probably walked over there. He leaned across the bed and picked up the bedside extension. The Stewarts' number was taped across the front, along with the police and the firehouse, to call in case of emergency. He dialed the number eagerly, impatient to hear Iris's voice, so he could tell Anna that he was back. The phone began to ring and then continued ringing, as he realized, with a sinking heart, that there was nobody home.

No answer. She wasn't there after all. Thomas dialed

again, just to make sure, but there was no answer. He slammed the phone down on the receiver and sat dejectedly on the edge of the bed.

He could not think of where else she might have gone. Maybe she had gone out somewhere with Iris, he thought. That was possible. Maybe they had gone out to search for the boy. He rubbed his eyes and stared at the phone. Or they might be out on the grounds somewhere. That could be. He thought of going over to check. They could be sitting out by the pool. But through the window he could see that it was growing darker. And it was getting chilly, too. The air already felt like fall. He walked over to the bedroom window, which was open a few inches, and closed it. Then he shook his head. Anna wouldn't be out reclining by the pool with Paul lost to her. He considered taking a walk over. If Iris were there, she might know something. Then he thought of Edward. He did not much like the idea of running into him. Edward always made him feel as welcome as a case of hepatitis.

Thomas lay back on the bed. Tracy might call at any minute, and he had promised to pick her up. And then there was Buddy. He would be calling, too. Try to rest, he told himself. There's nothing you can do but wait. Maybe if you take a nap, she'll be back when you wake up. He closed his eyes and tried to will himself to relax, although, as he did so, a vein began to throb in his forehead. Relax, he told himself. Any minute now the phone will ring. He began to rub the knot which had formed in the base of his neck as he covered his eyes with his other hand.

Using her bound feet and hands to make tiny, jerky pushes, Anna rolled her body across the cold stone floor toward the hot plate. The path was strewn with the flammable debris which Edward had collected. She forced herself to tumble over it, crushing a half-finished hull into splinters that stabbed through her clothes and tangling her limbs in the rags. Papers slid away as she bumped them, and she bruised her side on the cold head of a hammer which lay on the floor. Her rotating feet caught the leg of a chair, which tipped over, and the cardboard box on top of it, which was filled with tiny silken sails, overturned. Trian gles of bright fabric floated down and landed on the glowing ring of the hot plate. It flared up and flamed brighty for a few moments, casting a small but eerie glow in that corner before it turned to ash on the ring.

The edge of the rag left by Edward was flaming now, little licks of flame dancing on its blackened edges, eating in toward the center of the cloth. Anna hesitated, tempted to try to extinguish the rag, but she was nearer the cord of the hot plate. She looked up at the outlet where it was plugged. If she could lift her head up enough to grab the cord between her teeth, she thought, she could pull it from the wall. The thought of putting that cord in her teeth was chilling; but the rag was burning vigorously now, and she had to cut off the threatening burner.

"What are you doing?" Paul called out from above.

"Hang on, honey," she said. "I'm going to stop this burner."

"Be careful," he cried.

Anna stared resolutely at the cord. Then, dragging herself up on one raw elbow, she caught the cord in her mouth, carefully covering the sheath of the cord with her tongue as well as she could. Cocking her head to one side, she wedged a loop of the cord between her chin and her shoulder blade. Here goes, she thought. Don't bite down.

Anna squeezed her eyes shut and jerked her body away

from the wall. The plug resisted and then came free from the wall. The violent motion pulled the hot plate off its perch on a low bench, and it overturned, a foot away against the treadle of the sewing machine.

Anna quickly dropped the cord from her mouth. "It worked," she cried. "I unplugged it."

"Good work, Mom," he cried.

Anna felt a moment's giddy pleasure at the fact that he had called her Mom, but she was instantly sober again. "Now I'm going to put these ropes on my hands against the coils as they cool down and try to burn through them, if I can."

"Be careful," he said.

"First, though," she said, "I have to put that rag out."

The tails of the rag were aflame, and Anna dreaded what she had to do next; but she felt there was no choice. It might take awhile to free herself, and they would not be safe unless the rag was out. Once it was extinguished, she could concentrate on her bonds. The hot plate would not cool off that quickly. Now, however, she knew she had to smother the flames, and there was only one conceivable way to do it. She began to work her way toward the burning cloth, determined to crush it like a steamroller and flatten the flames before they could spread.

Anna tensed her body, prepared to roll. She hoped she could land squarely on it, so that it would be over in one try. She whispered a prayer and then drew back for momentum.

The little flames working in toward the center of the rag suddenly reached a brown, stained patch. In that instant the rag exploded with a burst that shot licks of fire out across the room.

Anna checked her forward motion with a cry, her face

seared by the intense and sudden heat. She shot backward as Paul let out a yelp. "What happened?"

"The rag," she gasped. "It exploded."

Shards of the flaming rag landed in different spots in the small space. A few hissed on the cold floor and died. Others landed on hospitable boxes and other piles of rags and papers. One fell on a broom, propped up against the wall. The flames ate their way hungrily down the bristles as Anna watched helplessly. There were small fires all around her now as smoke began to rise in the windmill.

Edward's fingers trembled as he knotted his tie, but otherwise he felt relatively calm. The ringing of the phone awhile before had unnerved him, but he had ignored it. It was just as well. Whoever was calling would be able to testify that he had not even been at home when they tried to reach him. He pulled on his jacket and checked himself in the mirror to be sure he was properly dressed. He always enjoyed dining at the club without Iris. When she was with him, no matter how well he looked, she always looked just dowdy enough to embarrass him as they walked through the dining room. Tonight, though, it would be perfect. It was a spot where he would be highly visible. He would eat, drink, and socialize, and by the time he returned from the evening all his problems would have turned to ashes. The windmill would be an inferno or a smoking shell. Inside, the searchers would find the remains of mother and son, the victims of a tragic mishap, their bonds incinerated in the blaze.

It was a bold plan, staging the accident right here on his own property, but he had finally decided it was the right move. It had infuriated him that Anna had stumbled into the middle of his perfect setup, and he had considered trying to dispose of two corpses instead of one, as he had originally planned. But the more he thought about it, the better it seemed to have them killed right here. Aside from the fact that he had no motive that anyone knew of, he felt sure that no one would ever believe that he would start such a fire on his own property. Anyone who knew him at all knew how attached he was to that windmill. In fact, it was his one regret that he had to sacrifice it in order to get rid of the boy and his snooping mother.

The Langes, he further reassured himself, were just the kind of people to come trespassing on his property, letting themselves into the windmill. It was one of their lowbrow habits to turn up, uninvited. Iris could certainly attest to that. He would tell the police that he had urged the boy to make use of the windmill anytime he pleased. He would be as blameless as could be. A victim, in fact, of their carelessness.

But now, he thought, it was time to get on the road. Edward picked up the keys to the Cadillac on the dresser and then opened the dresser drawer. Inside were his gold money clip and a leather billfold full of cash. He stuffed some bills into the clip and slipped it into his pocket. Then he snapped off the lamp and started out the door and down the hall to the stairs. He was halfway down the staircase when he heard the knock at the front door.

Edward froze, staring down at the door. For one moment he considered not answering it, thinking that perhaps whoever it was would go away. But then he realized that the person might go around to the back of the house instead, and he could not take that chance. He doubted whether there would be any sign of the fire yet, but he couldn't risk it. He would simply have to open the door and get rid of whoever was there. He reminded himself that he was a busy man on the way to his club. It was probably someone collecting for something.

Edward quickly took the remaining stairs. He peered out through one of the front windows but did not see a car in the drive. After walking softly to the front door, he pulled back one of the curtains surrounding the lead windows a fraction of an inch and looked out.

Thomas Lange stood on the doorstep.

Edward's heart constricted in his chest, and he felt the sweat pop out on his forehead. What is he doing here? he thought. He was in Boston. Be calm, he ordered himself. Anna must have summoned him home. Behave normally. He is looking for Anna, and you have not seen her since this afternoon. Edward straightened up and brushed a piece of lint off the front of his suit. Then he opened the door.

"Thomas," he said pleasantly, "what can I do for you? I'm just on my way out."

"Can I come in for a minute?" said Tom. "I'm so glad to find you home."

Edward looked pointedly at his watch, but Thomas seemed too agitated to notice. "Well," he said hesitantly, "for a minute, certainly."

Tom passed by him and into the living room, checking his sneakered feet to be sure he wasn't tracking dirt on the cream-colored carpet.

"Tom," said Edward, following him into the room, "I thought you were on a trip. When Anna called this morning, she said she was seeing you off at the airport."

Thomas shook his head wearily. "I went up to Boston, but then I got a message from Anna at my hotel that Paul was missing again. So I came home. And now Anna's nowhere to be found either."

"Oh, I'm sure she's not far," said Edward soberly.

"I was trying to take a nap and just wait for them, but it was driving me out of my mind. I had to come over and see if you or Iris knew anything about what happened or where Anna is."

"Well, Iris is away for a few days. I saw Anna earlier this afternoon, but not since then, I'm afraid."

"What did she want?" Thomas asked.

"She was looking for the boy," Edward said. "My goodness, what a terrible time you've all had."

Thomas frowned slightly.

"What's the problem?" Edward asked.

Thomas looked at him closely. "I called before. No one answered."

"I've been in and out," Edward explained, looking at his watch.

"I guess I'm keeping you," said Thomas. "I suppose I ought to be getting home."

"No, no, you don't," said Edward, aware that Thomas would be much too close for comfort if he went home, even though the house was a good distance away. He still might smell the smoke from there. "I'll tell you what," said Edward. "I have an idea. Why don't I take you out and we'll drive around town and look for Anna?" I'm sure you're in no mood to drive yourself right now."

"I couldn't," said Tom, surprised by the offer. "It's too much trouble. We wouldn't even know where to look."

"No trouble," Edward assured him. "I'd like to help. What do you say?"

"No, I can't," said Thomas. "I have to pick up Tracy in a while."

"We can get her on our way. Then, we'll swing by the police station and see if they have any news."

Thomas hesitated, suddenly looking extremely weary.

"You're right," he said. "I can't just sit home by the telephone, doing nothing about this situation. It's driving me nuts."

"That's right," said Edward, gripping Thomas by the elbow. "You come along with me."

Thomas allowed Edward to steer him to the front door, and the two men walked out toward the garage."

"I hate to drag you away from what you were doing," Thomas said.

"I was only going to the club for dinner," Edward said. He glanced back behind the house in the direction of the windmill. There was nothing to give him away. The smoke was not yet rising. "Believe me, I can do that anytime. It's not every day you can help out a friend." The two men entered the garage, and Edward unlocked the door to the Cadillac on the passenger side. Thomas looked at him incredulously for a moment, and then he shrugged and got in the passenger side. He's as cold a fish as ever, Tom thought, but at least he's making an effort.

A sense of elation and smugness filled Edward as he opened his own side and slid back behind the wheel. He tried to compose his face to appear properly serious as he turned on the engine and looked sympathetically at his neighbor. These people are so simple, he thought. They're like sheep.

The car, which was facing forward, rolled silently out of the garage and down the driveway.

The combined heat of the various fires was intensifying, causing the inside of the windmill to feel like a warming oven. With a recklessness born of desperation, Anna rolled back toward the hot plate, smothering the flames in her path.

Squirming up against the leg of the sewing machine, she groped behind her for the hot plate. At first she burned her fingers, noting with indifference that she felt the pain, but it no longer mattered. She held her bonds against the ring and tugged at them.

"Please," she whispered as a flaming rag torched the cane seat of a chair by the workbench. "Please."

She wriggled her hands against the burner, pulling and tugging at the ropes which held her. It was becoming more difficult to breathe as smoke began to fill the room. Her eyes were smarting, and she squeezed them shut.

"Mom," Paul cried from the loft. "Help." She heard him begin to cough.

The burning broom fell over, igniting a pile of notebooks. Anna tried to jerk her hands apart, but the hot plate was cooling now, its mission accomplished.

"Mom," the boy cried again.

Don't give up, she ordered herself. He needs you. Don't give up. But the scene before her streaming eyes was like a vision of hell. She mustered all her breath. "Try to cover your nose and mouth," she cried, straining to be heard above the crackle in the room. "Try not to breathe the smoke." She could feel the beads of water evaporating on her cheeks. Her eyes were watering uncontrollably now, but whether from smoke or from tears, she was unable to tell.

"Do you hear me?" she cried. "Paul!" But there was no answer from the loft above.

CHAPTER TWENTY-FOUR

"I'm sure there's some perfectly simple explanation," said Edward smoothly as he started down the lengthy drive, "although it's a shame you have to go through all this."

Thomas, who was slumped in the seat beside him, did not appear to be listening.

"If I know Anna," Edward went on, "she probably couldn't sit still either. She's probably out looking—"

"Wait a minute," said Thomas. "Stop the car."

Edward's head jerked around, and he stared at his passenger. "Whatever for?" he demanded.

Thomas sat upright in his seat. "The telephone is ringing in your house," he said. "Stop the car."

"You're hearing things," said Edward, halfheartedly applying the brake.

"I tell you it's ringing," Thomas insisted.

"Oh, it's probably just the Alisons, calling about dinner," said Edward. "I don't care if I miss their telephone call. Whoever it is can just call back later."

"It could be Anna," said Thomas excitedly. "She might have tried our house first and couldn't get me. You have to answer it."

Before Edward could prevent him, Thomas had jumped

from the car and was sprinting back toward the house. Edward pulled up the emergency brake and slid out of the car to follow him.

He reached the front door of the house some seconds after Thomas and leaned against it, panting from lack of breath. Thomas stood with his ear pressed to the door.

"It's still ringing," said Thomas. "I'm sure it's Anna. Open the door."

Edward glared at Thomas as he struggled to catch his breath. He glanced out toward the windmill and saw a faint plume of smoke rising in the air. "Don't be ridiculous," said Edward.

"She might need me. Maybe she had an accident. I don't know. Open the door."

"I think you're overreacting a little," Edward said coolly, "don't you?"

Thomas turned to his neighbor with eyes that were wholly determined. "You said you wanted to help me," said Thomas in a voice colder than Edward's. "If you want to help me, then open this fucking door, or I'll break a window and let myself in."

The two men stared at each other for a moment. Edward struggled to check his fury and not to bash in Thomas's insolent face. If Thomas broke the window, it would set off the alarms in the police station, and there would be squad cars here all too soon. The phone continued to sound its bell insistently. If he could satisfy Thomas, he might still get him out of here in time. In the end he'll pay for this, Edward reminded himself. He turned, his face pale, and put the key in the lock. "You're acting irrationally, Thomas," he said, turning the doorknob and opening the door.

Tom pushed past him and into the house, running for the phone, with Edward following him. He picked up the receiver, then hesitated and handed it to Edward. Edward did not look at him as he put the receiver to his ear. "Hello."

"Mr. Stewart," said Tracy, "I'm sorry to bother you, but do you know where my parents are? There's nobody answering at my house."

"Just a moment," Edward said. He turned to Thomas. "It's for you."

Thomas grabbed the phone from him, and yelled into it, "Yes?" as Edward walked back out into the foyer. There was no time to waste. No time at all. He had to get Thomas safely out of there before the fire began to blaze. Edward looked at his watch again.

"That was Tracy," said Thomas, coming into the foyer.

Edward turned to face him, forcing himself to smile, "I know. I suppose she needs her ride. We should get going and pick her up."

Thomas did not reply but preceded Edward out the door. He waited for Edward down by the driveway. Edward fished in his pocket for the keys and locked the front door again. Then he followed in Thomas's path.

"Look, Edward," said Tom, "thanks for the offer, but I think I can drive myself. I'm going to take a ride down and pick up Tracy, and she and I can drive around for a while and look for Anna."

Edward was about to protest, but then he thought better of it. Any which way that Thomas left the house was fine with him. Just as long as he got out of there. "Are you sure?" he asked stiffly. "I really don't mind."

Thomas shook his head. "Thanks anyway."

"Well, then, let me at least give you a ride home," said Edward, opening the door to the car.

"I'll walk home," said Thomas politely. "I don't want to trouble you any further."

"Don't be silly. Let me drive you. I'm on my way out."

Thomas raised a hand in protest. "I've already made you late. You go ahead without me. I can use the walk."

Edward could feel his face reddening, but he spoke calmly. "It's a long walk from here," he said. "Why don't you just get in the car?"

"It's not that far," said Tom. "I'll cut through the back."

Edward felt his heart pounding in his chest. He had to persuade him to get in the car. He could not let him walk through the back. Not now. He was sure to see the smoke. "No," Edward insisted. "I'll drive you."

Thomas sighed wearily. "Look, I'd rather walk. I think I've about exhausted your generosity as it is." He turned and started toward the back.

Edward clenched his jaw, and then he shouted, "How dare you?"

Thomas stopped short and stared at him.

"How dare you assume you can go trampling and trespassing over my property anytime you please? You and the members of your family treat this estate like a public park, and I won't have it."

Thomas stared at him for a moment, trying to think of something sufficiently scathing to say to make Edward regret what he had just said. You arrogant, pompous ass, he thought. You can't talk that way to me. So much for the neighborly gesture. Now I know how you really feel about us, and it's just what I suspected.

The thoughts raced through his head, but Thomas could not find words for them, for he did not want to sound hurt and petulant like a child. Edward was trembling from head to toe, but he did not take his imperious gaze from Tom's face.

Suddenly Tom realized that there was only one way to respond to Edward's outburst, and that was with calm defiance. "Sorry, neighbor," Thomas said slowly. "I feel like taking the shortcut."

With a deliberate stride he started around the side of the house.

Edward raced after him. "Stop this minute," he cried.

Thomas continued on a few more strides, and then he did stop. Slowly he turned and faced Edward, who was right behind him.

The two men stared at each other. Then Thomas spoke. "There is smoke," he said evenly, "coming from the direction of your windmill. It looks as if there's a fire out there."

Edward's features sagged, and his eyes were suddenly anxious. "Oh, nonsense," he said. "Get off my property."

"Don't you even want to look?" Thomas asked quietly.

Edward tore his eyes away from Thomas's disbelieving gaze. "No. You're crazy."

"No, I'm not," said Thomas. "Why didn't you want me to see it?"

Suddenly Edward lunged at him, grabbing Thomas by the neck of his shirt. For a moment Thomas was thrown off-balance, and Edward began to punch at him, his eyes blazing.

With a powerful swing of his right arm Thomas caught Edward in the side of the head and knocked him to the ground. Before Edward could scramble to his feet again, Thomas had disappeared around the back of the house and emerged on the patio. He could see the gusts of smoke more clearly now, gray against the darkening sky. He began to run.

The pulse in his ear and his heartbeat thundered while he ran, his sneakers making dents in the manicured lawn as he flew up over the rolling landscape of the estate. He leaped over a stone wall, staggered for a few steps, and then ran again.

The windmill was obscured from view by a bank of trees, but as he approached the trees, he could see an unnatural brightness beyond them. He pushed his way through and then stopped short and stared.

Sam, Paul's cat, was sidling near the door of the burning building, but the animal's approach was being thwarted by the heat. The cat turned at the sound of Tom's arrival and looked at him with huge eyes.

Tom looked from the cat's eyes to the burning building. Flames were licking the frames of the tiny windows, and smoke issued from them. The area around the door was already beginning to blacken. And from inside he could hear the crackling and the faint sound of a familiar cry, which made his blood turn icy. Tears sprang to his eyes, although he did not know it. His chest rose and fell in a rapid motion. "Anna," he said. Then he ran for the door.

He put his fingers on the doorknob but pulled them back again, burned by the heat it conducted. Tearing off his jacket, he wrapped it around the doorknob and jerked it open.

Heat and smoke billowed out, blackening his face and his shirt. Inside, he could see flames in clumps burning up piles of junk and climbing the walls. The heavy smoke made the air in the room opaque, except where it was punctured by flames.

"Anna!" he screamed. "Anna!"

Through the growing roar of the fire, he heard an answering groan. He pushed into the windmill, knocking over piles of burning debris and brushing off the flaming scraps that tried to settle on him. "Anna!" he cried. "Where are you?"

As his eyes adjusted to the gathering inferno, he saw a dark mass huddled behind the sewing machine. He lurched toward it, covering his mouth with the tails of his shirt, and bent down to see his wife, bound by ropes, crumpled in the corner, with one sleeve already on fire. She lifted her gaze to his, and then her eyes rolled back. After beating her flaming garment out with his hands, Thomas crouched down and carefully put his arms under her to lift her up. As he pulled her toward him, a line of flames burst into view where her arm dangled behind her. He gathered her stiff arms in close to him and tried to untie the knots which bound her hands. The sight of her bound revolted and enraged him. But the flames were spreading, and he was coughing from the smoke that filled his lungs.

He glanced up toward the door and saw that the path was alive with fingers of flame that he would have to skirt. Clutching Anna close to him, Thomas rose carefully to his feet, teetering under his burden. He murmured to her nonsensically as he tried to plan a path through the flames. They were all around him now, burning piles of rubbish raising the temperature in the windmill to an unbearable heat, raging and hungry for the fuel that was everywhere.

Like a man treading in a snake pit, Thomas picked his way through the fire, aiming for the door, his wife bundled in his arms like a child. A chunk of flaming wood fell from the loft above him, narrowly missing Anna's legs. Thomas jerked her clear of the blazing projectile and pushed his way through the fire to the door, disregarding the singeing on his flesh where licks of flame had whipped him like a lash and left their mark.

As they reached the doorway, a flaming hull from one of Edward's ships fell into his path. Tom jumped back, then over it, and they were through the door and out on the lawn. He staggered a few yards away from the windmill and then, gulping in air, dropped on his knees to the ground, carefully placing Anna down on the well-tended grass. Anna moaned, lying on her side, her arms and feet still bound behind her. Tom rested for a minute, and then he turned to her and put his head to her chest. She was coughing and breathing hard, but without grave difficulty. He reached over and began to untie her.

Anna started to stir as her bonds were removed, and then her eyes opened and she rolled over. She looked up at the soot-smudged face of her husband, smiling down at her.

"Are you all right?" he asked between coughs.

She reached her hand up, and he grabbed it and held it to his cheek. Anna struggled to sit up, and then she looked around.

"Paul," she croaked in a voice hoarse from smoke.

Thomas looked at her blankly.

The dazed expression in Anna's eyes turned to one of frantic alarm. "Tom, he's in the windmill," she whispered, an occasional normal tone breaking through the hoarse, anxious croak.

Thomas shook his head. "I didn't see him."

She grabbed his shirt. "In the loft," she cried.

Without another word Thomas sprang to his feet and ran back to the door of the windmill. Anna could see the flames shooting from the windows, framing the door as smoke poured forth.

She clutched her hands to her mouth, shaking her head

slowly from side to side, as she watched her husband hesitate and then plunge back into the inferno. Tears began to trickle down her face, leaving tracks in the soot on her cheeks.

It took several seconds after Thomas had bolted away from him for Edward to realize that he was ruined. Thomas would discover that his wife and son had been imprisoned in the windmill. It wouldn't be possible to kill them all. Not now.

Wiping his face on his sleeve, Edward staggered back toward the house. He would lose everything now, he thought numbly. His mind could not absorb the possibility. His perfect plan was ruined, and there was no time to think of another. With that realization Edward was jolted again into an awareness of his predicament. Running was his only hope. He charged into the house, not knowing what to grab first. He thought of the money in the dresser drawer. He raced up the stairs, yanked out the drawer roughly, and stuffed the money into his pants pockets. His next thought was for his boats. He grabbed the suitcase full of boats, which he lugged down the stairs, clutching the bag like a life preserver. In the foyer, at the foot of the stairs, he stopped, looking around at all the expensive things he owned. For a moment he thought that he could not leave them. Then, with an effort, he started to move.

Alternately running and walking, he reached the car where it was parked in the driveway. He was out of breath as he put his hand on the door handle and slipped inside. He placed the suitcase full of boats in the back seat. With trembling fingers he switched on the ignition and pressed his foot down on the gas. For one second he glanced behind him and saw the smoke rising from behind the house. He faced forward and gripped the wheel tightly. He did not have much time.

With all his weight he pressed down on the gas pedal. The car shot forward and began to career down the long driveway. He whizzed past the manicured grounds which had been his refuge for so long. Edward kept his eye on the drive, thinking about which way to go. He decided to head for the Millgate Parkway and head north. He was unable to think about any more than that.

The car approached the end of the drive, and Edward turned the wheel, applying the brakes so that the tires squealed as he made the corner. He glanced left and saw no one coming, as he had expected. The car, which had been going at a considerable speed, took the turn in a wide arc. As the Cadillac swung out into the road, Edward looked to his right and saw the police car, a few hundred feet from him, coming at a clip.

He spun the wheel frantically, trying to get the Cadillac back into its lane, but the automobile was out of control now and spun out wide, starting to jackknife. The police car tried to swerve out of the way but was unable to avoid the Cadillac. The two cars collided, and both cars jerked to a halt.

For a moment Edward sat, stunned, in his seat. Then, as he saw the door to the squad car open, he was revived to action. Throwing the gearshift into reverse, he pressed down on the gas, and the Cadillac jumped back and away from the crushed front of the police car. Panting now, he jammed the gearshift back into drive and turned the wheel so he could pass the vehicle he had just struck.

From the corner of his eye he could see the startled expression on the face of the cop, emerging from the car. Edward recognized Buddy Ferraro, the detective who was always hanging around the Langes. Edward gunned the engine, and his car shot forward, avoiding the police car but nearly hitting the detective, who had stepped out into the street with a hand raised.

"Halt," the officer called out, but Edward ignored the summons. The Cadillac accelerated quickly, and the car began to tear down the road. The crack of a pistol rang out, but Edward paid it no heed. He kept his eyes on the corner of the street. It was not far away now. If he could just make it to the parkway . . .

He could feel the fear in him now, gnawing at him. His breath was coming in short gasps, his chest aching from the tumultuous beating of his heart.

You've lost everything, he thought as he swallowed the lump in his throat. Suddenly, as he pressed on the gas, he thought he saw a child in the road ahead, staring up at him with innocent, wondering eyes. Nausea gripped his stomach, but he did not let up on the gas pedal. He could not stop now. He was almost to the corner. It was too late to stop. It always had been.

He heard the report of the gun again, and in that instant the mirage of the child disappeared. With a sudden feeling of elation he raced toward the end of the street. Then, to his shock, he felt the jolt as the back tire blew out. The car swerved crazily over the road, and Edward tried to think what to do. It was only a moment, but it was as if it were happening in slow motion, as he felt the huge, powerful machine start to spin out of control.

I'm going too fast, he thought. He tried to jam on the brakes, but it only sent the speeding car careening off the road.

A huge, shady elm tree loomed up ahead of him, just beside the entrance to Hidden Brook Lane. Edward could see the golden eagle on his hood flying toward it at an incredible speed. The sound of crunching metal reached his ears as the eagle rammed the tree and was sheared off. It bounced up over the hood and the shattered windshield, which were crushed like a paper cup by the impact.

Edward's last thought as he saw the tree coming toward him was that he would head for the sea and pay some yachtsman to take him aboard his boat. Once he was out of the harbor, he would take over the command. No one knew boats as he did. He would be the greatest captain who ever lived. The ocean would be his.

"Mine," he cried, as the impact jerked him forward, and the steering column rammed him through the chest.

I should never have let him go back in there, she thought. He'll never get out alive. I'll lose them both. I have to go after them.

Anna tried to stand but couldn't. She couldn't hoist herself up any higher than her hands and knees. Her head felt like a cannonball on her neck. She tried to crawl forward, toward the burning building, but collapsed almost immediately. Tom, she thought. Paul. She had to go after them.

Then she thought of Tracy. She still had a daughter, who needed her. Maybe God had left her alive for Tracy. "Please save them," she whispered.

Anna groaned as another window of the windmill burst into flames. Her arms trembled under her weight, and her wrists felt as if they could snap. She struggled up and sat back on her heels, her bruised knees digging into the ground. He had been gone too long. Too long. There were no human sounds.

The urge to go in rose in her again. Part of her wanted to

plunge in and throw herself on the flames like a grieving widow on the funeral pyre. The idea was almost tempting. It would be a way to relieve the horror. "Tom," she wailed. But she thought of Tracy again, and she knew she wouldn't do it.

Somewhere in the distance the sirens of fire engines began their plaintive wail. Anna heard them keening, but in her distraction she did not understand that they were coming to her. The sound grew louder as they came closer, and then she realized it.

Suddenly, in the doorway of the windmill, a dark, crouching figure burst forth, carrying another. Anna let out a cry of relief at the sight of her husband, grimy and gasping for breath.

"Tom," she cried, lurching to her feet. "Darling."

Then she looked at the burden in his arms. The boy was utterly still, except for his head, which bobbed lifelessly as Thomas carried him from the fire. On parts of his limp body the flesh appeared to be smoking through charred tissue. His eyes were closed, his mouth thrown open as if he had been crying out for the precious air that never came.

Anna looked from the boy to her husband, and then she raised her hands as if to ward off a blow. She began to scream.

Thomas placed the boy gently on the ground and looked up at her.

"No, Anna," he whispered, coughing hard into his hand. "He's alive. He is. Believe me."

Anna clapped her hands over her mouth and sank to her knees as Thomas bent over Paul's body and began to try to resuscitate him. She watched, transfixed, as Thomas placed his mouth over his son's and exhaled his own breath into him, turning his head to the side and listening for a response after each puff. On about the tenth breath the boy's chest moved, and Thomas looked up and met her eyes.

"See," he said.

Anna nodded and closed her eyes. She placed one hand on the boy's arm and the other on her husband. Thomas bent over Paul's body again, holding his head back in preparation for breathing.

"Can you do that?" Anna demanded. "Do you have the strength?"

Thomas only nodded, not wanting to waste the oxygen. Once again he put his mouth on Paul's and continued to breathe into the boy's mouth, while Anna watched as the boy's chest began to rise and fall in a steady rhythm and a semblance of color returned to his face. There was a commotion in the distance now as the fire engines and ambulance which Buddy had summoned on the police radio converged in the Stewarts' driveway.

"Tom, look," said Anna as Paul's eyes opened and rolled around to her. Thomas straightened up beside her. They both looked worriedly down at the boy and smiled at him.

"You okay?" Anna asked softly.

The boy nodded and then began to cough as if he would choke.

"Tom," said Anna grabbing his arm, "I think he's choking."

"No, he's got to get the smoke out." Thomas gripped Paul's hand as he coughed until the spasm ended. "He'll be all right. You're stubborn, right? You're a fighter."

Paul managed a feeble smile and wrapped his fingers around his father's. Tom smiled at Anna. "I think he gets that from you." Tom lowered his head to the boy's ear and spoke softly. "We'll get you to the hospital in no time, don't worry." Even as he spoke, the fire trucks and the ambulance came screeching up over the Stewarts' well-manicured grounds.

Paul nodded and closed his eyes, which were bloodshot and still tearing from the smoke. Tom gazed down, studying his son's haggard face. "I wonder what he gets from me," he said with a sad sigh.

Anna put her arm around him and watched her son's steady breathing. "Everything there is," she said gently. "Every good thing there is."

Dell Bestsellers

☐ **ELIZABETH TAYLOR:** The Last Star
  by Kitty Kelley $3.95 (12410-7)

☐ **THE LEGACY** by Howard Fast $3.95 (14719-0)

☐ **LUCIANO'S LUCK** by Jack Higgins $3.50 (14321-7)

☐ **MAZES AND MONSTERS** by Rona Jaffe ... $3.50 (15699-8)

☐ **TRIPLETS** by Joyce Rebeta-Burditt $3.95 (18943-8)

☐ **BABY** by Robert Lieberman $3.50 (10432-7)

☐ **CIRCLES OF TIME** by Phillip Rock $3.50 (11320-2)

☐ **SWEET WILD WIND** by Joyce Verrette $3.95 (17634-4)

☐ **BREAD UPON THE WATERS**
  by Irwin Shaw $3.95 (10845-4)

☐ **STILL MISSING** by Beth Gutcheon $3.50 (17864-9)

☐ **NOBLE HOUSE** by James Clavell $5.95 (16483-4)

☐ **THE BLUE AND THE GRAY**
  by John Leekley $3.50 (10631-1)

At your local bookstore or use this handy coupon for ordering:

Dell DELL BOOKS
P.O. BOX 1000, PINE BROOK, N.J. 07058-1000

Please send me the books I have checked above I am enclosing $ _____ (please add 75c per copy to cover postage and handling) Send check or money order—no cash or C.O.D.'s. Please allow up to 8 weeks for shipment.

Mr /Mrs /Miss _____

Address _____

City _____ State/Zip _____

The members of the Mobile Army Surgical Hospital are certified as hell-raising nuts by the army bureaucracy, which they turn into outright bedlam. It is a judgment confirmed by an assortment of individuals unfortunate enough to be victims of their pranks. They include:

A forgetful chaplain who writes all-is-well letters to the families of mortally wounded G.I.'s.

A despondent dentist who threatens to commit suicide once too often.

And Major Hot Lips Houlihan, the pompous Chief Nurse at the 4077th Mobile Army Surgical Hospital.

"This is lusty, uninhibited man-stuff with *no* holds barred. It is also extremely funny."
—*Publishers Weekly*

Books in the MASH Series

Published by POCKET BOOKS

MASH

by

RICHARD HOOKER

PUBLISHED BY POCKET BOOKS NEW YORK

**POCKET BOOKS, a Simon & Schuster division of
GULF & WESTERN CORPORATION**
1230 Avenue of the Americas, New York, N.Y. 10020

Copyright © 1968 by William Morrow & Company, Inc.

Published by arrangement with William Morrow & Company, Inc.
Library of Congress Catalog Card Number: 68-29610

ISBN: 0-671-82673-5

First Pocket Books printing November, 1969

34   33   32   31   30   29   28   27   26   25

Trademarks registered in the United States and other countries.

Printed in the U.S.A.

FOREWORD

MOST OF THE DOCTORS who worked in Mobile Army Surgical Hospitals during the Korean War were very young, perhaps too young, to be doing what they were doing. They performed the definitive surgery on all the major casualties incurred by the 8th Army, the Republic of Korea Army, the Commonwealth Division and other United Nations forces. Helped by blood, antibiotics, helicopters, the tactical peculiarities of the Korean War and the youth and accompanying resiliency of their patients, they achieved the best results up to that time in the history of military surgery.

The surgeons in the MASH hospitals were exposed to extremes of hard work, leisure, tension, boredom, heat, cold, satisfaction and frustration that most of them had never faced before. Their reaction, individually and collectively, was to cope with the situation and get the job done. The various stresses, however, produced behavior in many of them that, superficially at least, seemed inconsistent with their earlier, civilian behavior patterns. A few flipped their lids, but most of them just raised hell, in a variety of ways and degrees. This is a story of some of the ways and degrees. It's also a story of some of the work.

The characters in this book are composites of people I knew, met casually, worked with, or heard about. No one in the book bears more than a coincidental resemblance to an actual person.

MASH

1

WHEN RADAR O'REILLY, just out of high school, left Ottumwa, Iowa, and enlisted in the United States Army it was with the express purpose of making a career of the Signal Corps. Radar O'Reilly was only five feet three inches tall, but he had a long, thin neck and large ears that left his head at perfect right angles. Furthermore, under certain atmospheric, as well as metabolic, conditions, and by enforcing complete concentration and invoking unique extra-sensory powers, he was able to receive messages and monitor conversations far beyond the usual range of human hearing.

With this to his advantage it seemed to Radar O'Reilly that he was a natural for the communications branch of the service, and so, following graduation, he turned down various highly attractive business opportunities, some of them legitimate, and decided to serve his country. Before his enlistment, in fact, he used to fall asleep at night watching a whole succession of, first, sleeve stripes, and then shoulder insignia, floating by until he would see himself, with four stars on his shoulders, conducting high-level Pentagon briefings, attending White House dinner parties and striding imperiously to ringside tables in New York night clubs.

In the middle of November of the year 1951 A.D., Radar O'Reilly, a corporal in the United States Army Medical Corps, was sitting in the Painless Polish Poker and Dental Clinic of the 4077th Mobile Army Surgical Hospital astride the 38th Parallel in South Korea, ostensibly trying to fill a

1

straight flush. Having received the message that the odds against such a fortuitous occurrence open at 72,192 to 1, what he was actually doing was monitoring a telephone conversation. The conversation was being conducted, over a precarious connection, between Brigadier General Hamilton Hartington Hammond, the Big Medical General forty-five miles to the south in Seoul, and Lieutenant Colonel Henry Braymore Blake, in the office of the commanding officer of the 4077th MASH, just forty-five yards to Radar O'Reilly's east.

"Listen," Radar O'Reilly said, his head turning slowly back and forth in the familiar scanning action.

"Listen to what?" Captain Walter Koskiusko Waldowski, the Dental Officer and Painless Pole, asked.

"Henry," Radar O'Reilly said, "is trying for two new cutters."

"I gotta have two more men," Colonel Blake was shouting into the phone, and Radar could hear it.

"What do you think you're running up there?" General Hammond was shouting back, and Radar could hear that, too. "Walter Reed Hospital?"

"Now you listen to me . . ." Colonel Blake was saying.

"Just take it easy, Henry," General Hammond was saying.

"I won't take it easy," Colonel Blake shouted. "If I don't get two . . ."

"All right! All right!" General Hammond shouted. "So I'll send you the two best men I have."

"They better be good," Radar heard Colonel Blake answer, "or I'll . . ."

"I said they'll be the two best men I've got," Radar heard General Hammond say.

"Good!" Radar heard Colonel Blake say. "And get 'em here quick."

"Henry," Radar said, his ears aglow now from the activity, "has just got us two new cutters."

"Tell 'em not to spend it all before they get here," Captain Waldowski said. "You want another card?"

Thus it was that the personnel of the 4077th MASH learned that their number, and perhaps even their efficiency, would shortly be augmented. Thus it was that, on a gray, raw morning ten days later at the 325th Evacuation Hospital in Yong-Dong-Po, across the Han River from Seoul, Captains Augustus Bedford Forrest and Benjamin Franklin Pierce,

2

emerging from opposite ends of the Transient Officers' Quarters, dragged themselves, each hauling a Valpac and trailing a barracks bag, toward a jeep deposited there for their use.

Captain Pierce was twenty-eight years old, slightly over six feet tall and slightly stoop-shouldered. He wore glasses, and his brown-blond hair needed cutting. Captain Forrest was a year older, slightly under six feet tall, and more solid. He had brush-cut red hair, pale blue eyes and a nose that had not quite been restored to its natural state after contact with something more resistant than itself.

"You the guy going to the 4077th?" Captain Pierce said to Captain Forrest as they confronted each other at the jeep.

"I believe so," Captain Forrest said.

"Then get in," Captain Pierce said.

"Who drives?" Captain Forrest said.

"Let's choose," Captain Pierce said. He opened his barracks bag, felt around in it and extracted a Stan Hack model Louisville Slugger. He handed the bat to Captain Forrest.

"Toss," he said.

Captain Forrest tossed the bat vertically into the air. As it came down Captain Pierce expertly grabbed it at the tape with his left hand. Captain Forrest placed his left hand above Captain Pierce's. Captain Pierce placed his right hand, and Captain Forrest was left with his right hand waving in the air with nothing to grab.

"Sorry," Captain Pierce said. "Always use your own bat."

That was all he said. They got into the jeep and for the first five miles they did not speak again, until Captain Forrest broke the silence.

"What are y'all anyway?" Captain Forrest asked. "A nut?"

"It's likely," Captain Pierce said.

"My name's Duke Forrest. Who are y'all?"

"Hawkeye Pierce."

"Hawkeye Pierce?" Captain Forrest said. "What the hell kind of a name is that?"

"The only book my old man ever read was *The Last of the Mohicans*," Captain Pierce explained.

"Oh," Captain Forrest said, and then: "Where y'all from?"

"Crabapple Cove."

"Where in hell is that?"

"Maine," Hawkeye said. "Where you from?"

"Forrest City."

3

"Where in hell is that?"

"Georgia," Duke said.

"Jesus," Hawkeye said. "I need a drink."

"I got some," Duke said.

"Make it yourself, or is it real?" Hawkeye asked.

"Where I come from it's real if you make it yourself," Duke Forrest said, "but I bought this from the Yankee government."

"Then I'll try it."

Captain Pierce pulled to the side of the road and stopped the jeep. Captain Forrest found the pint in his barracks bag and opened it. As they sat there, looking down the road, flanked by the rice paddies skimmed now with November ice, they passed the bottle back and forth and talked.

Duke Forrest learned that Hawkeye Pierce was married and the father of two young sons, and Captain Pierce found out that Captain Forrest was married and the father of two young girls. They discovered that their training and experience had been remarkably similar and each detected, with much relief, that the other did not think of himself as a Great Surgeon.

"Hawkeye," Captain Forrest said after a while. "Do y'all realize that this is amazing?"

"What's amazing?"

"I mean, I come from Forrest City, Georgia, and y'all are a Yankee from that Horseapple . . ."

"Crabapple."

". . . Crabapple Cove in Maine, and we've got so much in common."

"Duke," Hawkeye said, holding up the bottle and noting that its contents were more than half depleted, "we haven't got as much of this in common as we used to."

"Then maybe we'd better push on," the Duke said.

As they drove north, only the sound of the jeep breaking the silence, a cold rain started to fall, almost obscuring the jagged, nearly bare hills on either side of the valley. They came to Ouijongbu, a squalid shanty town with a muddy main street lined with tourist attractions, the most prominent of which, at the northern outskirts, was The Famous Curb Service Whorehouse.

The Famous Curb Service Whorehouse, advantageously placed as it was on the only major highway between Seoul and the front lines, had the reputation of being very good because all the truck drivers stopped there. It was unique for its methods of merchandising and outstanding for its contribution to the venereal disease problem faced by the U.S. Army Medical Corps. It consisted of a half dozen mud and thatch huts, prefaced by a sign reading: "Last Chance Before Peking" and surmounted by an American flag flying from its central edifice. Its beckoning personnel, clad in the most colorful ensembles available through the Sears Roebuck catalogue, lined the highway regardless of the weather, and many drivers who made frequent trips to the front and back fastidiously found their fulfillment in the backs of their trucks, rather than expose themselves to the dirty straw and soiled mattresses indoors.

"You need anything here?" asked Hawkeye, noting the Duke saluting and nodding as the jeep chugged through the waving, cooing colorama.

"No," the Duke said. "I shopped in Seoul last night, but something else bothers me now."

"You should know better, doctor," Hawkeye said.

"No," Duke said. "I've been wondering about this Colonel Blake."

"Lieutenant Colonel Henry Braymore Blake," Hawkeye said. "I looked him up. Regular Army type."

"You need a drink?" Duke said.

Out of sight of the sirens now, Hawkeye pulled the jeep to the side of the road once more. By the time they had finished the bottle the cold, slanting rain was mixed with flat wet flakes of snow.

"Regular Army type," the Duke kept repeating. "Like Meade and Sherman and Grant."

"The way I see it, though, is this," Hawkeye said, finally. "Most of these Regular Army types are insecure. If they weren't, they'd take their chances out in the big free world. Their only security is based on the efficiency of their outfits."

"Right," the Duke said.

"This Blake must have a problem or he wouldn't be sending for help. Maybe we're that help."

"Right," the Duke said.

"So my idea," Hawkeye said, "is that we work like hell when there's work and try to outclass the other talent."

"Right," the Duke said.

5

"This," Hawkeye said, "will give us enough leverage to write our own tickets the rest of the way."

"Y'all know something, Hawkeye?" the Duke said. "You're a good man."

Just beyond a collection of tents identified as the Canadian Field Dressing Station, they came to a fork in the road. The road to the right led northeast toward the Punchbowl and Heartbreak Ridge; the road to the left took them due north toward Chorwon, Pork Chop Hill, Old Baldy and the 4077th MASH.

About four miles beyond the fork, a flooded stream had washed out a bridge, and a couple of M.P.'s waved them into a line with a dozen other military vehicles, including two tanks. They waited there for an hour, the line lengthening behind them until the line ahead began to move and Hawkeye guided the jeep down the muddy river bank and across the floorboard-deep stream.

As a result, darkness was settling on the valley when, opposite a sign that read "THIS IS WHERE IT IS— PARALLEL 38," another, smaller marker reading "4077th MASH, WHERE I AM, HENRY BLAKE, LT. COL. M.C." directed them to the left off the main road. Following directions, they were confronted, first, by four helicopters belonging to the 5th Air Rescue Squadron and then by several dozen tents of various shapes and sizes, forlornly distributed in the shape of a horseshoe.

"Well," Hawkeye said, stopping the jeep, "there it is."

"Damn," Duke said.

The rain had changed to wet snow by now, and off the muddy road the ground was white. With the motor idling, they could hear the rumble of artillery.

"Thunder?" Duke said.

"Man-made," Hawkeye said. "They welcome all newcomers this way."

"What do we do now?" Duke said.

"Find the mess hall," Hawkeye said. "It figures to be that thing over there."

When they walked into the mess hall there were about a dozen others sitting at one of the long, rectangular tables. They chose an unoccupied table, sat down, and were served by a Korean boy wearing green fatigue pants and an off-white coat.

6

As they ate they knew they were being looked over. Finally one of the others got up and approached them. He was about five feet eight, a little overweight, a little red of face and eye, and balding. On the wings of his shirt collar were silver oak leaves, and he looked worried.

"I'm Colonel Blake," he said, eyeing them. "You fellows just passing through?"

"No," replied Hawkeye. "We're assigned here."

"You sure?" the Colonel asked.

"Y'all said you all needed two good boys," Duke said, "and we're what the Army sent."

"Where you guys been all day? I expected you by noon."

"We stopped at a gin mill," the Duke told him.

"Let me see your orders."

They got out their papers and handed them to the Colonel. They watched him while he checked the papers and then while he eyed the two of them again.

"Well, it figures," Henry said finally. "You guys look like a pair of weirdos to me, but if you work well I'll hold still for a lot and if you don't it's gonna be your asses."

"You see?" Hawkeye said to Duke. "I told you."

"You're a good man," Duke said.

"Colonel," Hawkeye said, "have no fear. The Duke and Hawkeye are here."

"You'll know you're here by morning," Henry said. "You go to work at nine o'clock tonight, and I just got word that the gooks have hit Kelly Hill."

"We're ready," Hawkeye said.

"Right," Duke said.

"You're living with Major Hobson," Henry said. "O'Reilly?"

"Sir?" Radar O'Reilly said, already at the Colonel's side, for he had received the message even before it had been sent.

"Don't do that, O'Reilly," Henry said. "You make me nervous."

"Sir?"

"Take these officers . . ."

"To Major Hobson's tent," Radar said.

"Stop that, O'Reilly," Henry said.

"Sir?"

"Oh, get out of here," Henry said.

Thus it came about that it was Radar O'Reilly, who had been the first to know they were coming, who led Captains

7

Pierce and Forrest to their new home. At the moment, Major Hobson was out, so Hawkeye and Duke each selected a sack and lay down. They were just dropping off to sleep when the door opened.

"Welcome, fellows," a voice boomed, followed by a medium-sized major, who entered with a warm smile and offered a firm handshake.

Major Hobson was thirty-five years old. He had practiced a good deal of general medicine, a little surgery. and every Sunday he had preached in the Church of the Nazarene in a small midwestern town. The fortunes of war had given him a job for which he was unprepared, and associated him with people he could not comprehend.

"You fellows certainly are welcome," he intoned. "Would you like to look around the outfit?"

"No," said Duke. "We been stoned all day. Guess we'll get a little sleep."

"We've gotta fix the President's hernia at nine o'clock," Hawkeye said. "We're Harry's family surgeons. We'd ask you to assist, but the Secret Service is worrried about Chinese agents."

"Yankee Chinks from the north," Duke said. "Y'all understand."

Jonathan Hobson was shocked and confused, and there was much he didn't understand. Soon after nine o'clock he understood even less. The gooks had indeed hit Kelly Hill, the casualties were rolling in, and the five men on the 9:00 P.M. to 9:00 A.M. shift had their hands full.

When 9:00 A.M. arrived, it was clear that the most and best work had been done by Hawkeye Pierce and Duke Forrest. Among other things, the two, functioning as if they had been working across the table from each other for years, did two bowel resections, which means removing a piece of bowel damaged by such foreign bodies as fragments of shells and mines. Then they did a thoracotomy for control of hemorrhage, which means they opened a chest to stop the bleeding caused by the entrance of a similar body, and they topped this off by removing a lacerated spleen and a destroyed kidney from the same patient.

The ease with which they handled these and several more minor cases naturally stimulated considerable comment and speculation about them. With their chores done, however,

Hawkeye and Duke were too tired to care, and right after breakfast they headed across the compound for Tent Six.

As the components of the 4077th MASH were arranged around the horseshoe, the operating tent, with its tin Quonset roof, was in the middle of the closed end. The admitting ward and laboratory were to the left and the postop ward to the right. Next to the laboratory was the Painless Polish Poker and Dental Clinic, then the mess hall, the PX, the shower tent, the barber shop, and the enlisted men's tents. On the other side, and strung out from the postop ward, were the tents were the officers lived, then nurse country, and finally the quarters for the Korean hired hands. Fifty yards beyond these domiciles was a lonely tent on the edge of a mine field. This was the Officers' Club. If one walked carefully and obliquely northwesterly for another seventy-five yards beyond the Officers' Club and didn't fall into old bunkers, he'd reach a high bank overlooking a wide, usually shallow, branch of the Imjin River.

"Southern boy," Hawkeye was saying as they approached their tent, "I'm going to have myself a butt and a large shot of tax-free GI booze and hit the sack."

"I'm with y'all," Duke was saying, as Hawkeye opened the door affixed to the front of the tent.

"Look!" Hawkeye said.

Duke looked where Hawkeye was pointing. In one corner, kneeling on the dirt floor with his elbows on his cot, a Bible in front of him, his lips moving slowly, and oblivious to all about him, was Major Jonathan Hobson.

"Jesus," Hawkeye said.

"It don't look like Him," Duke said.

"Do you think he's gone ape?"

"Naw," Duke said. "I think he's a Roller. We got lots of them back home."

"We've got some back at the Cove, too," Hawkeye said. "You've gotta watch 'em."

"Y'all watch him," Duke said. "It would bore me."

While Major Hobson maintained his position, they had a large drink and then one more. Then, in loud, unmelodious voices, they sang as much as they could remember of "Onward Christian Soldiers" and crawled exhausted into their sleeping bags.

When they awoke, darkness had come again, and so had

another load of casualties. The casualties continued to pour in without letup for a whole week, and the new surgeons did more than their share of the work. This naturally aroused a growing respect among their colleagues, but it was respect mixed with doubt and wonder, for they fitted no recognizable pattern.

2

NINE DAYS AFTER the arrival of Captains Pierce and Forrest at the Double Natural, as the 4077th was called by the resident crapshooters, two things happened. There came a lull in business, and the shifts changed so that the two were working days. Both men much preferred this combination of circumstances except that now, each morning as they arose for breakfast, they were forced to witness and walk around their tentmate, Major Jonathan Hobson, kneeling in prayer beside his cot.

"Major," said Hawkeye one morning, as the lengthy ritual came to an end, "you seem to be somewhat preoccupied with religion. Are you on this kick for good, or is this just a passing fancy?"

"Make fun of me all you want," replied the Major, "but I'll continue to pray, particularly for you and Captain Forrest."

"Why, y'all . . ." the Duke started to say.

Hawkeye broke him off. It was obvious that the Duke did not wish to accept salvation from a Yankee evangelist, so Hawkeye motioned him to follow and they left the tent.

"Let's get rid of him," the Duke said, when they were outside. "I don't like that man, and he's stuntin' our social growth, too."

"I know," Hawkeye agreed. "He's such a simple clunk that I kind of hate to roust him, but I can't put up with him, either."

"What are we gonna do?" Duke said.

"We are going to ditch the Major," Hawkeye said, "But let's be quiet about it. No use kicking up too much of a fuss."

Hawkeye and Duke knocked on the door of Colonel Blake's tent and were told to enter. After they had made themselves comfortable, Hawkeye opened the conversation.

"How are you today, Colonel?" he said.

"That's not what you two came to ask," the Colonel said, eyeing them.

"Well, Henry," Hawkeye said, "we don't wish to cause any trouble, but we strongly suspect that something that might embarrass this excellent organization could occur if you don't get that sky pilot out of our tent."

"*Your* tent?" Henry started to say, and then he thought better of it. He sat there in silence for almost a minute, while the surge and counter-surge of his emotions played across the red of his face in iridescent waves.

"I have been in this Army a long time," he said finally, measuring his words. "I know just what you guys are up to. You figure you have me over a barrel, and to a certain extent you do. You do your jobs very well. We're going to lose our other experienced men and get a bunch of greenhorn replacements. You two are essential, but you can hold me up for just so much. If I go along with you now, where is it going to end?"

"Colonel," Hawkeye said, "we appreciate your position."

"Right," Duke said.

"I will define ours," Hawkeye said. "It reads about like this: As long as we are here we are going to do the best job we can. When the work comes our way we will do all in our power to promote the surgical efficiency of the outfit because that's what we hired out for."

"Right," Duke said.

"We'll also show reasonable respect for you and your job, but you may have to put up with a few things from us that haven't been routine around here. We don't think it will be anything you can't stand, but if it is you'll just have to get rid of us in any way you can."

"Boys," said the Colonel, after a moment's reflection, "I'm not sure what I'm getting into, but Hobson will be out of your tent today."

He reached under his cot and came up with three cans of beer.

12

"Have a beer," he said.

"Why, thank y'all," Duke said.

"Then there's one other small thing," Hawkeye said.

"What's that?" the Duke said to Hawkeye.

"The chest-cutter," Hawkeye said to the Duke.

"Yeah," Duke said to the Colonel.

"What?" the Colonel said.

During the quiet period that had settled upon the western Korean front, few shots had been fired in anger, and the only casualties had resulted from jeep accidents and from soldiers invading mine fields in search of pheasant and deer. Hawkeye and Duke had handled the lower extremity and abdominal damage of the hunters with their customary ease. When it came, however, to the depressed fractures of the sternum and multiple broken ribs with attendant complications sustained by the jeep jockeys, they both wished that they had had more formal training in chest surgery.

"That's right," Duke said to the Colonel. "Y'all better get us a chest-cutter."

"Stop dreaming," Henry said, "and drink your beer."

"We've been thinking," Hawkeye said, "that maybe you could trade two or three of these Medical Service clowns around here for somebody who can find his way around the pulmonary anatomy when the bases are loaded . . ."

". . . and it's the ninth inning," Duke said.

"Listen," Henry said. "I'll give it to you just the way the General would give it to me. Do you guys think this is Walter Reed? You're doing fine."

"We are like hell," Hawkeye said. "We're swinging with our eyes closed, and . . ."

". . . and up to now we've just been lucky," Duke said.

"Forget it," Henry said. "How's the beer?"

"Forget it, hell," Hawkeye said. "You're evading the issue. We have more chest trauma right here than any hospital at home and we need somebody who really knows how to take care of it. We're learning, but not enough. You know that just as well as we do."

"That's right," Duke said.

"Forget it," Henry said, "and by the way, with Hobson out of your tent as of now, please put in a little time for him in the preop ward."

It had long been customary at the 4077th for the surgeons

13

on duty to spend their time, when not called upon to operate, in the preoperative ward. On quiet days this was unnecessary. The arrival of casualties was always known in advance, no one could get more than three hundred yards away, and thus each doctor was available in minutes.

The logic of this had never gotten through to Major Hobson, however, and as titular head of the day shift he had attempted to impose the useless vigil upon Captains Pierce and Forrest as soon as they had joined his section. Hawkeye and the Duke had failed to comply, letting it be known that they would usually be available at the poker game that ran perpetually in the Painless Polish Poker and Dental Clinic, where Captain Waldowski, of Hamtramck, Michigan, and the Army Dental Corps, supplied cards, beer and painless extraction for all comers, twenty-four hours a day.

"I don't know, Henry," Hawkeye said now. "That's asking a lot, but if you get us that chest-cutter . . ."

"Get out of here!" Henry said. "Just finish your beers and get out of here!"

When not in the poker game, Hawkeye and Duke were likely to be in their tent. That very afternoon, shortly after lunch while all was quiet, Hawkeye was in the game, but Duke was in what was now their private quarters, propped up on his cot, a writing tablet on his knees. Every day he faithfully wrote his wife, a very time-consuming procedure, and he was thus engaged when Major Hobson came charging into the tent and demanded that Captain Forrest come to the preoperative ward immediately.

"Are there any patients?" Duke asked.

"That's neither here nor there," the Major replied austerely.

"If there ain't no patients there I stay here."

"Come to the preoperative ward immediately!" yelled the Major. "That's a direct order!"

"Y'all get out of here," was Duke's quiet answer.

The Major advanced like an avenging angel. The Duke came off his sack like the Georgia fullback he had once been, and Major Jonathan Hobson found himself prostrate in the snow and slush six feet from the tent door.

"That, you ridiculous rebel," said Hawkeye when he heard about it and got back to the tent, "was about as bright as Pickett's Charge. This will be trouble."

The expected arrival of Colonel Blake was forthcoming

14

within minutes. The door opened, Colonel Blake entered, and the door slammed shut behind him.

"You guys have had it!" he shouted, purple-faced and suffused with military indignation. "I'm having you court-martialed!"

"Henry," said Hawkeye, "I had nothing to do with it. It was all this dumb southern boy. However, I'll gladly participate in the consequences. Where do we get court-martialed? Tokyo, or maybe San Francisco?"

"San Francisco, hell. You get court-martialed here and now. You're both confined to the post for one month. This is a summary court-martial, and I've just held it."

"But y'all can't . . ." the Duke started to say.

"Look, Henry," Hawkeye said, "be reasonable. I wouldn't know how to get off this post if I wanted to, but I'd like to keep the way open in case they make me Surgeon General of the United States."

"Me too," Duke said.

With a grunt, the commanding officer departed, and it is possible that the penalty would have stood, except that the very next day Major Hobson, his ego restored and perhaps even enlarged by the Colonel's legal action, extended his activities. He began praying in the mess hall for fifteen minutes before each meal.

"That'll do it," Hawkeye predicted to the Duke.

It did. Colonel Henry Blake was endowed with more human understanding than is required of a Regular Army Medical Officer, but after three days of this he left his lunch uneaten, went to his tent, called 8th Army Headquarters, arranged orders for Major Hobson, drove him to Seoul and put him on a plane for Tokyo and home where, a few weeks later, the Major's enlistment would expire. Honorably discharged, he would return to his general practice, his occasional excursions into minor surgery and his church.

Returning from Seoul on the night of his Great Delivery, Colonel Blake was very tired and slightly mulled, but he mixed himself a drink and then collapsed on his cot. Before he could find sleep, however, Hawkeye Pierce and Duke Forrest entered. Apparently contrite, they silently helped themselves to a drink. Then they knelt in front of their commanding officer and started to pray.

"Lordy, Lordy, Colonel, Sir," they wailed, "send our asses home."

"Get your asses out of here!" yelled Colonel Blake, rising in wrath.

"Yes, sir!" they said, salaaming as they went.

3

SEVERAL WEEKS AFTER the departure of Major Hobson, it was again first reported by Radar O'Reilly and then announced by Colonel Blake that a new surgeon had been assigned to the 4077th MASH. The only available information was that he was a chest surgeon and he was from Boston.

"Great!" exulted Hawkeye.

"Goddam Yankee," said Duke.

"Undoubtedly a good boy," said Hawkeye.

He arrived on a cold and snowy morning about nine o'clock. Henry brought him to the mess hall for coffee and introduced him to the other surgeons, most of whom, because the gooks had been quiet for three days, were there.

The new boy was six feet tall and weighed about a hundred and thirty pounds. His name was John McIntyre. The fatigue suit and parka he wore prevented anyone from getting much of a look at him. He acknowledged introductions with noncommittal grunts, he sat down at a table, pulled a can of beer out of a pocket and opened it. Then his head disappeared into the parka like a turtle's into its shell, and the beer followed it.

"Seems like a nice fella," Duke said, "for a Yankee."

"Where you from, Dr. McIntyre?" someone asked.

"Winchester."

"Where did you go to school?

"Winchester High," from somewhere inside the parka.

"I mean medical school."

"I forget, I guess."

"That," said Hawkeye to the Duke, "ought to stop the conversation for a while. I got a feeling I've seen this thing before. Wish he'd come out of the cocoon."

Captain Ugly John Black, the chief anesthesiologist, apparently decided to smoke him out. During his long working hours, when operating-room technique required that the anesthesiologist attending the patient be separated from the rest of the operating team, Ugly John was often lonesome for conversation. The new man's laconic responses were at least more talk than Ugly John could get back from his anesthetized patients.

"Have a good trip over?" he asked.

"Nope."

"Fly?"

"Nope."

Ugly scratched his head and figured he'd play the guy's own game.

"So what did you do, walk?"

"Yep."

"Great idea," Ugly said. "I wonder why I didn't think of it."

The head came out of the parka and looked Ugly over with great care.

"I don't know," it said.

By now it seemed fairly obvious to the group that they had some kind of a nut on their hands, and all, including Duke and Hawkeye, departed with haste. During the day, while the new boy was being oriented and supplied with this and that, most of the outfit went to Henry and asked him not to put Captain McIntyre in any of their tents—all except Duke and Hawkeye.

"Let's see what happens," Hawkeye said.

"Yeah," Duke said.

Late that afternoon it happened. The door of the tent swung open, and in came the new boy, bag and baggage. The baggage was dumped on one of the empty cots, and the new boy lay down. A hand went into the depths of the parka, came out with a can of beer, went back in and came out with an opener. The new boy opened the beer, and for the first time he looked at his new tentmates.

"It's a small place," he said, "but I think I'm going to love it."

18

"My name's Pierce, and this is Duke Forrest," Hawkeye said, getting up and offering his hand.

The newcomer didn't budge.

"Seen you before, haven't I?" asked Hawkeye.

"I don't know. Have you?" answered McIntyre.

"For Chrissake, McIntyre, are you all this friendly all the time?" demanded the Duke.

"Only when I'm happy," answered McIntyre.

Hawkeye went out, filled a bucket with snow and mixed martinis. He poured two, thought a moment, shrugged his shoulders, and asked the new boy if he would like one.

"Yep. Got any olives?"

"No."

The hand disappeared into the parka and came out with a bottle of olives. An olive was removed and placed in the martini.

"You guys want an olive?"

"Yeah."

An olive was doled out to each. The Duke gave a contented sigh.

"McIntyre," he said, "you're a regular perambulatin' PX."

Hawkeye laughed loudly. The martini and the head came out of the parka, looked at him, then disappeared again.

Duke and Hawkeye were on night duty, and the new boy was assigned to their shift. A Canadian unit had spent the day getting shot up a few miles to the west, so the night was a busy one, and there were several chest wounds. About all Duke or Hawkeye or anyone else at the Double Natural knew about the chest was what they had learned by bitter and difficult experience in recent weeks. The new boy didn't say much, but he did come out of the parka and show them what to do.

In the third chest that he opened he went right to and repaired a lacerated pulmonary artery, and he did it like Joe D. going back for a routine fly. When morning came the night shift went to the mess hall, their curiosity aroused more than ever by the new chest surgeon from Boston. At breakfast, another can of beer materialized from the recesses of the parka and, once opened, disappeared back into it.

At the Double Natural a rag-tag squad of Korean kids waited on tables, and one of them placed a bowl of oatmeal

19

and a cup of coffee in front of Dr. McIntyre. The head shot out of the parka, and two glaring eyes focused on the boy.

"What's that?"

"Oatmeals, sir."

"I don't want oatmeals. Bring me bean."

"Bean hava no."

"OK. The hell with it."

Breakfast was quiet after that, and, as soon as the three had made it back to Tent Number Six, they went to bed, the new boy still in his parka.

At 4:00 P.M., Duke and Hawkeye got up, dressed and washed. From deep down in the parka, which had shown no previous signs of life, came the words:

"How about a martini?"

Hawkeye mixed, and again the olives were produced. After the first martini the new boy got up, took off the parka for the first time, washed his face, combed his hair, and got back into the parka. This look at him confirmed the impression Duke had formed the night before in the OR that Dr. McIntyre was about as thin as a man could get, and for the second time he addressed his new associate.

"Hey, boy, y'all got the clap?"

An immediate answer was not forthcoming. The head did come out of the parka, however, and look vaguely interested.

"What in hell makes you think he's got the clap?" Hawkeye asked. "Even a clap doctor can't diagnose it through a parka."

"What y'all don't know," replied Duke, "is that I'm a graduate of the Army Medical Field Service School at Fort Sam Houston, Texas, where I won high honors. I learned that the only thing that can go wrong with a soldier is for him to get shot or get the clap. He ain't bleeding so he's gotta have the clap."

"Well, when you put it that way," Hawkeye said, "it does make sense. However, he may be an exception to the rule."

"I don't have the clap," said the parka.

"See? What did I tell you?" said Hawkeye.

In the days that followed, John McIntyre continued to be an enigma. He and Hawkeye Pierce talked a little and looked each other over a little, and Hawkeye continued to have the nagging thought that he had seen him somewhere before.

One afternoon, about a week after the new doctor's arrival,

with the snow temporarily gone, some of the boys were throwing a football around. As Hawkeye and McIntyre emerged from their tent, a wild throw brought the ball to rest at the latter's feet. He leaned over very, very slowly and picked up the ball. With a lazy wave of his hand he motioned Hawkeye downfield. When the Hawk was thirty yards off, McIntyre whipped a perfect pass into his arms. They continued their walk to the mess hall in silence, but Hawkeye was bothered again by memories he couldn't quite bring into focus.

"Where'd you go to college, John?" he asked over a cup of coffee.

"It was a small place, but I loved it. Where'd you go?"

"Androscoggin."

McIntyre grinned, but he didn't say anything.

By midafternoon it had started to snow again. The Duke, between complaints about the Yankee weather, was writing his wife, and Hawkeye was reading *The Maine Coast Fisherman* when McIntyre got up from his cot and headed for the door.

"Where you goin'?" asked Hawk.

"To the Winter Carnival."

With that he headed out of the tent in the general direction of the mountain to the west. Half an hour later he was seen halfway up it.

"That," said Duke Forrest, "is the strangest son-of-a-bitch I ever did see. If he wasn't the best chest-cutter in the Far East Command, I'd kick his ass out of this here tent."

"Just wait," Hawkeye said.

Martini time came. Duke and Hawkeye were having their first, Hawkeye deep in thought.

"I know I've seen that guy before," he said finally, "and before long I'm going to remember where. I figure he went to Dartmouth, with all this Winter Carnival crap. Also Daniel Webster said, 'It's a small place,' and so forth. Which reminds me, did I ever tell you how I beat Dartmouth single-handed?"

"Yeah, but only sixteen times. Tell me again."

"Well, it was just a midseason breather for the Big Green, but a blizzard blew up and it was 0–0 going into the last minute. They had this boy who was supposed to be a great passer so he threw one, snow and all, and—"

Just then the door opened, and in came McIntyre covered with snow.

"Where's the martinis?" he asked.

Hawkeye looked at him, and suddenly the intervening years and the nine thousand miles dissolved and memory functioned. Perhaps it was the snow or the thought of Dartmouth or both. He jumped up.

"Jesus to Jesus and eight hands around, Duke!" he yelled. "You know who we been living with for the past week? We been living with the only man in history who ever took a piece in the ladies' can of a Boston & Maine train. When the conductor caught him in there with his Winter Carnival date she screamed, 'He trapped me!' and that's how he got his name. This is the famous Trapper John. God, Trapper, I speak for the Duke as well as myself when I say it's an honor to have you with us. Have a martini, Trapper."

"Thanks, Hawkeye. I wondered when you'd recognize me. The minute I saw you I knew you were the guy that intercepted that pass. Lucky you didn't have your mouth open or it would have gone down your throat."

"Trapper, Trapper, Trapper," Hawkeye kept saying, and shaking his head. "Say, what you been doing since then?"

"Not much. Just living on my reputation."

The Duke got up and shook hands with Trapper.

"Right proud to know y'all, Trapper," he said. "Are you sure y'all don't have the clap? Y'all look right peaked."

"I got over the clap. I'm so skinny because I don't eat."

"Why not?"

"Got out of the habit."

"Don't let it worry you," Hawkeye said.

"It could happen to anybody," Duke said.

And so the Trapper was one of them. An hour later the three tentmates weaved into the mess hall, arm in arm.

"Gentlemen," yelled Hawkeye, "this here is Trapper John, the pride of Winchester, Dartmouth College, and Tent Number Six, and if any of you uneducated bastards don't like it you'll have to answer to Duke Forrest and Hawkeye Pierce."

4

FOR SEVERAL WEEKS following the identification of Captain John McIntyre as Trapper John things settled down into an orderly routine. The work during the twelve-hour shifts was often intense, sometimes lacking, and usually somewhere in between.

Although many of the casualties were brought in from the Battalion Aid Stations by ambulance and might arrive at any hour, the most seriously wounded were flown in by helicopter. This meant that daylight was the frequent arrival time because the choppers did not fly at night. When the night shift had worked steadily from 9:00 P.M. to 4:00 A.M. and finally had everything cleaned up, some of its members could usually be seen as the first light of day seeped into the wide valley, peering north beyond the mine field and the river with its railroad bridge, hoping against hope that no choppers would materialize out of the mist.

When casualties were heavy, the regular schedule was ignored and every man worked as long as he could stay on his feet, think and still function. Finally, overcome by fatigue, he would grab a few hours of sleep and then go back to it again. When things were under control, however, there was leisure time and, particularly in winter and early spring, very little to do with it.

Tent Number Six, the home of Forrest, Pierce and McIntyre, became a center of social activity. It also became known as The Swamp, partly because it looked like the kind of haunt one might come across in a bog and partly because Hawkeye Pierce, while in college and unable to afford a dormitory room, had lived just off the campus in a shanty that his classmates had called The Swamp. The words, in big capital letters—THE SWAMP—were painted in red on the door of Number Six.

Cocktail hour at The Swamp began at 4:00 P.M., the hour at which the night shift normally awakened and had a few before supper, and the hour at which the day shift, if unemployed, could begin to relax. Cocktails consisted of better booze than most of the crew had ever had at home, and martinis were a favorite, served in water glasses filled to the brim.

A frequent visitor to The Swamp parties was the Catholic chaplain of the area, Father John Patrick Mulcahy, a native of San Diego and former Maryknoll missionary. He was lean, hungry-looking, hook-nosed, red-haired, and, in the eyes of the Swampmen, one of a kind.

The occupants of The Swamp had loose religious affiliations. Hawkeye claimed he had been brought up to be an all-over Baptist but that he had lost his nerve at the last minute. Duke was a foot-washing Baptist, and Trapper John was a former mackerel-snapper who had turned in his knee-pads. It was the Duke who hung the name of Dago Red on the Father, and the Father accepted it with good humor.

Prior to being in the Army, Dago Red had spent five years in China and seven years on the top of a mountain in Bolivia. His contacts had been limited. With Duke and Hawkeye and Trapper John he found stimulation in conversation that included politics, surgery, sin, baseball, literature and religion. Dago Red combined the dignity of his profession and the wisdom, understanding and compassion of an honest missionary with the ability to tolerate the Swampmen. He became one of them.

At two o'clock one morning, Hawkeye and Trapper John were fighting what seemed to be a losing battle in the OR with a kid who had been shot through both chest and belly. Despite control of hemorrhage and administration of blood, the patient, whose peritoneum had been contaminated for ten hours by spillage from his lacerated colon, went deeper and deeper into shock.

"Maybe we'd better get Dago Red," said Hawkeye.

"Call Dago," ordered Trapper John.

A corpsman went for him. Within minutes he appeared.

"What can I do for you fellows?" asked the Father.

"Put in a fix," said Hawkeye. "This kid looks like a loser."

Father Mulcahy administered the last rites. Shortly thereafter, the patient's blood pressure rose from nowhere to 100, his pulse slowed to 90, and he went on to recover.

From then on Dago Red put in many a fix. With the Swampmen it was mostly a gag, but one they could not quite bring themselves to forgo when things were rough. As far as Red was concerned, of course, it was no joke. He spent many sleepless nights applying fixes and feeding beer, whiskey, coffee or consolation to distraught surgeons whose patients had not responded to the fix or who were waiting for the fix to take.

This was all to the good, except that Duke Forrest became somewhat bothered. Protestantism was strong in him, and close association with an accredited representative of the opposition caused occasional qualms.

"Y'all seem to be a mighty effective bead-jiggler, Dago," he said one night, "but how do I know one of my boys couldn't do as well?"

"I'm sure he could," Red answered calmly.

"Tell y'all what I'm gonna do," Duke said. "I'm gonna get Shaking Sammy to put in a fix the next time I need one."

Shaking Sammy was the Protestant chaplain. His headquarters were in an engineering outfit down the road. He was called Shaking Sammy because he so dearly loved to shake hands. Whenever he hit the hospital, Shaking Sammy started shaking hands as soon as he came in and kept right on shaking. On one great morning, people whose hands were shaken by Sammy as soon as he entered the compound maneuvered into his path again and again as he made his rounds and shook his eager hand again and again. It took Sammy two hours to make the circle, and he had shaken hands three hundred times with fifty people.

Despite repeated warnings, Shaking Sammy also had the bad habit of writing letters home for wounded soldiers without inquiring into the nature of their wounds. One day, before Duke had a chance to invite him in for a fix, Sammy wrote a letter for a boy who died two hours later. The letter told his mother that all was well and that he'd be home soon. It had been written with no investigation of his surgical situation. The nurse had managed to see the letter, and she told Duke and Hawkeye. They escorted Shaking Sammy out of the hospital and, as he left, they shot all four tires of his jeep with their .45's. That was the last of Shaking Sammy for a while.

"Guess I'll have to stick with the bead-jiggler," said the Duke that afternoon. "Do you suppose we could convert him?"

Discussion of conversion was cut short by the arrival of a chopper with two seriously wounded soldiers. One of them, it seemed clear from the wound of entrance, the distended abdomen, and the severe degree of shock, had a hole in his inferior vena cava or possibly in the abdominal aorta. Since the inferior vena cava and the abdominal aorta drain blood from and supply blood to the lower half of the body, he was not long for this world.

Hawkeye, Duke and Trapper John went to work. They got blood going, and they gave him Levophed to raise his blood pressure. Ordinarily they would have waited for things to stabilize, but now there was no time.

Ugly John Black, the anesthesiologist, placed the tube in the trachea, through which he gave and controlled the anesthesia. Hawkeye Pierce was at the knife, and in they went. They tied off the vena cava faster than would have been considered proper in civilian surgery. Hawkeye jammed a large bore needle into the aorta so that they could pump blood through the real main line.

"Get Dago Red quick," yelled Hawkeye at the first lull.

Father Mulcahy was already entering the OR.

"What will it be, boys?" he said.

"All the Cross Action you got, plain or fancy, but make it good," said Hawkeye.

With continued blood replacement and with Levophed, hope began to emerge from what had been desperation and chaos. The patient's youth and vigor, plus rapid surgery and the remarkably effective Cross Action from Dago Red, added up to a virtual miracle.

Duke and Hawkeye were off duty the following Saturday night, and they had, perhaps, a few more than were necessary.

"We got to do something for Dago Red," said Duke. "I

mean to show our appreciation for all the good fixes, bead jiggling, and skillful Cross Action."

"There's no doubt about it," replied Hawkeye. "Did you have anything in mind?"

"Ain't nothing jelled exactly, but it's gotta be something impressive."

"How about a human sacrifice?"

"Hawkeye," said the Duke, "y'all are purely a genius. Let's get Shaking Sammy."

"A wise choice," replied the Hawk. "You get a jeep, and I'll round up Trapper John."

Within minutes they were streaking through the darkness down the road toward the engineer outfit where Shaking Sammy made his home. Sammy was taken in his sleep, bound, gagged and tossed into the back of the jeep.

At six o'clock on Sunday morning, as Dago Red appeared at the chaplain's tent to conduct early Mass, a frightening sight confronted him. He saw a cross. Lashed to it was his Protestant colleague, Shaking Sammy. Surrounding him on the ground was a pile of hay, assorted flammable junk and a couple of old mattresses. Lying on the mattresses were Captains Pierce, Forrest, and McIntyre.

"What's going on here?" asked Father John Patrick Mulcahy.

"It's something we gotta do," answered Trapper John.

"You guys are drunk!" the Father bellowed.

"We had a drink or two," the Duke said.

"Break this up before you get in trouble," the Father said, and then he saw the fifth in Duke's hand. "Give me that bottle, Duke."

"This ain't no bottle, Red," said Duke, showing him the rag stuffed in the neck of the bottle. "I'm chairman of the Fiery Cross Committee, and this here's a Molotov cocktail."

"This is in your honor, Red," said Hawkeye. "Step back and enjoy it. The time has come."

He lifted a gasoline can and poured the contents on the debris surrounding Shaking Sammy and some on Sammy himself. By now a crowd had gathered, sleepy, perplexed, but beginning to take interest.

"Dr. John Francis Xavier McIntyre will say grace," announced Hawkeye Pierce, "or whatever the hell you call it."

27

"I don't care if it rains or freezes," intoned Trapper John, "Sammy'll be safe in the arms of Jesus."

Although several people lunged at the Duke, he lit the wick of the Molotov cocktail and hurled it into Shaking Sammy's funeral pyre. Sammy screamed, and the Swampmen took off for The Swamp. As the crowd surged forward the Molotov sizzled and went out.

Pouring three shots, Hawkeye said, "You know, the silly bastard really thought it was gasoline we poured on him. After that letter and God only knows how many others he's written, I'm kinda sorry it wasn't."

"This is going to mean trouble," said Trapper John. "Nobody will put up with that kind of crap."

"Not ordinarily," said Hawkeye, "but we'll get away with it."

"Why?" asked Duke.

"Because at seven o'clock tonight three companies of Canadians are going for Hill 55. When they do, this place will be flooded with casualties. Personally, I don't plan to work if I'm under arrest."

"Who says?" said Trapper.

"The Canadian colonel told me last night."

"Well, we'll see," said Trapper. "Barricade that door, and let's go to bed."

When they awakened at four o'clock in the afternoon, all was quiet. Duke peeked out the door and closed it quickly.

"What do the initials M.P. stand for?" he inquired.

"Shore Patrol," answered Trapper John.

Hawkeye peeked through the rear of the tent and saw that the back was unguarded. He washed, combed his hair, put on clean clothes, a hat, captain's bars and all the appurtenances of military costume he had hardly ever worn. He went under the rear tent flap, and his tentmates quickly tied things back in place. A few moments later, a smiling Captain Pierce approached the two M.P.'s and returned their salutes.

"Colonel Blake says you can go back to your outfit, boys," he told them. "It's all blown over. You'd better get going before it's too dark."

The day was cold, and they took off gratefully. An hour later, after one leisurely martini apiece, the men of The Swamp strolled into the mess hall and sat down. The Colonel stared at them, spluttered, and pounded his fist on the table.

"Where are those M.P.'s?" he screamed. "You guys are confined to your tent until they come for you from Seoul."

"Y'all mean the Shore Patrol?" asked Duke innocently.

Henry shook. His mouth moved but no words came.

"What M.P.'s, Henry?" inquired Hawkeye. "Somebody screw up? We been in bed all day. Bring us up to date."

"Grab them!" yelled Henry, forgetting in his frenzy that no one else was present at the moment except nurses.

Nobody moved.

"Y'all heard your Cuhnnel," said Duke to the nurses. "Grab us."

"I'll try anything once," said Trapper John.

"I'm hornier than a three-balled tom cat," agreed Hawkeye. "Clear the tables for action."

At this point Dago Red walked in.

"Come with me," he ordered, pushing and shoving them out of the mess hall and herding them back to The Swamp. There, disillusioned and disappointed, he scolded, pleaded and insisted that they apologize to Shaking Sammy.

"Red," said Hawkeye, "I'm perfectly serious now. I'm not going to apologize to Shaking Sammy. I despise quack doctors, and for the same good reasons I despise quack sky pilots and all the screwballs on the fringe of the do-gooding business. So forget it."

Before the discussion got any further, the rumor of Canadians attacking 55 was borne out. Ambulances and helicopters disgorged dozens—of wounded. The Swampmen forgot the problems arising from human sacrificial ceremonies and went to the OR. To no one's surprise, no one tried to stop them. For the next four days they worked with little letup, and no mention was made of the sacrificial ceremony of the previous Sunday.

After five days the worst was over, the preop ward was cleaned out, and no new casualties were coming. The Swampmen had a drink at nine-thirty on a bright warm morning and put on their cleanest clothes. They borrowed handcuffs from the supply sergeant. They got three of their enlisted men friends to cuff them together and guard them with rifles. They sat huddled on the ground in front of Colonel Blake's tent, passed a bottle back and forth, and chanted their version of "The Prisoner's Song."

If we had the wings of a Colonel,
We'd fly to the high Pyrenees,
And open an open air laundry,
Specializing in Blake's B.V.D.'s.

Colonel Blake came out to see what was going on.

"Hey, Henry!" yelled Hawkeye. "Can officers get broads into Leavenworth?"

In times of stress Colonel Blake sometimes stuttered.

"You c-c-crazy bastards, get the h-h-hell out of here. They don't have any replacements for you, but if you don't get out of my sight so h-h-help me C-C-Christ I'll have you s-s-shot."

5

CAPTAIN WALTER KOSKIUSKO WALDOWSKI, of Hamtramck, Michigan, and Dental Officer of the 4077th MASH, was a very good dentist. He took care of the tusks of hundreds of troops, most of whom, before they met him, would have preferred to storm a gook bunker barehanded rather than go to a dentist. He wired fractured jaws and extracted teeth with a dexterity that few of the medical personnel had ever witnessed at home. That he should be called The Painless Pole was so obvious that no one would own up to being the originator of the nickname.

The Painless Pole ran the only truly popular Dental Clinic in the Far East Command, or at least in Korea. This clinic had a real poker table. It had a small portable pool table, a record player, a large supply of beer and other potables, and also one dental chair. At times of maximum surgical-military stress there were short intervals when the perpetual poker game might cease for a few brief hours. This was rare, however, for even when work was most intense, the poker game would often be the same. The players might change every fifteen minutes, but there were always players. Some were trying to relax enough to sleep. Some were trying to wake up. At any given time, a few of the players were likely to be patients. Perhaps they were waiting for Painless to get out of the OR; perhaps they were bleeding from an extraction and passing the time until the hemorrhage was definitely controlled. Other participants were wanderers from here and

31

there who knew they could always find a game at the Painless Polish Poker and Dental Clinic.

As a consequence, Captain Waldowski was widely known in the area and the most popular man in the outfit. Unlike most of the medical officers, he had been in private practice prior to being drafted. Unlike most of the medical officers, he had actually made a living, a state of grace almost inconceivable to his associates. He liked everyone, and was seldom without company.

His greatest hobby and interest, however, aside from managing the Poker and Dental Clinic, was women. As he was unmarried, it would have been perfectly natural for him to play the local nurses and patronize the flesh emporia in Seoul, but he passed these up much as a major league ballplayer would pass up a sandlot baseball game. Back home in Hamtramck, his reminiscences made clear, he had the highest lifetime batting average in the history of the league. At the present time he was engaged to, as best he could remember, three young lovelies, and while this sort of talk is so common in any military organization that it is automatically written off as malarkey, in his case it could not be written off, even by the most skeptical.

The Painless Pole, beyond any shadow of a doubt, was the best-equipped dentist in the U.S. Army Dental Corps. He was the owner and operator of the Pride of Hamtramck. Officers and enlisted men from the entire area frequently visited the 4077th MASH, supposedly to take advantage of the shower facilities, but actually they came in hope of catching a glimpse. In fact, Dr. Waldowski's dental assistant, a Corporal Jones, significantly enhanced his lowly wages by informing certain troops in advance of the Captain's intention of bathing. In the shower, popeyed officers and enlisted men viewed the Pride wistfully, and one day a corporal from Mississippi spoke for them all.

"Ah'd purely love," he said, "to see it angry."

Unfortunately, about once a month, the Painless Pole underwent a period of depression lasting no less than twenty-four hours and seldom more than three days. The usual activities of the Clinic continued, but except when forced to work, Walt just lay in his sack and stared at the walls. Radar O'Reilly, of course, was able to predict the advent of these episodes several days in advance, so that the clients of the

Clinic were forewarned, but it was Hawkeye Pierce who spread the first word of what turned out to be Captain Waldowski's most serious seizure.

On this afternoon Hawkeye had been working continuously for twelve hours and, having finally finished and found it to be bathing time, he had gone to the shower tent. He undressed slowly. His stethoscope fell out of the rear pocket of his fatigue pants, and he hung it on a nail along with the pants. He stepped under the shower, luxuriated in its warmth, relaxed and dreamed dreams of Crabapple Cove. Returning to reality, he walked back to the bench where he had left his clothes. He found Captain Walter Waldowski, The Painless Pole, sitting on the bench. All the Dental Officer had on was Hawkeye's stethoscope and a look of great alarm. He was listening to the Pride of Hamtramck.

"What's the matter, Walt?" asked Hawkeye.

"I think it's dead," Walt answered and, in a trance, he walked to the nearest shower with the stethoscope still dangling from his ears.

That evening The Painless Pole entered The Swamp and sat down. He was given a drink, which he accepted with indifference.

"I thought you guys oughta know," he announced.

"Know what?"

"I'm going to commit suicide."

There was a moment of silence. Finally Trapper John leaned from his sack and grasped Walt's hand.

"We'll miss you, Walt," he said. "I hope you'll be happy in your new location."

"Hey, Walt, how about you all leaving me your record player?" requested Duke.

"When are you making the trip?" inquired Hawkeye. "You oughta give Henry a little warning so he can get a replacement."

Throughout the interrogation, The Painless Pole sat numbly and made no effort to answer.

"How do you figure to go?" continued Trapper. "You gonna do the .45 between the eyes, or are you planning something a little more refined?"

"That's what I wanted to ask," Walt finally said. "What would you guys recommend?"

"The .45 will do it." Duke answered. "There's no question

33

about that, but it can be sloppy. How about the black capsule?"

"What's that?"

"It's a never miss, easy, pleasant ride," explained Hawkeye. "You have a few drinks, take the black capsule, and the next thing you know you're listening to the heavenly chorus singing the Hamtramck High School victory song."

"You guys got any black capsules?"

"For a buddy like y'all," the Duke told him, "we'll sure as hell get some, if that's what you want."

"That's what I want. I gotta go make out my will. Duke, you can have the record player. I'm closing the Clinic in the morning. Tomorrow night is it. You guys come up. We'll have a few drinks, and I'll take a black capsule, or maybe two."

The Painless Pole left. Hawkeye followed him.

"Relieve me in three hours," he instructed the Swampmen as he departed. "We'd better watch the foolish bastard until he gets over this one."

The next morning Henry heard about it. He was all upset and making plans to evacuate Painless, and came to The Swamp to discuss it.

"What in hell's wrong with him anyhow? Why do I have to get saddled with all the screwballs in the whole U.S. Army? Where in hell am I going to get another dentist?"

Trapper was in the Dental Clinic doing guard duty, but Duke and Hawkeye argued Henry out of his evacuation plans.

"Y'all don't need to get rid of him, Henry," said Duke. "He'll get the hell over it."

"Christ, Henry," Hawk added, "if you get rid of him, some head-shrinker will just give him shock treatments and probably send him to another outfit. We can give him some shock treatments right here!"

"I'm afraid not, boys," Henry said. "This sort of thing is dynamite. If he pushed himself over up here, I'd never hear the end of it."

"Henry, you surely are aware," Hawkeye continued, "of the immense prestige which the presence of the Pride bestows upon the unit. Furthermore, the Pride is the greatest drawing card any military shower tent ever had. You must realize that the personnel of our hospital and all nearby troops, in their zeal to view the Pride of Hamtramck, have become the cleanest goddam soldiers in Korea. Henry, in the name of

34

sanitation and personal hygiene, will you just give us twenty-four hours to cure Painless Waldowski?"

"Yeah, Henry," Duke said. "Will y'all just do that?"

"I'm crazy. I'm just as crazy as you guys: Go ahead, cure him, and let me the hell out of here!" he cried, leaving.

"So," Hawkeye said to the Duke, "how are we going to cure him?"

"Easy," the Duke said. "We'll get some kind of black capsule, like we told him, stick about fifteen grains of amytal in it, get him loaded, and give him the capsule. By the time he wakes up, he oughta be O.K."

"We better have some benzedrine or something around in case he looks like he won't wake up."

"Yeah, I guess so."

"We should fancy up the procedure a little, too. We can work that out today. Let's start by lining up Dago Red."

They ambled over to the chaplain's tent, entered and opened two of Father Mulcahy's beers.

"How they goin', Losing Preacher?" asked Hawkeye. "Whadda you hear from the Pope?"

"What do reprobates want?"

"We came to invite y'all to the Last Supper," explained the Duke.

"The Painless Pole," Hawkeye explained, "plans to cross the Great Divide about eleven tonight and wishes his friends and cronies to break bread and wine with him beforehand. He has also requested that Losing Preacher Mulcahy come prepared to administer the last rites of the bead-jiggler Church. He has been somewhat slack in his devotion to the Church in recent years and wishes you to grease the skids a little."

"Why don't you guys leave me alone? What's this all about anyway?" Dago asked wearily.

"We're serious, Red," Hawkeye said. "Painless has parted his mooring. We don't want to have him evacuated because he's a good guy and we like him and we figure we need him. We think we can get him straightened out, but we need a little help."

"What do you want me to do?"

"Just what we said. Come up, have supper, a few drinks, put in one of your well-known fixes, and don't get annoyed at anything you hear or see."

"OK, boys, I'll trust you," Father Mulcahy agreed, "but I hope the big guy in Rome never gets wind of it."

"He sure as hell won't hear it from me," Hawkeye assured him.

They went to the supply sergeant and commissioned the construction of a coffin.

"Who you planning to kill?" the sergeant asked.

"Nobody. We need the coffin for Painless. He is going to commit suicide."

"He can't do that!" protested the sergeant.

"Why can't he?"

"Dentists we got lots of, but there's only one Pride of Hamtramck."

"So what?"

"So what? It belongs to the world! You gotta stop him."

"Don't worry, we're not gonna let him do it. You seen Radar O'Reilly around?"

"Radar went to Seoul to get some blood. He'll be back this afternoon. Whadda you want with him?"

"We may need him. Send him over to The Swamp as soon as he gets back."

In the pharmacy a black capsule was prepared. Then the two trooped over to the mess hall and found the celebrated chef, Sergeant Mother Divine. Sergeant Mother Divine was a Negro boy from Brooklyn who, during his military career, had distinguished himself through a variety of accomplishments, not all of them culinary. As president of the Brooklyn and Manhattan Marked-Down Monument and Landmark Company, and equipped with picture postcards and impressive papers suggesting ownership of various public edifices, statuary and parks, he had, for months, been running a thriving sales business. Just two days before the visit of Hawkeye and Duke, in fact, he had sold the Brooklyn Botanical Garden for two hundred dollars to a Caucasian private from Mississippi.

"Man," one of his less sophisticated kitchen colleagues had said to him, more in awe than admonition, "how could you do that?"

"Man," Mother Divine said, "it was easy. That cat wouldn't buy the bridge because he said he'd heard in the family for years that his grandpappy had bought it a long time ago."

36

"Mother," Hawkeye said to him now, "how would you like to win the Medaille d'Honneur des Chevaliers d'Escoffier de France?"

"Man," Mother said, "what is it?"

"It's a gold medal," Hawkeye said.

"Man," Mother said.

"It's awarded in Paris every year," Hawkeye said, "to the man voted the Chef of the Year."

"And how do I get voted to that?" Mother asked.

"By preparing for this evening an especially sumptuous . . ."

"Oh no, man," Mother said. "I ain't caterin' to no special parties. That ain't in the regulations. In the regulations I just gotta provide three . . ."

"Mother," Hawkeye said, "you like Captain Waldowski, don't you?"

"That's right," Mother said. "In fact, there's somethin' about that man I greatly admire."

With that as his cue, and with the Duke nodding assent, Hawkeye launched into an explanation of the emotional and mental state of the Painless Pole and then an impassioned plea. When he finished, Mother Divine agreed to do his part to save the Pride of Hamtramck.

In the Clinic that evening the poker game was stopped, and the poker and pool facilities, along with the dental chair, were removed. Two long tables were transported from the mess hall, candles were lighted and the Swampmen tended bar. The guests—doctors, chopper pilots, enlisted men—began to warm up, but Painless Waldowski sat unhappily in a corner, barely acknowledging the greetings of his friends and admirers.

At the stroke of midnight the Last Supper was served, and no finer meal had ever been prepared at the 4077th MASH. This was due not only to the inspired efforts of Mother Divine but also to the fact that a Canadian supply truck had been hijacked a few miles to the south that very afternoon. As a result, smoked Gaspé salmon was followed by Pea Soup Habitant, roast beef sliced to the individual's preference, three vegetables, tossed salad, baked alaska, coffee or tea, Drambuie and Antonio y Cleopatra cigars.

Painless drank reluctantly and little, but Duke saw to it that the drinks were high in alcoholic content. Painless ate without appetite and at the conclusion of the meal, as each guest rose to make a short speech of fondness and farewell, he barely acknowledged the tributes and good wishes.

When the speeches had been completed, the coffin was carried in. It was lined with blankets and supplied with three fresh decks of cards, a box of poker chips, a fifth of Scotch, several basic dental instruments and pictures of Painless Waldowski's three fiancées. For the first time Painless showed some interest.

"What's that?" he asked.

"The coffin for y'all," the Duke informed him.

"But I'm not even dead yet."

"Yeah, but you're a pretty big guy," Hawkeye said. "We don't want to have to lug you around after you take the black capsule. We figured you could get in the box and then take it. Really, Painless, it'll be a helluva lot more convenient."

Painless looked doubtful.

"Hey, Painless," someone else asked, "which way do you think you'll go? Up or down?"

"I've asked the Father to arrange that," he said, glancing at Dago Red.

"You sure you still got an inside track, Red?" asked Trapper John. "If there's any chance of a slip-up, Painless might change his mind."

"My mind's made up," asserted the Painless Pole.

Father Mulcahy administered the last rites. As he concluded, there was a murmur of approval. This had been one of Red's best and most elaborate fixes.

"Well stroked," said the Duke.

As Painless prepared to enter the coffin and take the black capsule, Trapper and Hawkeye were watching the door anxiously. Suddenly it was thrown open and Radar O'Reilly burst in upon the gathering and, gasping for breath, yelled, "Hold everything!"

"What's the matter?" Hawkeye said.

"I just got the message," Radar said. "Painless needs a parachute. The fix didn't take, and he goes down."

A low, sudden rumble of discontent swept the room. The group turned its attention to Father Mulcahy.

"What's wrong, Red?" demanded Trapper John. "You lose your stuff?"

"Never mind the recriminations," said Hawkeye. "Let's get on with it."

38

He produced a parachute, and one of the chopper pilots helped him get Painless Waldowski into it. By now Painless was feeling the booze.

"I don't want to be a parachute jumper," he complained. "I might get killed."

"You just might," Hawkeye consoled him. "Get in here, Painless. It's time for take-off."

Complete with parachute, Painless got into the coffin. He took the black capsule and washed it down with a shot of Scotch. Within five minutes, he was in dreamland.

Trapper John came forward with a blue ribbon. Reverently, but loosely, he tied it around the Pride of Hamtramck, and the poker game started. At frequent intervals, one or another of the Swampmen got up to check their dentist's pulse, respiration and blood pressure.

On one occasion, when Painless seemed a little deeper than desirable, he was given a small dose of stimulant. By daybreak, he showed signs of recovery. He was removed from the coffin and taken to a waiting helicopter of the 5th Air Rescue Squadron parked just behind the preop ward. At a height of about fifty feet over the ballfield, directly in front of The Swamp, he was given a large shot of benzedrine intravenously and lowered from the chopper by a rope. A string attached to the ripcord was pulled, and the chute opened. A rescue crew waited below holding a blanket. The pilot released the rope. Painless and his parachute, to the cheers of the gathering, plummeted eight feet into the blanket.

While the chute was being removed, Painless rubbed his eyes, looked around and said, "What the hell's going on, boys?"

"That's what we'd like to know," said Hawkeye. "Come into The Swamp."

"You look dry," said Trapper, handing him a can of beer. "Where you've been, I hear you can get a thirst. Tell us about it. How'd you get back?"

"I'll be with you in a minute," said Captain Waldowski, leaving the tent after downing the beer in three gulps.

Upon his return, Painless, obviously proud and holding a blue ribbon in his hand, informed them, "I don't know where I've been, but wherever it was I sure as hell won first prize. How about a game of poker?"

39

6

THE OTHER DOCTORS in the 4077th spent a great deal of time in discussion of the men of The Swamp. When Duke's name was mentioned, it was generally agreed that he was the most amiable, and therefore likeable, of the three. Trapper John's consummate skill as a surgeon earned him the most respect, but when it came to Hawkeye Pierce there was a great divergence of opinion.

The man who hated Hawkeye the most was Captain Frank Burns. He had good reason. He was persecuted by Hawkeye Pierce. Captain Burns was the boss of one surgical shift, and Hawkeye of the other. Working times frequently overlapped, so some contact was inevitable. The more contact they had, the more they hated each other.

Frank Burns was the son of a general practitioner and surgeon in a medium-sized Indiana town. After one year of internship, and as heir apparent, he had joined his father in practice for three years before being drafted. He owned a thirty-five-thousand-dollar house and two automobiles.

Hawkeye Pierce had spent the same three years in a surgical residency, without salary, and had been supported by his wife and hospital poker games. In Hawkeye's opinion, Frank Burns, despite a definite technical competency, seldom thought and was a fake. In Frank Burns's opinion, Hawkeye Pierce was an uncouth yokel who failed to understand that learning surgery from a father who didn't know any was better than formal training in a teaching hospital.

41

Captain Burns, born to affluence, accustomed to authority, was very definitely the boss of his shift. He found the enlisted men exasperating. At least once a week, it was necessary for him to report someone to Colonel Blake for dereliction of duty. It then became necessary for Captain Pierce to intercede in behalf of the enlisted man, which he always did successfully. This annoyed Captain Burns, and one day he approached Captain Pierce and attempted to discuss the subject.

"Frank," Hawkeye said, "you stink. I haven't decided what to do about you, but sooner or later I'll come to some sort of decision. Now I suggest that you go to bed and lull yourself to sleep counting your annuities or something, before you precipitate my decision, to the sorrow of us both."

Frank ran to Colonel Blake and complained. Colonel Blake came to The Swamp.

"Pierce," he asked, "what ails you?"

"Well," said Hawkeye, "the guy from the Sox who looked me over once said that, in addition to having a very weak throwing arm, I'd never hit big-league pitching."

"Jesus," said Henry, "you *are* crazy. Anyhow, you leave Burns alone. I know what you mean about him, but surgeons of any kind are hard to find. Leave him alone, or it's gonna be your ass."

"Yes, my leader," agreed Hawkeye meekly, as Henry stormed out.

That night when Hawkeye went to work he encountered Frank.

"Hey, Frank," he said, "one of my kid brothers just got out of jail. I wrote him and told him to go out to Indiana and burn down your thirty-five-thousand-dollar house."

Again, Frank ran to Colonel Blake who visited Hawkeye in the morning.

"Pierce, have you flipped?" he demanded.

"Whadda ya mean?" asked Hawkeye, who had forgotten all about it.

"I heard what you said to Frank last night about your brother burning his house down."

"Which brother? I got six."

"The one who just got out of jail."

"Well, for Chrissake, Henry, I can't keep track of things from here. It could be any of them. They all sort of rotate in

42

and out. Forget it. None of them could find Indiana on the best day he ever had."

When Hawkeye, for the moment and to placate Colonel Blake, let up on Captain Burns, it was Duke Forrest who took over, again in behalf of the enlisted men. This time it was in behalf of Private Lorenzo Boone, the dunce of the Double Natural.

In his nineteen years, Private Boone had been exposed to very little, so his real abilities were difficult to assess. He couldn't seem to do anything right, which may have been why the Army assigned him to a Mobile Army Surgical Hospital, where he was given the job of third assistant bedpan jockey in the postop ward. Inept though he was, he did try hard, and he improved with time.

For a while Private Boone was assigned the simple job of computing the liquid intake and output of the more severely ill patients. This was really quite easy. Most of the patients received only intravenous fluids for intake, and they all had catheters in their bladders, so there was no problem in measuring the urinary output. In accordance with medical custom, Private Boone was supposed to measure these quantities in cubic centimeters (cc's), of which there are one thousand to a quart.

After a few days, the intake figures recorded by Private Boone became open to the question. Several patients were alleged to have taken only one cc, two cc's, or in extreme cases four or five cc's in a given twenty-four-hour period, and no output at all was recorded. The ensuing revelation that Private Boone thought cc's stood for cups of coffee solved part of the problem but did little to increase his efficiency.

It was shortly after this that Captain Burns was taken ill. In fact, he was so indisposed that he spent three days in his tent and, although the nature of his illness was never widely known, its origins were as follows:

Captain Burns was addicted to a common failing in the surgical dodge: if a patient died, he claimed it was (1) God's will or (2) someone else's fault. One day he spent six long, hard hours operating on a severely wounded soldier, who'd been in deep shock throughout most of the procedure. Half an hour after surgery, the patient died in the postoperative ward. His final gesture was to vomit and aspirate some of the vomitus.

Private Boone, on his own initiative, quickly brought in a suction machine. It was not functioning, but neither was the patient as Captain Burns appeared and observed Private Boone's futile efforts.

"Boone," he said, "you killed my patient!"

Private Boone turned white. He walked away and went to a dark corner and cried. The Captain said he'd killed a man, and the Captain was a doctor and he ought to know.

Duke Forrest caught it. To Captain Burns he said, "Frank, may I speak to y'all outside for a moment?"

Korean nights can be dark. Often you can't see your hand in front of your face. Captain Burns never saw the hand that broke his nose, split his lip, or the knee that made him terribly uncomfortable for three days to come.

Trapper John was next in line to take on Captain Burns, and it had to do with cardiac massage. Cardiac massage is manual compression of a heart that has stopped. It is done through a hole hastily made in the chest in the hope, usually forlorn, that the heartbeat will resume and the patient will recover. The administrator of cardiac massage compresses and releases the heart between the fingers of one hand with a rhythm designed to approximate the normal heartbeat, and Captain Frank Burns was, without doubt, the leading cardiac masseur in the Far East Command.

At breakfast one morning Trapper John McIntyre, leaving the mess hall, encountered Captain Frank Burns entering the mess hall. Trapper John traveled a fast right to Frank's jaw, and Frank dropped on the sand floor like a poleaxed steer.

This was the second time within a month that Frank had been assaulted by a Swampman. The first time had been clandestine, but this was public, and again an irate Henry entered The Swamp.

Standing over Trapper John, who was sipping a beer in his sleeping bag, Colonel Blake yelled his usual question. "What's wrong with you, anyhow?"

"I'm wondering the same thing, Henry," replied Trapper. "I hear the son-of-a-bitch got up. I guess I've lost my punch."

Trapper rolled over and ignored Henry.

"You wanta know what it's all about, Henry?" volunteered Hawkeye.

"Yeah, I sure do!"

"Well, you remember, yesterday morning was pretty busy.

The most minor injury was a kid with a shell-fragment wound in his right thigh. It didn't look like much. Frank decided to get him out of the way so they could get on with the others. As usual, he didn't think. He took the kid in with a pressure of eighty over fifty, had them give him anesthesia, and started to debride the wound. It turned out the kid's femoral artery was lacerated and he bled a lot. Then he had a cardiac arrest, and Frank rubbed his heart. It came back, he stopped the bleeding and got some blood into him, and by midafternoon he looked OK. By the time we came on duty last night the kid was in shock again. Trapper took over, figured he was bleeding from the chest wound Frank made, got his pressure up, and opened his chest again to stop the bleeding.

"Now the kid's OK," Hawkeye said, "but because that bastard Burns didn't observe a few basic principles, the boy almost died. Instead of cussing himself out for almost losing a patient, Frank thinks he's a big hero because he did a sucessful cardiac massage. Therefore Trapper John administered a knuckle sandwich."

It took a femme fatale, however, to restore peace, more or less, to the 4077th MASH. She was Major Margaret Houlihan, new Chief Nurse, and one June morning she emerged, not out of a scallop shell like Botticelli's Venus, but out of a helicopter. She was tallish, willowish, blondish, fortyish. She had a nice figure. In fact, she was a nice-looking, forty-year-old female.

Within the prescribed twenty-four hours following her arrival, Major Houlihan made a point of seeking out the boss of each shift and attempting to discuss nursing problems with him. Captain Burns was in starched fatigues and his most gracious mood, but he mentioned several nurses whose performance was inadequate and made a variety of suggestions for improvement. The Major was quite impressed with Captain Burns.

She was less impressed with Captain Pierce. She found him in the mess tent in soiled fatigues having a late breakfast. She introduced herself, and Hawkeye invited her to join him over a cup of coffee.

"Captain Pierce," Major Houlihan said, "I observed the night shift and I was not at all impressed with some of our nurses. How do you feel, Captain, about the nursing situation here?"

45

"Major," Hawkeye said, "this is a team effort. I'm responsible for my team. It consists of doctors, nurses and enlisted men. We've been working as a unit for six months with little change in personnel. I'm satisfied with them."

"Well," she said, "Captain Burns isn't at all satisfied."

"Mother," said Hawkeye Pierce, "Captain Burns is a jerk, and if you don't know it by now you . . ."

Major Houlihan arose. "I wonder," she asked, "how anyone like you reaches such a position of responsibility in the Army Medical Corps."

"Honey," answered Hawkeye, "if I knew the answer to that I sure as hell wouldn't be here."

"Very well, Captain," Major Houlihan said. "It appears that we are not going to get along. Nevertheless, I want you to know that I will attempt to cooperate with you in every possible way."

"Major," Hawkeye said, smiling, "I appreciate that, so would you consider another cup of coffee?"

Reluctantly she sat down again and resumed the talk. She was still terribly upset, so Hawkeye tried to explain a few things.

"Major," he said, "you're watching both shifts. Watch them with an eye to which shift does the most work with the least fuss. Watch them with an eye to how many people work happily or unhappily."

"I observed last night that both nurses and enlisted men addressed you as 'Hawkeye'."

"That's my name."

"Such familiarity is highly improper," declaimed Major Houlihan, "and inconsistent with maximum efficiency in an organization such as this."

"Well, Major," said Hawkeye as he got up and left, "I'm gonna have a couple shots of Scotch and go to bed. Obviously you're a female version of the routine Regular Army Clown. Stay away from me and my gang, and we'll get along fine. See you around the campus."

Having been summarily dismissed by Captain Pierce, Major Houlihan took her problems to the commanding officer. The interview was quite unsatisfactory. Colonel Blake told her, after she'd bothered him enough, that he'd rather get rid of Captain Burns than Captain Pierce, but couldn't afford to lose either one.

Major Houlihan was quite upset, but withheld final judgment for a week. By the end of that period she was completely convinced that the Swampmen, Pierce in particular, exerted an evil influence upon the Colonel and upon the whole outfit. Captain Burns, she learned from frequent observation, was a brilliant technical surgeon. His behavior was military, his dress and bearing were military. He was, she felt, an officer, a gentleman and a surgeon.

The obvious continued to escape her. For months Captain Burns's group had been getting into difficulties. Some of its members, when in doubt, bypassed Frank Burns and asked the Swampmen for help. As a result, Colonel Blake finally decided to create a Chief Surgeon, whose duty, in addition to doing his fair share of the work, would be to assist each shift in the management of the most difficult cases. Everyone in the organization except Captain Burns and Major Houlihan recognized that this job could logically be given only to Trapper John, and so it was.

Upon learning of the Colonel's decision, and certain that the commanding officer was bereft of his senses, Major Houlihan invited Captain Burns to her tent for a council of war. She gave Frank a drink. He explained to her the tragedy of turning the organization over to the riff-raff and, since she agreed with him, extolled her perspicacity. Then, over her signature, they composed to General Hammond in Seoul a letter that he would never receive because Hawkeye had the mail clerk censoring the Major's outgoing correspondence. After that the Major gave Frank another drink, and Frank embraced and kissed her. Then they departed, reluctantly, for the mess tent. It was supper time.

In The Swamp, meanwhile, a party in honor of the newly appointed Chief Surgeon was in progress. Attendance was high, and at five-thirty it was suggested by someone and agreed upon by all that a Chief Surgeon should be treated with more than usual respect. Trapper John went along with this and requested that he be properly crowned and transported to the mess hall by native bearers. This presented complications, as crowns are hard to come by in the Korean hinterlands, and the Korean houseboys, when asked to serve as native bearers, protested that they had not hired out as such. Instead, a bedpan was fastened to Trapper John's head with adhesive tape, and Hawkeye, Duke, Ugly John and the Painless Pole picked up the sack upon which the newly crowned Chief Surgeon rested and, with the others following, bore it and him to the mess hall.

"Now y'all hear this!" the Duke announced to the assembled diners. "This here is your new Chief Surgeon. He has just been crowned, so y'all do him honor."

Then the members of the Chief Surgeon's court broke into song:

> "Hail to the Chief,
> And King of all the surgeons.
> He needs a Queen,
> To satisfy his urgins."

"That's right," Trapper John, still reclining on his sack, said. "And who's that over there?"

He pointed toward the back of the mess hall. There, sitting apart from the others and evidencing complete disgust, were Major Houlihan and Captain Burns.

"Oh them, Your Highness?" Hawkeye said. "That's just the goose girl and the swine herd."

"I don't like the swine herd," Trapper John said, "but I might get to like the goose girl."

Major Houlihan and Captain Burns retreated to console each other and plot their revenge. They retreated to the Major's tent, where they consoled and plotted until 1:30 A.M. At least that was the report which Corporal Radar O'Reilly submitted in the morning.

The Swampmen were at breakfast when Major Houlihan and Captain Burns entered. As the two started to pass the table, eyes front, Duke spoke up.

"Mornin', Frank," he said.

"Hiya, Hot Lips," said the Chief Surgeon to the Chief Nurse. "Now that I'm a chief, too, we really oughta get together."

Frank stopped, turned and made one menacing step toward the Swampmen.

"Join us if you wish, Frank," invited Hawkeye. "Looks like a great day to set a hen."

Captain Burns thought better of it. He escorted Major Houlihan to a distant table, but his moment came that night when he and Hawkeye found themselves together in the utility room, next to the OR, where coffee was available. Hawkeye had just poured himself a cup and was seated at the table, sipping and smoking, when Captain Burns entered and approached the coffee pot.

"Hey, Frank," said the Hawk, "is that stuff you're tappin' really any good?"

"One more word out of you," Frank erupted, screaming it, "and I'll kill you!"

"So kill me," Hawkeye said.

At that moment Colonel Henry Blake entered, and what he saw was enough to do it. He saw Captain Pierce sitting peacefully with a cup of coffee and a cigarette. He saw Captain Burns, on the other side of the room, pick up the coffee pot and hurl it at Captain Pierce, who ducked. Then he saw Captain Burns follow the coffee pot and start flailing away at Hawkeye with his fists. Hawkeye, having spotted the Colonel, did nothing but cover his head with his arms and scream.

"Henry!" he screamed. "Help me, Henry! He's gone mad!"

The next day Captain Burns was reassigned to a stateside hospital. Although the Swampmen were happy, Colonel Blake wasn't, and entered The Swamp to define his unhappiness.

"OK," he said. "You guys win another round. You ditched Frank. I could have put up with him screwing Hot Lips, if he was, which I doubt, but you guys had to have your way. I just want you to know that I know what you did. He was a jerk, I admit, but he was needed, and now we don't have him and it's your fault."

"Henry," said Hawkeye, "for Crissake, sit down and relax. Nobody needs guys like him. You're all concerned with numbers of people. The clown created more work than he accomplished. We're better off without him."

"Maybe so," Henry sighed. "I don't know."

"Henry," Duke asked, "if I get into Hot Lips and jump Hawkeye Pierce can I go home, too?"

7

EACH DOCTOR'S tent at the MASH had a young Korean to clean it, keep the stove going, shine shoes, and do the laundry and other chores. He was called a houseboy.

Naturally The Swamp's houseboy was called a Swampboy. His name was Ho-Jon. Ho-Jon was tall for a Korean. He was thin. He was bright. Prior to the war he had attended a church school in Seoul. He was a Christian. His English was relatively fluent.

Ho-Jon thought Hawkeye Pierce, Duke Forrest and Trapper John McIntyre were the three greatest people in the world. Unlike other houseboys, he was allowed to spend a lot of his spare time in the tent. The Swampmen helped him with reading and writing English, had books sent to him from the States, and gave him a good basic education in a few short months. Ho-Jon had a mind like a bear trap. It engulfed everything that came its way. During bull sessions in The Swamp, he sat quietly in a corner and listened. During busy periods, he was brought to the OR and trained to assist the Swampmen as a scrub nurse.

The Swampmen thought as much of Ho-Jon as he did of them. On his seventeenth birthday, however, despite the attempt of Colonel Blake, urged on by the Swampmen, to intercede with the Korean government, Ho-Jon was drafted into the Republic of Korea Army. Unhappiness and a feeling of despair and frustration prevailed in The Swamp on the day of Ho-Jon's departure. The Swampmen gave him clothes,

51

money, canned food, and cigarettes. Hawkeye himself drove Ho-Jon to Seoul. There the two went to see Ho-Jon's family who lived in a dirty shack on a filthy street and whose reaction to the largesse showered upon their son by the American doctors was awe-inspiring and pathetic.

Hawkeye left hastily. He found an Air Force Officers' club where he drank moodily and disinterestedly without getting any emotional benefit from the good Air Force Scotch. He never expected to see Ho-Jon again. He thought of Crabapple Cove and wondered how he could ever have thought his material benefits and opportunities limited. Compared to Ho-Jon, he'd had everything.

As it turned out, Captain Pierce did see Ho-Jon again. It was six weeks later, when Ho-Jon returned in the uniform of a private in the ROK Army. The uniform was covered with blood. Deep in Ho-Jon's chest was a mortar fragment.

At the Double Natural, as at every MASH, all wounds were first hastily assessed in the admitting ward and then the seriously wounded were brought into the preoperative ward. There blood was typed, nurses and corpsmen took blood pressures, started transfusions, inserted Foley catheters in bladders and Levin tubes in stomachs, and hung the X-rays on a wire in front of each patient's cot.

Arriving for duty on this morning and finding the preop ward full, Hawkeye, Duke and Trapper John had gone down the row of wounded and started to make their plans. When they reached the last cot a corpsman said, "This kid is pretty bad."

Hawkeye looked at the X-ray. He saw a large shell fragment deep in the boy's chest.

"This one's for you, Trapper," he said. "I'll help you, and Duke can take that belly back there."

Then Captain Pierce took his first look at the patient.

"Christ!" he said. "It's Ho-Jon."

Trapper looked.

"OK. It's Ho-Jon. We'll fix him."

Ho-Jon opened his eyes. He saw his friends and smiled.

"You'll be OK, boy," said the corpsman.

"I know," Ho-Jon whispered. "Captains Pierces and Captains McIntyres will help me."

"You know it, Ho-Jon," Captain Pierce said. "You just rest, and we'll do it after you've had one more pint of blood."

The Duke was about to become occupied in a bad belly, so they decided not to tell him. They went out for a butt.

"How do we go, Trapper?" asked Hawkeye.

"Right chest, just like the missile. He's lost some blood. I'm afraid it's hit more than just the lung. It's in deep."

"Trapper, you remember how we used to wonder what a kid like Ho-Jon might do if he had a chance to get an education?"

"Yeah," Trapper answered dully.

"If we squeeze him through, I'm going to get him into Androscoggin College."

"We'll squeeze him through and right into Dartmouth," said Trapper, grinding out his cigarette. "If all he wants to do is catch lobsters, he can learn that here."

A grim pair of surgeons went to work on Ho-Jon.

"We'll need room," said Trapper. "The sixth rib goes."

"Never mind the conversation. Do it, Dad."

They opened the pleura, put in the rib spreader, and aspirated the blood from the chest cavity. Ho-Jon's pulse and blood pressure held steady. Trapper reached down toward the inferior vena cava where it empties into the right atrium of the heart. He felt the missile.

"I got it," he said. "Here, feel."

Hawkeye felt.

"I don't feel anything."

"Oh, Jesus," moaned Trapper, and felt again.

"What happened?"

"The mother must have gone in. I can't feel it."

"I don't get it," said Hawkeye nervously.

"It must have been in the cava, and the hole sealed itself off. When I felt it I must have jiggled it just enough to turn it loose. I can't feel it in the heart. I don't feel it in the right pulmonary artery. It must be in the left pulmonary artery."

"Whadda we do?"

"Close and get an X-ray and fight another day."

"OK," Hawkeye said unhappily.

The X-ray confirmed Trapper's guess. The shell fragment was in the left pulmonary artery. Three days later Ho-Jon was out of bed, happy, proud to have been operated on by two of his three heroes and, unaware of the odds against him, not at all upset at the prospect of further surgery.

Taking a missile out of a pulmonary artery is no great

trick, but few surgeons in Korea were familiar with such techniques. Cardiovascular surgery was in its infancy, and such procedures were not usually done in tents. Ordinarily this sort of case would have been evacuated to Tokyo, but no one seriously thought that any other surgeon in the Far East was better equipped to do the job than Trapper John. Colonel Blake did mention the possibility of evacuation once, but dropped the subject when Hawkeye gave him a very direct look.

In The Swamp the next week the tension grew. Humor was nonexistent. Unmilitary behavior tapered off. One evening Hawkeye passed around a bottle of Scotch, feeling that, for the sake of efficiency, they should attempt some sort of comeback.

"When do we go for it, Trapper?" he asked.

"June 2."

"Why June 2?"

"That's the day I shut out Harvard on two hits."

Trapper John did not say another word that night. He lay on his sack, sipped his drink and just looked straight up.

Ho-Jon, at the start of his big day, lay on the operating table, expectantly but confidently gazing up at Ugly John. Ugly John said, "Now, Ho-Jon, you just take it easy. Everything will be all right."

Ho-Jon smiled and said, "I know, Captains Blacks."

Ugly John started the Pentothal and curare, and three minutes later inserted the intratracheal tube through which Ho-Jon would do all his breathing while his friends worked on him. Then Ho-Jon was turned onto his right side and draped, and Trapper John, assisted by Hawkeye and Duke, removed Ho-Jon's fifth rib. With that out of the way, Trapper entered the pleural cavity, and easily located the missile wedged in the left pulmonary artery. After opening the pericardium, which surrounds the heart, he then dissected his way around the origin of the artery and placed umbilical tapes as temporary ties above and below the missile.

"How is he?" Trapper asked Ugly John.

"Nice," said Ugly. "Get on with it."

While Hawkeye applied traction on the tape above the shell fragment and Duke did the same below, Trapper incised the artery, removed the fragment, and resutured the artery with 5-0 arterial silk.

54

"Ease off on those tapes, and let's see how much it bleeds," said Trapper. He had to place one extra suture, and then there was no more bleeding.

"How's he doing?" Trapper asked the anesthesiologist.

"Nice," Ugly John assured him.

The Swampmen looked at one another, and Trapper said, "Boys, we're home free."

For the rest of the day relaxation ruled, and recollection of it is indistinct in the minds of the survivors, who included Ho-Jon. Soon Ho-Jon was up and around, back at his job as Swampboy, his English improving. He was losing the Korean habit of putting an "s" on the end of every word. He eagerly read all that the Swampmen provided for him.

"Now," said Hawkeye one day, "I gotta get him into Androscoggin College."

"Dartmouth," said Trapper John.

"Georgia," said Duke.

"Boys," said Hawkeye, "it's gotta be Androscoggin. Dartmouth is too big and too expensive. At Androscoggin he can start a little more slowly and get more attention. If he's as good as I think he is, he can move into the big leagues later, and I don't think Georgia is the place even if the Klan doesn't have a chapter house there any more."

The Swampmen agreed on Androscoggin College. "Guess I'll write to the Dean," said Hawkeye and sat down to do so. He wrote:

Dr. James Lodge
Dean, Androscoggin College
Androscoggin, Maine
Dear Mr. Lodge:

A few years having passed, perhaps you'll be willing to read a letter from me, although I seem to recall that when I left for the Army back in 1943 you indicated no great feeling of loss. The United States Army, in its infinite wisdom, allowed me to partake of the medical education for which I was so well prepared at Androscoggin.

Now I am in Korea as a surgeon in a Mobile Army Hospital. To make a long story short, I know a Korean kid that I want to get into Androscoggin. You took a chance on me. If you could do that you have twice as much reason to take a chance on my boy, Ho-Jon. He is a winner.

I'm just as serious as I can be. If you'll consider the deal at all, let me know what it will cost, and I'll see what I can do to get up the loot.

Your former outstanding undergraduate,

Hawkeye Pierce

An answer arrived three weeks later:

Dear Hawkeye:

As Dean of the College, I naturally remember you very well. In my job one has to take the bitter as well as the sweet, and I've had my share of both.

My natural expectation is that, if I accede to your request, I will soon have on my hands some illiterate seventy-year-old refugee from a leper colony. Despite the possibility of your having matured slightly in the last nine years, that is really what I expect.

However, this sort of thing is popular these days. If you feel your boy can do college work and if you can get him over here and supply him with a thousand dollars a year, we will give him a chance. Enclosed is an application for Ho-Jon to complete.

Sincerely,

James Lodge

Dean, Androscoggin College

"Boys," said Hawkeye, "it's going to cost us at least five or six grand, figuring travel and one thing or another."

"I know we'll get it up, but I don't know how," said Duke.

Dago Red entered. He had some pictures he had taken of the Swampmen during the winter. At the time Trapper John had been sporting a beard and a large crop of unbarbered hair. Several of the pictures were of Trapper John.

"Look at The Hairy Ape," said Duke.

"No," said Red, "he doesn't look like The Hairy Ape. With that thin, ascetic face and the beard and the piercing eyes, he almost looks like our Blessed Saviour."

Taking another look, he crossed himself and thought better of it.

"If that's what He looks like," said the Duke, "I'm gonna try Buddha."

"Lemme see that picture," said Hawkeye Pierce.

He looked. "By Jesus, it does look like Him," he agreed and lapsed into pensive silence.

A while later Hawkeye sat up, lit a butt, and said, "Hey, Trapper, how fast can you grow that beard back?"

"Couple weeks. What do you have in mind?"

"Money for Ho-Jon."

"How's that Yankee growin' a beard gonna get money for Ho-Jon?" asked Duke.

"Easy. We'll get a good picture of him, have copies made, and sell actual photographs of Jesus Christ at a buck a throw. If we make out with that, he can make a few personal appearances."

Trapper looked interested. "Always knew I'd make good," he said, "but I never thought I'd get to the top so fast."

"I'm movin' to another tent," wailed the Duke. "You crazy bastards are gonna get me in trouble."

"Now wait a minute, boys. You can't do this," pleaded Dago Red.

"Maybe not, Red," answered Hawkeye, "but we gotta get some money. This idea is crazy, but there are a lot of screwballs in an army. Trapper's picture will sell, and a lot of people will buy them for laughs and souvenirs. It won't hurt anybody, and it's a good cause. All we gotta do is work out the details."

Two weeks later the beard had grown, pictures had been taken and seven thousand prints made. Trapper John spent two days autographing them. Dago Red was frantic. They were ready for action. The enlisted men were fond of the Swampmen and were delighted to buy pictures of Trapper J. Jesus Christ McIntyre at a dollar a copy.

"We got us two bills," said Duke who in a day had unloaded 200 copies. "Let's go to Seoul and see if we can run it up in a crap game."

"Hell with that," declared Hawkeye. "If tomorrow is quiet, we'll get a truck from the motor pool and hit the sawdust trail."

At eight o'clock the next morning, the Swampmen ate a substantial breakfast. A truck was obtained. A large cross that Hawkeye had commissioned the supply sergeant to construct was hidden under blankets in the rear. Also hidden under the blankets was a nearly naked, bearded, long haired, fuzzy chested Trapper John, two dozen cans of beer and a thermos jug full of ice. In the cab were six thousand eight hundred photographs bearing the signature: *Jesus Christ.*

They visited medical corps collecting stations, battalion aid stations, artillery units, and other outfits. As they approached, the cross was erected behind the cab of the truck with straps binding Trapper John in the proper and accepted position. Hawkeye was at the wheel. After a turn or two around an outfit they halted. At nearly every stop, as Trapper peered beseechingly at the sky, an officer would step forward and demand, "What the hell is going on here?"

"Passion play," Hawkeye would explain. "Raising some dough to send our houseboy to college. For a buck you get an autographed picture of the Man, himself, or a reasonable facsimile thereof."

Trade was brisk. No one seemed to object to the performance until, late in the afternoon, they hit a Mississippi National Guard outfit. By this time Trapper, spending most of the hot day hidden beneath blankets in the rear of the truck, had consumed a lot of beer. He was still hot and still dehydrated despite the beer, however, when he once again assumed his position on the cross, so while Duke peddled autographed pictures, Hawkeye surreptitiously slipped Trapper a sip from a cool tin of brew. Four Guardsmen, attempting to obtain samples of wood from the cross as souvenirs, and observing this, became indignant. The indignation spread. The Swampmen departed in haste and returned to the 4077th, where the day's take was found to be a satisfying three grand.

That night they decided to push their luck. The moon was bright, making helicopter flying possible, so the chopper pilots of the Air Rescue Squadron were enlisted. Hawkeye and Duke, with pictures, traveled by jeep to prearranged points where troops were in fair quantity. They announced the availability of personally autographed photographs of Jesus Christ, and their timing was perfect. At each point, as the sales talk ended, a brilliant phosphorus flare would be lit, and a helicopter would appear. Spread-eagled on a cross dangling beneath the chopper and illuminated by the eerie light of the flare was the loinclothed, skinny, bearded, long haired, and pretty well stoned Trapper John.

Any good act swings. The pictures sold. Back in The Swamp at 1:00 A.M. the loot was counted again. They had six thousand five hundred dollars.

"Let it go at that," said the Duke. "We got what we need."

The next day Hawkeye Pierce arranged for five thousand dollars to be sent to his father, Benjamin Franklin Pierce, Sr., along with a note:

Dear Dad:
    This five thousand dollars is for my friend, Ho-Jon, to go to Androscoggin College. Look after him and the money until I get home.

                                        So long,
                                        Hawkeye

Within the next month Hawkeye received two letters. The first was from his father:

Dear Hawkeye:
    I deposited five thousand dollars in the Port Waldo Trust Company for Ho-Jon. How come you can send some forcigner to college and leave me to bail your brothers out of jail? I always encouraged you to go to school, and now look what happens. Your brother Joe got took up for drunken driving. Mother is well.

                                        Your father,
                                        Benjy Pierce

The second letter was from the Dean of Androscoggin College, Dr. James Lodge:

Dear Hawkeye:
    We have received Ho-Jon's application, and his record appears to be outstanding, although somewhat unusual. The letter accompanying his application was particularly impressive and influenced our decision to accept him. My suggestion that you might have written it for him was quickly squelched by members of the English Department who remember you.
    Yesterday a truckful of lobster bait, departing from

campus roads, drove directly to the front door of the administration building. A large gentleman, who identified himself as your father, disembarked and gave us one thousand dollars on account for Ho-Jon. We killed a pint of Old Bantam Whiskey which he happened to have with him. Today I have a big head, and the building smells like a lobster boat. Nevertheless, we look forward to Ho-Jon's arrival.

> Very truly yours,
> James Lodge
> Dean, Androscoggin College

The money left over bought clothes and tickets for Ho-Jon. On August 20, 1952, he concluded his duties as Swampboy. He arrived at Androscoggin College on September 10. Soon after, Hawkeye Pierce's old fraternity, assured by Hawkeye that Ho-Jon's prep school education had included martini mixing and crapshooting, pledged him.

8

TRAPPER JOHN MCINTYRE had grown up in a house adjacent to one of suburban Boston's finest country clubs. His parents were members, and, at the age of seventeen, he was one of the better junior golfers in Massachusetts.

Golf had not played a prominent role in Hawkeye Pierce's formative years. Ten miles from Crabapple Cove, however, there was a golf course patronized by the summer resident group. During periods when the pursuit of clams and lobsters was unprofitable, Hawkeye had found employment as a caddy. From time to time he had played with the other caddies and, one year, became the caddy champion of the Wawenock Harbor Golf Club. This meant that he was the only one of ten kids who could break ninety.

In college Hawkeye's obligation to various scholarships involved attention to other games, but during medical school, his internship and his residency he had played golf as often as possible. Joining a club had been out of the question, and even payment of green fees was economically unsound. Therefore he developed a technique which frequently allowed him the privilege of playing some public and a number of unostentatious private courses. He would walk confidently into a pro shop, smile, comment upon the nice condition of the course, explain that he was just passing through and that he was Joe, Dave or Jack Somebody, the pro from Dover. This resulted, about eight times out of ten, in an invitation to play for free. If forced into conversation, he became the pro from Dover, New Hampshire, Massachusetts, New Jersey, England, Ohio, Delaware, Tennessee, or Dover-Foxcroft, Maine, whichever seemed safest.

There was adequate room to hit golf balls at the Double Natural, and with the arrival of spring Trapper and Hawkeye had commissioned the chopper pilots to bring clubs and balls from Japan. Then they had established a practice range of sorts in the field behind the officers' latrine. The Korean houseboys were excellent ball shaggers, so the golfing Swampmen spent much of their free time hitting wood and iron shots. They began to suspect that if they ever got on a real course they'd burn it up, at least from tee to green, but that possibility seemed as remote as their chances of winning the Nobel prize for medicine.

The day after The Second Coming of Trapper John, however, a young Army private, engaged in training maneuvers near Kokura, Japan, had, when a defective grenade exploded, been struck in the chest by a fragment. X-rays revealed blood in the right pleural cavity, which contains the lung, the possible presence of blood within the pericardium, which surrounds the heart, and a metallic foreign body which seemed, to the Kokura doctors in attendance, to be within the heart itself.

Two factors complicated the case: (1) there was no chest surgeon in the area and (2) the soldier's father was a member of Congress. Had it not been for the second complication, the patient would have been sent to the Tokyo Army Hospital where the problem could have been handled promptly and capably.

When informed immediately of his son's injury, however, the Congressman consulted medical friends and was referred to a widely known Boston surgeon whose advice in this matter would be the best available. The Boston surgeon told the Congressman that, regardless of what the Army had to say, the man to take care of his son was Dr. John F. X. McIntyre, now stationed at the 4077th MASH somewhere in Korea. Congressmen make things move. Within hours a jet was flying out of Kokura and then a chopper was whirling out of Seoul, bearing X-rays, a summary of the case, and orders for Captain McIntyre and anyone else he needed to get to Kokura in a hurry.

Unaware of all this excitement, Trapper John and Hawkeye

were hitting a few on the driving range when the chopper from Seoul arrived. They first heard, then saw, it approaching, but as they were off duty and it was coming from the south, anyway, they ignored it. Trapper, still taken with his new image, had not gotten around to shaving his beard or having his hair cut, and he was bending over and teeing up a ball when the pilot, directed to them, walked up.

"Captain McIntyre?" the pilot said.

"What?" Trapper John said, straightening up and turning to face his visitor.

"God!" the pilot said, stunned by his first look at the man whose importance had set a whole chain of command from generals down to clerk-typists into action.

"His son," Hawkeye said. "Would you like to buy an autographed picture for . . . ?"

"*You're* Captain McIntyre?" the pilot said.

"That's what the Army calls me," Trapper said. "Take off your shirt, stick out your tongue and tell me about the pain."

Completely bewildered now, the pilot silently handed over the white envelope containing orders and the explanatory letter from General Hamilton Hartington Hammond and with it the large brown manila envelope containing the X-rays of the chest of the Congressman's son. Trapper read the first and handed them over to Hawkeye and then, as Trapper held the X-rays up to the sunlight, the two looked at them.

"I don't think the goddam thing's in his heart," said Hawkeye, without great assurance.

"Course it isn't," affirmed Trapper John, "but let's not annoy the Congressman. Let us leave for Kokura immediately, with our clubs."

Delaying only long enough to clear it with Henry, they lugged their clubs to the chopper, boosted them in and climbed in after them. At Seoul, Kimpo airport was shrouded with fog and rain, which did not prevent the chopper from landing but which precluded the takeoff of the C-47 scheduled to take them to Kokura. To pass the time in pleasant company, the two surgeons ambled over to the Officers' Club where, after the covey of Air Force people at the bar got over the initial shock, they made the visitors welcome.

"But you guys are a disgrace," said one, after the fourth round. "You can't expect the Air Force to deliver such items to Japan."

"Our problem," Hawkeye explained, "is that right now we've got the longest winning streak in the history of military medicine going, so we don't dare get shaved or shorn. What else can you suggest?"

"Well, we might at least dress you up a little," one of the others said.

"I'm partial to English flannel," Hawkeye said.

"Imported Irish tweed," Trapper said.

The flyboys had recently staged a masquerade party in their club and they still had a couple of Papa-San suits. Papa-San suits take their name from the elderly Korean gentlemen who sport them, and they are long, flowing robes of white or black, topped off by tall hats that look like bird cages.

At 2:00 A.M., Trapper and Hawkeye climbed aboard the C-47 resplendent in their white drapery and bird cages, their clubs over their shoulders. Five hours later they disembarked at Kokura into bright sunlight, found the car with 25th STATION HOSPITAL emblazoned on its side, crawled into the back and awakened the driver.

"Garrada there," the sergeant said.

"What?" Trapper said.

"He's from Brooklyn," Hawkeye said. "He wants us to vacate this vehicle."

"I said garrada there," the sergeant said, "or I'll . . ."

"What's the matter?" Trapper said. "You're supposed to pick up the two pros who are gonna operate on the Congressman's son, aren't you?"

"What?" the sergeant said. "You mean *you* guys are the *doctors?*"

"You betcher ever-lovin' A, buddy-boy," Hawkeye said.

"Poor kid," the sergeant said. "Goddam army . . ."

"Look sergeant," Trapper said, "if that spleen of yours is bothering you, we'll remove it right here. Otherwise, let's haul ass."

"Goddam army," the sergeant said.

"That's right," Hawkeye said, "and on the way fill us in on the local golfing facilities. We gotta operate this kid and then get in at least eighteen holes."

The sergeant followed the path of least resistance. On the way he informed the Swampmen that there was a good eighteen-hole course not far from the hospital but that, as the

Kokura Open was starting the next day, the course was closed to the public.

"So that means we've got a big decision to make," Trapper said.

"What's that?" Hawkeye said.

"The way I see it," Trapper said, for the benefit of the sergeant, "we can operate on this kid and then qualify for this Kokura Open, or we can qualify first and then operate on this kid, if he's still alive."

"Goddam army," the sergeant said.

"Decisions, decisions, decisions," Hawkeye said. "After all, *we* didn't hit the kid in the chest with that grenade."

"Right!" Trapper said. "And it's not *our* chest."

"It's not even our kid," Hawkeye said. "He belongs to some Congressman."

"Yeah," Trapper said, "but let's operate on him first anyway. Then we'll be nice and relaxed to qualify. We wouldn't want to blow that."

"Good idea," Hawkeye said.

"Goddam, goddam army," the sergeant said.

Delivered to the front entrance of the 25th Station Hospital, Trapper and Hawkeye entered and approached the reception desk. Behind it sat a pretty WAC, whose big blue eyes opened like morning glories when she looked up and saw the apparitions before her.

"Nice club you've got here, honey," said Hawkeye. "Where's the pro shop?"

"What?" she said.

"What time's the bar open?" Trapper said.

"What?" she said.

"You got any caddies available?" Hawkeye said.

"What?" she said.

"Look, honey," Trapper said. "Don't keep saying 'what.' Just say 'yes' instead."

"That's right," Hawkeye said, "and you'll be surprised how many friends you'll make in this man's army."

"Yes," she said.

"That's better," Trapper said. "So where's the X-ray department?"

"Yes," she said.

They wandered down the main hallway, people turning to look at them as they passed, until they came to the X-ray

65

department. They walked in, put their clubs in a corner and sat down. They put their feet on the radiologist's desk and lighted cigarettes.

"Don't set fire to your beard," Hawkeye cautioned Trapper John.

"Can't," Trapper said. "Had it fire-proofed."

"What the . . .?" somebody in the gathering circle of interested X-ray technicians started to say.

"All right," Trapper said. "Somebody trot out the latest pictures of this kid with the shell fragment in his chest."

No one moved.

"Snap it up!" yelled Hawkeye. "We're the pros from Dover, and the last pictures we saw must be forty-eight hours old by now."

Without knowing why, a confused technician produced the X-rays. The pros perused them carefully.

"Just as we thought," said Trapper. "A routine problem."

"Yeah," Hawkeye said. "They must have a hair trigger on the panic button here. Where's the patient?"

"Ward Six," somebody answered.

"Take us there."

Led to Ward Six, the pros politely asked the nurse if they might see the patient. The poor girl, having embarked from the States many months before fully prepared in her mind for any tortures the enemy might inflict upon her, was unprepared for this.

"I don't know," she said. "I don't think I can allow you to see him without the permission of Major Adams."

"Adams?" Trapper said. "John Adams?"

"Adams?" Hawkeye said. "John Quincy Adams?"

"No. George Adams."

"Never heard of him," Trapper said. "Come on now, nice nurse-lady. Let's see the kid."

They followed the hapless nurse into the ward and she led them to the patient. A brief examination revealed that, although the boy did have a two-centimeter shell fragment and a lot of blood in his right chest and that removal of both was relatively urgent, he was in no immediate danger. His confidence and well-being were not particularly enhanced, however, by the bearded, robed, big-hatted character who had dumped a bag of golf clubs at the foot of his bed and had then started to listen to his chest.

"Have no fear, Trapper John is here," Hawkeye assured him in a loud voice, and then, privately, he whispered in the patient's ear: "Don't worry, son. This is Captain McIntyre, and he's the best chest surgeon in the Far East and maybe the whole U.S. Army. He's gonna fix you up easy. Your Daddy saw to that."

When they asked, the Swampmen were told by the nurse that blood had been typed and that an adequate supply had been cross-matched. They picked up their clubs and, following directions, headed for the operating area where they found their way barred by a fierce Captain of the Army Nurse Corps.

"Stop, right where you are!" she ordered.

"Don't get mad, m'am," Hawkeye said. "All we want is our starting time."

"Get out!" she screamed.

"Look, mother," Trapper said. "I'm the pro from Dover. Me and my greenskeeper want to crack that kid's chest and get out to the course. Find the gas-passer and tell him to premedicate the patient, and find this Major Adams so he can get his spiel over with. Also, while you're at it, I need a can of beans and my greenskeeper here wants ham and eggs. It's now eight o'clock. I want to work at nine. Hop to it!"

She did, much to her own surprise. Breakfast was served, followed immediately by Major Adams who, after his initial shock, adjusted to the situation when it developed that all three had a number of mutual friends in the medical dodge.

"I don't know about the C.O., though," Major Adams said, meaning the Commanding Officer.

"Who is he?" Hawkeye said.

"Colonel Ruxton P. Merrill. Red-neck R.A. all the way."

"Don't worry about him," Trapper said. "We'll handle him."

At nine o'clock the operation started. At nine-oh-three Colonel Merrill, having heard about the unusual invasion of his premises, stormed into the operating room. He was without gown, cap or mask, so Hawkeye, deploring the break in the antiseptic techniques prescribed for OR's, turned to the circulating nurse and ordered: "Get that dirty old man out of this operating room!"

"I'm Colonel Merrill!" yelled Colonel Merrill.

Hawkeye turned and impaled him on an icy stare. "Beat it,

Pop. If this chest gets infected, I'll tell the Congressman on you."

After that there was no further excitement, and the operation, as the Swampmen had surmised, turned out to be routine. Within forty-five minutes the definitive work was done, and only the chest closure remained.

When the operation had started, the anesthesiologist of the 25th Station Hospital had been so busy getting the patient asleep in order to meet the deadline imposed by the pros from Dover that he had not been introduced. Furthermore, he had not seen them without their masks—nor had they seen him—but when he had a chance to settle down and relax, the shell fragment and the blood having been removed to the perceptible betterment of the patient's condition, he wrote at the top of his anesthesia record the name "Hawkeye Pierce" in the space labeled "First Assistant." He wrote it with assurance and with pleasure.

The anesthesiologist was Captain Ezekiel Bradbury (Me Lay) Marston, V, of Spruce Harbor, Maine. In Spruce Harbor, Maine, the name Marston is synonymous with romantic visions of the past—specifically clipper ships—and money. The first to bear the name captained a clipper, bought it and built three more. The second commanded the flagship of the fleet and bought four more. Number III was skipper of the *Spruce Harbor*, which went down with all hands off Hatteras some three years after number IV had been born in its Captain's cabin forty miles south of Cape Horn. Number V was Me Lay Marston, the only swain in Spruce Harbor High who could say, "Me lay, you lay?" and parlay such a simple, unimaginative approach into significant success with the young females of the area.

Hawkeye Pierce thought of it first, and last, but Me Lay Marston had also gone around for a while with the valedictorian of the Class of '41 at Port Waldo High School. In November, 1941, after Spruce Harbor beat Port Waldo 38–0, Pierce and Marston engaged in a fist fight which neither won decisively. In subsequent years they belonged to the same fraternity at Androscoggin College, played on the same football team, attended the same medical school and, during internship, they shared the same room. Me Lay was an usher when Hawkeye Pierce married the valedictorian, and Hawkeye provided a similar service when Me Lay did the same for the Broad from Eagle Head, whom Hawkeye had also dated for a while.

During his adolescence and earliest manhood, Me Lay had been proud of his name. Now, circumstances having forced him to correct his behavior, he was merely resigned to it. By 1952, however, he had not been addressed as Me Lay for three years. He had not seen Hawkeye Pierce for three years.

So on a bright, warm day in Kokura the fifth in a series of Captain Marstons looked up from his chart and asked, "May I have the surgeon's name, please?"

Hawkeye Pierce answered, "He's the pro from Dover and I'm the Ghost of Smoky Joe."

"Save that crap for someone else, you stupid clamdigger," answered Captain Marston.

The surgeons stopped. The first assistant leaned over and looked at the anesthesia chart and saw his name. He knew the writing and recognized the writer. He took it in his stride.

"Me Lay, I'd like you to meet Trapper John."

"The real Trapper John? Your cousin who threw you the pass and went on to greater fame on the Boston & Maine?"

"The one and only," affirmed Hawkeye.

"Trapper, you are in bad company," said Me Lay, "but I'll be happy to shake your hand if you'll hurry up and get that chest closed. You still workin' the trains?"

"Planes mostly. May take a crack at rickshas. You still employing the direct approach?"

"No, not since I married the Broad from Eagle Head. I've been out of action now for four years."

"Then what the hell do you do around here?" asked Hawkeye. "It doesn't look like you're very busy. You mean to tell us you don't chase the local scrunch?"

"I don't seem to be interested in it from that angle. The first month I was here all I did was wind my watch and evacuate my bladder. Now I'm taking a course in Whorehouse Administration."

"Under the auspices of the Army's Career Management Plan?" inquired Trapper.

"No, all on my own."

"It was Yankee drive and ingenuity that built the Marston fortune," Hawkeye pointed out. "I'm proud of you, Me Lay. Where are you taking the course?"

"At Dr. Yamamoto's Finest Kind Pediatric Hospital and Whorehouse," Captain Marston informed him.

"Cut the crap, Me Lay. This sounds like too much even for you."

"I'm serious. This guy practices pediatrics, has a little hospital and runs a whorehouse, all in the same building."

"What are you? A pimp?"

"No. I keep the books, inspect the girls and take care of some of the kids in the hospital. Occasionally I tend bar and act as bouncer. A guy needs well rounded training to embark on a career such as this."

The chest got closed, despite the conversation. In the dressing room the Swampmen got back into their Papa-San suits and continued the reunion with Me Lay Marston.

"What's with this Colonel Merrill?" asked Trapper.

"Red-neck R.A. all the way," Captain Marston said. "He'll give you a bad time if you let him."

A messenger entered and stated that Captains Pierce and McIntyre were to report to the colonel's office immediately. Me Lay gave them the address of the FKPH&W and suggested that they meet him there at seven that evening for dinner and whatnot.

"OK," Hawkeye said, and then he turned to the messenger waiting to guide them to the colonel's office. "Got any caddy carts?"

"What?" the messenger said.

Sighing, they slung their clubs over their shoulders and followed the guide. The colonel was temporarily occupied elsewhere. so rather than just sit there during his absence and read his mail, the Swampmen decided to practice putting on his carpet.

"You men are under arrest," the colonel boomed, when he stormed onto the scene.

"Quiet!" Trapper said. "Can't you see I'm putting?"

"Why, you . . ."

"Let's get down to bare facts, Colonel." Hawkeye said. "Probably even you know this case didn't demand our presence. Be that as it may, your boys blew it. We bailed it out, and a Congressman is very much interested. We figure this kid needs about five days of postop care from us, and we also figure to play in the Kokura Open. If that ain't okay with you, we'll get on the horn to a few Congressmen."

"Or one, anyway," Trapper John said.

It was mean but not too bold, and they knew it would work. They took their clubs and walked out. At the front door of the hospital they found the car which had brought them from the airport. It was the colonel's car, and the sergeant was lounging nearby, awaiting the colonel. Trapper John and Hawkeye got into the front seat.

"Hey, wait a minute," the sergeant said.

"The colonel is lending us his car," Hawkeye informed the Sergeant. "We'll give it back after the Open."

"That's right," Trapper said. "He wants you to go in now, and write some letters for the Congressman's son."

"Goddam army," the sergeant said.

They drove to the golf course and parked, unloaded their clubs and walked into the pro shop. Although most of the golfers were members of the American and British armed forces, the pro was Japanese and he greeted the appearance of two Korean Papa-Sans with evident hostility.

"How do we qualify for the Open?" asked Hawkeye.

"There twenty-five dollar entry fee," the pro informed him, eyeing him coldly.

"But I'm the pro from Dover, and this here is my assistant," announced Hawkeye, handing the Japanese his Maine State Golf Association handicap card.

"Ah, so," the Japanese hissed.

"We're just in from visiting relatives in Korea," Trapper informed him. "Our clothes got burned up. We can't get any new ones until we win some dough in your tournament."

"Ah, so," hissed the pro, much relieved, and he promptly supplied them with golf shoes and two female caddies.

With the wide-eyed girls carrying the clubs, they trekked to the first tee. There, waiting to tee off, they were taking a few practice swings, to the amusement of all in their vicinity, when they observed four British officers, one of them a colonel, approaching. In a matter of minutes two things became evident. Judged by his own practice swings the British colonel was not on leave from his country's Curtis Cup team, and judged by the disdain evident on his face when he eyed the Swampmen he was not in favor of any Papa-Sans sharing the golf course with him.

"Damn this get-up," Hawkeye was saying to Trapper. "It doesn't do much for my backswing."

"Good," Trapper said, increasing the awkwardness of his own efforts.

"What do you mean, good?" Hawkeye said.

"Keep your voice down," Trapper said, "because I think we're about to hook a live one."

"See here, you two!" the British colonel bleated, walking up to them at that moment. "I don't know who you think you are, but I think . . ."

"Think again," Trapper said.

"I want you to know I'm Colonel Cornwall . . ."

"Cornwallis?" Hawkeye said. "I thought we fixed your wagon at Yorktown."

"I said Cornwall."

"Lovely there in the spring," Trapper said. "Rhododendrons and all that."

"Now see here!" the colonel said, red in the face now. "I don't know what you're doing here, but rather than make an issue of it, if you'll just step aside and allow us to tee off . . ."

"Look, Corny," Hawkeye said. "You just calm down, or we'll tee off on *you*."

"I'll tell you what we'll do, Colonel," Trapper said. "You look like a sporting chap, so to settle this little difficulty in a sporting way, we'll both play you a ten pound Nassau."

"I beg your pardon?"

"You heard him," Hawkeye said.

"Excuse me a moment," the colonel said, and he turned and rejoined his companions to get their opinion of the proposition.

"What do you think?" Hawkeye said.

"We got him," Trapper said, manufacturing as awkward a swing as he could without making it too obvious.

"Here he comes now," Hawkeye said.

"All right," the colonel said. "You're on, and we'll be watching every shot you hit."

The Swampmen hit drives designed to get the ball in play, with no attempt at distance, and they were down the middle about 225 yards. Trapper reached the green in two and got his par four. Hawkeye hit a nice five-iron but misjudged the distance and was long, hit a wedge back but missed a five-footer and took a bogey.

The second hole was a short par three that gave them no

trouble. Both bogied three and four, however, as it became clear that driving range experience at the Double Natural had sharpened their hitting ability but done little for their judgment of distance or their putting. Nevertheless, the girl caddies were quite impressed, particularly by Trapper John, whose every move they watched with rapt fascination.

Approaching the seventh, a par five, they were both three over par, and as the day was getting warmer, Trapper took off the long, flowing top of his Papa-San suit and his hat. This left him with long hair, a beard, a bare torso, and long, flowing trousers, and seemed to move him up another notch in the eyes of the girls.

On the seventh, he was down the middle a good 260, with Hawkeye not far behind him. Hawkeye's second shot wasn't much, however, and he had a full five-iron left. Then Trapper cranked out an awesome two-wood with a slight tail-end hook which hit the hard fairway, bounced over a trap, and came to rest within two feet of the pin.

"Jesus!" exclaimed Hawkeye. The caddies, hearing this, looked knowingly at each other, and it dawned on the Swampmen what their mounting excitement was all about. Happily, Hawkeye had several of the autographed pictures in his wallet and, with a grand gesture, he bestowed complimentary copies upon the girls who, their suspicions confirmed, were overcome. Hawkeye had to lead them aside to calm them down, explaining as best he could that the Master's game was a little rusty and that He wanted to get in at least eighteen holes before making His comeback generally known.

"These bimboes," he explained to Trapper, approaching the eighth tee, "are on a real Christian kick, so don't disappoint them."

Trapper grabbed his driver, winced and looked at his hands. "Goddam nail holes," he complained.

The rest of the way around, Trapper played even par on the not too difficult and not too long course to finish with a seventy-three. Hawkeye couldn't figure the greens and found himself needing a ten-footer on the eighteenth for a seventy-eight. Trapper blessed the ball and the cup before Hawkeye essayed the putt, which went in like it had eyes. The caddies, bowing their way out, departed to spread the word.

"Now," Trapper said, "let's prepare to lighten Corny's load

73

a little. If that hacker breaks eighty I'll take it to the World Court."

The Swampmen, with Trapper back in full uniform, found the bar. They were on their second Scotch when they noticed the Japanese faces peeking through the window and then Colonel Cornwall and his three colleagues pushing their way through the crowd at the door.

"I say now," the colonel was saying, brushing himself off. "Does anyone know what this is all about?"

"Ah, yes," Hawkeye said, motioning toward Trapper, who was bowing toward the faces at the window and door. "Mighty High Religious Personage is greeting followers."

"Of course, of course," the colonel was saying now, starting to rock with laughter. "I say! That's rather droll, isn't it?"

"What's that, sir?" one of his colleagues asked.

"Chap here," he said, nodding toward Trapper. "Why, the chap here's portraying John the Baptist!"

"Colonel," Hawkeye said, handing him one of the autographed pictures, "you can't tell the players without a score-card."

"Oh, I say!" the colonel was roaring now. "That *is* good, isn't it? I *do* get it now. Say, you chaps, do have a drink on me. Oh, I say!"

The Swampmen had several drinks on him and, when they got around to comparing cards, the colonel, who had shot an eighty-two, paid up willingly.

"Corny," Hawkeye heard himself saying, "how about you and these other gentlemen joining us for dinner at Dr. Yama-moto's Finest Kind Pediatric Hospital and Whorehouse?"

"Oh, I say!" the colonel said. "That sounds like sport!"

Shortly after 7:00 P.M., Me Lay Marston, idly sipping a martini in the bar of the FKPH&W, heard a commotion outside. Going to the door, he found Hawkeye, the British contingent and then Trapper John bringing up the rear. Trapper was trying to disentangle himself from the converts and the just curious.

"Me Lay," Trapper said, when he got inside, "I've had enough of this. Get me a pair of scissors and a razor."

In time Trapper John was shaved, shorn and showered, and dinner was solicitously served by the young ladies. While the visitors sipped after-dinner cordials, Me Lay excused himself to make his rounds at the adjoining hospital. In a few minutes he returned with a worried look.

"What had you guys planned for tonight?" he asked.

"Well," answered Trapper, "we thought we'd get some . . ."

"How about looking at a kid for me?"

"Look, Me Lay," Hawkeye said, "you're supposed to be the intern in this . . ."

"Shut up, and come look at this kid."

"What's the story?" asked Trapper.

"Well, one of our girls got careless, and two days ago she gave birth to an eight pound Japanese-American male."

"What's wrong with him?"

"Every time we feed him, it either comes right back up or he coughs and turns blue and has a helluva time."

"We don't have to see him," Trapper said. "Call that half-assed Army Hospital and tell them to be ready to put some lipiodal in this kid's esophagus and take X-rays."

"But it's ten-thirty at night. We can't get everybody out for a civilian. They won't do it."

"How much you wanna bet, Me Lay?" inquired Hawkeye Pierce. "Get on the horn and tell them the pros from Dover are on their way with a patient. Better tell the OR to crank itself up, because I got a feeling that you're going to pass some gas while I help Trapper close a trachco-csophageal fistula."

"Oh, I say," Colonel Cornwall wanted to know, "what's that?"

"It's a hole between the esophagus and the trachea, where it doesn't belong," Hawkeye explained.

"And you chaps can repair that?"

"Well," said Me Lay. "We can try."

At the 25th Station Hospital, the Officer of the Day received a call from Captain Marston saying that an emergency was coming in for X-rays. Soon after, Hawkeye and Trapper, in Papa-San suits and followed by Me Lay carrying the baby, entered the X-ray department.

Captain Banks, the O.D., arrived and asked, "What's this all about?"

"It's all about this baby," Hawkeye informed him. "We want to X-ray him and we want to do it right now, and we do not wish to be engaged in useless conversation by officious military types, of which you look like one to me."

"But, we can't . . ."

Hawkeye sat Captain Banks on the edge of a desk and handed him the phone.

"Be nice, Captain. Call the X-ray technician. If you give us any kind of a bad time, me and Trapper John are going to clean your clock. We are frustrated lovers and quite dangerous."

Captain Banks called. While awaiting the technician, Trapper and Me Lay placed a small catheter in the baby's esophagus. A few minutes later, radio-opaque oil was injected through the catheter. It revealed the abnormal opening between the esophagus and the trachea but no significant narrowing of the esophagus. This meant that anything the baby ate could go into his lungs but that, happily, once the opening was closed, the esophagus would be able to accommodate the passage of food. It required careful preparation, proper anesthesia, early and competent surgery and good luck.

"Me Lay, let's you and me get a needle into a vein," Trapper said, and then, turning to Captain Banks, he said, "You there, in the shiny shoes, tell the lab to do a blood count and cross-match a pint. We won't need that much, but it's a term they'll understand. Then tell the OR to get set up for a thoracotomy. We're going to operate in about two hours. Hawkeye, you stick close to Alice, or whatever his name is, and see that he performs efficiently."

The Officer of the Day had no choice but to perform efficiently. The nurses were routed out, not at all pleased at the prospect of operating a second time with the pros from Dover. There was, in fact, outright grumbling which Hawkeye Pierce brought to a rapid conclusion.

"Ladies," he said, "we are sorry to get you out at this time of night. However, we stumbled upon this deal, and we can't walk away from it, no matter whose rules are broken. This baby will die if we don't fix him, so let's all be nice and just think about the baby."

Fortunately, nurses succumb to this kind of pitch. They gave up any show of resistance, particularly after they saw the baby, but Hawkeye caught Captain Banks calling Colonel Merrill.

"Now, Captain," he chided him, "I may give you a few lumps, but first I must call the Finest Kind Pediatric Hospital and Whorehouse."

76

So doing, he talked to Colonel Cornwall, explained their situation and made a few suggestions. Fifteen minutes later, as Colonel R. P. Merrill stormed into the hospital, he was met by four British officers who loaded him unceremoniously into their Land Rover and returned to the FKPH&W.

After Captain Banks had been stripped naked, and locked in a broom closet by the two Swampmen, the operation was finally started. Me Lay's anesthesia was excellent, the nurses cooperated completely, and Trapper and Hawkeye indulged in none of the by-play that had marked their first local appearance. After an hour and a half of careful work, Trapper had closed the fistula. They shed their gowns and discussed the postoperative care.

"I think we better leave him here," said Trapper. "You can't take care of anything like this in that whorehouse hospital of yours, can you, Me Lay?"

"Not too well, but I don't see how we can keep him here. Merrill will be all over us in the morning."

"Leave the kid here," Hawkeye said. "We'll be in and out and can look after both him and the boy we did this morning. I know how to keep Merrill off our backs."

At 3:00 A.M., back at the FKPH&W, they had a drink with the British officers who told them that Colonel Merrill was upstairs asleep, having been coaxed into having a drink and a sedative.

"But what about when he wakes up?" asked Me Lay.

"Send a naked broad into his room and take some pictures," suggested Hawkeye.

"Oh, I say!" Colonel Cornwall said.

A few minutes later, Colonel Merrill began to stir and awaken as the girl joined him in bed. Witnesses to the scene filled the doorway while Trapper John leisurely shot a roll of film.

"I told you so! I told you so!" chanted Hawkeye. "He's a dirty old man. A disgrace to the uniform."

"The blighter should bloody well be cashiered from the service," asserted Colonel Cornwall indignantly.

"I'd say that depends on his behavior from now on," said Trapper John, pocketing the film.

The Swampmen were to tee off in the Kokura Open at ten o'clock the next morning. One of Me Lay's assistants was instructed to obtain proper clothing, since they did not wish to wear Papa-San suits forever.

Awakening at 8:00 A.M., weary but determined to be ready for the tournament, they drank coffee, ate steak and eggs served in bed by the ladies of the house, and donned sky blue slacks and golf shirts.

On the way to the course, they visited their two patients. The baby was far from out of the woods, but the Congressman's son was doing well. Before leaving, they entered the colonel's office.

"Where's that dirty old man?" Hawkeye asked the secretary.

The colonel came out, but he didn't roar.

"Colonel," said Hawkeye, "we've qualified for the Kokura Open so we're going to the course. We expect your people to watch that baby we operated on last night like he was the Congressman's grandson, which for all we know he may be. We expect to be notified of any change for the worse, and if we find anything wrong when we come back this afternoon, we'll burn down the hospital."

The Colonel believed them.

They arrived at the golf course at nine-thirty, practiced putting and chipping, took a few swings and, with their English confreres there to cheer them on, they pronounced themselves ready to go. They weren't. The activities of the previous days, and nights, had taken too much out of them, and by the end of the third day, what with having to check repeatedly on the Congressman's son and the baby, they were hopelessly mired back in the pack.

"I guess that does it," Trapper said, as they sat in the bar at the club. "We might have a chance if three guys dropped dead and a half dozen others came down with echinococcosis."

"What's that?" Colonel Cornwall wanted to know.

"The liver gets so big you can't get your club head back past it," Hawkeye said, "so we've got no chance."

"We're proud of you anyway," the colonel informed them. "You gave it a good go, you did. I must say, though, I shouldn't give up surgery for the professional tour if I were you."

"I guess we figured that out already," Trapper said, "but what I can't figure out is what we're going to do about this baby we're stuck with."

78

"But you chaps have done all you can," the colonel said.

"No, we haven't," Trapper said. "After the big deal we made saving his life, what do we do now? Leave him in a whorehouse?"

"Leave it to me," Hawkeye said. "I think it'll be safe now to take the kid back to Dr. Yamamoto's Finest Kind Pediatric Hospital and Whorehouse."

They went to the 25th Station Hospital, said good-bye to the Congressman's son who was well on his way to recovery, and picked up their small patient. Riding the Land Rover back to the FKPH&W, Trapper had a thought.

"We oughta name the little bastard," he said.

Hawkeye had considered this problem twenty-four hours earlier. He had even laid a little groundwork.

"I have named him," he said.

"What is it?"

"I'm not sure how much I can con Me Lay Marston into," Hawkeye said, "but the name is Ezekiel Bradbury Marston, VI."

"Oh, I say," Colonel Cornwall said.

"Obviously you are either nuts or you know something," Trapper John said eventually. "Which is it?"

"I know something. I know that Me Lay and the Broad from Eagle Head have one daughter and that's all the kids they're ever going to have. I'll save you the next question. Remember I was away for a while last night? I went to one of those overseas telephone places and called the Broad from Eagle Head, whom I've known longer than Me Lay has. To make a long story short, she agrees that a name like Ezekiel Bradbury Marston must not die!"

"Hawkeye, you are amazing," admired the Colonel.

"For once, I gotta agree," agreed Trapper.

At the FKPH&W, they placed Ezekiel Bradbury Marston, VI, in a laundry basket, left instructions for his care and returned to the bar where they found the unsuspecting parent, Me Lay Marston.

"What are we going to do with this kid, Me Lay?" asked Trapper.

"I don't know."

"Well, Jesus, Me Lay, you're not much of a whorehouse administrator if you don't have some ideas on the subject."

"Good-looking kid," said Hawkeye. "What's his mother like?"

"A nice intelligent girl. She asked me this morning what we'd do with the baby. I've been looking into a few possibilities, but I'll tell you right now there aren't any good ones."

"Too bad. The little chap's half American," said Colonel Cornwall. "Any way to get him to the States?"

"Only one way," said Me Lay.

"What's that?"

"Get somebody to adopt him."

Hawkeye said, "Me Lay, why don't you adopt him?"

Me Lay looked miserable. He lit a cigarette and sipped his drink.

"That idea's been popping into my head ever since we operated on him," he said, finally, "but how can I do it? Am I supposed to call up my wife and say I'm sending home a half-breed bastard from a Japanese whorehouse?"

"You don't have to," Trapper told him. "Hawkeye called your wife last night. The deal's set. All you have to do is arrange the details."

Hesitating only a moment, Me Lay got up, went to the hospital area, picked up the baby and brought him to the bar.

"What's his name, Me Lay?" asked Trapper.

"Gentlemen, meet my son, Ezekiel Bradbury Marston, VI, of Spruce Harbor, Maine."

Late that night a flyboy who'd been in Seoul earlier in the day brought word of increasing action on Old Baldy. The next morning the pros from Dover, having withdrawn from the tournament, but still clad in sky blue slacks and golf shirts, boarded a plane for Seoul.

9

In the middle of a hot, humid and bloody afternoon Lt. Col. Henry Blake finished a bowel resection, assessed the grief in the admitting and preop wards and then stepped outside to smoke, pace back and forth and, about once every ten seconds, look hopefully to the south. From the number and nature of the casualties, and with the privileged information from Radar O'Reilly that the situation on Old Baldy would get worse before it got better, he knew that he—that all of them—were in trouble. Between his looks to the south he swore at the Army for taking two of his three best cutters to Kokura and not getting them back in time.

As he ground out his butt, drew a deep breath and made a half-hearted attempt to square his sagging shoulders, he took a last look down the valley and saw it—a cloud of dust. Henry smiled and, for the first time in twenty-four hours, relaxed because he knew that just ahead of just such a dust cloud had to be a jeep driven by Hawkeye Pierce. Seconds later Hawkeye and Trapper, in sky blue slacks and golf shirts, jumped from the jeep.

"Hail, gallant leader!" Hawkeye said, snapping off a salute.

"The organization looks busy," observed Trapper John to Hawkeye, "so I wonder what its gallant leader is doing, just standing here and dilly-dallying in the sunshine."

"Beats me," Hawkeye said.

"You guys get your asses to work!" yelled Henry.

"Yes, sir," Trapper said, saluting.

"Sure, Henry," Hawkeye said, "but we'd appreciate it if you'd get our clubs out of the jeep and clean them."

They ran for the preop ward where the scene informed them that they were in for the busiest day of their lives. What they were yet to learn was that they, and the entire personnel of the 4077th MASH, were in for the busiest two weeks the Double Natural had ever known. For a full two weeks the wounded would come and keep coming, and for a full two weeks every surgeon and every nurse and every corpsman, as the shifts overlapped, would work from twelve to fourteen to sixteen hours a day, every day, and sometimes some of them would work twenty out of the twenty-four.

It could have been chaos, and it almost was. They came in by helicopter and they came in by ambulance—arteries, lungs, bowels, bladders, livers, spleens, kidneys, larynxes, pharynxes, bones, stomachs. Colonel Blake, the surgeons, Ugly John, Painless Waldowski, who, when he wasn't extracting shattered bone and wiring jaws, was passing gas to back up Ugly John, were in constant hurried communication, trying to maintain some order to the flow. Their objective was to provide each patient with the maximum preparation for and the proper timing of his surgery. This was controlled, of course, by the availability of the operating tables and the surgeons. As each new chopper brought new emergencies, plans and timing constantly had to be changed because some cases had to be moved directly from chopper to admitting ward to OR.

From one flight of choppers the Swampmen found eight new arrivals, all of whom needed maximum and immediate attention. The worst was an unconscious Negro private who was the bearer of a note from the doctor in the Battalion Aid Station. The note stated that the patient had been knocked out when a bunker had collapsed, had awakened and then had slowly subsided into unconsciousness again. This was a neurosurgical problem, but the 4077th had no neurosurgeon because such cases were supposed to be sent to the 6073rd MASH, which had several.

Trapper John looked at the note and then at the boy. He looked in his eyes. The right pupil was dilated and fixed. His pulse was slow, his blood pressure negligible.

"I'm afraid this one has an epidural hematoma," he said. "Duke, haven't you been that route a little?"

"Yeah," Duke said, "but not enough to be a pro."

"You're a pro now," Trapper said.

Duke quickly examined the patient. He found indications of pressure on the brain from blood accumulating between the skull and the outer brain lining.

"Right now," he ordered, "lug this one into the OR."

The Duke ran ahead of the stretcher. In the OR he encountered, fortunately, the boss, chief, honcho, leader and head coach of the operating room nurses, Captain Bridget McCarthy of Boston, Massachusetts.

"Quick, Knocko," he commanded, "y'all get me gloves, knife, hammer, chisel, Gelfoam and a drain."

Captain Bridget McCarthy was maybe thirty-five years old, five feet eight inches of solid maple, and she did not ordinarily tolerate much lip from the Swampmen or her immediate superior, Major Hot Lips Houlihan, either. This last endeared her to the Swampmen who did not call her "Knocko" for nothing, for they knew she could take out any one of them in a head-on. More than anything, however, she was also a nurse who had come specifically to be a nurse, so when Duke gave orders with fire in his eye she asked no questions and said, "Yes, sir."

The right temporal area was quickly shaved and scrubbed, and Duke incised down to the bone. He had no desire to go through the skull with a hammer and chisel, but he also had no choice. The appropriate drills for making burr holes were at the 6073rd with the neurosurgeons, so he did the best he could. With luck, or skill born of need, he cracked a jagged hole in the skull in less than a minute. As he broke through, blood flowed out in a torrent. The torrent quickly diminished to a dribble and then Duke exercised highly commendable surgical wisdom. The wise surgeon, particularly when out of his field, knows when to quit, so Duke refrained from looking for hemorrhage beneath the dura mater. He settled for the drainage of the epidural hemorrhage, and the pressure on the brain was relieved. He stuffed Gelfoam down toward the bleeding site, put in a rubber drain, closed the skin with silk sutures, and the soldier began to stir and moan. As his breathing improved and his pulse picked up, the Duke spake the words that, if they ever name a medical school after him, may be carved in stone over the entrance to the administration building:

83

"He might make it, even if all I really did was hit him in the head with an axe."

As Duke went, then, to the postop ward to write orders on his patient, Captain Bridget McCarthy went to the other end of the operating tent to find out what the excitement was. The excitement was the patient who'd arrived on the same chopper with the epidural hematoma. Hawkeye had looked at him quickly, found him to be in shock, semiconscious but not, it seemed, in immediate danger. His clothes were saturated with mud, as was his hair, and there was a muddy, bloody bandage around his neck.

"Get that bandage off so I can see what the hell's underneath," Hawkeye told a corpsman, and he went on to the patient on the next stretcher.

The corpsman removed the bandage. The patient turned his head to the left. Blood shot two feet into the air from the hole in his right neck where a mortar fragment had entered. The soldier yelled.

"Mama, Mama!" he yelled. "Oh, Mama, I'm dying!"

It looked like a gushing well, and a fascinated group gathered to watch. As the well crested and the blood descended, it fell on the face of the soldier and into his mouth. He coughed, spraying his rapt audience with blood.

Hawkeye ran over. In haste, and instinctively, he stuck his right index finger down the hole, blocking off the severed common carotid artery. He had stopped the flow of blood, but he had also tied up his right hand, and he wondered: "What the hell do I do now?"

"Bring him to the OR right on this stretcher," he yelled. "I can't take my finger out. Find Ugly John and get his ass in here!"

As Knocko McCarthy followed Hawkeye into the OR, she had no chance to ask questions. Hawkeye was still sounding off orders.

"Start somebody cutting off his clothes . . . Tell the lab to come in with a couple of low titre O, and type and cross match him for five or six more . . . Get somebody to do two cutdowns and start the blood . . . Come to think of it, get somebody to start rounding up donors, and send some cowboys to Seoul for all the goddam blood they can get . . . And get that Christly gas passer in here!"

"I'm here," Ugly John said.

"Good," Hawkeye said. "I guess you'd bettter get him asleep and a tube in him if you can. His common carotid is cut, and I can't do anything with the son of a bitch jumping all over the place. We haven't got time for any of the preoperative pretties."

"Mama, Mama!" the patient was yelling. "I'm dying."

"Hold still," Hawkeye said, "or I'll guarantee it."

Ugly John did a cutdown and got into a vein. He got some blood started, as well as Pentothal and curare, and inserted his intratracheal tube. It was still a toss-up. Although the patient had survived the induction of anesthesia, Hawkeye still had to get the carotid clamped off, and as soon as possible.

"Get help," he ordered Knocko McCarthy. "I gotta keep a finger on this or we lose him, and I can't expose it and get it clamped with one hand."

He tried though. Grabbing a scalpel with his left hand, he enlarged the wound around the bare, dirty right index finger which had to stay in the neck. Next he tried to slide a Kelly clamp down his finger into the wound and clamp the artery, but it didn't work. Then he got a retractor and, managing to hold it in the wound with his left hand, he improved the exposure. He was still in desperate need of help.

"Look, Ug," he said to Ugly John who was busy enough with the anesthesia and the new blood, "grab a Kelly, and from where you are I think you can ride it down my finger, grab, and we'll have this mother under control."

Ugly did as told. Reaching the bottom of the wound, he opened the clamp as wide as he could. Sensing that he was around something substantial, he closed the clamp vigorously, asserting, "I got it! I got it!"

He had clamped the end of Hawkeye's finger. Hawkeye, by reflex, removed his finger—and the blood flew. When it did Hawkeye went back in, but this time with his left index finger, and now, with luck, he was able to get a clamp on the artery.

"I'm OK for now," he told Knocko McCarthy and one of the surgeons from the other shift who came running up with her, "but get the Professor."

Most of the surgeons had some locally acquired experience in the care of arterial injuries, but they were still beginners. Therefore the Army had sent a Professor of Vascular Surgery from Walter Reed Hospital in Washington to give lessons throughout Korea. Fortune had placed him, at this time, at the Double Natural, and he bailed the patient, and Hawkeye, out.

Trapper John, meanwhile, had delved into a chest and Duke was now occupied with several feet of small bowel which were no longer useful to the owner. Hawkeye returned to the preop ward where Colonel Blake had taken charge.

"What's the score now?" Hawkeye asked.

"A major case on every table and ten more that are bad and about thirty that can wait till things quiet down."

"Who's ready?"

"That one over there," said Henry, pointing.

That one turned out to be a very black Negro who was one of Ethiopia's contributions to the UN forces. Hawkeye repaired the damage to the liver and bowel there just in time to assist Trapper John who had gone into another chest. From Trapper he went to help Duke remove the right kidney and a section of colon belonging to a Corporal Ian MacGregor.

"What type we got here?" Hawkeye asked the Duke.

"Don't y'all know you're operating on a member of Princess Patricia's Canadian Light Infantry?" the Duke said.

"Finest kind," Hawkeye said.

That was the way they played it, day after day. As soon as someone finished a case he had to assist elsewhere until another case of his own was brought in. Then, briefed by Colonel Blake, he'd step in and do his best. When the last of the serious cases was allotted, the surgeons, as they became free, would start working on the minor things—debridement of extremity wounds, some with fractures, some requiring an amputation of a finger, a toe, a foot or a leg, but minor as compared with what had gone before. Meanwhile they, and everyone else, would listen for, and dread, the sound of the six o'clock chopper.

The six o'clock chopper, either morning or evening, was always unwelcome because the very fact that the pilot was risking the trip in half-daylight meant that the soldiers lying in the pods were seriously wounded. So twice each day, at dawn and at dusk, as six o'clock approached, everyone—surgeons, nurses, lab technicians, corpsmen, cooks and mostly Lt. Col. Henry Blake—would listen, and during the time of the Great

Deluge, they would hear, not one six o'clock chopper but three or four.

"What the hell is going on up there, anyway?" Colonel Blake asked no one in particular one 6:00 P.M., the roar of the choppers filling the postop ward, where the colonel was assessing results with the Swampmen.

"The Chinks," Trapper John said, "are obviously holding a Gold Star Mothers membership drive."

"And it's up to us," Hawkeye said, "to stamp out that organization, so let's get to it."

"Right," Duke said. "We can fix 'em just as fast as they can shoot 'em."

"Right, hell," Henry said. "You guys can't go on like this forever. You haven't had any sleep."

"Right," Duke said.

"How the hell do you feel?" Henry said.

"Better than the patients," Duke said.

"Then what the hell are you doing, standing around here?" Henry said.

The new group was truly international. Hawkeye drew a Turk, and repaired his lacerated colon. Duke took off the right leg of a Puerto Rican kid, portions of whose femur, shattered by a mortar up on Pork Chop Hill, had punctured the chest of his fox hole buddy, who was now on the next table under Trapper's knife. When Trapper finished there, he closed the ruptured diaphragm of a Chinese prisoner of war, while Duke assisted the Professor of Vascular Surgery who was trying to save the left leg of a Netherlands private by fashioning an arterial graft out of a segment of vein from the other leg, and Hawkeye, with Pete Rizzo assisting him, went into the belly of an Australian.

"Dammit," he said, after about a half hour of it, "we just need more hands."

"I know," Pete Rizzo said, "but I only got two."

"Knocko!"

"Yes, sir?" Captain Bridget McCarthy answered.

"Put on a pair of gloves and help us for a few minutes, will you?"

"Can't, Hawk," Captain Bridget McCarthy said. "I've just got too much to do already."

"Then find somebody else."

"Yes, sir."

87

Ten minutes later, Hawkeye was aware of the help—gowned, capped, masked and gloved—at his left. Without looking up he reached over and put the new assistant's hands on a retractor.

"Pull," he said.

"How, Hawk?" he heard Father Mulcahy say. "This is a little out of my line."

For days, now, and for nights, too, Dago Red had been doing his part. All day and all night he had been going from patient to patient—black, white, yellow—friend and foe. Some of them didn't know who he was, but they all knew the side he was on. A confident patient does better in surgery, and so does a confident surgeon, and Dago Red had the right words for both.

"Just pull," Hawkeye was saying now. "Right there, and toward you. More. Good. And when we get out of this you can put in the first sterile fix in the history of surgery."

And still they came. Bellies, chests, necks, arteries, arms, legs, eyes, testicles, kidneys, spinal cords, all shot to hell. Win or lose. Life and death. At the beginning of it, all of the surgeons, and particularly the Swampmen, had experienced a great transformation. During periods of only sporadic employment they often drank far too much and complained far too much, but with the coming of The Deluge they had become useful people again, a fulfilled, effective fighting unit and not just a bunch of semi-employed stew bums stranded in the middle of nowhere. This was fine, as far as it went, but it was going too far. By the end of the second week they were all wan, red-eyed, dog-tired and short of temper, and it was obvious to all of them that their reflexes had been dulled and that their judgment had sometimes become questionable.

"This can't go on," Lt. Col. Henry Blake was saying at five forty-five one afternoon, for the fifieth or sixtieth time within the last three or four days. "Goddam it and to hell, but this just can't go on."

Henry was standing, with the Swampmen, just outside the door of the postop ward. Once again, somehow, they had managed to take care of all the major cases, and the debridements and fractures and amputations were now being handled by others. They had ostensibly stepped out for a smoke, but each knew that they were all there to post a watch to the

88

north and hope against hope against the appearance of the six o'clock choppers.

"It's gotta end sometime," Henry was saying. "It's gotta end sometime."

"All actions and all wars," Trapper John said, "eventually do."

"Oh, hell, McIntyre," Henry said, "what good is that? When? That's the question. When?"

"I don't know," Trapper said.

"But who the hell does know?" Henry said. "I call three times a day, but those people in Seoul don't know a damn thing more than we do. Who the hell does know?"

"I don't know," Hawkeye said, "but maybe Radar . . ."

"O'Reilly, sir," Radar O'Reilly said, at the colonel's elbow.

"Goddam it, O'Reilly," Henry said, "don't do that!"

"Sir?"

"What the hell are you doing out here, anyway?"

"I thought you called for me, sir," Radar said.

"Look, O'Reilly . . . ," the colonel started to say.

"Look, Henry," Hawkeye said, "maybe I'm going off my nut . . ."

"Maybe we all are," Henry said.

"Then maybe Radar can help us."

"We *are* crazy," Henry said, shaking his head. "We're absolutely mad."

"Look, Radar," Hawkeye said. "What we . . ."

"Let me handle this, Pierce," Henry said. "O'Reilly?"

"Sir?"

"Now don't lie to me . . ."

"Why, sir! You know that I never . . ."

"Never mind that, O'Reilly," Henry said. "I don't want to listen to any of that, but I want to know something."

"What, sir?"

"Goddam it," Henry said, turning to the others. "I haven't really gone out of my mind, have I?"

"No you haven't, Henry," Trapper said. "Go ahead."

"Yeah, go ahead," Duke said.

"Look, O'Reilly," Henry said, looking right at Radar. "What do you hear?"

"Nothing, sir."

"Nothing!" Henry said. "What the hell do you mean, nothing?"

"I don't hear anything, sir."

"Well, what does that mean?"

"I believe it means, sir," Radar said, "that the action has subsided in the north."

"Good!" Duke said.

"Look, O'Reilly," Henry said. "Are you telling the truth?"

"Why, sir! You know that I never . . . ."

"Stop that, O'Reilly!"

"Yes, sir."

"Radar," Hawkeye said. "Tell us something else."

"Yes, sir?"

"Do you hear the six o'clock choppers?"

"No, sir."

"You sure?"

"Yes, sir."

"Well, how the hell are you going to hear them, anyway, standing here?" Henry said, and he pointed toward the north. "You should be listening out there."

"Yes, sir," Radar said.

Radar started to walk slowly toward the north then, and they followed him. They formed a small procession, Radar in the lead, his ears at the right-angle red alert, his head turning on his long, thin neck in the familiar sweeping action. They walked across the bare ground the fifty yards to the barbed wire, beyond which lay the mine field, and they stopped.

"Well?" Henry said.

"Nothing, sir."

"Keep trying."

"Yes, sir."

To the north the valley was blanketed in shadow now, the hills to the left dark, but the sunset colors still bathing the tops of the hills to the east. They stood behind O'Reilly, where they could watch him and the sky at the same time, and they maintained absolute silence. As they watched, the last of the colors left the eastern hills, the dusk mounted in the valley and only the sky held light.

"O'Reilly," Henry said, "it's six o'clock."

"Nothing, sir."

"It's six-oh-five."

"Nothing, sir."

"O'Reilly," the colonel said, at about six-fifteen, "I can't see my watch any more."

"Nothing, sir."

"Glory be!" the Duke said.

"Good work, O'Reilly," the colonel said. "Dismissed."

"Thank you, sir."

"And by the way, Radar," Hawkeye said, "stop by The Swamp tomorrow for a bottle of Scotch."

"Thank you, sir," Radar said. "That's very kind of you, sir, but you were thinking of two."

"OK," said Hawkeye. "You're right, and you've got two."

"Thank you, sir."

"We're all crazy," Henry said.

There was no jubilation. They were all too tired. In fact, they were exhausted, completely spent, and the Swampmen hit their sacks. When 6:00 A.M. came and went, and there were no choppers, they slept on, and at 8:00 A.M., when Radar O'Reilly, accompanied by an associate lab technician, entered The Swamp, he could have made any of the three the victim of his desperate need, not for two fifths of Scotch, but for a pint of A-negative blood, quantities of which were on order from Seoul but had not arrived.

"Captain Forrest?" he said, shaking the Duke. "Sir?"

"Not now, honey," the Duke mumbled. "Gobacksleep."

Gently, Radar straightened Duke's right arm. Deftly, he injected Novocaine over a vein. Duke stirred but did not awaken, and while the assistant tightened the sleeve of Duke's T-shirt to serve as a tourniquet, Radar skillfully inserted a No. 17 needle into the vein and joyfully extracted a pint.

"Where'd you get it?" Colonel Blake asked, after Radar had hurriedly cross-matched it and proudly presented it to his chief. "Twenty minutes ago you said there wasn't any."

"I found a donor, sir," said Radar.

"Good boy," said the colonel.

Two hours later the colonel himself was a visitor to The Swamp. By now Hawkeye was in the middle of Muscongus Bay between Wreck Island and Franklin Light. He and his father, Big Benjy Pierce, were hauling lobster traps.

"Finest kind," Hawkeye was saying.

"C'mon, Pierce," Henry was saying, shaking him. "C'mon. Wake up!"

"What's wrong, Pop?"

"Pop, hell!" Henry said. "It's me."

"Who?" Hawkeye said.

"Listen, Pierce," Henry said. "There's a Korean kid in preop with a hot appendix. Who's going to take it out?"

"You are," Trapper John said, rolling over in his sack.

"Why me?" Henry said.

"Because," Trapper mumbled, "although you are a leader of men, there are no men left."

10

THE BUSINESS of doing major surgery on poor-risk patients can be trying and heartbreaking at any time, and when it is done regularly it can have an increasingly deleterious effect upon those who are doing it. It was therefore inevitable that The Deluge should have its after-effects, not only on the patients who survived but also on the surgeons who contributed to that survival. The first of the Swampmen to give outward evidence of what they had all been through was Hawkeye Pierce, and the first man to get caught in the fall-out was the anesthesiologist—Ugly John.

A good anesthesiologist is essential to any important surgical effort. Without one, the greatest surgeon in the world is helpless. With one, relatively untalented surgeons can look good. If the man at the head of the table understands the surgical problem and the surgeon's needs, if he understands the physiology and pharmacology of carrying a patient through a hazardous procedure, if he can have the patient under deep and controlled anesthesia when it is needed and awake or nearly so at the end of the operation, he is an anesthesiologist and a boon to all mankind. If all he can do is keep the patient unconcious, he is just a gas-passer. There were more gas-passers than anesthesiologists in Korea, but in Captain Ugly John Black, limpid-eyed, dark-haired, and the handsomest man in the outfit, the 4077th had an anesthesiologist.

Ugly John probably worked harder than anyone else in the unit. Theoretically his responsibilities consisted only of supervising the anesthesia service. Actually, as the only one formally trained in anesthesiology, he was morally if not militarily bound to be available at all times. Too often this involved day after day of twenty-four hour duty, with only an occasional catnap. During busy periods like The Deluge the surgeons were constantly aware of his almost perpetual state of exhaustion and his greater than average effort. Nevertheless, when they had a tough one, they either wanted Ugly John to give the anesthesia or they wanted him to be around to check on it. Just his presence, or the knowledge that he was sacked out around the corner in the preop ward, was emotional balm to the man at the knife.

One of the most consistent customers of the 4077th MASH was the Commonwealth Division, consisting of British, Canadian, Australian, New Zealand and other assorted British Empire troops a few miles to the west. Captain Black had an intense, burning, complete, unremitting hatred for all the medical officers in the Commonwealth Division. His reason was very simple: they gave half a grain of morphine and a cup of tea to every wounded soldier. If the soldier was incapable of swallowing the tea, he still got the half grain of morphine. As a result of this treatment, it was frequently necessary to wait for the morphine to wear off before a patient's condition could be assessed. If early surgery seemed reasonable or mandatory, Ugly John, in the process of getting the patient to sleep, often caught the tea in his lap. Frequently the patient had holes in his stomach or small bowel. In this situation, Ugly did not catch the tea in his lap. The surgeon would aspirate it from the abdominal cavity where it had leaked through the holes. The surgeons of the 4077th had the largest series of tea peritonitis cases in recorded medical history.

When leisure came his way, Ugly's first duty was to repair his intratracheal tubes. These are tubes placed in a patient's windpipe through the mouth and attached to a machine, controlled by the anesthesiologist, which delivers oxygen and anesthetic agents in the concentrations desired. Inside the windpipe the tubes are held in place by small balloons which are inflated after their introduction.

The balloons on Ugly's intratracheal tubes, like all balloons, kept blowing out. The supply of new tubes was limited or nonexistent, for reasons never quite clear, so it was up to

Captain Black to keep them in constant repair. There was only one source of new balloons.

Every week or ten days the PX received a shipment of the various things PX's receive shipments of. This always caused a line to form, and the line always included most of the nurses. At the head of the line, however, would be Ugly John Black. As the PX opened for business, Ugly John would step up and announce in a loud, clear, purposeful voice: "I'll take sixty rubber contraceptive devices. I hope to hell they're better than the last batch. They all leaked." Then he'd turn around and look austerely at the interested throng, few of who knew what he did with sixty such items a week.

When not working or blending intratracheal tubes and contraceptives into efficient units, Ugly was known to have a drink or two. In these situations, he usually wound up in The Swamp and vented his spleen upon the entire medical profession of the British Empire.

"Those lousy bastards!" he would yell. "There isn't a god-damned one of them would shake hands with his grandmother. He'd rather knock her on her ass with half a grain of morphine and then drown her with a cup of tea."

Such a man was bound to be held in high esteem by the Swampmen and was considered a warm and welcome friend. Actually, the incident involving Hawkeye and Ugly John was a minor one—at least, as it concerned them—but it was the first sign of things to come.

In The Swamp, every problem case ever done at the 4077th was discussed, dissected and analyzed from every possible angle and in every conceivable detail. The Deluge had left much for discussion, and two nights after its end the Swampmen were thus engaged when the door opened and a corpsman stuck his head in.

"Hey, Hawkeye," he said, "they want you in the OR."

"I'm not on duty. Tell them to go fry their asses."

"The Colonel says to get your ass over there."

"OK."

Over in the OR, two of the night shift had the typical difficult war surgical problem with major wounds of chest, abdomen and extremities. The abdominal wounds alone made it a bad risk, and there was little margin for error. They needed help and advice. Hawkeye scrubbed up and was briefed by Ugly John.

95

"So how much blood," Hawkeye wanted to know, "did they give him before they started operating?"

"One pint," said Ugly.

"For Chrissake, John, why in hell do you let these cowboys start a case like this on one pint?"

"Well," Ugly started to say, "they . . ."

"Look, goddamit," Hawkeye went on. "You know as well as I do he should have had another hour and at least three pints before they brought him in here. What the hell's the matter with you, anyway?"

"I can't do everything around here," Ugly said. "I'm just the goddamned anesthesiologist."

"That doesn't stop you from thinking, does it?"

"The surgeons said he was ready," Ugly said. "These guys have been doing OK, so I haven't been arguing with them . . ."

"Then don't argue with me," Hawkeye said.

"So you're right," Ugly said, "but I'll tell you this. You're getting pretty hard to live with, Pierce."

"And that kid on the table may be pretty hard for someone to live without," Hawkeye said.

Then he got into the case and took it over. He concluded it as quickly as possible. He used every trick he'd learned in ten months of war surgery, and then he called in Dago Red to put in a fix.

"Please, Red," he said, "bring him in."

Too much is too much. Despite all efforts and fixes, the boy died an hour after surgery.

Father Mulcahy led Captain Pierce to Father Mulcahy's tent, gave him a cigarette and a canteen half full of Scotch and water. Lying on Red's sack, Hawkeye dragged on the butt, swallowed the drink and said, "Red, my curve's hanging, and I lost the hop on my fast ball."

"Speak English, Hawk. Maybe I can help you."

"Listen to Losing Preacher Mulcahy," Hawkeye said. "You'd like to get me snapping the mackerel, wouldn't you?"

"Oh, come off it, Hawk," Dago Red said. "You know me too well to say something like that."

"Yes, I do, Red. I'm sorry. I seem to be a little overextended these days, but I'll get over it. I can be a little nutty now and then, but I ain't a nut."

"I know you're not," Dago Red said, "but you people in

The Swamp have got to get over the idea that you can save everyone who comes into this hospital. Man is mortal. The wounded can stand only so much, and the surgeon can do only so much."

"Red, that lousy can't-win-'em-all philosophy is no good. In The Swamp the idea is that if they arrive here alive, they can leave alive if everything is done just right. Obviously this can't always be, but as an idea it's better than fair, so spare me all the rationalizations."

"Hit the sack, Hawk," Father Mulcahy said. 'You still need sleep."

Hawkeye hit the sack, but the sleep he found was troubled and restless. At nine o'clock the next morning he entered the life and abdomen of Captain William Logan.

Captain William Logan, the still fairly youthful manager of a large supermarket, had joined the Mississippi National Guard soon after his release from five years of service in World War II. When the Mississippi National Guard was summoned to Korea, Captain Logan had left the supermarket, his wife, his new set of Ben Hogan matched clubs and his three kids to go with them.

Captain Logan, Major Lee, who was an undertaker, and Colonel Slocum, who owned the Cadillac distributorship, were all from the same town. They belonged to the same Masonic Lodge and the same country club. Colonel Slocum, Major Lee and Captain Logan were very disturbed the morning the gooks lobbed one in on Captain Logan's 105mm howitzer battery, and Captain Logan's abdomen got in the way of a couple of shell fragments.

When Hawkeye Pierce operated on Captain Logan he had had enough sleep, and too much of everything else. He removed a foot of destroyed small bowel and re-anastomosed it, that is, reunited the ends of the remaining intestine. When done, he thought that the anastomosis might be too tight but he elected to leave it. That was a mistake, but only one of two.

For the next eight days Captain Logan did poorly. Each day he was worse. Hawkeye watched him, worried and worked, and every time he turned around he encountered Colonel Slocum and Major Lee who wanted to know how things were going.

"Not too well," Hawkeye kept telling them.

"Why not?" they asked.

On the eighth day, they asked three times why things weren't going too well.

"Because, goddamn it, I did a lousy anastomosis," Hawkeye informed them.

On the ninth day, Hawkeye took Captain Logan, now desperately ill, back to the OR. He fixed the inadequate anastomosis, discovered at the same time that he had missed a hole in the rectum, did a colostomy, and five days later Captain Logan, much improved and out of danger, was evacuated. This was Saturday, and on Saturday night people from everywhere came to the tent which served as an Officers' Club for the 4077th.

Hawkeye Pierce, having learned a valuable lesson, having retrieved Captain Logan from the brink but still disgusted with himself, entered. Standing at the bar with a bottle of fine Scotch whiskey were Colonel Slocum and Major Lee, who beckoned to him.

Hawkeye's spirits plummeted even lower. His head hung. "The bastards are going to beat me up," he thought, "and they got a right to." He walked to the bar and joined them.

"Captain Pierce," Colonel Slocum said, handing him a drink, "there's something we want to tell y'all."

"I figured as much."

"We want to tell y'all that it makes us men up on the line feel mighty good to know that there are doctors like you around to take care of us if we get hurt."

Hawkeye was dumbfounded. He took a big pull on the Scotch and said, "For Christ sake, Colonel, don't you realize that I blew this one? I almost killed your buddy with bad surgery. I got him out of trouble, but he never shoulda been in it!"

"We been watchin' you, Pierce," Colonel Slocum said, with Major Lee at his side nodding assent. "Y'all worried about that man like he was your own brother, and he's OK now. That's all we need to know. We don't even care if you're a Yankee. Have another drink, Hawkeye!"

"Jeezus!" Hawkeye said. He put his glass down on the bar, turned his back on Colonel Slocum and Major Lee, and walked away from them and out the door.

It was three days later that Trapper John and the Duke caught the kid named Angelo Riccio, out of East Boston.

Private Riccio didn't look too bad. He was alert. His pulse was a little rapid. His blood pressure was strong enough at one hundred over eighty. He had a variety of shell fragment wounds, only one of which seemed important.

Duke Forrest, coming in to work the night shift and drifting down the line of wounded, had been unimpressed by Angelo until he saw the X-ray. Angelo's heart looked too big. Examining the wounds again, Duke decided that one of the shell fragments could have hit the heart, causing hemorrhage into the pericardium, which surrounds and contains it.

Duke found Trapper John in the mess hall, watching a movie he had already seen twice in the States. Trapper came. He looked at the X-ray, and he and Duke sat down next to Angelo.

"How do you think the Sox'll make out this year?" Trapper asked the kid.

"Without the big guy they got nothin'," said Angelo, "and the big guy's over here somewhere."

"That's right," Trapper said. "Does that make you feel good, knowing that even a guy like that is over here?"

"Are you kiddin', Doc?" Angelo said. "I wouldn't wish this kind of thing on a dog. I'd feel much better if he was back over there bustin' up a few ball games for us."

"Well, he will be again," Trapper said, "and you'll be there to see him."

"Where you from, Doc?" Angelo asked.

"Winchester."

"You know my cousin, Tony Riccio? He's about your age."

"Sure I know him, Angelo. He caught for Winchester High."

"Yeah," Angelo said. "The Sox were interested in him, and then he threw out his arm."

Old Home Week ended.

"Angelo, we're going to operate on you," said Trapper.

"OK," Angelo said, "so operate on me. You're the Doc."

Trapper and Duke operated on him. Trapper lined it up ahead of time. "He's got blood in his pericardium. Before we open it we've got to have control of the vena cavae. We've got to have plenty of blood. Once we get to the heart we've got to close the holes quick or we lose."

They did it all as right as they could, but when they opened the pericardium everything went to hell. The shell fragment had made several small holes in the right atrium. Trapper and Duke handled it better than any other two people in Korea could have, but they and Angelo needed three or four more minutes.

Angelo died. He would never see Ted Williams step to the plate again, and half an hour later Dago Red found Trapper John McIntyre wandering around in the dark, took him to his tent and gave him a can of beer. Then he went in search of Duke Forrest and found him alone in The Swamp. The Duke had already opened a can of beer, but he wasn't drinking it. He was crying into it.

"And a Yankee, too," the Duke said, to cover his embarrassment when he looked up and saw Dago Red. "You know somethin'? The way I'm goin' I shouldn't even be operatin' on Yankees."

It was obvious that something had to be done for the Swampmen. It was obvious, of course, to Dago Red, and it was obvious to Colonel Blake who realized that he had a serious problem on his hands—his problem boys were too exhausted and too dispirited to create their usual problems. It was also obvious to Radar O'Reilly who, tuned in as he was to everyone, was the most empathic member of the 4077th MASH, and who came up with two solutions.

The first of these was Dr. R. C. Carroll. Dr. R. C. Carroll had arrived at the Double Natural about five weeks before, was from deepest Oklahoma and somehow, while acquiring a medical education and two years of post-graduate training, had remained curiously unexposed to certain elements of human existence. Trapper John, most urbane of the Swampmen, had put the handle on Dr. Carroll.

"I thought I lived with the two biggest rubes in Korea," Trapper John said, "until this jeeter came along."

"Jeeter" became his name. Being new in the outfit he was not yet a member of the inner circle that gathered regularly at The Swamp for a drink before supper, but he did drop in occasionally. One afternoon, during the depth of the depression that followed The Deluge, he knocked on the door and was bade to enter. The Swampmen were alone.

"Excuse me," Jeeter said, "but Corporal O'Reilly said you fellas wanted to see me."

"Radar," said Hawkeye, who had been mooning into his martini, "must have his wavelengths mixed."

"Don't pay any attention to Captain Pierce," Trapper John said, handing Jeeter a water glass filled with a martini he had mixed for himself. "Sit down and have a drink."

"What is it?" Jeeter inquired.

"A martini, more or less," Trapper said.

"It looks like water," Jeeter said.

"That's right," Trapper said, "and it's sort of like water, but you don't drink it when you're thirsty."

"Right," the Duke said.

"Oh," Jeeter said.

Perhaps Jeeter was thirsty. He finished the drink in five minutes and indicated his need for another. Trapper gave him another, although somewhat reluctantly.

"You know somethin'?" Jeeter said.

"What?" the Duke said.

"Ah only been here a little over a month," Jeeter said, "but ah'm hornier than a bitch in heat."

"Good," the Duke said.

"Yeah," Hawkeye said. "That just indicates you're healthy."

"Oh," Jeeter said.

"So what's your problem?" Hawkeye said.

"Well," Jeeter said, "what do ah do?"

"Did you ever think of the nurses?" Hawkeye said.

"All the time, but ah figured they were all took or didn't put out."

"I'll give you a word on nurses, Jeeter," volunteered Captain Pierce. "They're human, just like us."

"Oh," Jeeter said.

"Some of them do all of the time, some of them do some of the time, and observation over a period of many months convinces me that very few of them are queer."

"Oh," Jeeter said, halfway through his second martini now, "but how do ah go about it?"

"Don't ask me," said Trapper. "Captain Pierce, here, seems to be the big authority."

"Well," Hawkeye said, warming to the assignment, "there are two methods. One is the simple, staid, stateside, hackneyed, civilian approach where you devote all your spare time for a week, softening the broad up with drinks, eating with her, taking her to Seoul on her day off, to our so-called

Officers' Club on Saturday night, getting her stoned and then escorting her to a tent or down to the river with a blanket."

"Oh," Jeeter said.

"But if you go with the blanket," Hawkeye said, "under no circumstances should you proceed more than ten yards north from the O Club because you might place the blanket on top of a mine. An exploding mine may give the protagonist and his partner the impression that he's Thor, the God of Thunder, but actually it's the worst form of coitus interruptus."

"Right," the Duke said.

"And, of course," Hawkeye said, "this method doesn't guarantee success. You may strike out. The flower of femininity you select may require not one but two weeks of cultivation, and then you run into the law of diminishing returns. Our leading tacticians recommend a week at the outside for this method."

"Oh," Jeeter said, indicating a desire for martini number three, "but what's the second method?"

"The second method is quicker and statistically almost as sound. You talk to the broad for a few minutes in some social situation, preferably over a drink, and you say, 'Honey, let's go somewhere and tear off a piece.' Either she says OK, or she takes off like a candy-assed baboon. The big plus of this method is that you either score fast or lose fast, and if you lose you can go on to the next blossom without further waste of time, effort and good booze."

"But which do you recommend?" asked Jeeter.

"Well, I don't really know," said Hawkeye. "This is mostly theory with me. What do you think, Trapper?"

"Well," Trapper said, "maybe he should announce his availability. Most of them will be in the mess hall swilling coffee, so let's go eat."

Jeeter, by now finding even ambulation a difficult exercise, was assisted to the door of the mess hall. Most of the nurses were indeed present, and Jeeter, silhouetted in the doorway but with the Swampmen out of sight on either side of him, made his announcement.

"Ah'm gonna screw every goddam nurse in the place!" he proclaimed loudly.

"Starting with Hot-Lips Houlihan," Trapper John whispered to him.

"Startin' with Hot-Lips Houlihan!" Jeeter shouted.

The Swampmen did not follow him in. They went back to The Swamp, had a short one and ate later. The next morning Jeeter knew only that he felt terrible and, after Colonel Blake had chewed him out, that he was in disgrace. It remained for Roger the Dodger Danforth, in a matter of hours, to take him off the hook.

Roger the Dodger Danforth was a surgeon at the 6073rd MASH, twenty-five miles to the East. Roger and Ugly John Black had trained together in the States, so Roger and the Swampmen were all well acquainted. In fact, they shared a mutual disrespect for most things held dear by others and a mutual respect for each other, and although Roger the Dodger was not considered, by observers of both phenomena, to be a greater menace than the three members of The Swamp, he was held to be at least their equal.

"Thank God," Colonel Blake would say, after Roger the Dodger's visits, "that that sonofabitch isn't assigned here, too."

On the day following Jeeter's pronunciamento in the portal of the mess hall, Roger the Dodger arrived about noon. Hawkeye had just finished amputating the leg of the only customer of the morning—a Korean who had thought himself immune to minefields—and he had gone to the mess tent for a light lunch.

"Where are the boys?" he asked Dago Red.

"Roger the Dodger is here," Dago Red said. "He and Ugly and your boys are over in The Swamp, and may the Lord have mercy on us all."

"Second the motion," Hawkeye said, "and I better have a large lunch."

After the large lunch, Hawkeye headed for The Swamp with an equal mixture of anticipation and reluctance. Halfway across the ball field that separated The Swamp from the mess tent he was greeted by Roger the Dodger, who stood in the doorway of The Swamp with a glass in his hand and yelled: "Hi, Hawkeye, you old shitkicker! Screw the Regular Army! How they goin'?"

"Finest kind," Hawkeye said.

"Have a drink," Roger the Dodger invited. "Brung two bottles of my own."

"What the hell are you doing here, anyway?" Hawkeye wanted to know.

"I don't know," Roger the Dodger said. "All I know is, last

night I had a call from some goddam Colonel O'Reilly who said to come . . ."

"Who?" Hawkeye said.

"I don't know," Roger the Dodger said. "The only O'Reilly you got in this outfit is some corporal looks like a goddamn weathervane. What difference does it make? Have a drink."

"I just might," Hawkeye said.

They all had several, and a glow of amiable incandescence began to suffuse The Swamp. All might have gone well, except that Roger the Dodger, apparently the recipient of a call to take this light out into the world, insisted on stepping to the door every fifteen minutes to yell: "Screw the Regular Army!"

Daily at 3:00 P.M., and for an hour, the showers at the 4077th MASH were reserved for the nurses. The nurses, some past the first bloom of youth, some not on diets, had to pass The Swamp en route to and from their ablutions, and it was a portion of this processional that crossed the field of vision of Roger the Dodger on one of his trips outdoors to exhort the populace to violation.

"All the nurses," Roger the Dodger yelled now, "are elephants!"

Then he switched the call to: "All the elephants have clap!"

"And Hot-Lips Houlihan," Trapper John suggested, "is the head mahout, and must be held responsible."

"And Hot-Lips Houlihan," Roger the Dodger yelled, "is the head mahout, and must be held responsible!"

That had the expected result. For the past two hours Colonel Henry Blake had been sitting in his tent listening to the exhortations and hoping against hope. He had called in Father John Patrick Mulcahy and, over beers, they had discussed possibilities.

"Frankly," Colonel Blake had said, "I'm scared. Any commanding officer with half a brain wouldn't let this go on."

"I disagree with you, Colonel," Father Mulcahy had said. "Something had to break, and I was afraid it was going to be our friends over there."

"I know," the Colonel said. "The other day that Duke called me 'sir.' At any moment I've been expecting Hawkeye Pierce to salute me. They're not well, I tell you. They've been pressed too hard, and that's why I let that Roger the Dodger in there again. Something's got to happen."

"And it's about to," Father Mulcahy said as the two, aghast, heard Roger the Dodger invoke the name of the Chief Nurse. "I think I'll go over to my place, or would you rather I stay?"

"No," Colonel Blake said. "It's all my fault, so I'll handle this Amazon alone."

Father Mulcahy had no sooner departed than Major Margaret Houlihan arrived. She arrived right from the showers, the ends of her hair still wet and the strap of her shower cap trailing from one end of her rolled towel. She was irate, and try as he might, Henry could not tune her out.

"This isn't a hospital," he heard his Chief Nurse screaming at him. "It's an insane asylum, and you're to blame . . ."

"Now, just a minute, Major," Henry started to say. "You . . ."

"Don't you minute-major me," his Chief Nurse went on. "If you don't stop those beasts, those THINGS, that one they call Trapper John from addressing me as Hot-Lips and stirring up those others, I'm going to resign my commission and . . ."

"Oh, goddammit, Hot-Lips," Henry heard himself saying, "resign your goddamn commission, and get the hell out of here!"

Five minutes later, Radar O'Reilly was awakened from a sound sleep. He was awakened by a telephone conversation between Major Houlihan and General Hammond, in which Major Houlihan was pouring out a lively story of a military hospital with everything out of control. This was followed by a conversation between General Hammond and Colonel Blake, in which Radar heard General Hammond say: "Henry, for Christ's sake, what the hell's going on up there? You get down here tomorrow morning at 0930, and your story better be a goddamn good one."

Radar hastened to The Swamp. By now Roger the Dodger, having added another chapter to his legend, had departed for his hospital, leaving the Swampmen and Ugly John to clean up the carnage. Radar filled them in on what he had heard.

"You know, Henry might really be in trouble," Hawkeye said, after Radar had finished his report and left. "That damn fool nurse has finally become a real menace."

105

"That's right," the Duke said.

"Trapper," Hawkeye said, "why do you always have to call her 'Hot-Lips'?"

"I don't always have to call her 'Hot-Lips.' This morning I was nice to her. I called her 'Major Hot-Lips'."

"What'll we do?" asked the Duke.

"Well," Trapper said, "I guess that if I hadn't called that bomber 'Hot-Lips' and then treed her with Jeeter and Roger the Dodger, the General wouldn't be on Henry's ass. Therefore, I'll go down and square it with the General."

"We'll go with you!" chorused Forrest and Pierce.

They made an appointment with the General for nine o'clock the next morning but appeared in his outer office at eight-thirty. They were wearing fatigues that had that lived-in look, without insignia, and they sat down on the bench that ran along one wall. Three quite attractive members of the Women's Army Corps—a lieutenant and two sergeants—occupied the working space of this outer part of the General's sanctum.

"Well," Trapper John said, after a few minutes, "shall we?"

"Why not?" Hawkeye Pierce said.

Each of the Swampmen produced from the recesses of his clothing a bottle labeled Johnny Walker Black Label. Earlier, back at the Double Natural, these bottles had been filled with tea by Sergeant Mother Divine, and now Duke Forrest rose from the bench and approached the WAC lieutenant.

"Y'all got any paper cups, honey?" he asked politely.

Confused, the lieutenant produced paper cups. The cups were filled, and cigarettes were lighted.

"Think the broads might like some tea?" wondered Trapper John in a stage whisper.

"They ain't broads," answered Hawkeye. "They're two sergeants and a lieutenant."

"Which are higher, sergeants or captains?" inquired the Duke. "Do we outrank them?"

"I dunno," said Trapper.

"Even if they outrank us, they might like some tea," said Hawkeye.

Duke rose again, the complete southern gentleman.

"Pardon, ladies, but would y'all care for some tea?"

"No, thank you," the lieutenant answered frostily.

The Swampmen sipped their tea in silence. Suddenly, the

silence was shattered by Trapper John: "I bet generals get plenty."

The lieutenant shot from behind her desk.

"Who are you people?" she demanded in great indignation.

"Don't get overheated, honey," Hawkeye said. "We're just a bunch of screwups from up the line. We gotta see the General at nine o'clock, civilian time, to chew him out."

"The General is supposed to see three medical officers at nine o'clock," she snapped, regaining a trace of composure.

"That's us, ma'am," spoke up Duke Forrest. "If you ladies don't happen to feel well, we'd admire to give y'all an examination."

Despite the rigid training required to reach officer and upper enlisted rank in the WAC, the lieutenant and her troops were totally unprepared for this sort of situation. They deserted in the face of the enemy.

"Must be a coffee break," observed Hawkeye.

After a few minutes of idle chatter, the Swampmen found time hanging heavy. Hawkeye produced a pair of dice and a crap game started.

At eight fifty-nine General Hammond arrived. As he walked through the outer sanctum toward his inner sanctum he was annoyed to find his secretarial force gone, and the spectacle of three disheveled crapshooters and three bottles of Johnny Walker Black Label annoying him even more.

"Hiya, General, how they goin'?" Hawkeye inquired.

The General stood transfixed.

"The Duke's trying to make a four," Trapper John informed the General.

"Little Joe," Duke begged the dice.

"Duke can't make fours," Hawkeye assured the General. "He'll crap out in a minute and we'll be with you."

Duke sevened and stood up. "Nice to see y'all, General," he said. "Y'all sure got it knocked—three nice lookin' WAC's workin' for y'all, and comin' to work in the middle of the mornin'."

"We got here early," Trapper John explained, "because we spent the night in a whorehouse, and we had to get out before the day shift took over. Have a shot of tea?"

He offered his bottle to the General. The General remained transfixed.

"Come in," he finally commanded. Followed by the

Swampmen, the General stalked into his office. Safely behind his desk, the General scowled at them.

"I've heard about you people," he said, "but I didn't really believe it. Now I do."

"You got some nice looking stuff working in your office, General," Hawkeye said.

"Shut up!" roared the General.

"General," Trapper said, "I'd like to change the tenor of this interview and be very serious. We've been in every hospital you have. The 4077th is the best you've ever had, and the biggest reason is Colonel Henry Braymore Blake. It was me that got that dizzy nurse mad when Henry had already had more than any of us needed. Do anything you want with us, but you'd be a damn fool to get rid of your best MASH commander because Hot-Lips Houlihan doesn't like her name."

The General grunted, took a nervous sip of water and lit a cigarette.

"Do you men really mean it?"

"General," said Hawkeye, "we know what we're talking about. We've seen more of the inside of these places than you have. We wouldn't be going out of our way for a Christless Regular Army Colonel if we didn't mean it! Begging your pardon, of course, General. I forgot."

"I'll bet," said the General, thinking hard now. "Suppose I replaced Henry with someone else? What would happen?"

"The guy'd never last," Trapper John informed him.

"Positively not," Hawkeye said.

"Right," the Duke said.

"OK," said the General. "I appreciate your coming. Don't worry about Henry."

The Swampmen scurried out one door, just before a harassed, scared and premature Henry, seemingly hurrying to his own execution, burst through another.

"Glad to see you, Henry," the General greeted him. "I probably shouldn't have made you come all the way down here. Fact is, I'm bored with the company around here. I wanted someone to have a couple of drinks and some lunch with."

"But what about Major Houlihan?" gulped Henry.

"You mean Hot-Lips?" asked the General. "Screw her."

"N-n-no th-thanks, G-General," replied Henry.

108

11

THE TEMPERATURE at noon, day after day, was between 95°
and 100°. The temperature at midnight, night after night,
was between 90° and 95°. As the tempo of the war picked
up again, the wounded soldiers kept coming by ambulance
and helicopter, and the Double Natural was too busy and
too hot.

Surgery in the steaming heat beneath the tin roof of the
Quonset hut was hard on the surgeons and not good for the
patients. Both lost fluids and electrolytes. Captain Ugly John
Black, the anesthesiologist, claimed that after any long case
the patient, who'd been receiving the appropriate intravenous
fluids, was usually healthier than the surgeon. Sleep for the
weary workers was absolutely necessary but nearly impossible, particularly for the Swampmen, who were working the
night shift and trying to sleep during the day. They gave up
any idea of sleeping in The Swamp. Instead they went to the
river a few hundred yards north, launched air mattresses, and
slept half submerged, in the shade of the railroad bridge
where the gentle current kept them wedged against the
pilings.

Then two things happened. First, the fighting and therefore
the surgery slacked off. Second, Colonel Henry Blake was sent
to Japan for temporary duty at the Tokyo Army Hospital and
replaced for the three weeks by Colonel Horace DeLong,
another Regular Army doctor whose permanent assignment
was at the Tokyo Army Hospital.

The period of hard work and the heat had put tempers on edge. About midnight, soon after Colonel DeLong arrived, a soldier was brought in with shell fragment wounds involving his belly and chest. The chest wounds weren't major but still required that a drainage tube be inserted in the chest for re-expansion of the lung. The abdominal wounds were major, but routine for the organization—the kind of case demanding a sensible plan of preoperative preparation, well controlled anesthesia, reasonably rapid, technically careful surgery, and an awareness, as Captain Hawkeye Pierce had learned again in the case of Captain William Logan, of how easy it is to miss one little hole in the bowel when there are ten or twelve.

Hawkeye Pierce was the gunner again in this one. He saw the X-rays, looked at the patient, knew what had to be done and when would be the best time to do it. He and Ugly John figured this would be about 3:00 A.M., after the patient had had some blood, after the closed thoracotomy had had its effect, and after the patient's pulse and blood pressure had stabilized.

By one-thirty there were indications that the patient was coming around and that 3:00 A.M. was a fairly shrewd call. At one-thirty, Hawkeye Pierce stepped into the Painless Polish Poker and Dental Clinic to pass the time until the knife dropped. At one-forty-five Colonel DeLong entered the Clinic and carried on as became his rank.

"Captain Pierce," he stated, "you have a seriously wounded patient for whom you are responsible. I find you in a poker game."

Hawkeye knew the Colonel had years and overall experience on him, but he also knew that few people had the reflexes for this kind of surgery unless they'd been doing it day in and day out for a while. He understood the Colonel's unhappiness but, choosing to be unpleasant and uncooperative, he answered, "You betcher ass, Dad."

"What?" said the Colonel.

"Gimme three," said Hawkeye to Captain Waldowski.

The Painless Pole gave him three.

"Pierce," yelled Colonel DeLong, "the soldier requires emergency surgery."

"You betcher ass, Colonel."

"Well, Captain, are you going to take care of your patient, or are you going to play poker?"

110

"I'm going to play poker until 3:00 A.M. or until the patient is adequately prepared for surgery. However, if you'd like to operate on him yourself right now, be my guest, Colonel. I get the same pay whether I work or not."

The Colonel just stood there. Hawkeye held a pair of aces, didn't draw anything worth while, waited till the bet came to him and dropped out, knowing by then that the Painless Pole had filled either a straight or a flush.

The Colonel still stood there. Hawkeye lit a cigarette and ignored him. The Colonel said, "Pierce, I want to talk to you."

Hawkeye said, "Look, Delong, my mood and my tenure of office in this organization add up to I don't want to talk to you. As far as I'm concerned, you're just another Regular Army croaker, and you all give me the red ass except maybe Henry Blake. Why don't you either take the case yourself or join me at three o'clock?"

Ignored by the poker players who were more interested in the game than in the side show, Colonel DeLong retreated. At two-forty-five Hawkeye left the game. The patient was taken into the operating area. Ugly John started putting him to sleep.

"Send for Colonel DeLong," Hawkeye told a corpsman.

The Colonel arrived and joined Hawkeye at the scrub sink. Hawkeye was beginning to feel a little contrite.

"Colonel," he said, "at one-thirty this guy had had less than a pint of blood, and he'd lost two or three. His pulse then was 120, and his blood pressure was about 90. Now, at three o'clock, he's had three pints of blood. His pulse is 80 and his blood pressure 120. His collapsed lung is expanded. He's had a gram of Terramycin intravenously. We can operate on him safely. We should do it quickly, but we don't have to do it frantically or carelessly."

The operation went the usual route. Numerous holes had to be repaired, and one piece of small bowel had to be removed. After an hour all the apparent damage had been corrected.

"Now, Colonel," said Hawkeye, "I'm going to sandbag you. Do you figure we're ready to get out of this belly?"

"Obviously you don't think so, and I don't know why," admitted Colonel DeLong.

"Well, Dad, we haven't found any holes in the large bowel. They've all been in the small bowel, but the smell is different.

111

I caught a whiff of large bowel, but it ain't staring us in the face, right?"

"Right," the Colonel said.

"So if it ain't staring us in the face it's got to be retroperitoneal," Hawkeye said, meaning that the perforation had to be in a portion of the large intestine hidden in the abdominal cavity. "Therefore, and from the look of the wounds, I figure he's got a hole in his sigmoid colon that we won't find unless we look for it."

They looked for it and found it. The Colonel was impressed. They closed the hole, did a colostomy and closed the belly.

Afterwards, over a cup of coffee, the Colonel said, "OK, Pierce, that was a nice job, but you must realize that I can't afford to tolerate the rudeness and insubordination you demonstrated when I tried to talk to you during the poker game."

"So don't afford it," suggested Hawkeye.

"Pierce, you don't like me, do you?"

"For Christ's sake, Colonel," exploded Hawkeye, "why don't you go to bed? Right now I don't even like myself, and all I need to set me off is to be bugged by a Regular Army medical officer."

The Colonel went to bed. There wasn't much else he could do.

Two days later there was no work at all. The heat persisted. It was too hot to drink. It was too hot to sleep. It was too hot to play baseball. It was too hot to play poker. The Swampmen made a halfhearted effort at rehabilitation. They'd been reading some Somerset Maugham stories about Malayan rubber plantations. At 9:00 A.M. they got their ice cube tray out of the refrigerator in the laboratory. Soon they were sitting in chairs in front of The Swamp holding tall glasses of Pimm's #1 Punch and making believe they were Malayan rubber plantation foremen. Whenever a Korean houseboy came into sight, they yelled at him to get to work and start turning out the rubber, and they were thus laconically passing the time when Colonel DeLong sauntered by.

"Good morning, gentlemen," he greeted them.

"You just out from home?" asked Trapper John.

"No, I've been in Tokyo for some time."

"Y'all married?" asked the Duke.

"Yes."

"Bring your wife with you?" asked Hawkeye.

"Of course not."

"I say, I wish I knew how you fellows get away with it," said Trapper. "We three have our brides along, and it's pure grief. They can't stand the beastly climate, and they won't let us commingle with the native girls. You don't know how lucky you are!"

"I believe I'll wander down to the pool for a dip," said Hawkeye. He got his air mattress from the tent and headed for the river. The others followed, leaving the Colonel standing with his mouth open.

"Oh, I say, Colonel," Trapper called back to him, "perhaps you'd join us for a set or two of doubles later, after the heat has abated?"

So they went to the river, swam a little and slept a little. By 3:00 P.M., Hawkeye Pierce was awake, pensive and bored. He lay belly down and naked on his air mattress, peering into the murky water below.

"Hey, Duke," he asked, "whadda ya know about mermaids?"

"Nothin'," Duke assured him.

Trapper John, a leading authority on many subjects, joined the conversation. "In my opinion, there are mermaids in this river."

"I'm forced to keep an open mind on that," said Hawkeye. "Certainly if there are mermaids in this river, we'd be just plain foolish not to grab a few of them."

"How y'all gonna catch a mermaid?" asked Duke.

"In a mermaid trap, naturally," said the Hawk.

"How do you make a mermaid trap?"

"Just like a lobster trap, only bigger."

"Let's get goin' on it."

"OK"

They paddled ashore, dressed, went to the supply tent, where a cooperative sergeant provided material and tools. Hawkeye Pierce, in his boyhood, had built many lobster pots. For a man of his experience and background, the construction of a mermaid trap didn't seem to present a major problem, and the next morning found the Swampmen well along on their project when again Colonel DeLong dropped by.

"What are you doing here, gentlemen?" he asked.

"Buildin' us a mermaid trap," Duke informed him. "Y'all want to help?"

The Colonel was trying to blend into the environment. "I see," he said. "Where do you expect to catch mermaids?"

"The river's alive with them," answered Trapper.

"I see," said the Colonel again. "Assuming that you are able to catch one of these creatures, what do you propose to do with it?"

Hawkeye gave the Colonel a look of impatience and scorn. "We're gonna screw the ass off her," he stated.

The Colonel was desperately trying to hang in there. "Do you have reason to believe that mermaids may be effectively utilized for that purpose?"

"Oh, Finest Kind," Hawkeye assured him.

"Numero Uno," said Trapper John.

"Yeah," said the Duke.

Colonel DeLong retreated to his tent to think. Colonel Blake, before departing for Toyko, had deliberately and perhaps maliciously not briefed him on the Swampmen.

Meanwhile, Hawkeye had words with the Duke and Trapper John, which went something like this: "I haven't built a lobster trap in years, and I've lost the touch. This mermaid trap has already become bigger than I am. Let's change the game. We got this guy DeLong buzzing anyhow. Let's convince him we're nuts, and maybe he'll ship us out for awhile until Henry gets back and catches on. They got psychiatrists in Seoul, and we'll be close enough to get back if business picks up."

Trapper took the cue. He went to the next tent and spoke to Rafael Rodriguez, a lieutenant in the Medical Service Corps.

"Rafe," he said, "we'd like a little help. Would you be willing to go tell Colonel DeLong we've flipped and suggest emergency psychiatric care?"

Rafael Rodriguez had been on The Swamp's list of nonsurgical good boys for several months, and now he justified the faith bestowed upon him. He went to Colonel DeLong's tent, knocked respectfully and was bade to enter.

"Sit down. Have a beer, Lieutenant," the Colonel urged him.

"Thank you, Sir. Sir, you look troubled. Perhaps I could be of help. I've been here for some time, you know."

"Perhaps you could, Rodriguez," the Colonel said. "I'm new. This is a strange and unusual situation for me. I'm very worried about three of our surgeons: Pierce, McIntyre and Forrest. Their work, in the little time I've been here, has impressed me, but the last day or two their general behavior has caused me considerable concern."

"Sir, I don't blame you. In fact, that's why I've come to see you. I've known them since they came. They have been good men, but I'm compelled to say that I'm disturbed about them. Sir, I know them intimately. Something has happened. Sir, I think they need psychiatric care."

"That's all I need to hear," said Colonel DeLong. "I thought so, but I needed the confirmation of a reliable observer who's been on the scene longer than I. I'll take the responsibility of telling them about it."

"Thank you, Sir," said Rafael Rodriguez. "I don't think I'd be able to do it."

"I understand, Lieutenant," said Colonel DeLong.

Rafe took a back route to The Swamp, poured a Scotch and gleefully informed the occupants that they were to undergo psychiatric evaluation. He left after one Scotch, lest the Colonel catch him there. Half an hour later, Colonel DeLong entered The Swamp.

"Gentlemen," he said, "I'll come directly to the point. I am informed that your work here has been of exceptional quality. However, my own observations, confirmed by others, indicate that now you need help. Apparently prolonged responsibility in this situation, along with the heat and the isolation, has taken its toll. I've arranged for you to go to the 325th Evac tomorrow for a few days rest and to be seen by the psychiatric service. They will determine what happens next."

Hawkeye Pierce looked at Trapper John. "I always knew you was foolish," he said.

Duke Forrest whined, "I cain't go to no hospital. I gotta get me a mermaid."

Trapper John rose from his sack. "Colonel, if I could catch a mermaid tonight, you'd let me take her to the hospital with me, wouldn't you?"

"Of course!" said the Colonel.

"Colonel," said Hawkeye, "I'll go along with this for only one reason. A few days down there will give me a shot at the epileptic whore, which has become one of my life's ambitions,

115

and in this general geographical location that's the only thing that interests me more than a mermaid."

Colonel DeLong desperately, all of a sudden, wanted to ask about the epileptic whore but restrained himself. "Transportation has been arranged," he told them. "You'll be picked up at 0800 hours."

"Finest Kind," agreed Hawkeye, as the Colonel left.

Duke and Trapper turned to Hawkeye.

"What's this about an epileptic whore?" they demanded.

"It just popped into my head. I got a buddy back home who's a psychiatrist. He had a patient who was an epileptic, and every time her husband tried her she threw a fit. All the guy had to do was plug himself in and the world went crazy. To me it always sounded like a great bit. For all I know, they may have an epileptic whore in Seoul. Anyway we might be able to use the idea. How do we handle the psychiatrist?"

Trapper was thinking, which was vaguely recognized by his colleagues, so silence ensued for several minutes. Finally he spoke.

"We tell the headshrinker nothing except name, rank, serial number, and we want to get fixed up with the epileptic whore."

Silence again, while Duke and Hawkeye mulled it over.

"Whadda you think?" asked Trapper.

"I think Henry'll be back in four days," said Duke, "and that's how long we'll get away with this crap."

"I think it's OK," said Hawkeye. "Let's tell the shrink the broad's at Mrs. Lee's. I don't figure to spend four days down there without some psycho-sexual-physiological relief."

"I believe," said Trapper John, "that the group is in full accord in that area."

Trapper mixed another round of drinks. A few moments passed before Hawkeye spoke again.

"I figure we'd better think this over a little more," he said. "Psychiatrists are never overly troubled with the smarts, but even the dumbest one is going to smell a rat if we all go in and say the same thing. I kind of have a yen for this deal. Why don't you guys tell the shrink that you're OK, that you've been riding along to protect me, and that I've suddenly become much worse. I think I can drive whatever simple son-of-a-bitch we encounter out of his mind."

116

"I guess you're right, Hawk," Trapper agreed. "You got the ball."

"How y'all figure to handle it?" asked Duke.

"Easy," said the Hawk. "I'll talk gibberish to him. All you guys got to do is be very serious, impress him with your virtue, and emphasize that I've been effective and valuable until now, and you love me dearly. After an interview with him I'll meet you at Mrs. Lee's."

As Colonel DeLong had promised, the transportation arrived at 8:00 A.M., and the nuts were taken to the psychiatric section of the 325th Evacuation Hospital in Yong-Dong-Po. Duke and Trapper walked in, solicitously leading Hawkeye. They were to see Major Haskell, the Chief of Psychiatry. Fortunately he had only been in Korea for two weeks, and news of the 4077th MASH had not reached him.

Trapper and Duke arranged to meet him first, explained that they had gone along with the mermaid gag in the hope of straightening Captain Pierce out, and that they had submitted to this ordeal themselves in the hope that he would snap out of it at the last moment. However, it was clear, just from his behavior in the last twelve hours, that Pierce's sanity had deteriorated alarmingly. They hoped that the Major would do everything possible to see that proper treatment was obtained without delay.

"We've been close to this man, Major," said Duke. "He's been a dedicated surgeon. He's been a tower of strength to us. Now he needs help. We know you'll do your best."

"I appreciate your help, gentlemen," Major Haskell assured them, "and I have some idea of how close the three of you have been. I understand the emotional involvement that men in your situation develop with one another. However, I can tell from the way you've presented this story that you have a grasp of the problem. I think you realize, and if you don't I must warn you, that this is a serious problem. It sounds to me like some form of schizophrenia, and in this sort of case, with the sudden deterioration you've described, the prognosis is usually not good."

"Oh," the Duke said.

"By the way," the Major continued, "I have Colonel DeLong's report here. He mentions something about an epileptic whore. What's that all about?"

"They got one at Mrs. Lee's," Trapper told him. "I hear

117

she's real wild. We'll appreciate whatever you can do for Captain Pierce."

Duke and Trapper left, and Hawkeye was led in. The Major invited him to sit down and offered him a cigarette.

"How do you feel today, Captain?"

"I have sounded forth the trumpet that shall never call retreat. I am lifting out the hearts of men. Hey, you got any Harry James records?"

Major Haskell took a deep breath and ignored Captain Pierce's question.

"Tell me about yourself, Captain. Who are you?"

"Hawkeye Pierce."

"I know, but beyond that, what are you?"

"I'm the world's greatest short putter, to say nothing of being a descendant of Robert Ford."

"Who was he?"

"The dirty little coward who shot Mr. Howard."

"Why have you come down to see me today?"

"I ain't come down to see you. I came for the action."

"Do you mean the epileptic whore?"

"You betcher ever-lovin' A, Major."

"Captain, we're getting away from our subject. Something seems to have happened to you since Colonel DeLong took over your hospital."

"That's right, Sir. He's against me."

"What makes you think so?"

"The dirty mudder was gonna steal my mermaid."

"Is there anything else about Colonel DeLong that bothers you?"

"Yeah. He reminds me of my old man."

"I see," said Major Haskell. "Now perhaps we are getting somewhere. In what way does he remind you of your father?"

"He doesn't play tennis."

"Why doesn't your father play tennis?" Major Haskell asked, sort of by reflex, and regretted the question even before the answer.

"Because the harpies of the shore have plucked the eagle of the sea," Hawkeye explained. "He can't take the ball on the rise no more. They have laid poor Jesse in his grave."

"I see," answered the Major. "Captain Pierce, tell me about yourself. Feel free to talk. I want to help you. Perhaps if you'd just relax and open up and let the words come, you'd feel better and I'd be able to help you."

"Dad, I feel great."

"Talk to me anyhow, Captain. Just talk about anything that comes into your head."

"Death is an elephant, torch-eyed and horrible, foam-flanked and terrible," Hawkeye commented.

Major Haskell lit a cigarette.

"You nervous or something?" asked Hawkeye.

"Not at all," the Major replied, nervously.

"Hey, Dad, I'll give you a nice buy on an elephant. Velly clean. Takes penicillim. Finest kind."

"Captain Pierce, what are you up to? Frankly, I can't decide whether you're crazy or just some kind of screwball."

"Well, why don't you mull it over for a while. You got anything to trade in?"

"What do you mean?"

"I mean you want a clean deal on a clean elephant, or you got some kind of used up elephant you wanta stick me with in return for my best elephant?"

"Look, Captain Pierce—"

"You hate me, don't you?" said Hawkeye. "Just like Duke and Trapper hate me."

"I'm sure no one hates you, Captain."

"They sure as hell do."

"Why?"

"Because I'm a great mahout. I'm an elephant boy. That's all I ever wanted to be but because the elephants like me so good, the people all hate me."

"Captain Pierce, I think we'll send you to the States for treatment."

"Finest Kind," said Hawkeye, rising, and added: "Be swift my soul to answer him, be jubilant my feet," and cut out on swift, jubilant feet for Mrs. Lee's where he found Duke and Trapper John at lunch, or rather at pre-lunch martinis. They appeared unusually happy.

"Here's the nut," said Trapper. "How do they handle you hopelessly deteriorated schizophrenics nowadays?"

"The shrinker said he was gonna send me back to the States," Hawkeye informed them. "Maybe I oughta take him up on it. I don't know how they treat it, and I don't plan to find out. Now tell me why you guys look so happy."

"You'll never believe it, Hawk," Trapper filled him in, "but Mrs. Lee actually has an epileptic whore, or at least a babe who has some kind of convulsion every time she entertains a client. She's been scaring the customers silly, but with proper publicity she should go good."

Duke and Trapper had already told Mrs. Lee of the potential value of her convulsing employee. They had predicted that there would be some phone calls before long, inquiring as to her existence and availability. When the phone rang, it was answered by Mrs. Lee, whose round cherubic face broke into a wide smile as she nodded her head rapidly.

"Epileptic whore hava yes," she assured the party on the other end of the phone. "Velly clean, school teacher."

Mrs. Lee described all her girls as "velly clean." Beyond that, they were divided into three subcategories: movie actresses, cherry girls and school teachers. A girl's status varied with Mrs. Lee's usually shrewd estimate of the customer's needs.

There was a commotion at the front entrance as Major Haskell appeared with two M.P.'s. Hawkeye was led to an area of seclusion by Mrs. Lee as Major Haskell and his troops entered the dining room.

"Has Captain Pierce been here?" he demanded of Trapper and Duke.

"Hell, no," said Duke. "We figured you all had him under wraps. How'd he get away?"

"I don't know," said Haskell, "but that boy is way out. It's imperative that I find him."

"If I were you, I'd search the waterfront," suggested Trapper. "He might be looking for mermaids."

"How about you fellows helping out? You said he meant everything to you. I should think you'd help me find him before he harms himself or someone else."

"If he's all that crazy, the hell with him," said Trapper.

"Yeah," the Duke said. "We got appointments with the epileptic whore anyway."

"I'm tired of hearing about the epileptic whore," stated the Major. "What's it all about anyhow?"

"Epileptic whore hava yes, Major," smiled Mrs. Lee. "Velly clean, school teacher. Finest Kind."

Major Haskell perked his ears at the last expression, but before he could draw any conclusions Trapper started talking.

"Major," he said, "a guy in your business really should take a crack at this broad out of professional interest. It's an opportunity that's unlikely to come your way again. You could make a name for yourself writing papers about her."

The Major sat down, ordered a drink and excused the M.P.'s. "You may have a point, gentlemen. Can you fix me up? It should be quite an interesting case."

"The fastest ride in the Far East Command," Trapper assured him.

"And y'all may have my reservation," Duke told him. "I was on for three o'clock, but I can see that it'll mean more to you all."

"That's very kind of you, Captain," replied Major Haskell.

They had a few more drinks, ate an extended lunch, and at 3:00 P.M. Major Haskell went to keep his appointment.

"Good luck," said Trapper. "Don't break your stem."

"Y'all watch out when she sunfishes," warned Duke.

Within fifteen minutes the Major, looking somewhat pale and drawn, reappeared and nervously ordered a double Scotch.

"That was quick," said Duke. "Major, y'all must be one of them short-time skivvy boys."

The Major did not reply.

"Come on, Major," urged Trapper, "how was it?"

"I don't think it's epilepsy. I think it's a purely hysterical convulsion," replied the Major.

"Yeah, but how was it?" insisted Duke.

"Tremendous," said the Major and departed.

For the next two days, business at Mrs. Lee's was big. The epileptic whore was in popular demand. The Swampmen hung around, observed with interest, interviewed many of the survivors, but did not avail themselves of her services.

On the second day, Hawkeye asked, "When are you guys gonna try her?"

"Maybe tomorrow," answered Trapper.

"What's the hurry?" asked Duke. "When y'all gonna try her yourself?"

"Never," said Hawkeye. "I'm a man of simple needs, which have already been adequately fulfilled for the time being."

On the third day Colonel Henry Blake, returning to his duties as C.O. of the 4077th MASH, stopped at the 325th Evac, called his outfit and requested transportation. He spoke to Colonel DeLong, who told him that the Swampmen were undergoing psychiatric evaluation at the 325th Evac.

Henry laughed with delight, but to himself. He sought out Major Haskell, who told him that McIntyre and Forrest were at Mrs. Lee's but that Pierce had dropped from sight.

"Don't worry, Major, they're all at Mrs. Lee's. I'll go over there. When my driver comes would you be kind enough to send him to pick us up?"

"I'm sorry, Colonel, but even if Pierce can be found, I couldn't possibly allow him to return to duty. I'm sure, when you see him, you'll agree with me."

"Pierce isn't any crazier now than he's ever been," Henry assured him. "Don't let him worry you, Major."

"I'll come with you if I may," said Haskell.

They found the Swampmen in Mrs. Lee's bar.

"Hiya, Henry. How they goin'?" asked Hawkeye. "I bet you got plenty in Tokyo, didn't you?"

"Shut up, Pierce. What's this all about?"

"I went ape," said Hawkeye, nodding to Major Haskell. "Ask him."

"I think you'd better come with me, Pierce," said Major Haskell.

Trapper joined in. "Henry doesn't believe you, Hawk. Say something in schizophrenic."

"My father was the keeper of the Eddystone light. He slept with a mermaid one fine night. Out of that union there came three—a porpoise and a porgy, and the other was me," replied Hawkeye.

"See what we mean?" said Duke.

Colonel Blake turned to Major Haskell. "I'll be responsible for him. Believe me, you've been had. Consider yourself lucky. I've been putting up with this kind of crap for months. You're only had a couple of hours of it."

Hawkeye summoned Mrs. Lee and whispered in her ear. Mrs. Lee asked to see the Colonel in private and led him upstairs to a certain room as Hawkeye ordered drinks for all and spoke to Major Haskell: "I hate to disappoint you, Dad, but I'm not quite as foolish as I led you to believe. I'm going back to the MASH with the rest of them as soon as Henry has enjoyed the Fastest Ride in the Far East Command. Have a drink with me, and let there be no moaning at the bar ere we leave Mrs. Lee."

"OK," said Haskell, "but I still don't think you're normal."

"I ain't. Normal people go crazy in this place."

While they were all on their second round of drinks, Colonel Blake returned.

"Well?" said Trapper John.

" 'Beware the Jabberwock, my son!' " said Colonel Blake, addressing Major Haskell, and then: " 'The jaws that bite, the claws that catch! Beware the Jubjub bird and shun the frumious Bandersnatch!' "

"Major," Hawkeye said to Haskell, "this looks like something right down your alley."

"Yeah, Major," the Duke said, "y'all been educated to handle this kinda thing, and we gotta get out of here."

12

WITH THE END of summer, the baseball that the Swampmen had tossed and batted around occasionally to get some exercise and kill some time, took on air and a new shape. It became a football and an object of pursuit as, in their idle moments, they passed and kicked it back and forth and ran one another from one end of the ball field to the other to cries of: "How to go!"—"Nice grab!"—"Hawk, this time I'll fake to the Duke and you fake the block on the tackle and I'll hit you with it over the middle."—"Way to go!"—"Way to throw! Who ever heard of Sammy Baugh?"

"You know what we ought to do?" Hawkeye said, as they came puffing back into The Swamp one afternoon.

"Have a drink," the Duke said.

"No," Hawkeye said. "We oughta get us up a football team."

"And play who?" Duke said.

"The Chicago Bears," Trapper said. "It'd be a way to get home."

"No, thanks," Duke said. "I'd rather get killed over here."

"Listen, you guys," Hawkeye said. "I'm serious. We're all starting to get stirry again. We need something to do. There's that big guy named Vollmer over in Supply played center for Nebraska. Jeeter was a second string halfback at Oklahoma . . ."

"God help us," Trapper said.

"There's Pete Rizzo."

"He was a Three-I infielder," Duke said.

"But he played football in high school."

"But who do we play?" Duke said.

"Hot-Lips Houlihan's Green Bay Pachyderms," Trapper said.

"I want Knocko McCarthy on our side," the Duke said.

"Now, wait a minute," Hawkeye said. "I'm serious. They've got some kind of a league over here. The 325th Evac in Yong-Dong-Po claim they're champions because last year they beat two other teams. I know where we can get a real ringer, and if we can beat them we can clean up on some bets."

"You're nuts," Trapper said.

"Yeah," the Duke said, "and who's the ringer?"

"You ever hear of Oliver Wendell Jones?" asked Hawkeye.

"No," Trapper answered.

"Sounds like a nigra," said Duke.

"Never mind the racial prejudice. You ever hear of Spearchucker Jones?"

"Yeah," Trapper said.

"Maybe the best fullback in pro ball since Nagurski," Hawkeye said.

"Okay," Trapper said, "but what's he got to do with us?"

"You haven't read much about him lately, have you?" Hawkeye said.

"Probably just a flash," Duke said.

"Flash hell," Hawkeye said. "You want to know why you haven't heard about him?"

"Yeah," Duke said. "Tell us."

"No, don't tell us," Trapper said. "We'd like to spend all our spare time guessing."

"You haven't heard of Spearchucker Jones lately," Hawkeye said, "because his real name is Dr. Oliver Wendell Jones, and he's the neurosurgeon at the 72nd Evacuation Hospital in Taegu."

"Damn," Trapper said.

"Yeah," Duke said.

"But how come," Trapper, mixing the drinks now, wanted to know, "you're such an expert on all this?"

"Because," Hawkeye said, "when I was in Taegu before they dragged me kicking and screaming up here I roomed with Spearchucker. He went to some jerkwater colored college, but he did well enough to get into med school. He had played football in college, but no one had ever seen him. When he got out of med school he got married, and he wanted to take a residency. He needed some dough so he started playing semi-pro ball on weekends around New Jersey. Somebody scouted him and the Philadelphia Eagles signed him. He was great even though he couldn't work at it full time. He kept it a secret about being a doctor, but it would have leaked out fast if he hadn't been drafted just as he was getting a reputation."

"And you're the only one over here who knows this?" Trapper said.

"A few of the colored boys know who he is, but they won't talk because he's asked them not to."

"Good," Trapper said. "You really think we can get him?"

"Sure," Hawkeye said.

"Now, wait a minute," Duke said. "I know how you Yankees think. Y'all wanta get this nigra up here to live in The Swamp. Right?"

"Right," Hawkeye said.

"OK," Duke said. "If y'all can live with him, so can I. I'm washed up at home anyway, after living with two Yankees."

"So how do we get him?" Trapper said.

"Easy," Hawkeye said. "We tell Henry we can't exist any longer without a neurosurgeon. If he doesn't go for that we tell him the truth. There's a little of the opportunist in Henry, too."

"Okay," Trapper agreed. "Let's make our run at him right now."

"But is this nigra in shape?" Duke wanted to know.

"This big bastard has to be a long way out of shape before anybody around here will stop him," Hawkeye assured him. "He's also a helluva guy."

Five minutes later Colonel Henry Blake, on his hands and knees on his tent floor, rummaging through his foot locker for some personal papers, was interrupted by the Swampmen who entered without knocking.

"Oops!" Trapper said, as Henry looked up. "Wrong address. This must be some kind of Shinto shrine."

"Looks like it," Hawkeye said. "Pardon us, oh Holy Man."

"Knock it off," Henry said, getting up. "What do you bastards want now?"

"A drink," Trapper said.

"You've got drinks where you live," Henry said, eyeing them. "What else do you want?"

"Here." Trapper said, handing Henry a Scotch, while Hawkeye and Duke helped themselves. "Relax."

"Henry," Hawkeye said, "you're not the only one caught up in this religious revival. We just had a revelation, too."

"What is this?" Henry started to say. "What . . . ?"

"Henry," Trapper said, "it just came to us. We gotta get us a neurosurgeon."

"Right." Duke said.

"You're out of your minds," Henry said.

"After all we've done for the Army," Trapper said, "is that too much to ask?"

"Please," Hawkeye said, genuflecting in front of Henry. "Please, oh Holy One, get us a neurosurgeon."

"We're serious." Trapper said.

"Right." Duke said.

"Okay." Henry said, still eyeing them. "What's the game?"

"Football."

"What?"

"Football."

"Football, hell," Henry said.

"We mean it," Hawkeye said, "and it's very simple. We want a football team, and we want to challenge the 325th Evac for the championship of Korea, and to do it we need a neurosurgeon Wouldn't you like the 4007th MASH to be the football champions of Korea? Who knows? We might be invited to the Rose Bowl!"

"The hell with that," Trapper said. "Just think of the dough we can make with a little judicious betting on ourselves."

"Explain." Henry said, perking up now. "And what the hell has a neurosurgeon got to do with it?"

"Ever hear of Spearchucker Jones?" Hawkeye said.

"Yeah. Colored boy. Plays pro football. So what?"

"He's not playing pro football right now, and we can get him."

"We can? How?"

"Tell General Hammond you gotta have a neurosurgeon, and you want Captain Oliver Wendell Jones of the 72nd Evac."

It took a moment for it to sink in.

"You mean it?" Henry said. "You really mean it?"

"You see?" Hawkeye said to the others. "I told you Henry believes in free enterprise, too."

"You're damn tootin'," Henry said. "You really think we can get him?"

"Sure," Hawkeye said. "Nobody else over here knows who he is, except a few of his friends who aren't talking."

"Good," Henry said, starting to pace the floor now. "Good thinking. Now you want to know something else?"

"What?"

"That Hammond," Henry said, pacing. "He flashes that star around and calls himself coach of that 325th Evac. Why, he's still back in the Pudge Heffelfinger era of football. He doesn't know the first damn thing about how the game is played today."

"Good," Trapper said.

"All he did was pull rank," Henry said.

"Then we can do it?" Hawkeye said.

"Yes," Henry said. "On one condition."

"What's that?"

"I want to be coach," Henry said.

"Anything you say, Coach," they assured him in unison.

"Hammond," Henry said. "Where'd he ever get the idea he's a coach?"

The next day Hawkeye composed a letter to Captain Oliver Wendell Jones, apprising him of the plan. He extolled the congenial working conditions at the Double Natural, described in glowing terms the friendly atmosphere of The Swamp, of which he invited Captain Jones to become the fourth member. Then he pointed out the benefits, financial as well as physical, that could accrue from playing a little football against the innocents of the 325th Evac. At the same time Colonel Henry Blake, chuckling to himself all the while, made the proper request to General Hamilton Hammond, and ten days later Captain Jones appeared, filling the doorway of The Swamp.

"My God!" Trapper said. "Darkness at noon. Look at the size of him!"

"And he drinks double bourbon and coke, Trapper," Hawkeye said, jumping up and shaking Captain Jones' hand. "Welcome, Spearchucker, welcome!"

"You sure I'm in the right place?" Captain Jones said, grinning.

"You sure are," Hawkeye said. "Shake hands with the Trapper. Shake hands with the Duke. Now shake hands with that double bourbon."

Captain Jones did. In fact, he shook hands with several double bourbons while the others made their usual display of affection for Trapper's martinis. Hawkeye and Captain Jones kicked around a few memories, and then Trapper John got into it.

"Tell me something," he said to Captain Jones. "Where'd you get that Spearchucker handle?"

"I used to throw the javelin," Jones told him. "Somebody started calling me that, and the sports writers thought it was good and it stuck."

"How come you and the Hawk here got to be such big buddies down in Taegu?"

"Well," said Jones, "I got assigned there and there weren't any other colored and they didn't have a room for me all by myself. Hawkeye went to the C.O. and said: 'Tell that big animal he can live with me if he wants to.'"

"That was nice," Trapper said, "but let's not give him the Legion of Merit."

"Nobody's handing out any medals," Spearchucker said, "but there are so goddamn many phonies around. The worst are the types who knock themselves out to show you that your color doesn't make any difference, and if it wasn't for your color they wouldn't pay any attention to you. They're part of the black man's burden, too."

"Understood," Trapper said.

"Anyway," Spearchucker said, "there are a lot of colored boys over here, and I know quite a few. Every now and then some of them would drop in to visit me. Now and then Hawkeye would stay around but most often he'd cut out. One day I said: 'Hawkeye, how come you don't care for some of my friends?'"

"So this guy," Spearchucker said, nodding toward Hawkeye, "says to me: 'Do you like all the white boys around here?' I said: 'No, Hawkeye, and thank you.' That's what I mean."

"The hell with this," Hawkeye said now. "Let's talk about something else."

"In a minute," the Duke said, and up to now he had been just monitoring the conversation. "I want to say something."

"What?" Spearchucker said, looking right at him.

"I'm from Georgia," Duke said.

"I know that," Spearchucker said.

"If you and I had a problem," Duke said, "we'd be the only ones who could understand it. These Yankees couldn't, but what I wanta say is that I don't have a problem, and if y'all do, tell me now."

Captain Jones sipped his drink and grinned and looked at the Duke.

"No problem with me, Little Duke," he said.

"Wait a minute," the Duke said, eyeing Captain Jones. "How come y'all call me Little Duke?"

"Well," Spearchucker said, "Hawkeye wrote me about you two guys and he said you're from Forrest City, Georgia. Right?"

"Right," Duke said, "but . . ."

"Your daddy a doctor?"

"Yeah."

"He used to own a little farm north of town?"

"Oh, no," Trapper John said. "Please."

"Wait a minute," Duke said. "He's right. Let the man talk."

"Who tenant-farmed that place?" asked Captain Jones.

"John Marshall Jones," Duke said.

"I should have been a lawyer," said Oliver Wendell Jones. "What happened to John Marshall Jones?"

"He got knifed by another nigra," Duke said.

"What happened to his family?"

"They went north."

"That's right," Captain Jones said. "They went north. You know where they got the money for the trip?"

"No."

"The doctor sold the farm, paid the family's debt and gave my mother a thousand dollars. They called him The Big Duke. Now how do you like that, Little Duke?"

Captain Forrest said nothing. He just sat there, looking at Captain Jones and shaking his head.

"You see why I got no problem?" Spearchucker said.

"Duke," Hawkeye said, "as Grant said to Lee at Appomattox: 'You give up?' "

"Yeah," the Duke said.

13

COLONEL HENRY BLAKE was busier than he had been since The Deluge, and happier than he had been since his arrival in Korea. The first thing he did on the morning after his new neurosurgeon reported was call General Hammond in Seoul and, still chuckling to himself, wonder if, by any chance, the football team of the 325th Evacuation Hospital would care to meet an eleven representing the 4077th MASH.

General Hammond was delighted. The previous year his team had administered such thorough hosings to the only two pickup elevens in Korea foolish enough to challenge his powerhouse that both of those aggregations had abandoned the game. This had left him with a winning streak of two straight, visions of some day joining the company of Pop Warner, Amos Alonzo Stagg and Knute Rockne—and no one to play. The date was set for Thanksgiving Day, five weeks away, on the home field of the champions at Yong-Dong-Po.

The next thing Colonel Blake did was write Special Services in Tokyo and arrange for the use of two dozen football uniforms, helmets, shoes and pads, all to be airlifted as soon as possible. Then he dictated a notice, calling for candidates to report at two o'clock the next afternoon, and copies were posted in the messhall, the latrines, the showers and in the Painless Polish Poker and Dental Clinic. After that he showed up at The Swamp.

"Now," he said, after he had finished his report, "when do we start getting our dough down?"

133

"Why don't we wait a while, Coach," Trapper John suggested, "until we see what we've got for talent?"

"It doesn't matter what we've got," Henry responded. "That Hammond doesn't know anything about football."

"But if we seem too eager, Coach," Hawkeye said, "we may tip our hand."

"I guess you're right," Henry agreed.

The following afternoon, at the appointed hour, fifteen candidates appeared on the ball field. The equipment would not arrive for several days, so Henry, a whistle suspended from a cord around his neck, and as previously advised by his neurosurgeon, ran the rag-tag agglomeration twice around the perimeter of the field and then put them through some calisthenics. After that he just let them fool around, kicking and passing the three available footballs, while he and the Swampmen sized them up.

"Well," Henry said, at cocktail hour that afternoon in The Swamp, "what do you think?"

"Can we still get out of the game?" the Duke said.

"Yeah," Hawkeye said. "Whose idea was this anyway?"

"Yours, dammit," Trapper said.

"God, they looked awful," Hawkeye said.

"They'll look fine," Henry said, "once the uniforms get here."

"Never," the Duke said.

"Listen," Spearchucker said. "The coach is right, I don't mean particularly about the uniforms, but no team ever looks good the first few days. I noticed a few boys out there who have played the game."

"Besides," Henry said, "what does that Hammond know about football? It's like having another man on our side."

"The first thing we've got to do," Spearchucker said, "is decide on an offense."

"That's right," Henry said. "That's the first thing we've got to do. What'll it be? The Notre Dame Box?"

Trapper had been a T quarterback at Dartmouth, and Duke had run out of the T as a fullback at Georgia. Androscoggin, where Hawkeye had played end, had still used the single wing, but Spearchucker had played in the T in college and, of course, with the pros. Hawkeye was outvoted, 3 to 1, with Henry abstaining but agreeing.

"Now we've got to think up some plays," Henry said. "Why

don't you fellas handle that while I look after some of the other details?"

Spearchucker diagrammed six basic running plays and four stock pass plays, and that evening presented them to Henry, with explanations. Henry studied these, established a training table at one end of the mess hall and ordered his athletes to cut down on the consumption of liquor and cigarettes. The Swampmen settled for two drinks before dinner and none after, and reduced their inhalation of nicotine and tobacco tars by one half.

For the next days, Henry, with surreptitious suggestions from Spearchucker, had the squad first walk through and then run through the plays. When the uniforms arrived they turned out, to the dismay of the Duke, who had worn the red for Georgia, to consist of cardinal jerseys, white helmets and white pants. As the personnel sorted through the equipment and found sizes that approximated their own, Henry fretted. He could hardly wait to see them suited up.

"Great! Great!" Henry exulted, as they lined up in front of him on the field. "You men look great!"

"We look like a lotta goddamn cherry parfaits," Trapper said.

"Great!" Henry went on. "Wait'll that Hammond sees you. He's in for the surprise of his life."

"It'll be the last surprise he'll ever have," the Duke said. "He'll die laughin'."

Things were not as desperate, however, as the Swampmen seemed to believe. To the practiced eye of their newest member, in fact, it was apparent that his colleagues possessed at least some of the skills needed to play the game. Trapper John, after he took the snap from center, hustled back and stood poised to throw, looked like a scarecrow, but he had a whip for an arm and began to regain his control. Hawkeye, when he went down for passes, exhibited good moves and good hands. The Duke had the short, powerful stride a fullback needs, ran hard, blocked well and, during the few semi-scrimmages, showed himself to be imbued with an abundance of competitive fire. Sergeant Pete Rizzo, the ex-Three I League infielder, was a natural athlete and a halfback. Of the others, the sergeant from Supply named Vollmer, who had played center for Nebraska, was the best. Ugly John made a guard of sorts and Captain Walter Koskiusko Waldowski, the

Painless Pole, a survivor of high school and sandlot football in Hamtramck, was big enough, strong enough and angry enough to be a tackle. The rest of the line was filled out by enlisted men, with the exception of one of the end spots to which, over the objections of Trapper John, Dr. R. C. (Jeeter) Carroll was assigned.

The Spearchucker, of course, was kept under cover, except to jog around and catch a few passes. When anyone was watching he dropped them. No one guessed his identity, so scouts from the Evac Hospital could report to General Hammond only that the big colored boy was a clown, that whatever the Swampmen might have been once and were trying to be again, they had partaken of far too much whiskey and tobacco to go more than a quarter. Moreover, there were only four substitutes.

Hawkeye scouted the 325th. He went down one afternoon and tried to look like he was bound on various errands between the Quonsets that surrounded the athletic field, while he eyed the opposition.

"They got nothing," he reported on his return. "Three boys in the backfield looked like they played some college ball, but they probably aren't any better than Trapper, the Duke and me. They got a lousy passer, but their line is heavier than ours, and they got us in depth. I think that without the Spearchucker we could play them about even. With the Spearchucker they can't touch us."

"Good," Trapper said. "Then I suggest we do this: We hide the Spearchucker until the second half, and we hold back half our bets. We go into the half maybe ten points or two touchdowns behind, and then we bet the rest of our bundle at real odds."

"Great!" Henry said. "Everybody get his dough up!"

By the time everyone had kicked in—doctors, nurses, lab technicians, corpsmen, Supply and mess hall personnel— Henry had $6,000. The next morning—five days before the game—he called General Hammond, and when he came off the phone and reported to The Swamp it was apparent that he was disturbed.

"What happened?" Trapper asked. "Couldn't you get the dough down?"

"Yeah," Henry said. "I got $3,000 down."

"No odds?" Duke asked.

"Yeah," Henry said. "He gave me 2 to 1. He snapped it up."

"Oh-oh," Trapper John said. "I think I smell something."

"Me, too," Henry said. "That Hammond is tighter than a bull's ass in fly time. Whatever he's trying to pull, I don't like it."

"Tell you what we'd better do," Hawkeye said. "When I scouted those clowns they didn't look any better than we do but with them just as anxious to get their money down as we are, maybe I missed something. Spearchucker better go down tomorrow and nose around. He'll know a ringer if he sees one."

"Maybe I'd better go at that," Spearchucker said.

The next night Captain Jones returned from his scouting trip to Yong-Dong-Po. He didn't look any happier than Henry had the day before.

"What's the word?" asked Trapper John.

"They got two tackles from the Browns, and a halfback played with the Rams."

"That's not fair!" Henry said, jumping up. "Why, this game is supposed to be . . ."

"Wait a minute," Hawkeye said. "Are these guys any good?"

"Anybody ever ask you to play pro football, boy?" Spearchucker said.

"I get your point," Hawkeye said.

"My arm is sore," declared Trapper. "I don't think I can play."

"What do we do?" asked Henry.

"Y'all are the coach," Duke said. "How about it, Coach?"

"I guess we have to play," Henry said, his dreams of gold and glory gone.

"The bastards outconned ups," Hawkeye said.

"Maybe not," Spearchucker said. "We'll think of something."

"Like what?" Duke said.

"Like getting that halfback out of there as soon as we can," Spearchucker said.

"You know him?" Duke said.

"No," Spearchucker said, "but I've seen him. He played only one year second-string with the Rams before the Army got him. He's a colored boy who weighs only about 180, but he's a speed burner and one of those hot dogs."

"What does that mean?" Henry said.

"I mean," Spearchucker said, "that when he sees a little running room he likes to make a show—you know, stutter steps and cross-overs and all that jazz. He runs straight up and never learned to button up when he gets hit, so I think that, if you can get a good shot at him, you can get him out of there."

"Then let's kick off to them," the Duke said, "and get him right away."

"Good idea," Henry said.

"No," Spearchucker said. "He'll kill you in an open field. You've got to get him in a confined situation, where he hesitates and hangs up."

"Good idea," Henry said.

"Sure," Hawkeye said, "but how do we do that?"

"They'll run him off tackle a lot from strong right," Spearchucker said, "or send him wide. Hawkeye has to play him wide and turn him in, and when he makes his cut to the left he's gonna do that cross-over and Duke has to hit him high and Hawkeye low."

"Great idea!" Henry said. "That'll show that Hammond."

"Yeah," Duke said, "but can we do it?"

"It's the only way to do it," Spearchucker said. "If you don't get him the first time, he'll give you plenty of other chances."

"But when we unload him, if we can," Hawkeye said, "we'll have to break his leg to keep him from coming back in."

"Not necessarily," Trapper John said. "I got an idea."

"What is it?" Henry said.

"Tell you later," Trapper said, "if it works."

Trapper John excused himself, left The Swamp, walked over to Henry's tent and made a phone call. He talked for five minutes, and when he came back his teammates and their coach were dwelling on the problem presented by the two tackles from the Browns.

"We run nothing inside until I get into the game in the second half," Spearchucker was explaining. "These two big boys must be twenty or thirty pounds overweight. We run everything wide, except for maybe an occasional draw for

Duke up the middle to take advantage of their rush on Trapper when he passes."

"God help me," Trapper said.

"And me, too," Duke said.

"In other words," Spearchucker said, "the idea is to run the legs off 'em that first half. I think that will be all the edge I will require, gentlemen."

"Right," Henry said. "Imagine that Hammond, trying to pull something like that."

On the day of Thanksgiving the kick-off was scheduled for 10:00 A.M., so shortly after the crack of dawn the 4077th MASH football team, the Red Raiders of the Imjin, all fifteen of them, plus their coach, their water boy and assorted rooters, took off in jeeps and truck. The Swampmen rode together in the same jeep and in silence. No bottle was passed and no cigarettes were smoked, and when they arrived in Yong-Dong-Po and headed for the Quonset assigned to the team as dressing quarters Trapper John excused himself and disappeared.

"Where the hell have you been?" Hawkeye asked him, when their quarterback finally returned just in time to suit up and loosen his arm.

"Yeah," the Duke said. "We thought y'all went over the hill."

"Had to see a man about a hot dog," Trapper said. "Good old Austin from Boston."

"Who?" Duke asked.

"About what?" Hawkeye said.

"Tell you about it if it works," Trapper said. "You two clods just take care of the halfback."

"All right, men," Henry was saying. "I want you to listen to me. Let's have some quiet in here. This game . . ."

He went into a Pat O'Brien-plays-Knute Rockne, stalking up and down and invoking their pride in themselves, their organization, the colors they wore and their bank accounts. When he finished, out of words and out of breath, his face was as red as their jerseys, and he turned them loose to meet the orange and black horde of Hammond.

"Look at the size of those two beasts," Trapper John said, spotting the two tackles from the Browns.

"We know," Duke said. "We were out here before. This is gonna take courage."

"I ain't got any," Trapper said.

"Me neither," Jeeter Carroll said.

"God help us," Trapper said.

Hawkeye, because it had been his idea to play the game in the first place, was sent out now, as captain, to face the two tackles for the coin toss. When he came back he reported that he had lost the toss and that they would have to kick off.

"Now keep it away from the speed-burner," Spearchucker instructed the Duke. "Kick it to anybody else but him."

"That's right," said Henry, regaining his breath. "Kick it to anybody else but him."

"I know," the Duke assured them. "Y'all think I'm crazy?"

"Let's go get 'em men!" Henry said.

The Duke kicked it away from the halfback who had played a year of second-string with the Rams. He kicked it as far away from him as he could, but the enemy was of a different mind. The individual who caught the ball, by the simple maneuver of just running laterally and handing off, saw to it that the halfback who had played a year of second-string with the Rams got the ball. The next thing they knew, the Red Raiders of the Imjin saw an orange and black blur and they were lining up to try to prevent the point after touchdown, an effort which also failed.

"Stop him!" Henry was screaming on the sidelines. "Stop that man!"

"Yeah," the Duke was saying as they distributed themselves to receive the kick-off. "Y'all give me a rifle and I might stop him, if they blindfold him and tie him to a stake."

When the kick came, it came to the Duke on the ten and he ran it straight ahead to the thirty before they brought him down. On the first play from scrimmage Trapper sent Hawkeye, playing at left half until Spearchucker could get into the game, around right end. Hawkeye made two yards, and Pete Rizzo, at right half, picked up two more around the other flank.

"Third and six," Hawkeye said, as they came back to huddle. "I'll run a down and out."

"I'll run a down and in," Jeeter Carroll said, "but throw it to Hawkeye."

"My arm is sore," Trapper said.

"Y'all gotta throw," Duke said.

"God help us," Trapper said.

By the time he had taken the snap and hustled back, Trapper John knew that his blocking pocket had collapsed. He knew it because the two tackles from the Browns were descending upon him, and he ran. He ran to the right and turned and ran to the left.

"Good!" Spearchucker was calling from the sidelines. "Run the legs off those two big hogs!"

"Throw it!" Henry was shouting. "Throw it!"

Trapper threw it. Hawkeye caught it. When he caught it he lugged it to the enemy forty-nine. That was about as far as that drive went, and with fourth and five on the forty-four, Duke went back to punt.

"Don't try for distance," Hawkeye told him. "Kick it up there so we can get down and surround that sonofabitch."

"Yeah," Duke said, "if I can."

He kicked it high and, as it came down, the halfback who had played a year of second-string with the Rams, waiting for it on his twenty, saw red jerseys closing in. He called for a fair catch.

"A hot dog," Spearchucker said, on the sidelines. "A real hot dog."

"A hot dog," Hawkeye said to Duke as they lined up. "Spearchucker had him right."

"Yeah," Duke said. "Let's try to take him, like the Chucker said."

When the play evolved, it was also as Spearchucker had called it. The halfback who had played a year of second-string with the Rams went in motion from his left half position, took a pitch out, turned up through the line off tackle and tried to go wide. When he saw Hawkeye, untouched by blockers, closing in from the outside, he made his cut. He made that beautiful cross-over, the right leg thrust across in front of the left, and just at the instant when he looked like he was posing for the picture for the cover of the game program, poised as he was on the ball of his left foot, the other leg in the air and one arm out, he was hit. From one side he was hit at the knees by 200 pounds of hurtling former Androscoggin College end, and from the other he was hit high by 195 pounds of former Georgia fullback.

"Time!" one of the former Brown tackles was calling. "Time!"

It took quite some time. In about five minutes they got the

halfback who had played a year of second-string with the Rams on his feet, and they assisted him to the sidelines and sat him down on the bench.

"How many fingers am I holding up?" General Hammond, on his knees in front of his offensive star and extending the digits of one hand, was asking.

"Fifteen," his star replied.

"Take him in," the General said, sadly. "Try to get him ready for the second half."

So they took him across the field and into the 325th Evac. As the Swampmen watched him go, Trapper John was the first to speak.

"That," Trapper John said, "takes care of that. Scratch one hot dog."

"Y'all think he's hurt that bad?" the Duke asked.

"Hell, no," Trapper said, "but we won't see him again."

"I suspect something," Hawkeye said. "Explain."

"An old Dartmouth roomie of mine," Trapper explained, "is attached to this cruddy outfit. I called him the other night, after Spearchucker outlined the plot, and told him to put in for Officer of the Day today."

"I'm beginning to get it," Hawkeye said.

"This morning," Trapper went on, "I paid him a visit and cut him in for a piece of our bet. Right now Austin from Boston is going to place that hot dog under what is politely called heavy sedation, where he will dwell for the rest of the game and probably the rest of the day."

"Trapper," Hawkeye said, "you are a genius."

"Y'all know something?" the Duke said. "I think we can beat these Yankees now."

"Time!" the referee was screaming, between blasts on his whistle. "Do you people want to play football or talk all day?"

"If we have a choice," Hawkeye said, as they started to line up, "we prefer to talk."

"But you ain't got a choice," one of the tackles from the Browns said, "and you'll get yours now."

"What do y'all mean?" the Duke said. "It was clean."

"Yeah," Hawkeye said, "and you'll have to catch us first."

On that drive the enemy was stopped on the seven, and had to settle for the field goal that made it 10–0. For their part, the Red Raiders devoted most of their offensive efforts to pulling the corks of the two tackles, running them from one side of the field to the other. Midway in the second quarter they managed a score after Ugly John had fallen on a fumble on the enemy nineteen. Two plays later Hawkeye caught a wobbling pass lofted by a still fleeing Trapper John and fell into the end zone. Just before the end of the half the home forces rammed the ball over once more, so the score was 17-7 when both sides retired for rest and resuscitation.

"Very good, gentlemen," Spearchucker, who had been pacing the sideline helmeted and wrapped in a khaki blanket, told them as they filed in. "Very good, indeed."

"Yeah," Trapper John said, slumping to the floor, "but I gotta have a . . ."

". . . beer, sir?" said Radar O'Reilly, who had been serving during the time-outs as water boy.

"Right," Trapper said, taking the brew. "Thank you."

"Tell you what," Hawkeye said. "They got us now by ten, so we ought to be able to get two to one. Coach?"

"Yes, sir?" Henry said. "I mean, yes?"

"You better get over there quick," Hawkeye said, "and grab that Hammond and try to get the rest of that bundle down at two to one."

"Yes, sir," Henry said. "I mean, yes. What's the matter with me, anyway?"

"Nothin', Coach," Duke said. "Y'all are doing a real fine job."

Henry was back in less than five minutes. He reported that he had failed to get as far as the other team's dressing room. Halfway across the field he had been met by General Hammond who, having just checked on the health of his offensive star, had found him still under sedation. As Henry described him, the General was extremely irate.

"He was so mad," Henry said, "that he wanted to know if we'd like to get any more money down."

"Did you all tell him yes?" Duke wanted to know.

"He was so mad," Henry said, "that he said he'd give us three to one."

"And you took it?" Trapper said.

"I got four to one," a gleeful Henry said.

"Great, Coach!" they were shouting now. "How to go, Coach!"

"But," Henry said, the elation suddenly draining from his face, as he thought of something, "we still have to win."

"Relax, coach," Spearchucker assured him. "If these poor white trash will just give me the ball and then direct their attentions to the two gentlemen from Cleveland, Ohio, I promise you that I shall bring our crusade to a victorious conclusion."

Henry gave them then a re-take of his opening address. He paced the floor in front of them, waving his arms, exhorting, praising, pleading until, once more, his face and neck were of the same hue as their jerseys and once more, and for the last time, he sent them out to do or die.

As the Red Raiders of the Imjin distributed themselves to receive the kick-off, Captain Oliver Wendell Jones took a position on the goal line. The ball was not kicked to him, but the recipient, Captain Augustus Bedford Forrest, made certain that he got it. Without significant interference, Captain Jones proceeded to the opposite end zone. Captain Forrest then kicked the extra point, bringing the score to 17—14, and while the teams dragged themselves back upfield, the two tackles from the Browns were seen loping over to their sideline. There they were observed in earnest conversation with General Hamilton Hartington Hammond who, as the two lumbered back onto the field, was seen shaking his fist in the direction of Lieutenant Colonel Henry Braymore Blake.

"Those two tackles, sir," Radar O'Reilly informed his colonel, "told General Hammond that they recognize Captain Jones, sir."

"Roll it up!" Henry, ignoring both his corporal and his general, was screaming. "Roll it up!"

"Keep it down," advised Hawkeye. "We may want to do this again."

"We may not have to worry about that," Spearchucker, still breathing heavily, informed them. "I guess I'm not in the shape I thought I was. This may still be a battle."

It was. It was primarily a battle between the two tackles and Spearchucker, with certain innocent parties, such as Ugly John and the Painless Pole and Vollmer, the sergeant from Supply and center from Nebraska, in the middle. When the Red Raiders got the ball again they went ahead for the moment, as Spearchucker scored once more on a forty-yard burst, but then the enemy surged back to grind out another and, with three minutes to play the score was Hammond 24, Blake 21, first-and-ten for the home forces on the visitors' thirty-five-yard line.

"We gotta stop 'em here," Spearchucker said.

"We need a time-out," Trapper John said, "and some information."

"Time-out!" Hawkeye called to the referee.

"Radar," Trapper John said, when Radar O'Reilly came in with the water bucket and the towels, "do you think you can monitor that kaffee-clatch over there?"

He nodded toward the other team, gathered around their quarterback.

"I think I can, sir," Radar said. "I can try, sir."

"Well, goddammit, try."

"Yes, sir," Radar said, fixing his attention on the other huddle.

"What are they saying?"

"Well, sir," Radar said, "the quarterback is saying that they will run the old Statue of Liberty, sir. He's saying that their left end will come across and take the ball off his hand and try to get around their right end."

"Good," Spearchucker said. "What else are they saying?"

"Well, sir," Radar said, "now the quarterback is saying that, if that doesn't work, they'll go into the double wing."

"Good," the Duke said.

"Ssh!" Hawkeye said. "What are they gonna do out of the double wing?"

"Well, sir," Radar said, "they're having an argument now. Everybody is talking so it's confusing."

"Keep listening."

"Yes, sir. Now one of the tackles is telling them all to shut up. Now the quarterback is saying that, out of the double wing, the left halfback will come across and take the hand-off and start to the right. Then he'll hand off to the right halfback coming to the left."

"Radar," Hawkeye said, "you're absolutely the greatest since Marconi."

"Greater," Trapper John said.

"Thank you, sir," Radar said. "That's very kind of you, sir."

"Time!" the referee was calling. "Time!"

It was as Radar O'Reilly had heard it. On the first play the enemy quarterback went back, as if to pass. As he did, the left end started to his right, and the Red Raiders, all eleven of them, started to their left. The left end took the ball off the quarterback's hand, brought it down, made his cut and met a welcoming committee of ten men in red, only Ugly John, temporarily buried under 265 pounds of tackle, failing to make it on time.

"Double wing!" Spearchucker informed his associates as the enemy lined up for the next play. "Double wing!"

"Hut! Hut!" the enemy quarterback was calling. "Hut!"

This time the left halfback took the hand-off and started to his right. The eleven Red Raiders started to *their* right and, as the right halfback took the ball from the left halfback, ran to his left and tried to turn in, he, too, was confronted by ten men wearing the wrong colors. This time it was the Painless Pole who, tripping over his own feet, kept the Red Raiders from attaining perfect attendance.

The first man to hit the halfback was Spearchucker Jones. He hit him so hard that he doubled him over and drove him back five yards, and as the wind came out of the halfback so did the ball. It took some time to find the ball, because it was at the bottom of a pile of six men, all wearing red jerseys.

"Time!" Spearchucker called, and he walked over and talked with the referee.

"What's the matter?" Trapper John asked him, when he came back. "Let's take it to them."

"Too far to go, and we're all bushed," Spearchucker said. "I just told the referee that we're gonna try something different. We're gonna make the center eligible . . ."

"Who?" Vollmer, the sergeant from Supply and center from Nebraska said. "Me?"

"That's right," Spearchucker said. "Now everybody listen, and listen good. We line up unbalanced, with everybody to the right of center, except Hawkeye at left end. Just before the signal for the snap of the ball, Duke, you move up into the line to the right of the center and Hawkeye, you drop back a yard. That keeps the required seven men in the line, and makes the center eligible to receive a pass."

"Me?" Vollmer said. "I can't catch a pass."

"You don't have to," Spearchucker said. "Trapper takes the snap and hands the ball right back to you between your legs. You hide it in your belly, and stay there like you're blockin'.

146

Trapper, you start back like you got the ball, make a fake to me and keep going. One or both of those tackles will hit you . . ."

"Oh, dear," Trapper said.

"Meanwhile," Spearchucker said to Vollmer, "when your man goes by you, you straighten up, hidin' the ball with your arms, and you walk—don't run—toward that other goal line."

"I don't know," Vollmer said.

"You got to," Hawkeye said. "Just think of all that dough."

"I suppose," Vollmer said.

"Everybody else keep busy," Spearchucker said. "Keep the other people occupied, but don't hold, and Vollmer, you remember you walk, don't run."

"I'll try," Vollmer said.

"Oh, dear," Trapper John said.

"Time!" the referee was calling again. "Time!"

When they lined up, all of the linemen to the right of the center except Hawkeye, they had some trouble finding their positions and the enemy had some trouble adjusting. As Trapper John walked up and took his position behind the center and then Duke jumped up into the line and Hawkeye dropped back, the enemy was even more confused.

"Hut!" Trapper John called. "Hut!"

He took the ball from the center, handed it right back to him, turned and started back. He faked to Spearchucker, heading into the line, and then, his back to the fray, he who had once so successfully posed as The Saviour now posed as The Quarterback With the Ball. So successfully did he pose, in fact, that both tackles from the Browns and two other linemen in orange and black fell for the ruse, and on top of Trapper John.

Up at the line, meanwhile, the sergeant from Supply and center from Nebraska had started his lonely journey. Bent over, his arms crossed to further hide the ball, and looking like he had caught a helmet or a shoulder pad in the pit of the stomach and was now living with the discomfort, he had walked right between the two enemy halfbacks whose attention was focused on the trappings of Trapper John. Once past this checkpoint, about ten yards from where he had started and now out in the open, the sergeant, however, began to feel as conspicuous as a man who had forgotten his pants, so he decided to embellish the act. He veered toward his own sideline, as if he were leaving the game.

"What's going on?" Henry was screaming as his center approached him. "What's going on out there? What are you doing?"

"I got the ball," the center informed him, opening his arms enough for Henry to see the pigskin cradled there.

"Then run!" Henry screamed. "Run!"

So the sergeant from Supply and center from Nebraska began to run. Back upfield, the two tackles from the Browns had picked up Trapper John. That is, each had picked up a leg, and now they were shaking him out like a scatter rug, still trying to find the ball, while their colleagues stood around waiting for it to appear, so they could pounce on it. Downfield, meanwhile, the safety man stood, shifting his weight from one foot to the other, scratching an armpit, peering upfield and waiting for something to evolve. He had noticed the center start toward the sidelines, apparently in pain, but he had ignored that. Now, however, as he saw the center break into a run, the light bulb lit, and he took off after him. They met, but they met on the two-yard line, and the sergeant from Supply and center from Nebraska carried the safety man, as well as the ball, into the end zone with him.

"What happened?" General Hammond, coach, was hollering on one sideline. "Illegal! Illegal!"

"It was legal," the referee informed him. "They made that center eligible."

"Crook!" General Hammond was hollering at Lieutenant Colonel Blake on the other sideline, shaking his fist at him. "Crook!"

"Run it up!" Henry was hollering. "Run it up!"

"Now we just gotta stop 'em," Spearchucker said, after Duke had kicked the point that made it MASH 28, Evac 24.

"Not me," Trapper John said, weaving for the sideline.

And stop them they did. The key defensive play was made, in fact, by Dr. R. C. (Jeeter) Carroll. Dr. Carroll, all five feet nine inches and 150 pounds of him, had spent the afternoon on the offense just running passroutes, waving his arms over his head and screaming at the top of his lungs. He had run button-hooks, turn-ins, turn-outs, zig-ins, zig-outs, posts and fly patterns. Trapper John had ignored him and, after the first few minutes, so had the enemy. Now, with less than a minute

148

to play, with the enemy on the Red Raiders' forty, fourth and ten, Spearchucker had called for a prevent defense and sent for the agile Dr. Carroll to replace Trapper John.

"Let's pick on that idiot," Radar O'Reilly heard one of the enemy ends tell the enemy quarterback as Jeeter ran onto the field. "He's opposite me, so let's run that crossing pattern and I'll lose him."

They tried. They crossed their ends about fifteen yards deep but the end couldn't lose Jeeter. Jeeter stuck right with him but, with his back to play, he couldn't see the ball coming. It came with all the velocity the quarterback could still put on it, and it struck Jeeter on the back of the helmet. When it struck Jeeter it drove him to his knees, but it also rebounded into the arms of the Painless Pole who fell to the ground still clutching it.

"Great!" Henry was shouting from the sideline. "Great defensive play."

"That's using the old head, Jeeter," Hawkeye told Dr. Carroll, as he helped him to his feet.

"What?" Jeeter said.

"That's using the old noggin," Hawkeye said.

"What?" Jeeter said.

Then Spearchucker loafed the ball into the line twice, the referee fired off his Army .45 and they trooped off the field, into the waiting arms of Henry, who escorted them into their dressing quarters where they called for the beer and slumped to the floor.

"Great!" Henry, ecstatic, was saying, going around and shaking each man's hand. "It was a great team effort. You're heroes all!"

"Then give us our goddamn Purple Hearts," said Ugly John, who had spent most of the afternoon under one or the other of the two tackles from the Browns.

When General Hammond appeared, he was all grace. In the best R.A. stiff-upper-lip tradition he congratulated them, and then he took Henry aside.

"Men," Henry said, after the general had left, "he wants a rematch. Whadda you say?"

"I thought he was bein' awful nice," Spearchucker said.

"We might be able to do it to them again," Henry said, still glowing.

"Never again," Hawkeye said. "They're on to us now."

"Gentlemen," the Duke, slumped next to Hawkeye, said, "I got an announcement to make. Y'all have just seen me play my last game."

"You can retire my number, too," Trapper John said.

"Mine, too," Hawkeye said.

"Anyway, men," Henry said, "I told you so."

"What?" Hawkeye said.

"That Hammond," Henry said. "He doesn't know anything about football."

14

FOR THE NEXT two days, Henry spent his spare time distributing the profits of the betting coup to the financial backers of the Red Raiders. The way the money had been bet—half of it before the game at two to one and the rest at halftime at four to one—meant that the ultimate payoff was three to one, so when Henry stopped off at The Swamp on the second afternoon and handed each of the occupants his original $500 and then $1,500 more, the recipients were more affluent than they had been in a long while.

"And no place to spend it," the Duke said.

"Send it home," the colonel advised.

"No," Hawkeye said. "I got a better idea."

"What?" Henry said.

"You keep all the money, and send us home."

"No chance," Henry said.

"But why, coach?" Duke wanted to know. "With the time the Hawk and me put in before they sent us to y'all, we been over here longer than anybody but you."

"That's right," Hawkeye said, "and it ain't fair."

"Excuse me," Trapper John said, getting up, "but I've heard this before and I don't want to hear it again."

"I'll go with you," Spearchucker said. "I can't stand the sight of suffering, either."

"Soreheads!" the Duke called after them. "Just because we get out before y'all!"

"Seriously, Henry," Hawkeye said, "the Duke and I are

151

scheduled to get shed of this Army in March. That's only a little over three months away. Now, ever since we've been stuck out here at the tag end of nowhere we've watched a procession of our contemporaries come and go. Singles and doubles hitters, strike-out artists, long down the fairway or off into the woods, it didn't matter what they were, because they all got rotated back to stateside duty four—five months before they were to get sprung."

"That's right," Henry said.

"But why?" the Duke said.

"I know why," Hawkeye said. "It's because the Army always gets even."

"What do you mean?" Henry said.

"I mean," Hawkeye said, "that the Duke and I are two of the three biggest screwups over here, or four if you count Roger the Dodger . . ."

"I don't count him," Henry said. "I don't even think of him, and if that sonofabitch comes around here again I'm gonna have him shot on sight."

"Anyway," Hawkeye said, "you gotta admit it. We screwed up, so now the Army, defender of democracy and symbol of justice, is gonna take it out on us."

"No," Henry said. "You're wrong. You won't believe it, but it's not a punishment."

"Then what is it?" the Duke said. "It feels like a punishment."

"It's ironic," Henry said, "but it's because you two, like Trapper John, came here with more than average training and experience. You've done a good job when the chips were down, and now we can't afford to waste you. If you went home now you'd be of no use to anyone but your wives. Therefore, we've got to keep you here until your enlistments expire."

"Ain't that the damndest thing?" the Duke said.

"In short," Hawkeye said, "we screwed up in the wrong area. If we had dubbed it along in the working time and never given it the goddamn college try, we'd be back at some stateside hospital, living with our wives and behaving like officers and gentlemen? Is that right?"

"Yeah," agreed Henry with a broad grin.

"I couldn't stand a stateside Army hospital," the Duke said. "Too many jerks."

The next morning the two appeared in front of Colonel Blake's tent. When the colonel came out in answer to their calls, they announced that the Spearchucker had arranged for them both to be given $25,000 bonuses by the Philadelphia Eagles and they were leaving immediately for the City of Brotherly Love. They then departed by jeep, and were neither seen nor heard from for three days. Colonel Blake, of course, was aware that the other two occupants of The Swamp knew where they were and could have them back in two hours if a hint of heavy work arose.

Four days after they returned, the two, whose previous escapade had been ignored by Henry, appeared once again in front of their colonel's tent. Once again he went out to meet them.

"So where do you wise bastards think you're going this time?" he inquired.

"Paris," replied Hawkeye.

"Yeah," said the Duke.

"That's very interesting," said Henry. "What for?"

"We gotta get the Duke fixed," explained Hawkeye. "It's an emergency. He's been nice to me and Trapper and Spearchucker for three days in a row, and we think he's turnin'."

"Well," said Colonel Blake, "that certainly is an emergency, and we can't have that sort of thing around here, but why don't you just take him down to Seoul? It's so much closer."

"Why, Colonel," replied Hawkeye, "you can't be serious. Just two days ago you gave the enlisted men a lecture on how they should not get it in Seoul because there is so much neisserian infection. What applies to enlisted men must certainly apply to officers, and we do not wish to set a bad example. We hear that there is not too much of it in Paris, so that's where we are going."

With that they jumped into their jeep and disappeared for what turned out to be another three days. This time their colonel realized that, for the good of the organization if for no other reason, he would have to curtail the extracurricular excursions of his two transients. At the same time he realized that, as the two sweated out the termination of their enlistments and grew more itchy by the day, he needed some means of keeping them busier and thus happier in their home away from home. He might have prayed for an increase in battle casualties, but he was too fine a human being for that,

153

so he prayed for any other answer, and the next morning it appeared in two parts, named Captains Emerson Pinkham and Leverett Russell.

Captains Pinkham and Russell were replacements for two of Henry's surgeons who, having been nursed along to the point of being able to accept major responsibility, had unaccountably but not unexpectedly been whisked away. Henry greeted them, oriented them and then invited them to meet him and various members of his staff late that afternoon for cocktails at the so-called Officers' Club.

It was a pleasant, but in some ways disturbing, social occasion and confrontation. Trapper John, Spearchucker, Ugly John and the others who were not on duty found Captains Pinkham and Russell highly presentable. They were intelligent, polite, seemed to possess normal senses of humor and on the subject of surgery talked impressively. This last should not have surprised nor disturbed the veterans, for the surgical world changes rapidly and almost all surgical residents talk well, but the veterans had been so far removed from the mainstream of their profession for so long that, as the recruits expounded on new approaches and new techniques, at least several of the listeners wondered if, when they did get home, they would have to start all over again.

"Well," Henry said, as he, Trapper John and Spearchucker headed toward the mess hall at the party's end, "they seem all right. Good men."

"I think so," Spearchucker said, "for Ivy League types."

"I guess so," Trapper John said, "but we'll see what the Hawk and the Duke think, if they ever get back."

"Oh, they'll be back," Henry said, "and that gives me an idea."

Two days later, when Hawkeye and the Duke returned, Henry read them the Old Familiar. While the strains of that were still sounding in their ears, he launched into his project for the preservation of what remained of the sanity of Hawkeye and the Duke and the perpetuation of the efficiency of his organization.

"Now, while you two clowns were gone," he told them, "we picked up two new men. Their names are Emerson Pinkham and Leverett Russell."

"Sound like Ivy League types," Duke said.

"That's right," Henry said. "They are, but they're good

154

men. They're intelligent, they've had excellent training and they're abreast of certain new concepts of surgery that you and I have never even heard about."

"Good," Hawkeye said. "Then let them do all the work."

"No, goddammit," Henry said, the red rising to his hairline again. "Not for one minute. That's been the trouble with this organization. When we've been busy there hasn't been time to teach the new men the kind of hurry-up, short-cut or call-it-what-you-will surgery that you have to do in a place like this. When we've had time you people have goofed off, which is my fault, and as a result anybody who learned anything here just picked it up by accident. Well, that's gonna stop, and it's gonna stop right now. These new men are going to be taught everything they can be taught, and you two are gonna teach them!"

"Yes, sir," Duke said.

"OK," Hawkeye said. "I guess you're right."

At lunch that day, Henry introduced Hawkeye and Duke to Captains Emerson Pinkham and Leverett Russell, and the two veterans invited the two recruits to join them, Trapper John and Spearchucker at The Swamp for cocktails at four o'clock. At four o'clock the two appeared and were served libations. As before, they shaped up well in all the requisite areas. Since their arrival they had observed a number of operations and had performed two themselves, and this, of course, quite naturally invited a comparison between the methods being employed at the MASH and the techniques taught in the high-level stateside training hospitals.

"I think I can speak for Lev as well as myself," Captain Pinkham said at one point, "when I say that we are not, for a moment, regretting our presence here. There's a job to be done, and some men are giving their lives so, at the very least, we can give our time and our talents, such as they may be. At the same time, any surgeon, aware of everything that's going on in his field back home, has to regret it when he's sent to a place like this where about all he ever gets to do is meatball surgery. No offense, of course."

Hawkeye looked at Duke, Duke looked at Hawkeye, Trapper John and Spearchucker looked at their colleagues. The term was one that was used often in The Swamp, but now it had just been used by someone else, and a recruit.

"No offense," Hawkeye said. "Have another drink."

As it happened, the Double Natural was moderately busy at this time, and Henry had paired Captains Pinkham and Russell with Captains Pierce and Forrest on the night shift. On this very first night, in fact, there was even a six o'clock chopper, so after they had bolted down a quick meal, the two veterans escorted the two recruits over to view the passengers.

The chopper had brought two 4077th MASH Specials: both had belly and extremity wounds, and one had a minor chest wound. Hawkeye and Duke stood back while Captains Pinkham and Russell made their examinations, then informed the recruits that they would be ready and willing to assist when the patients had been prepared and moved into the OR. After that the two Swampmen retired to the lab where, a few minutes later, Captain Bridget McCarthy found them avidly engaged in questioning Radar O'Reilly who had recently been in communication with Jupiter.

"All right, you two!" Captain McCarthy ordered. "Get out of here!"

"What's your maladjustment tonight, Knocko?" asked Hawkeye.

"Listen," she said. "Your two Cub Scouts want to operate on those patients right away, and they're not ready to be operated on."

"Now just a minute, ma'am," Duke said. "Just where did y'all . . ."

"Attend medical school?" Knocko asked. "Right here."

"Yes, ma'am," Duke said. "We'll go help."

In the preoperative ward the two graduates of the ivory tower surgical training programs were showing their inexperience. The two cases that confronted them were well within the ability of the Double Natural, or any other MASH, to handle. Both patients were in moderate shock, but had no continuing blood loss. Both required preoperative resuscitation by a process well known even to the corpsmen and Korean helpers.

Captain Pinkham had the boy with the minor but significant chest wound. When Hawkeye and Duke wandered in, he was fussing around the patient, rapping on the chest and listening to it with a stethoscope. He was behaving, in other words, like a doctor and not a meatball surgeon, so Hawkeye took a look at the X-ray, assessed the situation and spoke.

"Doctor," he said, "this guy obviously has holes in his bowel and his femur is broken. It's not a bad fracture, but he's probably dropped a pint here. There's at least a pint in his belly and maybe a pint in his chest. Agreed?"

"Agreed," Captain Pinkham said.

From there Hawkeye went on to explain that the patient also had a pneumothorax, meaning that there was air in his pleural, or chest, cavity because his lung was leaking air and had collapsed. In addition, he suggested, the shock from the blood loss was probably augmented by contamination of the peritoneum, or abdominal, cavity by bowel contents.

"So what he needs," he said, "before you lug him in there and hit him with the Pentothal and curare and put a tube in his trachea, is expansion of his lung, two or three pints of blood and an antibiotic to minimize the peritoneal infection."

"I see," Captain Pinkham said, beginning to see a little light, "but we'll still have to open his chest as well as his belly."

"No, we won't," said Hawkeye. "The chest wound doesn't amount to a damn. Stick a Foley catheter between his second and third ribs and hook it to underwater drainage, and his lung will re-expand. If he were going to do any interesting bleeding from his lung, he'd probably have done it by now. We can tap it after we get the air out and his general condition improves. Right now we just want to get this kid out of shock and into the OR in shape to have his belly cut and his thigh debrided."

Two corpsmen brought what at the Double Nature passed for an adequate closed thoracotomy kit. It contained the bare essentials for insertion of a tube in a chest, and after Hawkeye had watched Captain Pinkham fiddle around with it for awhile, he spoke again.

"Look," he said. "All that's great, but there will be times when you won't have the time to do it right. Lemme show you how to do it wrong."

Hawkeye donned a pair of gloves, accepted a syringe of Novocain from a corpsman, infiltrated the skin and the space between the ribs and shoved the needle into the pleural cavity. Pulling back on the plunger he got air, knew he was in the right place, noted the angle of the needle, withdrew it, took a scalpel, incised the skin for one-half inch and plunged the scalpel into the pleural cavity. Bubbles of air appeared at

157

the incision. Then he grasped the tip of a Foley catheter with a Kelly clamp and shoved the tube through the hole. A nurse attached the other end to the drainage bottle on the floor, a corpsman blew up the balloon on the catheter and now bubbles began to rise to the surface of the water in the bottle. Hawkeye dropped to his knees on the sand floor and, as he began to suck on the rubber tube attached to the shorter of the two tubes in the bottle, the upward flow of bubbles increased as the lung was, indeed, expanding.

"Crude, ain't it?" said Hawkeye.

"Yes," said Captain Pinkham.

"How long did it take?"

"Not long," admitted Captain Pinkham, who couldn't help noticing that the patient's breathing had already improved.

Duke, meanwhile, watched Captain Russell apply his surgical resident's approach to the other soldier who, waiting for blood, was still in shock. Captain Russell, afraid that he'd miss something, was examining the patient centimeter by centimeter, fore and aft, while the corpsmen waited impatiently to start the transfusion.

"Excuse me," Duke said after a while, "but all you're doin' now is holdin' up progress. Why don't y'all let these folks get to work?"

"But don't you think . . ." Captain Russell started to say.

"What I think," Duke said to the corpsmen, "is that we better start the blood."

Having taken the recruits that far, the two veterans headed for the game in the Painless Polish Poker and Dental Clinic to pass the two hours until the patients would be ready for surgery. When they figured that the patients had been sufficiently transfused and adequately resuscitated, they headed back to the OR, scrubbed and joined their junior partners.

Duke and Captain Russell had a boy whose small bowel was somewhat perforated, requiring removal of two different areas and closure of several individual holes. This sort of work is done ritualistically in most surgical training programs, because it is basic to belly surgery and should never be learned incorrectly, and as a result, the surgical residents in their third and fourth years of training, particularly in good teaching hospitals, may still be at the ritualistic stage. Captain Russell surely was.

Duke having determined that all they had to do was fix the

small bowel and that time, up to a point, was not going to be a factor, decided to sweat it out. For two hours he stood there amusing himself by mildly insulting Knocko McCarthy, who wouldn't hurt him while he was scrubbed, and assisting in wonder as Captain Russell performed a small bowel resection as performed by the residents in a large university hospital.

"Do y'all mind if I do this one?" he asked, as Captain Russell finally advanced on the second area needing repair. "I lost twenty bucks in that poker game, and I'll never get even at this rate."

He didn't wait for an answer. In twenty minutes he removed the damaged segment of bowel and sewed the two ends together.

"Y'all probably noticed," he explained to Captain Russell as they were closing, "that when clamping and cutting the mesentery, I wasn't quite as dainty as y'all were. Y'all will recall that I didn't do the anastomosis with three layers of interrupted silk, like y'all did. I used an inner layer of continuous catgut and interrupted silk in the serosa. Where y'all put twelve sutures on the anterior side of yours, I put four. Y'all observed that the lumen in my anastomosis is as big as yours, I've got mucosa to mucosa, submucosa more or less to submucosa, muscularis pretty much to muscularis and serosa to serosa, and there ain't any place where it's gonna leak. It took y'all two hours, and it took me twenty minutes. Your way is fine, but y'all can't get away with it around here. Y'all will kill people with it, because a lot of these kids who can stand two hours of surgery can't stand six hours of it."

"But . . ." Captain Russell started to say.

"That's right," Duke said, "and if I'm really in a hurry I'll ride with just the continuous catgut through all the layers."

So it went, for several weeks. The recruits, being polite, listened and, being intelligent, learned. They had both, however, been born and bred, as well as formally educated, to be fastidious, so the shucking of old habits did not come easily. Captain Pinkham, in particular, still tended to get bogged down in detail. He would become completely absorbed in repairing damage to a hand and ignore or sublimate the obvious fact that the patient could die of his abdominal wounds. Once, in fact, on a busy night while Hawkeye was occupied elsewhere, he spent six hours on a case that should not have taken more than two hours and managed to miss a

159

hole in the upper part of the stomach. The patient almost died, early, from too much surgery and, later, from the missed hole. Hawkeye took that one back to the table and, two days later, with the patient well on the way to recovery, he was able to make this the case in point.

"Now I'll offer you some thoughts," he told the much relieved Captain Pinkham. "This is certainly meatball surgery we do around here, but I think you can see now that meatball surgery is a specialty in itself. We are not concerned with the ultimate reconstruction of the patient. We are concerned only with getting the kid out of here alive enough for someone else to reconstruct him. Up to a point we are concerned with fingers, hands, arms and legs, but sometimes we deliberately sacrifice a leg in order to save a life, if the other wounds are more important. In fact, now and then we may lose a leg because, if we spent an extra hour trying to save it, another guy in the preop ward could die from being operated on too late.

"That's hard to accept at first," he said, "but tell me something, doctor. Do you play golf?"

"I do," Captain Pinkham said, "but I haven't been getting much in lately."

"Then let me put it this way," Hawkeye said. "Our general attitude around here is that we want to play par surgery on this course. Par is a live patient. We're not sweet swingers, and if we've gotta kick it in with our knees to get a par that's how we do it."

"I can't argue against that," Captain Pinkham said.

"Good," Hawkeye said. "Come on up to The Swamp for a drink."

Colonel Blake, of course, was enormously pleased. He had not only hit upon a project that was at least partially intriguing Captains Forrest and Pierce during their final months, but also Captains Pinkham and Russell were obviously benefitting. He had established a kind of teaching hospital. Then Captain Pinkham came to see Colonel Blake and Colonel Blake came to see Captain Pierce.

"Have a drink, Henry," Hawkeye said.

"Yeah," the Duke said. "Join us."

"No, thanks," Henry said. "How's it going?"

"Good," the Duke said. "Can we go home now?"

"No," Henry said. "What I want to know is how Pinkham's been doing lately."

"Good," Hawkeye said, "although the last couple of days I've had the feeling that I'm starting to bore him."

"He's got a problem," Henry said.

"We all have," Hawkeye said.

"Not like his," Henry said.

"What's wrong with him?" the Duke said.

"His wife," Henry said.

"Too bad," Hawkeye said, "but he married the broad. You didn't, so why is he bothering you?"

"Yeah," the Duke said.

"Ever since he landed here," Henry said, "he's been getting letters from his wife saying she can't live with his parents and their kid is sick, she thinks, but the doctor doesn't, and why doesn't he come home and take her off the hook? The damn fool woman seems to think the guy can break it off over here any time he wants to."

The two Swampmen were silent. Henry looked from one to the other.

"Come on, you guys," he said. "You always got ideas. What the hell am I going to do? I didn't think I was sent over here to run a kindergarten."

"If I was y'all," said Duke, "I wouldn't do a goddamn thing."

"Sure," Henry said. "That's the obvious answer, but I have a hospital to run and you know how hard replacements are to get, and I have to make the ones we get as useful as I can. This guy was just starting to shape up, but this week he got four letters, all saying the same thing but each one worse than the one before. She'll drive him nuts."

"I don't know," Hawkeye said.

"Me neither," Duke said.

"Thanks a lot," Henry said, as he departed.

The next day Captain Pinkham received another and more desperate letter from his wife. This time he didn't tell anyone about it, but at 2:00 A.M. it was obvious to Hawkeye, who was watching him closely, that Captain Pinkham was trying to concentrate but that he was failing. Between cases he gave the Duke the word and they took Captain Pinkham to The Swamp, gave him a beer and asked: "What's the trouble? Anything we can do?"

161

Captain Pinkham showed them the letter. After reading it, they took him to his tent, gave him a sleeping pill and said: "Sleep and don't worry about the work."

The next day Captain Pinkham awakened still impaled on the horns of the kind of trouble only hardnoses can survive, and Captain Pinkham was no hardnose. Two days later, fortunately for all, salvation came. It came to Colonel Blake, via the Red Cross and the Army, in the form of orders to send Captain Pinkham home on emergency leave. His wife had folded and been placed in a private fool farm.

The two Swampmen found that they missed Captain Pinkham, who had proved himself willing to try, so they were particularly nice to Captain Russell, who missed his buddy even more. Between themselves the two made noises about how they would handle that kind of grief if it ever came their way, but they both had the same doubts. They thanked their good fortune for wives who didn't bug them from 9,000 miles away, and they sat down and wrote identical letters:

Darling,

I love you. I need you, I hope you love me and need me. If so, you can have me in two weeks by following these simple instructions:

(1) Go crazy.

(2) Notify the Red Cross.

Love,

15

THE DAYS PASSED, among them Christmas and New Year's. On Christmas, Dago Red said four Masses at nearby troop concentrations, another at the Double Natural where he also conducted a non-denominational service. Then he pulled all the strings behind the scenes at the party in the mess hall where a red-suited and white-bearded Vollmer, the sergeant from Supply and center from Nebraska, a pillow strapped to the stomach where the ball had once been cradled, handed out clothing, cigarettes and fruit to a gaggle of Korean house boys while their benefactors among the personnel of the 4077th applauded.

For dinner on both holidays, Mother Divine put down excellent repasts. Mother, still president of the Brooklyn and Manhattan Marked-Down Monument and Landmark Company, and still doing business with Caucasians from south of the Mason-Dixon Line, was in a beneficent mood. For a while during the autumn, business had slackened off, but the onset of the holiday season had brought on a gift-buying stampede, and Mother had even managed to unload two items in which little interest had previously been shown.

The first of these was the Soldiers' and Sailors' Monument at 89th Street and Riverside Drive. It was purchased by a Private First Class from Hodge, Alabama, who mailed the postcard picturing it to his fiancée, with the following message printed on the reverse side:

163

Huney:

   I just bot this for you. They will delivur it in a
cuple weeks. Have them put it in yur side yard and wen
we get marreed I'll get Puley to help me muve it to
our own place.

   Merry Xmas. Your frend and husbend to be.

His buddy, and near-hometown-neighbor from Dutton,
bought Fifth Avenue (Looking North From Forty-Second
Street) as a surprise for his father. On the back of the card,
circa 1934, he wrote:

Pa:

   Merry Christmus. I bout this strete for you. You
can see that all of the cars that use it are olden, so I
figger you can move the garege up there and will get
all the busines you can handel. I'll help wen I get home.
Merry Christmus agan.

The holidays over, time dragged for Hawkeye and Duke.
The 4077th was reasonably busy, so they had enough to do.
When Henry was afraid they didn't, and still on his teaching
hospital kick, he had them shepherding associates with less
experience over the rocky pastures of meatball surgery, until
one night, early in February, he entered The Swamp, kicked
the snow off his boots, helped himself to a large shot of Scotch,
made himself comfortable on one of the sacks and announced
to Captains Forrest and Pierce: "I've got orders for you two
eightballs to ship out of here a week from today."

Duke and Hawkeye jumped, laughed, hugged Henry,
hugged each other. Spearchucker, with two months left to go,
congratulated them warmly. In the far corner of the tent,
Trapper John McIntyre with almost six months of servitude
still ahead of him, lay on his sack and looked at the roof.

The last week was interminable. Preparation for leaving
involved very little so, considering the importance of the
event, The Swamp was pretty quiet. Finally, Duke and Hawkeye shaped up for their last night shift, and the demands it
made upon them brought them back to earth.

Arterial injuries were not unusual, but this night they
caught two. Trying to save the right leg of a G.I. from

Topeka, Kansas, and the left leg of a Tommy from Birmingham, England, Duke and Hawkeye did two vein grafts to bridge the arterial gaps blown out by gook artillery. When the shift was over, they started for The Swamp, tired, excited, and troubled. They had just done two operations on two legs belonging to young men, to each of whom a leg was important, and they were walking away knowing that, in all probability, they would never learn the fate of the legs.

At The Swamp, their two colleagues were waiting for them, bottle open. By 11:00 A.M. they had gone over for the third time plans, which each secretly suspected would never materialize, for meeting in the States as soon as possible after Spearchucker and Trapper John gained their releases.

"Look," Trapper John said finally, "aren't you guys going to say goodbye to Henry?"

"Naturally," Duke said. "We take kindly to the man."

"Well, why don't you do it now?"

"Yes, father," Hawkeye said.

At 11:15 A.M. Duke and Hawkeye, still in their soiled fatigues but wearing scrubbed and serious looks, arrived at the office of Colonel Henry Blake. Hawkeye approached Henry's sergeant, threw his shoulders back and stated, "Captain Pierce and Captain Forrest request permission to speak to Colonel Blake."

The sergeant, who had known them for eight months as Duke and Hawkeye, was shaken.

"What kind of bullshit is this?" he wanted to know. "Don't screw up now, for Chrissake."

"Don't worry," Hawk assured him. "Announce us."

The sergeant knocked on Henry's door and announced: "Captain Pierce and Captain Forrest request permission to speak to the Colonel."

Colonel Blake blanched. His knees shook.

"What are they up to?"

"Don't know, Sir."

"Well, let's find out. Send them in."

Duke and Hawkeye entered, saluted and stood at attention.

"Stop it, you two! Cut it out!" roared Colonel Blake. "You're making me nervous. What the hell have you got in mind now?"

"Tell him, Duke," Hawkeye, still at attention, said.

"You all tell him. I can't."

"Well, Henry," explained Hawkeye, "we haven't come to apologize for anything exactly . . ."

"Good," Henry said.

". . . but we wanted you to know that we know what you've had to put up with from us and that we appreciate it. We think you're quite a guy."

Duke stepped forward and offered a much-relieved but silent Henry his hand. Hawkeye also shook hands, and then they saluted, executed a perfect about-face and, solemn-faced and in step, departed.

Back at The Swamp, most of the outfit had showed up for a farewell drink. Ugly John, who would drive them to Seoul in the jeep, was there. So were Dago Red and the Painless Pole, Jeeter Carroll, Pete Rizzo, Vollmer, the sergeant from Supply and center from Nebraska, and the other survivors of the Thanksgiving Day Massacre, officers and enlisted men all milling around in a heterogeneous mass. Captain Leverett Russell thanked them for their patience during the past months. Radar O'Reilly presented them with his own version of their horoscopes. Mother Divine, who had just leased out the rowboat concession for the Central Park Lake, sent over a box lunch for them to take along, and Colonel Blake appeared just long enough to hand over two bottles of Scotch to be put in the jeep. Everyone wished them luck, pumped their hands, and gave them home addresses.

"Let's get the hell out of here," Hawkeye whispered to the Duke, finally. "I'm beginning to feel like Shaking Sammy."

"Me, too," the Duke said.

Hawkeye looked toward Trapper John's corner. Trapper had a bottle and a glass. He sat on the edge of his sack, alternately taking large gulps of the liquid and letting his head drop almost into his lap. Hawkeye went over, took the bottle and glass and put them on the washstand.

"All right, you bastards!" he announced to the others. "Out! We leave in two minutes."

The others pushed their way through the door, and the bottle was reclaimed from the washstand. The Duke poured four drinks, which were downed in silence. The Duke shook hands with Spearchucker and Trapper and left without a word. Hawkeye Pierce shook hands with Spearchucker, and then stuck out his hand for Trapper John.

"Hang in there," he said.

"Get the hell out of here," Trapper John said.

Outside, Ugly John waited at the wheel of the jeep, the others gathered around it. Hawkeye and Duke climbed into the back seat and, as Ugly John gave it the gun and they affected Nazi salutes, they made their turbulent departure from the cheering multitude.

"Don't look back," Hawkeye said.

"I ain't," the Duke said.

For five minutes the two did not look at each other, nor did they speak. Their first act to break the silence was to blow their noses.

"Well," said the Hawk finally, "when you live in this sort of situation long enough, you either get to love a few people or to hate them, and we've been pretty lucky. I don't know. I do know that nothing like this will ever happen to us again. Never again, except in our families, will we ever be as close with anyone as we were in that goddamned tent for the past year, and with Ugly here and Dago and a few others. I'm glad it happened, and I'm some jeezely glad it's over."

"Yeah," agreed the Duke, "and y'all know what I'm thinkin'? We came in a jeep, half in the bag, and now we're leavin' in a jeep, half in the bag."

In Seoul, the jeep carrying Captains Duke Forrest and Hawkeye Pierce and driven by Captain Ugly John Black found its way to an Air Force Officers' Club.

"I can't believe it. I just can't believe we're actually goin' home," Duke kept saying, as they stood at the bar.

"You lucky bastards," groaned Ugly. "I don't know if I can hold out one more month."

"You'll make it, Ug," Hawkeye said.

"Yeah," the Duke said. "It's good y'all came this far with us to see how it's done."

They had a supper of shrimp cocktail and filet mignon. Hawkeye, in fact, had two shrimp cocktails, two filet mignons, and pondered ordering a third round.

"You got worms?" Ugly wanted to know. "You hit those steaks like they're going to bite back if you don't swallow them fast."

167

"You mean these appetizers? Jesus, boy, you oughta see the meal my old man and the valedictorian will have for me when I get home!"

Dinner finally over, they returned to the bar. As they sipped their brandies, the conversation, which had been lagging, came to a halt.

"Let's finish these up and haul for where we spend the night," Hawkeye said finally. "I'm tired."

"Well," said Ugly, "when am I ever going to see you guys again?"

"Ugly," answered Hawk, "that's a painful subject. I hope it's soon, but I don't know. If you come to Maine, you'll see me. If we attend the same medical meetings we'll meet. From here it sounds great to say we'll all get together soon, but all I know is this: You can call me or the Duke fifty days or fifty years from now and we'll be glad to see you."

"Right," the Duke said.

"Yeah," Ugly said. "I know what you mean."

Ugly drove them to the Transient Officers' Quarters at the 325th Evacuation Hospital, from opposite ends of which, more than fifteen months before, the two had emerged to meet for the first time. They watched the jeep disappear into the darkness and head north and back to the Double Natural.

They opened the door of the Transient Officers' Quarters, walked in, stomped the snow off their feet and dumped their barracks bags on the floor. Looking around they saw a dismal but familiar military scene. A large room was almost filled with triple-decker bunks. The floor was littered with old copies of *The Stars and Stripes* and empty beer cans. There were two weak electric lights hanging from the ceiling, two bare wooden tables and a few flimsy chairs. In a corner, five young officers were seated around one of the tables talking earnestly, seriously, worriedly. Their clean fatigues and their general appearance indicated that they were coming, not going.

Duke selected one of the three-decker bunks. He examined it carefully, prodding it and poking it.

"Hawkeye," he said, "I think y'all better pour us some prophylactic snake bite medicine. This place is plumb full of snakes."

"I never argue about snakes with a man from Georgia,"

said Hawkeye, extricating a bottle and paper cups from his bag. "I will pour the necessary doses."

They sat at the wooden table, sipped the Scotch, smoked, and said little but looked happy. They had long hair, could have used shaves, and their clothes were dirty. Between them they owned one-half pair of Captain's bars, which Hawkeye wore on the back of his fatigue cap.

From the corner, the eager new officers watched them with interest. Finally one of them rose and approached.

"May I ask you gentlemen a question?" he inquired.

"Sure, General," said Hawkeye, who had turned his fatigue cap around so that the Captain's bars showed.

"I'm not a general, Captain. I'm a lieutenant. May I ask why you wear your cap that way?"

"What way?"

"Backwards."

Hawkeye took his cap off and inspected it.

"It looks OK to me," he said. "Course, I ain't no West Pointer, and frankly I don't give a big rat's ass whether it's on backwards or forwards. What's more, when I wear it this way, a lotta people think I'm Yogi Berra."

"Yogi Berra?" the lieutenant said.

"Hey, Duke," Hawkeye ordered. "Gimme my mask."

The lieutenant scuffed his feet and asked, "How long have you gentlemen been in Korea?"

"Eighteen months," Duke informed him. "Seems like just yesterday we came."

The lieutenant left and rejoined his group. "They're nuts," he told them.

"Jesus," said one of them, "I hope we don't look like that after eighteen months."

"Hawkeye," Duke said, "y'all hear what that boy said?"

"Yeah."

"Do y'all attach any significance to it?"

"Not much. We've done our jobs. I'm not ashamed of anything. I don't care what anyone thinks."

"Me neither," Duke said, "but y'all don't suppose we've really flipped, do you? Sometimes I'm not sure."

"Duke, wait'll you see your wife and those two girls. You'll be tame, docile and normal as hell. I wouldn't know you two months from now. Relax."

"Yeah," Duke said, pouring another drink, and then raising his voice, "but do y'all know something? This is the first day in eighteen months I ain't killed nobody."

"Like hell! You didn't get one on Christmas."

"That's right. I forgot, but y'all know it kind of gets in your blood. Guess I'll clean my .45 just in case any Chinks infiltrate this here barracks."

The Duke took out his .45, started to clean it and to look significantly at the new officers in the other corner. He poured another drink. "Hawkeye," he announced loudly, "those guys are Chinks in disguise, or at least I think they are. Guess I'll shoot 'em, just to be safe."

Hawkeye got up, his hat on backwards, and approached the new officers.

"Maybe you guys better cut out for a while," he suggested. "I only think I'm Yogi Berra, but my buddy has a more serious problem. After four drinks he knows he's the United States Marines."

Duke started to sing as he loaded his .45:

> From the Halls of Montezuma
> To the Shores of Okefenokee.

The new officers went through the door rapidly and into the snow. They found the 325th Evacuation Hospital's Officers' Club. If they hadn't been green, they'd have found it sooner. Excitedly, to an enthralled audience that included Brig. General Hamilton Hartington Hammond, the five described their experiences in the barracks.

"Leave those two alone!" General Hammond thundered, when someone suggested that the Military Police be summoned. "For Chrissake, just leave them alone! Just hope that train leaves in the morning with them on it. Assign these men other quarters!"

Ere long, Duke and Hawkeye grew lonesome.

"You scared our friends," said Hawk. "They left."

"Yeah," Duke said, "but that ain't important. I just don't believe that y'all are Yogi Berra. I ain't the United States Marines, either, because I'm Grover Cleveland Alexander. Let's get that buddy of Trapper John's who's stationed here to

170

find us a catcher's mitt. Then y'all can warm me up at the Officers' Club."

"Grover," Hawkeye said, "I think you got a fast ball like Harriet Beecher Stowe."

"What's Trapper's friend's name?" Duke said, ignoring him.

"I don't know," Hawkeye said. "I think he called him Austin From Boston."

"Good," the Duke said. "There can't be two people named that."

They finished their drinks and went out into the night. For forty-five minutes they tramped through the snow, traversing the various roadways while, at the top of their voices, they called for Trapper John's friend.

"Austin From Boston!" they called. "Oh, Austin From Boston! Where are you, Austin From Boston, Trapper John's friend?"

Their cries, of course, penetrated the Officers' Club where, at the bar, the five new men clustered now around General Hammond. They were afraid to request an armed escort to accompany them to their new quarters, and they were even more afraid of going out in the snow and dying alone so far from home.

"Goddammit, you men!" General Hammond said finally, tiring of playing mother hen as they pressed closer around him with each plaintive cry. "Why don't you go to your quarters and get some rest?"

"It must be terrible up there, Sir," one of the new men said.

"Up where?" General Hammond said, starting to swing his elbows now.

"Up at the front, Sir."

"Oh, Goddammit," the General said, giving up. "Do your mothers know you're over here?"

"Yes, Sir," they all replied.

Unable to find Trapper John's friend, who may well have heard their calls and wisely decided against responding, Hawkeye and Duke returned to the barracks where, as soon as they hit their bunks, they fell into sound slumber. Three hours later, Hawkeye was awakened by the Duke, who was fully dressed and fully packed. This had required very little effort, as he had neither undressed nor unpacked.

171

"Wake up, y'all. We're goin' home. That train leaves at seven."

"What time is it now?"

"Four."

"Jesus, are you out of your mind? I wanna sleep."

"Y'all can't sleep. I think we both got snakebit during the night. Have some medicine."

He handed Hawkeye a shot of Scotch and a lighted cigarette. While Hawkeye immunized himself, Duke filled a flask.

"The mess hall starts servin' at four-thirty," he announced. "We gotta eat hearty."

As soon as the mess hall opened, Duke and Hawkeye entered with barracks bags and proceeded to eat heartily. Over a cup of coffee, Hawkeye reached into a seldom used pocket for a fresh pack of cigarettes. With the cigarettes came a small piece of paper. On it was written, in the unmistakable hand of Trapper John McIntyre, the unmistakable poetry of Bret Harte:

> Which I wish to remark,
> And my language is plain,
> That for ways that are dark
> And for tricks that are vain,
> The heathen Chinee is peculiar,
> Which the same I would rise to explain.

And then: "It's a small place, and now I love it less. If the heathen Chinee should get lucky, just remember your old Dad, and know that he wouldn't have missed it for the world."

Hawkeye handed the note to Duke who read it and took out his flask. They drank reverently and headed for the nearby train.

The train ride to Pusan was a full twelve-hour journey. The two Swampmen slept for the first six hours; then Hawkeye read while Duke gazed out the window. At one point a sergeant of the Military Police, patrolling the aisle, requested politely that Hawkeye remove his captain's bars from the back of his fatigue cap and pin them on the front and Hawkeye, to his own surprise, politely acceded.

"Well, now," Duke said, after the sergeant had gone on.

"For a much-decorated, fierce, front-line fighting type like y'all, that was pretty peaceful. Y'all goin' chicken?"

"No," Hawkeye said, "but I've been thinking."

"It gives you a headache?"

"I've been thinking that you and I really have been living a life that few of the people we're gonna meet from here on in know anything about. Most of the combat and near front-line people like us fly out from Seoul, so we're gonna look like freaks to the clerk-typists and rear echelon honchos who have been living about as they would in a stateside Army camp. We'd better act at least half civilized. In fact, it wouldn't hurt if, the next chance we get, we even put on clean uniforms."

"I'll think about it," agreed Duke.

In Pusan they were directed to the Transient Officers' Quarters and assigned to one of the Quonset huts. The hut was divided into three compartments, and they were in one of the end divisions. Each area was heated by oil stove, and each cot had a mattress on it.

"Which reminds me of something else," Hawkeye said, as they examined their quarters.

"What's that?" Duke asked.

"I am reminded," Hawkeye said, "that back in The Swamp you were one of the most faithful observers of the night rules. Religiously you would leave your sack, walk three steps to the door and take the seven prescribed paces before initiating micturition. This is such a conditioned habit that I thought I'd mention it. It might not be appropriate tonight."

"I'll bear that in mind, too. Anythin' else, Aunty?"

Although the rest of the Quonset filled rapidly, there were, among the other guests, few other medical officers and none from MASH units. There were few people who had been up forward, so Duke and Hawkeye were satisfied to keep to themselves. After a reasonable number of drinks and at a reasonable hour, they decided to hit their sacks, but after fifteen months on hard cots a mattress atop a spring may seem uncomfortable. Duke, having tried his, dragged his mattress to the floor, where he went to sleep until approximately 3:00 A.M., when Hawkeye was awakened by a loud voice complaining in the next compartment.

"Hey, buddy," someone was protesting, "you can't do that in here!"

173

"I'm doin' it, ain't I?" Captain Pierce heard Captain Forrest reply, and shortly Captain Forrest returned to flop down on his mattress again and begin to snore once more, as the occupants of the next compartment continued to grumble and complain.

In the morning it was clear that their fellow officers considered Duke inapproachable. With misgivings they sought out Hawkeye and registered their complaints. Since neither Duke nor Hawkeye wore medical insignia, Hawkeye saw no reason to correct the impression that he and Duke were fierce, battle-hardened combat veterans. He was pleasant but firm.

"I'll do my best," he assured the committee, "but even I dasn't rile that man none. If I can get him home without him killin' anybody, or earnin' the Purple Heart for myself, I'll be lucky. He's got so he can't hardly tell a Chink from anyone else."

As Hawkeye finished his explanation, Duke joined the group and at the same moment a passing truck backfired. Hawkeye and the Duke hit the floor, simultaneously drawing their .45's and looking around for the enemy. Then, realizing their mistake, they arose, feigning embarrassment.

That night Hawkeye slept without interruption. When he awoke it was to the babble of another delegation of their neighbors, standing in the doorway and viewing with obvious distaste the Duke, still sleeping on his mattress on the floor.

"What's the matter?" Hawkeye, sitting up and rubbing the sleep from his eyes, asked him. "He didn't do it on the floor again, did he?"

"No, he did it on the stove."

"Why didn't you stop him?"

"We were afraid he'd do it on us."

That afternoon they embarked aboard a ferry for Sasebo. As the ferry left the dock, they leaned over the side, smoking and observing a crowd of Koreans and a Korean band cheering and serenading their departure. Hawkeye threw his cigarette into the swirling, dirty waters below.

"And now," he said, "as we leave the Beautiful Land of Korea, the grateful natives line the shores and chant: 'Mother————, Mother————.' "

"Y'all just about said it all," agreed the Duke.

174

As the ferry approached the Japanese shore, Sasebo materialized from the mist as a pretty town. There were mountains, evergreens and a rocky shoreline that, not that he needed any prodding, reminded Hawkeye of the coast of Maine. There were shops and Officers' Clubs and several thousand troops awaiting transportation home. The Swampmen abandoned fatigue uniforms, donned Ike jackets, adorned them with proper insignia and became recognizable as medical officers.

This was a mistake. Before any group of returnees was allowed to board a troopship, short-arm inspection was mandatory, and properly so. Returning medical officers were drafted for this duty, and when the Swampmen heard about this, they were shaken.

"Not me," said Hawkeye. "Let the pill rollers who been doing it all along do it. After eighteen months of being one of their knife artists, I ain't going to be demoted."

"Me neither," declared Duke.

A sergeant with a pad descended upon them. "You men medical officers?" he asked.

"Yes."

"May I have your names, please?"

"What for?"

"I'm making up the roster for short-arm inspection tomorrow."

"Oh, certainly, Sergeant," Hawkeye said. "My name is Captain George Limburger, and this is Captain Walter Camembert."

The sergeant started to write, and Hawkeye politely assisted him with the spelling.

"What time tomorrow?" Duke asked.

"You'll be notified."

Time passed slowly in the big, bare barracks. No one seemed to know when they'd ship out. After being placed on the short-arm roster, the Swampmen decided to go shopping. Popular items in the local shops were flimsy, transparent negligees known as skin suits. No red-blooded American boy wanted to return to his homeland without several skin suits for his loved one, or ones, and the local shopkeepers were hard put to meet the demand.

"I gotta get me some skin suits," said Hawkeye.

"Me too."

At the nearest shop they looked over the selection. The Duke insisted on having one with fur, preferably mink, around the bottom. After much haggling and consultation between employees and owners, the shop agreed to supply such a garment if given twenty-four hours. Their command of English didn't match their curiosity, and they couldn't completely grasp the Duke's simple explanation that he did not wish his wife's neck to get cold.

The next morning the sergeant who came in search of Captains Limburger and Camembert was a different sergeant. He went through the barracks shouting: "Limburger! Camembert?" Several officers inquired about the price. Some asked for crackers. The sergeant became annoyed. Finally he arrived in the area occupied by Duke and Hawkeye, who had just returned from shaving and had yet to don shirts or insignia.

"What do you want with those two guys?" Hawkeye asked him.

"They're supposed to hold short-arm inspection."

"You can't be serious!"

"Why not?"

"Don't y'all know," said Duke, "that those guys are the two biggest fairies in the Far East Command? That'll be the longest short-arm inspection y'all ever saw."

The sergeant perceived the logic of their argument. He consulted his list. "You know anybody named Forrest or Pierce?" he inquired

"Yeah," Duke told him. "They shipped out yesterday."

"Well, thanks a lot," said the sergeant.

Two days later the word came. They were to board a Marine transport for Seattle. They packed. They had a bottle of V.O. left, and booze was not allowed on troopships.

"What difference does it make?" asked Hawkeye. "How we going to get enough booze on board to last us to Seattle, anyway?"

"I got an idea," the Duke said. "Let's drink this jug and have our next drink in Seattle. If we can go that long without it, we'll know we're not dangerous alcoholics."

"The first sign of a stewbum," said Hawkeye, "but it's OK with me."

They boarded ship carrying pretty full loads. Having been

informed that short-arm inspection was also carried out at regular intervals on shipboard, they checked in under their own names, but then assumed new identities. The Caduceus of the Medical Corps was removed from the Eisenhower jackets. The simple cross of the Chaplain's Corps replaced it.

They shared a cabin with four other returning officers who were not particularly pleased to find two chaplains among them. The conversation was slightly stilted until, that evening, Duke and Hawkeye broke the ice.

"Do you gentlemen happen to have any Aureomycin?" asked Hawkeye. "The Reverend here seems to be developing a slight cold. In fact, gentlemen, the Reverend, I fear, has fallen from grace with a large splash."

"What do you mean?" asked one of their cabin-mates.

"The Reverend, God forbid, has come down with the clap."

Incipient laughter was cut short by a stern look from Hawkeye. "Be charitable, gentlemen. Help us. My colleague is a good man. It is just that he has been unusually bedevilled, and I must do something to remedy the tragic results of his excessive libido before he returns to Kokomo, where he is betrothed to the Bishop's daughter. Bishops, as a group, are opposed to gonorrhea, and this one has particularly firm views on the subject."

Meanwhile Duke, looking very pleased, began to leaf through a girlie magazine, a corner of which he had noticed protruding from a barracks bag.

"Stop looking at those pictures, Reverend," commanded Hawkeye.

One of the group, a big, tough, rough-looking first lieutenant, with the crossed rifles of the infantry on his collar and the look of the front line about him, was observing them quizzically. After a little more of the act, he began to grin.

"They ain't no chaplains," he exclaimed in a broad southern accent. "They're Duke and Hawkeye from the 4077th MASH. They saved my brother's life two months ago. What the hell's wrong with you guys?"

"We are traveling incognito," Duke told him. "We will do anything to avoid officiating at short-arm inspection, and we figure if we are chaplains there will be no one demanding that we view three thousand weapons."

177

"Yeah," quibbled one of them, "but they must have your names. It's a big boat, but in two or three weeks they're bound to track you down."

"Any of you guys want to be Forrest and Pierce of the U.S. Army Medical Corps between here and Seattle?" asked Hawkeye. "Tell you what we'll do. We'll pay you."

"How much?"

"Cent for each one you inspect."

"Pretty low wages," one of them, a red-haired artillery captain from Oregon, said.

"But it's an important contribution to public health," Hawkeye told him.

"I'll do it for two cents a weapon," the infantry man who had recognized them said, "not a penny less."

"You are hired," Hawkeye informed them, handing them their medical insignia. "You are now members of the Army Medical Corps."

"How do we go about it?" inquired the new physicians.

"It is very simple," Hawkeye explained. "You get a chair. You sit on it backwards with your arms clasped behind its back and your chin resting on the top. You gotta have a big cigar in your mouth. You sit there and look. Most of the guys will know what to do. If they don't you growl, 'Skin it and wring it, soldier.' Sound mean when you say it. If you think there is a suspicion of venereal disease, you make a gesture with your thumb like Bill Klem calling a guy out at the plate. Then somebody hauls the guy off somewhere. I never found out what happens to them. Every now and then, just so they know you're alert, you grunt, 'Don't wave it so close to my cigar, Mac!' If you follow these simple rules, you can't go wrong."

Just to be safe, Duke and Hawkeye kept the chaplains' insignia on their collars. Other doctors didn't interest them, and medical insignia invited medical conversation. However, the chaplains' roles soon became as burdensome. One Lutheran parson from central Pennsylvania was particularly interested in talking shop. He asked Duke what his reaction had been to his Korean experience. Duke cured him quickly. "Loved it," he answered. "Didn't do nawthin' but hoot, holler, drink rum and chase that native poon!"

On the fourth day out they became captains in the Medical

Corps again. Their two new friends had established themselves as short-arm inspectors, and they themselves had tired of being asked for spiritual guidance by soldiers who had flunked inspection.

"Now I know what happens to the guys who get thumbed out of the short-arm line," said Hawk. "They get a shot of penicillin and a ticket to see the chaplain."

The time passed slowly, but it did pass. Nineteen days out of Sasebo, in a fog so dense that nothing, not even Mt. Rainier, was visible, the troopship docked in Seattle.

Ten hours later in a taxi on the way to the airport, Captains Augustus Bedford Forrest and Benjamin Franklin Pierce nursed a fifth of whiskey. At the airport, everything was fogged in, so they went to the cocktail lounge.

As they sat there at the bar, it all seemed unreal. Two people who had been very important to each other were now almost totally preoccupied with thoughts of other people, and their conversation had become sparse and even a little stilted.

"We don't seem to be acting like Swampmen," observed Duke.

"I guess not, but I don't feel like it. It's just as well."

"Probably."

"Flight 401 for Pendleton, Salt Lake City, Denver and Chicago," blared the loud-speaker.

During the early morning hours, with the moon shining on the snow-covered Rockies, the stewardess addressed the former Swampmen, "I'll have to ask you gentlemen to put away that bottle."

"Sorry, miss," apologized Hawkeye. "We sort of don't know any better."

An hour later the stewardess spoke again to Captain Augustus Bedford Forrest. "Sir, if you don't put away that bottle, I'll have to ask the Captain to come back and speak to you."

"That'll be fine, ma'am. We'd be proud to meet him! My buddy here's a Captain, too."

Hawkeye grabbed the bottle and put it away. "Never mind your Captain, honey," he promised. "I'll take care of mine."

At 6:00 A.M., in the men's room of Midway Airport in Chicago, Duke and Hawkeye finished the jug and threw it in a trash can. They were too excited to be drunk. The flight to

Atlanta was announced. Duke put his arm around Hawkeye.

"I'll see y'all some time, you goddamned Yankee. Stay loose!"

"Helluva place to end an interesting association, Doctor," said Hawkeye Pierce, "but it's been nice to have known you."

Dr. Augustus Bedford Forrest boarded the plane for Atlanta, where he was met by a big girl and two little ones. Six hours later the valedictorian of the class of 1941 at Port Waldo High School and two small boys watched Dr. Benjamin Franklin Pierce disembark from a Northeast Airlines Convair in Spruce Harbor, Maine.

The larger of the two boys jumped into his father's arms and inquired, "How they goin', Hawkeye?"

"Finest kind," replied his father.